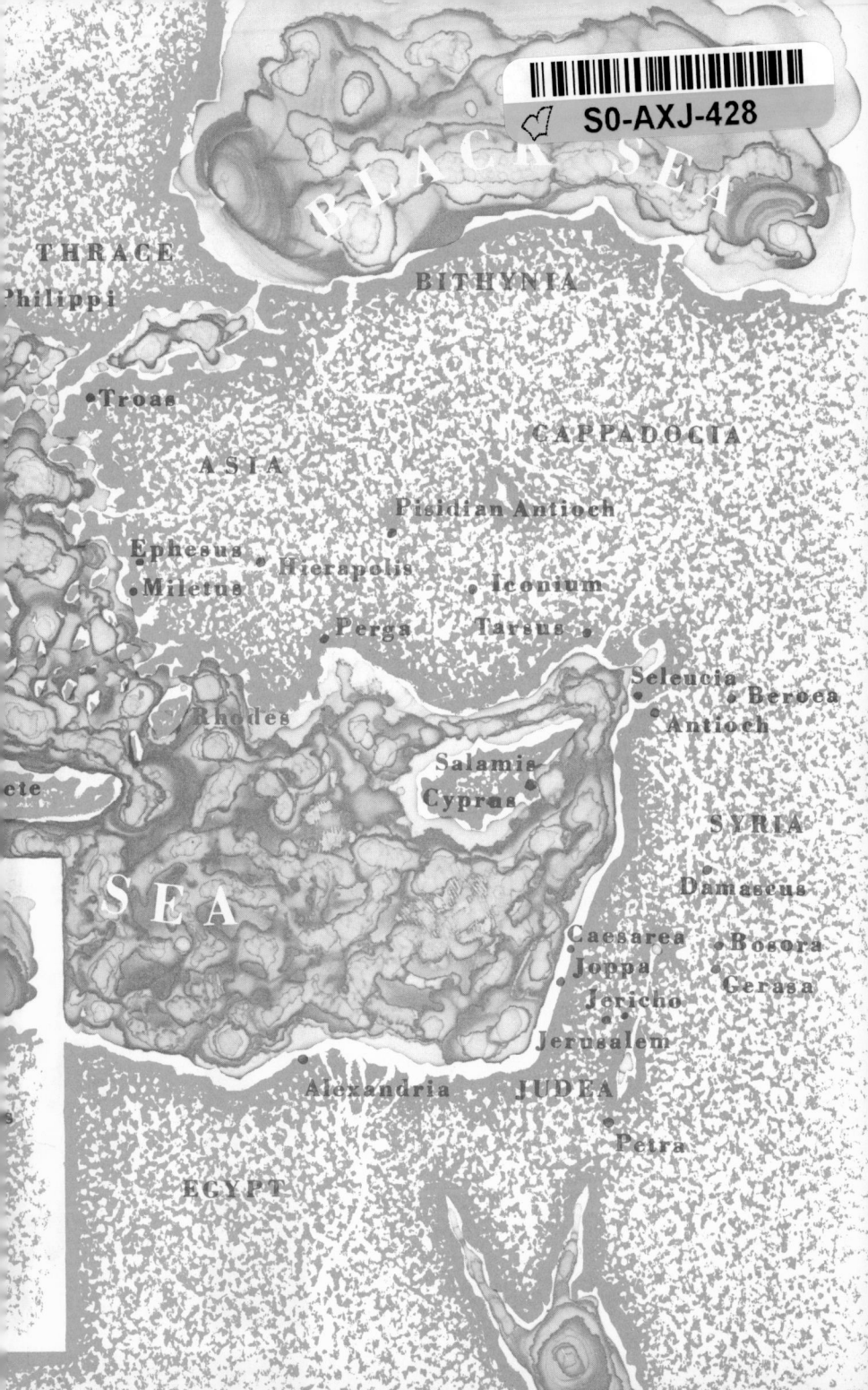

# BY FRANK G. SLAUGHTER

GOD'S WARRIOR  
SURGEON, U.S.A.  
CONSTANTINE  
THE PURPLE QUEST  
A SAVAGE PLACE  
UPON THIS ROCK  
DEVIL'S HARVEST  
TOMORROW'S MIRACLE  
DAVID: WARRIOR AND KING  
THE CURSE OF JEZEBEL  
EPIDEMIC!  
PILGRIMS IN PARADISE  
THE LAND AND THE PROMISE  
LORENA  
THE CROWN AND THE CROSS  
THE THORN OF ARIMATHEA  
DAYBREAK  
THE MAPMAKER  
SWORD AND SCALPEL  
THE WARRIOR  
THE SCARLET CORD  
FLIGHT FROM NATCHEZ  

THE HEALER  
APALACHEE GOLD  
THE SONG OF RUTH  
STORM HAVEN  
THE GALILEANS  
EAST SIDE GENERAL  
FORT EVERGLADES  
THE ROAD TO BITHYNIA  
THE STUBBORN HEART  
IMMORTAL MAGYAR  
DIVINE MISTRESS  
SANGAREE  
MEDICINE FOR MODERNS  
THE GOLDEN ISLE  
THE NEW SCIENCE OF SURGERY  
IN A DARK GARDEN  
A TOUCH OF GLORY  
BATTLE SURGEON  
AIR SURGEON  
SPENCER BRADE, M.D.  
THAT NONE SHOULD DIE  

## Under Penname C. V. TERRY

BUCCANEER SURGEON  
THE DEADLY LADY OF  
   MADAGASCAR  

DARIEN VENTURE  
THE GOLDEN ONES

GOD'S WARRIOR

# GOD'S WARRIOR

THE PATHWAY OF FAITH SERIES

*Frank G. Slaughter*

DOUBLEDAY & COMPANY, INC.
GARDEN CITY, NEW YORK, 1967

*With the exception of actual historical person-
ages, the characters are entirely the product of
the author's imagination and have no relation to
any person in real life.*

*Library of Congress Catalog Card Number 67-10379*
*Copyright © 1967 by Frank G. Slaughter*
*All Rights Reserved. Printed in the United States of America*
*First Edition*

*To my mother-in-law,*

MRS. PEARL KARNES MUNDY

*eighty-seven years young*

*and beloved by all who*

*know her.*

# CONTENTS

*I have fought a good fight,*
*I have finished my course.*
*I have kept the faith.*

II TIMOTHY 4:7

*I am verily a man which am a Jew, born in Tarsus, a city of Cilicia.*

THE ACTS 22:3

# Book I · Tarsus

Saul saw the stranger as soon as he stepped through the door and, putting down the needle with which he had been sewing, moved toward the front of the shop. Behind him the whir of spindles twisting the tough black goat's-hair thread for which Tarsus was famous and the slap-slap of the looms weaving it into the cloth called *cilicium* continued unabated.

The stranger paused in the doorway, blinking a little at the cool gloom of the busy tentmaker's emporium after the bright sunlight outside. A tall man with red hair, he appeared to be in his middle twenties—five or six years older than Saul. Relaxed and obviously sure of himself, he waited for his presence to be noted. That the newcomer was a Jew, Saul's quick appraising glance had already assured him. For even with the red hair and the height—both a little unusual in Jews—the steep planes of the visitor's face and the jutting strong profile of his nose was enough to identify his racial heritage.

"Shalom," Saul said politely in Aramaic. "Welcome to the shop of Joachim, the tentmaker. I am Saul, his son."

"I am Joseph of Cyprus." The stranger, too, spoke the Aramaic tongue.

"A seaman?"

"Yes. How did you know?"

"Your hair is bleached by the sun and your face is brown. There are crystals of salt in your eyebrows."

Joseph laughed. "It was stormy outside the harbor. Even after we anchored in the Rhegma, I felt as if I were still rising and falling with the waves."

"I have never taken a sea voyage," Saul said, a little wistfully.

"Ours is only a cargo boat sailing between Salamis, Tarsus, and Seleucia, hauling copper sheets and hides for sale in the market. A storm blew our sail to shreds, so the master sent me to ask whether you could make us another quickly."

"Of course," said Saul. "Does any of the sail remain that I could measure?"

"Enough for that but nothing else, I'm afraid."

"I'll go with you and write down the measurements. When my father returns, he will be able to give you a price." Saul turned toward the back of the shop. "I'm going to the harbor, Jepthah, to measure a sail," he called to one of the weavers. "Tell my father when he returns."

The Cypriot was forced to accommodate his stride somewhat to fit the pace of his shorter companion, as they walked along the street outside. Saul of Tarsus was barely of medium height. Broad of shoulder, his arms were well developed from handling the heavy looms that wove the goat's-hair thread into cilicium. His head was of noble proportions and in spite of his shorter stature, he gave an impression of strength, resourcefulness and maturity beyond his age. They moved southward along a street paralleling the River Cydnus toward where a marsh, which had formerly made the southern portion of Tarsus little more than a quagmire, had been dredged to form a large basin called the Rhegma around which the harbor had been built.

"Tarsus is a large city," Joseph of Cyprus said. "I have never been here before."

"It has been an *urbs libera* for more than a century."

"A free city! Then your father must be a Roman citizen."

"So am I. And so were my grandfather and great-grandfather before me."

"All of them tentmakers?"

Saul nodded. "My ancestors came here centuries ago in the time of the Seleucid Emperors, from Gischala in Galilee."

"I know of the town. My family came to Cyprus in a Phoenician ship, fleeing the conquest of Tyre by Alexander the Great. But the trade of seafaring has about run out in me." Joseph grinned. "Too many storms and too little money to be made hauling the kind of cargo we carry to Seleucia and Tarsus. Next Nisan, I shall go to Jerusalem for the Passover and remain there. I know something of metal working and an uncle is going to find a place for me in a shop. A better living can be made in Jerusalem selling jewelry and remembrances to rich Jews from Alexandria than by risking my life on a ship."

Saul's face had begun to glow at the very mention of the Holy City. "I shall visit Jerusalem some day. Have you been there before?"

"Once. When I was thirteen and became a Son of the Commandment."

"Is the temple really roofed with gold?"

"It shines like gold," Joseph assured him. "I have seen nothing like it anywhere, not even the Museum at Alexandria and the Temple of Artemis at Ephesus."

"The Museum of Alexandria!" Saul's extraordinarily brilliant eyes shone. "Tarsus has a fine university, but no library in the world equals Alexandria."

"You must be a scholar."

"I would like to go to Jerusalem and learn to be a scribe and a lawyer." The animation suddenly left Saul's face. "But I'm an only son and the men of our family have been tentmakers since before we left Gischala."

"Mine were seafarers, but I'm changing that," said Joseph. "I would rather eat as a silversmith—even though I don't have any particular love for the craft—than starve as a sailor."

"I would be willing to starve to become a teacher."

"I'm afraid that's not for me," said Joseph. "Even the details of the Law are beyond me. And, as for the Prophets—"

"Father let me attend a Greek school when Rabbi Eloichim couldn't teach me anything about geometry," said Paul. "Not many Jews in Tarsus do even that."

"If you're so anxious to become a scribe, why don't you go to Jerusalem and study under Gamaliel? You've heard of him, haven't you?"

"Of course. He's the greatest teacher in Israel."

"I notice that you have several weavers, so your shop must be prosperous. Couldn't someone else take it over?"

"Jepthah—he's my sister Miriam's husband—would like nothing better. But it would break my father's heart."

"I suppose I'm lucky that my mother was a Greek," Joseph said. "We Grecian Jews don't follow the old ways as closely as you seem to do. By the way, my uncle Sosipater teaches philosophy at Salamis and asked me to give his good wishes to a philosopher named Nestor here. Do you know him?"

"Everybody in Tarsus knows of Nestor," said Saul. "He inherited the mantle of Athenodorus, who was the tutor of Emperor Augustus. The university is in the northern part of the city, but we Jews have little to do with pag—with the Greeks."

"My uncle says Jews can learn much from Greeks," said Joseph. "But perhaps you'd better not go there with me."

"Perhaps not." To a strict observer of Mosiac Law, only the least possible contact with Gentiles was allowed. And even that brief contamination must be washed away by a strict regimen of ritual cleansing. "But I can show you where it is, after we measure the sail of your ship."

Since tentmakers in coastal areas were also sailmakers, the shop of Joachim was located not far from the southern edge of the Rhegma. Only shallow draft galleys ascended into the city itself; others tied up at the quays lining the lower harbor. But there was much shipping for Tarsus was a major seaport. Only a little less important than Alexandria or Antioch. To Saul, who came here often to measure sails or deliver the completed product to the shipmasters, the seaside activities were an old and familiar story. Today, however, perhaps because Joseph had spoken to him of Antioch, Alexandria, and Salamis—places which until then had been only names to him—he found himself studying the dockside with new eyes.

The sleek galley with its single bank of oars, squaresail amidships, and shield bearing the eagles of Rome—from which Saul

Once every hour, the weavers rose from the pit and walked about, to prevent the recurrent swelling of the ankles and enlargement of the veins of the lower leg known as "weaver's disease."

At the sight of Joseph, Saul dropped the wheel and, putting down the bag of goat's-hair, came to the front of the shop. Joachim, too, laid down the scissors he had been using to cut cilicium and came forward.

"This is Joseph of Cyprus, Father," said Saul. "I measured a sail for him yesterday, the one you were figuring on this morning."

"You are welcome, friend Joseph." Joachim was a sturdy gray-haired man with a long beard. "Saul has talked of nothing but you and your ship since yesterday."

"I'm afraid my business cannot bring much profit to you, sir," Joseph said. "We can afford only the cheapest of cloth for our sail."

Joachim raised his hands in a gesture of protest. "We do not use the word cheap in speaking of cilicium. Even the least costly is far better for a sail than Egyptian cloth or that of Byblos."

"I know that, sir," said Joseph. "The shipmaster sent me to you because the fame of Joachim has extended far beyond the walls of your shop."

"The Torah warns against being puffed up," Joachim smiled. "Do not tempt me to the sin of pride."

"Will you make a sail for me sir?"

"Of course. Saul is very good at figures and has even learned the geometry of Euclid—though I doubt if the good Rabbi Eloichim, his teacher, would approve. He will give you a price."

A period of brisk bargaining followed and in the end, a price agreeable to both was decided upon, though Joseph protested dutifully that the boat would have to be sold to pay for the sail, while Saul insisted that, since the sail was being sold at such a great bargain, the boat would be worth much more. The transaction completed, it was sealed with a glass of wine and everyone was happy.

"Are you familiar with our city, Joseph?" Joachim asked.

"No more than I've seen when docking and loading cargo along the Rhegma and yesterday when I came to your shop."

"Then you must enjoy our hospitality while your sail is being sewn. Saul will show you Tarsus. He's curious about everything and knows the district from the Cilician Gates all the way to the sea."

Saul wasted no time in getting his cloak and the two left the shop. "Can you take me to Nestor, the philosopher?" Joseph asked.

"He will be at the university. If we stay on this side of the Cydnus, we will pass it."

Soon they came to a rolling elevation upon which stood a rambling group of marble-columned buildings, separated by green grass and shady trees. "This is the university," Saul said. "I've never been inside."

"But would you like to?"

Saul hesitated only a moment. "I've often wondered what it's like," he confessed.

"Your father told you to show me the sights of the city," Joseph reminded him. "And you said yourself that no other university in the world can equal it."

The argument swept aside Saul's Pharisaic scruples against possible contact with anything that might be ritually forbidden. "We will have to ask for Nestor. I don't know where to find him."

"You need not speak to any Gentiles," Joseph assured him. "I meet them every day in buying and selling cargo and the master of my ship is a Phoenician, so I'm already defiled."

A graveled path led through the cool shadows beneath the trees. Saul drew back when a marble statue loomed up before them, averting his eyes instinctively against the nakedness of the youth. When he opened them again and looked at the statue more closely, he was so struck by the beauty of the chiseled form that he quite forgot his instinctive scruples.

"Greek cities are filled with such statues," said Joseph. "Herod the Great brought many like this to the outskirts of Jerusalem to adorn the hippodrome he built there for the games."

"Have you ever seen the games?"

"Once, in Antioch, I watched gladiators fight against wild beasts. But the men had swords and shields, while the animals had only claws. It was a poor show indeed."

Saul and Joseph had passed several walled enclosures that served as classrooms. They were empty, however, since it was too early in the day for most of the teachers to have gathered their students about them. Then they rounded a corner and found themselves at the entrance to a small open amphitheater, with seats of stone in curving rows along the side of a shallow ravine, half-surrounding a raised stage, likewise paved in stone. Perhaps fifty young men in the white robes usually worn by students were listening intently to an elderly man seated on a chair at the edge of the stage. The teacher's face had the sculptured lines, softened now with age, of the young athlete's statue they had passed. Saul drew back but just then the teacher saw them and beckoned imperiously.

"Do not fear knowledge, young men," he said in the bellow of the rather deaf. "Come and sit at the feet of Nestor."

Since they were in the presence of the man they had come to see, Saul had no alternative except to stay. Besides, if they fled now, the others would laugh at them and he had a strong aversion to being mocked by anyone. He and Joseph descended the steps and took seats at the end of a row where they could easily hear the speaker.

"Know that you are set free of all passions, when you have reached such a point where you ask naught of God that you cannot ask openly," Nestor continued his discourse. "I have made it a rule of my life to so live with men as if God saw— and men were listening."

Saul was intrigued by what the deaf old philosopher on the platform was saying. Though he had never seen Nestor before, he knew the high position the famous teacher occupied in the minds of men of learning, not only in Tarsus but elsewhere in the Empire.

"What is he saying?" Joseph asked in a whisper, for Nestor was speaking in Greek.

Saul shook his head without taking his eyes off the teacher, for Nestor was speaking again:

"Many of you aspire to be philosophers, so you will be fawned upon by others for your great learning. But I would give you rather the example of my own master, Athenodorus. Though wise enough to be the tutor of the Emperor Augustus, he still returned to Tarsus, when a decadent government threatened to destroy the city's greatness and send it into a decline. By choosing to place his wisdom in the service of men, Athenodorus knew he was placing it at the service of God, the highest calling to which man can attain.

"I counsel all of you then, to strengthen your minds by making yourself useful in politics to fellow citizens and the world. But in the degraded and envenomed state of politics, one must be content with the opportunity for free expression of the mind in benefiting one and all by educating them, by encouraging virtue, by teaching them to comprehend the will of God and to have a good conscience. Thus even in private life, one fulfills the perfect duty. The student lives well, not by renouncing humanity and society, but by drawing his friends around himself. He who lives and studies for his own benefit will from lack of work fall into mere misuse of the time nature requires us to spend. One must be able to give an account of one's time and prove one's old age by the amount of what one has done for the good of the world and not simply by the length of time one has lived."

When the teacher raised his hands in an unmistakable gesture of dismissal—the students began to file from the small amphitheater. Saul still sat in his place, rapt in contemplation of what he had heard; only when Joseph nudged him, did he get to his feet.

"You had better speak to Nestor now," he told Joseph. "There may not be another chance."

"But—" Joseph stopped, obviously overawed by his surroundings and the majestic presence of the great philosopher.

"Come on." Saul descended the steps and approached the chair where Nestor sat with his head bowed, as if spent from the exertion of teaching. "Noble sir," he said. "We would speak with you."

Nestor raised his head and Saul saw that he was very old;

in the sun and even established a city dedicated to Aton. he offended the priests of Ammon, who controlled the mon people of Egypt, so he was eventually destroyed and city with him."

aul knew he shouldn't be listening to such talk of Gentile ory, but his eager mind had been challenged and he found give and take of discussion with the old philosopher far more iting than the dreary memorizing of pages from the Torah ting down the minutiae of the Law, as taught in the school Rabbi Eloichim.

"We Stoics believe the guiding principle of the entire uni- rse is spiritual, a force we call the Logos or reason," Nestor ded. "Being divine and ultimate, the Logos is God and the telligence of man is only a fragment of that universal divine ason."

"Then every man would be a god!"

"Only if he attains the highest good described in the writings f Plato—which means living in complete harmony with the ogos guiding the universe, as I told my students just now. When a man does that, he truly takes on kinship with god nd becomes a son of god."

"But how shall we know—"

"In his heart and his conscience, every man carries a divine guide to life. But to follow reason fully, a man must gain full control over the emotions that seek always to undermine the Logos within him."

"The Prophet Jeremiah spoke of a time to come when the Law would be written in the hearts of all men, showing them the way to full kinship with him," said Saul. "Do you suppose he meant the same thing?"

"I'm sure he did. Your prophets were so filled with the spirit of God that they glimpsed truths mere men were not able to see. We Stoics seek the same revelation through reason." Nestor reached for the staff that lay on the stone platform beside his chair and pushed himself to his feet. "I thank God daily that my mind has been spared the decline of age, but I cannot say the same for my body. I must go now and seek some rest."

gossip in Tarsus said he was already in h[...]
but there was no dimming of the intelligenc[...]
from his eyes. "You are a Jew, young man," [...]
could you wish of me?"

"Knowledge," Saul said without hesitation. '[...]
only you can give."

"You are wrong there," said Nestor. "The [...]
before you, while my course is almost run. Wh[...]

"Saul, son of Joachim, the tentmaker."

"I know your family. Your grandfather was [...]
some of those you call Pharisees came from Jerus[...]
it was a breach of your Law for Jews to a[...]
Gentiles, so our friendship faded."

"That is the Law of the Most High," Saul sa[...]
now I heard you speak of other gods."

"Some Greeks still worship many deities, but we [...]
there is only one. You Jews believe he spoke to [...]
Moses on the mountain and gave him your Law, [...]
find many of those same edicts on tablets engraved [...]
of King Hammurabi, more than a thousand years [...]
Moses."

"But our people were selected—"

"Even as we Greeks believe we were selected. It [...]
thing for people to be proud of themselves, as long [...]
doesn't make them overbearing."

"Our god selected the Jews as his own people," [...]
tested. "We are the first—"

"Now you are in danger of being puffed up, young [...]
that, too, is against your Mosaic Law." Nestor's [...]
twinkled; he was obviously enjoying this duel of wit[...]
you know that a Pharaoh of Egypt conceived the idea of [...]
god long before your people came into what you call the [...]
ised Land?"

"N-no sir."

"Don't be downcast. Your ignorance is the result of th[...]
the Jews have tried to shut themselves and their faith [...]
from the rest of the world. The Pharaoh was Amenhotep I[...]
Akhenaten. He worshiped a single god manifested to the [...]

"Could I study with you, noble sir?" Saul asked impulsively. "For the first time I realize how little I know."

Nestor studied the eager young face looking so anxiously at him. "I suspect that students like you come to a teacher once in a lifetime if he is lucky, Saul ben Joachim," he said. "My mind may be too old to cope with you."

"But will you take me?"

"Your father may not approve. The Pharisees are jealous of all knowledge not contained in your Law."

"I will convince him," Saul promised. "Only say you will take me."

"You speak the common Greek. Do you write Greek also?"

Saul flushed. "I am but a poor scholar in the language; my teachers didn't encourage me to read it."

Nestor's eyes twinkled again. "For fear that you might begin to realize there is a world outside your faith, where men also strive for kinship with God?"

"I—I suppose so."

"Get your father's permission then, young Saul, and you may sit with my students. We Stoics force no one to believe as we do, but we always hope reason will lead everyone eventually to God."

Belatedly, Saul remembered why he and Joseph had dared to enter the confines of the university. "This is my friend, Joseph of Cyprus," he said. "He brings you greetings from a kinsman of his who once studied with you."

"So?" Nestor turned to Joseph. "Who is your kinsman?"

"My uncle, Sosipater. He knew you years ago, when you were both students of Athenodorus."

"Sosipater?" Nestor frowned. "A Jew?"

"A Greek. My mother's brother."

"I remember him now. We were young men together, just after Athenodorus came back to Tarsus from Rome. What is your uncle doing now?"

"He teaches Greek and numbers to the children of merchants in Salamis."

"A worthy occupation." Nestor turned to Saul. "Don't forget what I said just now about strengthening the mind by making yourself useful to fellow citizens. The man of intellect cannot separate himself completely from the rest of the world, else he loses touch with the spark of the divine that dwells in all of us."

The old philosopher started across the platform toward the exit at the far side, where a shaded path led to still another of the columned buildings at the university.

"Give my greetings to your uncle when next you see him, Joseph of Salamis," he said as the two younger men walked beside him. "I hope to see your face among my students one morning, Saul ben Joachim, but, if it is not there, be sure I shall understand. Because of the strictness of your Law and your conviction of a special purpose under God, you Jews have been able to keep yourselves a separate people for two thousand years, which may even be a good thing. I sometimes think the decline of Greece began when Alexander conquered the world and spread our love of learning and beauty so thinly that in many places it has disappeared altogether."

"But not here as long as you are alive, sir. We can all be thankful for that."

Nestor gave Saul a long and searching look. "As a Jew, confident of his selection by God and obeying your Law, you may be closer to him than those of us who call ourselves philosophers, young Saul. If because of my teachings you lose the pride and convictions of your faith, narrow though they may be, I shall have done you harm. Think well before you decide to join my students, lest by learning to think like a Greek, you destroy yourself as a Jew."

III

Work on Joseph's sail was already well advanced when Saul and the mariner returned to the shop. The cloth had been cut to the pattern and dimensions Saul had outlined on the waxed tablet, and skilled workers were sewing the seams around strands of the tough cilicium cord as a reinforcement for the fabric, making it less liable to tear. First the edge of the pattern was laid down, then the cord was placed upon it and the edge of the next piece lapped over it. Thus by sewing double rows of stitches with the tough thread on either side, the cord was embedded into the sailcloth.

Joseph had to return to the ship, so Saul took awl, needle and tough leather palm and joined his father. They worked for a while in silence; not knowing just how to approach his father with the request he had to make, Saul did not speak. But Joachim, knowing the driving force of his son's mind, realized something was troubling him and opened the way.

"Where did you and the Cypriot go?" he asked casually.

"Along the river—as far as the university." Saul looked at his father quickly to see whether or not Joachim was frowning. Seeing no sign of disapproval he added, "We even went inside."

"The university?"

"Joseph's uncle knows the philosopher Nestor and wished to be remembered to him."

"Nestor is a great man—but very old."

"We didn't thrust ourselves upon him, Father. We happened to stumble upon a small theater where he was teaching—so we had to listen until he finished and Joseph could speak to him."

Joachim smiled, having some idea of just how reluctant Saul had been to listen. More than once Rabbi Eloichim had complained that Saul spent the time when he should have been memorizing the six hundred and thirteen provisions of the ceremonial law reading scrolls containing forbidden Greek teachings.

"Nestor believes in God as we do, Father," said Saul.

"The philosopher is a good man. He is known to lead a blameless life."

"Then why are we Jews not supposed to associate with such as he?"

Joachim sewed a dozen stitches before he answered, punching a hole for each through the double layers of tough cloth with his awl and using the leather palm on his left hand to push the needle through, until he could seize it and pull the thread taut, drawing the fabric layers tightly together.

"The Most High knows well the frailty of men," he said finally. "And how prone we are to yield to temptation and worship other gods."

"As the children of Israel worshiped the golden calf of Baal before the mountain, even as the Lord was giving Moses the tablets of the Law?"

"Then—and at other times. Men at best are frail vessels, God gave us the Law as a bulwark against temptation to help make us worthy of eternal life."

"But the Greeks believe in eternal life, too, Father. Nestor says they seek it by uplifting reason—he calls it Logos—to where they are free of emotion and sin."

"I know little of philosophy," Joachim conceded, "though I believe it is true that the Stoics live lives of purity as we Pharisees do. But for every one of them, there are ten or more Greeks who engage in lustful rites like the worship of Diana at Antioch and Ephesus and of Dionysius elsewhere."

"Even as the Amhaaretz among our own people?" The "unclean ones," common people who had neither the time nor the inclination to observe strictly the written Law from the Torah—the first five books of the scriptures—or the Oral Law, a mass of interpretations covering every phase of a pious Jew's life developed by the Pharisees over the centuries, were looked at askance by ritually devout Jews.

"We who know the Law sin more quickly by breaking it than the Gentiles, who do not know it," Joachim admitted. "But I must warn you against letting the worship of knowledge become a form of idolatry. You have a questioning mind, Saul. Be sure it doesn't lead you into sin."

"Then I may study under Nestor?"

"If you wish. I rely on your own good sense and your upbringing to tell you whether you are being led astray."

The sail was finished the next day about noon. Placing it folded upon a cart, Saul led the donkey that drew the vehicle through the streets to the quayside, where the battered old vessel from Cyprus was docked. Joseph and the crew had been busy loading the ship since morning with a cargo of tents to be sold in Antioch. Saul helped lash the sail to the spar through the carefully stitched grommets. When that was finished, new sheet ropes were attached to the corners of the sail and secured to the rail with heavy pins of wood.

The new sail made even the battered old ship look good and, when a fresh breeze from the north sprang up as they were finishing, the captain decided to sail at once. Standing on the quay, holding the donkey lest the flapping of the sail disturb it, Saul watched Joseph handle the long steering oar at the stern. As the sail filled and the vessel started moving downstream under the impetus of the strong current of the Cydnus, they called farewell to each other.

"Don't forget to look for me when you come to Jerusalem," Joseph reminded him. "My uncle's shop is in the Street of the Jewelers." Then the wind tautened the sail and a sudden rise in the pitch of its humming through the rigging drowned out further words.

IV

The sun was not yet visible over the eastern side of the city when Saul awakened. Like most inhabitants of Tarsus, he slept on the flat roof of his home in warm weather. Pausing to wash his hands and face in the basin placed beside the stairway leading down to the lower floor and the street, he faced toward Jerusalem as he had done thousands of times before and murmured a prayer to the Most High God. Then picking up a handful of dates from a crock in the kitchen, he descended to the street.

Since it was not quite dawn, Tarsus had not yet begun to stir and the streets were empty. The moon hung in the sky to the west, its outline already growing pale from the coming dawn. Over much of the Rhegma a blanket of gray fog obscured the surface of the water, blotting out the hulls of the boats anchored there and making the spars and the sails seem like ghostly shadows suspended over the water without support.

The rhythmic tramp of feet came to his ears and a Roman detail on morning patrol rounded a corner ahead. Their helmets and armor were freshly polished, and their caligae, or half-boots reinforced with metal, struck sparks at times from the stone pavement. The decurion in charge of the detail gave Saul a sharp glance but, seeing only a youth who met his gaze without cringing, made no move to distrub him. Like most citizens of Tarsus who claimed the precious right of citizenship, Saul looked upon Rome and the Emperor, not as oppressors, but as bringers of the peace and economic security that helped to maintain the position of Tarsus as one of the great cities of the Empire.

It was still more than an hour before Nestor's first lecture of the day to his students. Being old, the philosopher preferred to teach in the early morning, when it was cool, and rest during the hot part of the day, leaving the evening free for dining and the discourses that were the most treasured part of university life for both teachers and students. Saul knew this last would be denied to him, for even his father would not approve of his consorting to that extent with Gentiles. Besides, Saul's own Pharisaic upbringing made him recoil with horror from the very idea of eating with those considered ritually unclean.

Walking along through the silent, still sleeping city, Saul stumbled upon the lowest of a set of steps at the end of the street and automatically began to ascend them. Only when he came out upon an upper level, did he suddenly become conscious of his surroundings and, with a gasp of dismay, realize that he had ascended to the temple of Zeus, father of all Greek gods. He had never come here and was on the point of turning to run down the steps, when the first rays of dawn breaking through the darkness to the east—visible here upon the highest point in the city before it could be seen at the lower levels—rooted him to the spot with wonder at the sheer beauty of the scene before him.

Tarsus lay so low that the Mediterranean was not visible even from the height of the temple podium. Carefully averting his eyes from the main structure of the temple, Saul crossed the platform to the northeast corner from which he could see the sunrise more clearly. At this elevation, he could look down upon the course of the Cydnus, winding through the coastal plain toward the sea from the mountains to the north and bisecting the city, before it widened in the southern area to form the enclosed lake and main harbor of Tarsus, known as the Rhegma.

To the north, the ground rose gradually in a series of low plateaus covered with vineyards, fields, and ripening crops, with the darker shadow of the Taurus Mountain range, its peaks still capped with snow, looming beyond. A natural barrier far more massive than any man-made fortification, it shut away the coastal plain from the Galatian uplands and such thriving centers as Lystra, Derbe, and Antioch-in-Pisidia, a former Roman frontier post, now a thriving city from which caravans often came southward to trade at Tarsus, bringing bales of the goat's-hair used in his father's shop.

To the northeast, the light of day was just breaking through the narrow mountain pass called the Cilician Gates, where great caravans from Syria and the countries of the Euphrates still farther eastward, passed daily to enter the coastal plain, bound for Tarsus—and—the other thriving cities of the area. Saul had been as far north as the Gates and had marveled at the road carved long ago from the living rock in the form of a passageway so narrow that there was barely room for the road and a stream beside it. To the west, the dun colored expanse of the Cilician Plain stretched toward Mersin, formerly a rallying point for pirates who preyed on shipping and even chased their prey at times into the otherwise safe harbor of the Rhegma—until Roman authority and Roman justice had all but stamped out their activities.

By now the sun was flooding the city with light. In the quarter of the Jews, who always tended to remain together, both for protection and to maintain their religious integrity,

Saul could see shoppers and artisans beginning to move about. By now, his father was probably taking down the heavy wooden shutters that had guarded the front of the shop. And in the back, where the living quarters were arranged around a court with a well in the center and the spreading branches of an ailanthus tree furnishing shade against the noonday sunlight, his mother, Naomi, would be putting out dates and goat's milk for the morning meal.

The Jewish quarter was a world Saul had known intimately since his babyhood, a protected world where each man respected the other and all were joined by the common bond of their worship of the same God and the all-encompassing Law of Moses, which not only held them together in life but promised eternal bliss after death to those who obeyed it. Around it was the city, a bustling metropolis that did not allow itself to doze and drift backward while dreaming of past glories.

Tarsians had cut a road through the Cilician Gates from the living rock so that great caravans and later the armies of Alexander and of Rome could pass through. Tarsians had enlarged the channel of the Cydnus and dredged out the mud flats of the Rhegma to give the city one of the finest harbors in the Empire. Tarsians had built a great university from which learned men went out to the far corners of the Empire. Tarsians had earned by their own energy the titles of *urbs libera* for their city and the much prized Roman citizenship for themselves. And, under the leadership of the great Athenodorus, they had cleaned out a corrupt local government, replacing it with men who put personal honesty above personal wealth.

Altogether, this was no small world in which Saul ben Joachim dwelt. And when he surveyed it again from the elevation of the temple of Zeus, his sandals crunching upon the stone pavement of the podium as he walked from one corner to the other to obtain a wider view, he felt a surge of pride. Yes, he told himself, he was a Tarsian, a citizen of no mean city and the equal of any. In addition, he was a Jew, member of a race chosen by God as his own and therefore doubly possessing the right to be proud. Buoyed by that thought and with the apprehension that had kept him from sleeping now alloyed, he ran down the steps of the temple and turned toward the cloistered halls of the university, lest he be late for his first lesson at the feet of Nestor.

## V

The small amphitheater was almost filled, when Saul made his way down an aisle and found a place at the end of one of the curving rows of seats. Most of the students wore draped white Grecian robes, aping their teachers in both dress and manner of speech. He had not noticed yesterday the difference between their robes and his somber short tunic, for Joseph had been with him then and the seaman's clothes had been even rougher than his own. But his trained eyes recognized at once that none here were of finer quality than his own and some much less, so he was not disturbed, even when he saw one of the students lean over to speak to another, obviously calling attention to his presence, and heard a snicker of amusement run down the line of young men.

Nestor was climbing the steps at one end of the stone platform now, supporting himself with his staff and the help of a disciple. The old philosopher crossed to the chair in the center of the stage and settled into it with an audible sigh. But when his eyes scanned the group before him, there was no sign of weariness in his gaze.

"A new student has come to join us," he announced. "Stand up and give your name, please, young man."

Saul got to his feet. "I am Sau—, Paulos," he said using the Greek version of his name.

"Where have you studied before, Paulos?"

"At the feet of Rabbi Eloichim."

A snicker swept through the audience but was suppressed immediately when Nestor said, "I know the rabbi well—by reputation. He is a great scholar of a race that was a civilized nation, fighting to keep Assyrian invaders from overrunning

Asia Minor and Greece, when our ancestors were tending goats in the Anatolian uplands."

Saul sat down with a warm sense of gratitude to the old scholar, who at once launched into his discourse to the students.

"When I spoke to you two days ago," he said, "it was concerning the duty of every man to attain individual peace and, through serving others, to gain stature within himself. Only in this way can he see the eternal light shining through the darkness of human evil to illuminate the lives of men and, by capturing some of that light within himself, approach the divine.

"You, being young, will be moved by passions which you must exorcise, as you would cast out an evil spirit. For only by removing the temptation of emotion can you strive toward the goal of an inner discipline that will not allow you to give way even to joy, since with it comes the temptation to excess. The one who would become truly wise learns first that there is no real evil in the world, only ignorance of divine purpose causing men to believe in evil. Since whatever happens is an expression of Logos—the eternal will—it must be good, when seen in the light of the whole. But one can see that light only by subjecting himself to the discipline that removes all emotions from his action."

Saul frowned as he sought to understand the philosopher's meaning. Yesterday he had been struck by the teachings of Nestor and the challenges thrown down to the minds of the students. But a philosophy that permitted no joy, naming it as reprehensible as anger, sorrow, or greed, was hard to understand.

"You, Paulos." Nestor's voice brought him upright in his seat. "Did I see you shaking your head?"

"Only because I seek to understand your thought, master," Saul stammered.

"You find it difficult?"

"Yes."

"You saw none of the others shaking their heads, did you?"

"I beg forgiveness if I have offended, sir."

"You have not offended, Saul ben Joachim. Instead you have paid a teacher the highest compliment a student can pay, the proof that you are thinking, seeking to grasp the ideas I have cast forth like—to use a proverb from your people, I believe— pearls before swine. Because I am old, and reputed to be wise, these others listen and do not question. My pearls of wisdom drop like stones into the currents of their minds—or shall I say the stagnant pools."

There was a burst of laughter, by which Saul judged that satirical thrusts such as this were not uncommon in the old fellow's way of teaching.

"They create no more disturbance in those stagnant pools," Nestor continued, "than a rock cast into the Rhegma. Only a momentary ripple and then nothing."

"But a large enough ripple can drive a ship against the quay and crush it, sir," said a tall, dark-haired young man sitting not far from Saul.

"True, Lucius," Nestor conceded. "Being the son of a ship-owner, you would be expected to think in such terms. I go on hoping one day to cast such a large stone into the stagnant pools of my fellow men's minds that just such a wave as you describe shall result. The noble Athenodorus, my preceptor, cast such a rock into the pool of Tarsus, when he used the powers vested in him by the Emperor Augustus to discipline an evil group of men led by one Boethus, who had taken control of this very city.

"One of Athenodorus' first acts was to revise the burgess rolls so that only men who had proved themselves worthy were allowed to retain their Roman citizenship and vote. Most of you here today—including our newest scholar, Paulos—are descendants of that group. I would remind you, therefore, as I did on another occasion, that he who seeks to reach the highest levels of intellect and thus achieve the divine wisdom, which is the ultimate goal of goodness, can best do so by placing his talents at the disposal of his fellows."

Nestor waved his hand in a beckoning gesture and his disciple, who had been sitting on the step just below him, poured a cup of wine from a flagon beside him and handed it up to the old philosopher, who drank it down with evident relish.

"While I speak of Athenodorus," he continued, "I would remind you again of a rule of conduct he recommended to all his students and which I have sought to observe ever since. Whenever you are tempted to speak in the heat of anger, pause first to repeat silently the letters of the alphabet. And having repeated them, you may find no need to utter words."

Saul stood with the other students until the old man had left the small amphitheater, then started to leave himself. But at the first row of seats above his own, he found a taller, broad-shouldered youth blocking his way.

"Answer me a question, Paulos—since you have decided to call yourself that," the heavy youth said. "What is a Jew, the son of a tentmaker, doing at the university of Tarsus?"

Saul felt an instant flash of anger at the deliberately insulting tone of the other but held it under control. He was not afraid of the older youth, but he had no wish to engage in an altercation on his first day as a student and give the university authorities an excuse to bar him from further study.

"I seek knowledge, even as you do," he said mildly.

"Does it take philosophy to weave cloth for a tent?" A burst of laughter greeted the jibe.

"Perhaps not philosophy." Saul held himself tense, waiting for the blow he knew the other was working himself up to deliver. "But the principles of Euclid can help in designing a sail."

"Euclid!" The heavy youth scowled. "What principle of Euclid, pray?"

Another voice spoke before Saul could answer. It was Lucius, the one student besides Saul himself who had engaged in an interchange of words with Nestor. "The proposition of Pythagoras, of course—the Bridge of Fools or Asses. Who should know that better than you, Timaeus?"

With the words, Lucius moved up beside Saul, holding out his hand in the Roman grip of friendship and greeting. "My father owns ships," he said. "I have often heard him say he will have no sails that were not sewn in the shop of Joachim, the tent-maker."

Saul breathed a deep sigh of relief at having been spared a fight with Timaeus. Other students came up to greet him then and the bully moved away.

"Pay no attention to Timaeus," Lucius advised as he fell into step beside Saul. "His father gives money to the university, so he can pose as a benefactor of learning but his son is a dolt. The authorities only let him pretend to be a student because of his father's gold."

"I'm glad you spoke when you did," Saul confessed. "The last thing I want is a fight my very first day at the university."

"I'll wager you'd give Timaeus a battle," said Lucius. "By the way, you made Nestor happy just now when you had the courage to disagree with him."

"It wasn't so much that I disagreed as that I didn't under-stand," Saul confessed. "Surely a philosophy that denies joy cannot bring much happiness to those who follow it."

"That's why the Stoics will never have a great appeal," Lucius agreed. "Except to a few who are of an ascetic turn of mind."

"Why study it then?"

"Everyone does at the university of Tarsus, but because you study a philosophy doesn't mean you follow its principles. Nestor is the greatest of the Stoics in Tarsus and perhaps in the world, yet he encourages us to doubt because only through doubt can we find the truth."

"How will we know it when we do find it?"

"That question continues to baffle philosophers." Lucius' voice was suddenly serious. "Is it true that in your religion there is no such thing as doubt?"

"The Law was given us by God through Moses. So long as we obey it, we cannot fail to do what he intends for us."

"And the reward?"

"The joy of living according to the Law—and life eternal."

"Greeks are not so sure of the way to Paradise," Lucius admitted. "Some seek it in the philosophy of the Stoics and the Epicureans, others through the rites of Dionysius or Eleusis.

A few even subscribe to the Egyptian religion of Isis and Osiris, but I suspect that you Jews are better off than all of us, for your way is already set."

"Only if we obey the Law."

"This law of yours. Does it cover everything a man does?"

"Yes."

"Surely there has to be change."

"No change is possible in the written Law, since God gave it to Moses more than a thousand years ago. But learned rabbis in Jerusalem interpret it in what we call the Oral Law."

"Then this Oral Law was not actually spoken by God himself?"

"No. It is made up of interpretations."

"By men like you and me?"

"They are wise men—and very learned."

"So are the Greek philosophers, but they are still men. It seems to me that you Jews can't be any more certain of what is right in your Law than we Greeks can be in our philosophy, since both come from the minds of men and both are therefore fallible."

"The argument you make is not valid," Saul said quickly, for to admit the truth of Lucius' words was to deny principles he had been taught to live by—and—render of no value the minute attention to the Law that was the very essence of the Pharisaism, in which he had been steeped since his birth—since the Law would then be as fallible as the men who had made the interpretation.

"Why?" Lucius demanded.

"We believe God speaks in the hearts of prophets and learned men, making his will known through them. To name their pronouncements fallible is blasphemy."

"I'm not familiar with the word—at least not in what appears to be its usage among the Hebrews."

"He who denies God speaks blasphemy—a mortal sin."

"For which a man can lose his chance of eternal life?"

"The Law demands that a blasphemer be stoned to death. Every man who hears his blasphemy must cast a stone."

"Who decides such a sentence?"

"The great court that sits at Jerusalem, the Sanhedrin."

"Is there any appeal?"

"No—except that nowadays the sentence of death must be approved by the Roman authorities before it can be carried out."

"This is a strange thing," said Lucius. "You say blasphemy is a mortal sin against God himself, yet the decision that a man has blasphemed is left to men, who are frail and subject to varying emotions. How can you be sure their pronouncements are indeed the will of God?"

"He—he speaks through them." The feeling of being driven into a corner by the probing of Lucius' logic was a new and disturbing experience for Saul, shaking the very foundations of things he would never thought of questioning a few days ago.

"When Zeus became angry with the acts of men, he destroyed them with thunderbolts from heaven," said Lucius. "Why doesn't your God strike down the blasphemer directly?"

"The Most High did that in other times. When Lot and his family were fleeing from Sodom and Gomorrah long ago they were forbidden to look back, but his wife looked and was turned into a pillar of salt."

"I would like to read the story of your people," said Lucius, "where can I find it?"

"Our scriptures have been translated into Greek for Jews of the Diaspora—like those here in Tarsus. Most of them don't even speak Hebrew any more, though we do learn to read it in our schools."

"Are there many in what you call the Diaspora?"

"Alexandria alone has more Jews than live in all of Syria Palaestina—the homeland."

"Yet all of you still look to Jerusalem for final decisions in questions of Law?"

"Of course. The temple is there and the Holy of Holies at its center is the dwelling place of God on earth."

"When you came to class today for the first time, Paulos, I saw you only as a Jew and a tentmaker. Even when I spoke up just now, it was so Nestor wouldn't lead you into something that might be over your depth. Yet you have told me things I never knew before."

"But you know so much more than I do—about so many things."

"Then since we both realize how ignorant we are, let us make a pact to help increase each other's knowledge. You can tell me about the history of your people, while I shall help you acquire more of the learning of the Greeks. I suspect we will both be better men because of it."

VI

At the stern insistence of his father, Saul did not let his new and exciting studies at the university of Tarsus interfere with the traditional education of a Jewish youth. Like all devout Jews, he had begun his schooling at the leading synagogue of Tarsus, where his father was one of the "rulers" of the congregation, an elder who sat with others upon an elevated platform in the center of the building during the religious services and guided both the temporal and religious affairs of the congregation.

Though inevitably influenced by the culture of the cities in which they lived, the Jews jealously sought to keep alive in the hearts of their children the knowledge of their glorious ancestry and the Law which set them apart from all nations. At the synagogue where Saul's family had been leaders for many generations, he had begun his schooling at the age of five. But even before that he had listened, eyes dancing with excitement, to the epic stories of his people's history. Moses floating as a baby in a tiny boat and discovered by Pharaoh's daughter, to be reared as a prince of Egypt; the flight of the Children of Israel from Egypt under his leadership, with the miraculous crossing of the Sea of Reeds; the giving of the Law on Mount Sinai; the death of Moses on Mount Nebo with the glorious vista of the land of Canaan promised by God to his people spread out before him; the thrilling military conquests of Joshua; the marvelous exploits of Samson; the tremendous feat of arms performed by David when he killed the Philistine giant, Goliath; the magnificence of Solomon; the dramatic confrontation of the priests of Baal by the Prophet Elijah on Mount Carmel—these and many other thrilling stories he had heard at his father's knee in the evening, when the looms were still and the spindles no longer whirred.

In the school of the synagogue, at the age of six he had learned to read while the teacher sat cross-legged upon a little platform with a scroll of the Law on a low rack before him and the students arranged in a half circle. Each in turn read in Hebrew from the Torah, beginning with the Book of Leviticus containing the Law and continuing until the five books were finished.

Saul's quick intelligence let him learn the words rapidly as they were repeated aloud, the entire classroom reverberating to the din of childish voices, with now and then a harsh correction or sharp whack from the teacher for an inattentive student. Each word must be pronounced correctly and with due reverence, but to many of the students, the learning of Hebrew was an unwanted chore, since it was used only in the synagogue during religious services. Aramaic—sometimes also called Syriac—was the language of ordinary life, while Greek was both spoken and written in carrying out business affairs, because it was understood even more widely than Latin, the language of the Romans.

After reading had come writing, which Saul had loved. Figures, too, were a challenge seized upon by his eager intelligence. Noting his natural aptitude for learning, the teacher had given him extra work and he soon outdistanced those students who would never go beyond a few years of study required of them in the synagogue school, barely enough to teach them to read the Torah and the Prophets stumblingly, when called on during the Sabbath services.

Saul's instruction had not ended with the elementary teaching of the synagogue, as it did with so many of his schoolmates. He had gone on to a larger school run by Rabbi Eloichim, where all the advanced Jewish students of Tarsus were brought together. Both the manner of teaching and the subject matter were still the same, however, the endless repetition of verses from the Books of the Law and the Prophets, until he could repeat them by heart with little stimulation to his active intelligence and his desire to learn other things.

Until he passed the age of twelve, Saul had sat during the Sabbath services with his mother, other women, and children behind a latticed grillwork separating a gallery on the second level from the main floor of the synagogue. But having become a man—in the eyes of the congregation—at twelve, he then entered the front door on the Sabbath morning with the other men, washing his hands briefly in the outer court before going to the meeting place to take his seat. Before him, near the center of the main floor, stood the Ark with the Scrolls of the Law and the prophets arranged across a space at the top.

At the beginning of the service, one of the rulers of the synagogue rose from his seat among the elders and climbed a low set of steps to a platform, where he sat behind the scrolls. From the elevated position he counted heads among the congregation and determined that the ten men required to be present before a service could be held were actually there. This having been done, he nodded to the rabbi of the day, who rose in his place, ascended to the platform and, hands uplifted, led the congregation in reciting the *Shema*, the creed of Israel beginning with the words:

> "*Hear, O Israel! The Lord our God, the Lord is one.*
> *You must love the Lord your God with all your heart,*
> *And with all your soul and with all your might.*"

Next, the ruler removed a scroll of the Law from the Ark and handed it down to the *chazan*, or custodian, who placed it on a reading desk before the rabbi. Being a center of trade and travel, as well as the home of a large and prosperous Jewish congregation, Tarsus was a favorite stopping point for traveling teachers, so there was a new one almost every Sabbath.

The rabbi on a Sabbath shortly after Saul began his studies at the university was named Samuel. He was a learned man, judging by the length and whiteness of his beard. What was more, he came from Jerusalem and had announced that he taught from the Porch of Solomon in the temple, giving his pronouncements added weight and authority.

Opening the silver case containing the scrolls, Rabbi Samuel kissed the cloth in which the parchment rolls were wrapped. Loosening its folds, he then spread the scrolls out upon the reading desk, separating the spindles upon which the thin strips of hide were wrapped, and turning them until he came to the selection for today's reading. It was from the Book of Exodus, the commandments given by the Lord to Moses on Mount Sinai. He read them slowly one by one and when he had finished, read the fourth a second time:

*"Remember the sabbath day and keep it holy. Six days you shall labor and do all your work, but the seventh day is the sabbath of the Lord your God: you shall not do any work, you, your son or daughter, your male or female slave or your cattle, or the stranger who is within your settlement. For in six days the Lord made them, and he rested on the seventh day; therefore the Lord blessed the sabbath day, and hallowed it."*

The reading in Hebrew finished, the rabbi translated it into Aramaic for those who had forgotten the small amount of Hebrew they had learned in school. Then he carefully rolled up the scrolls, kissed their cloth cover once again and, placing the whole in the silver case, handed it to the chazan, who gave it to the ruler for placing in the Ark. Taking his seat in a chair placed beside the reading stand, the teacher then began his address.

"Work is worthy and brings to all men the blessings of the Most High, as well as material rewards," he stated. "But as you have heard, work is forbidden on the Sabbath. To obey would be simple, if the commandments had specified the nature of the work that can or cannot be done but, since it does not so specify, the learned rabbis of Jerusalem—of whom I am proud to be a member—have had to interpret the Law."

Remembering how Lucius had questioned the right of mere men to interpret the Law of God, Saul pricked up his ears.

"Work," the teacher of the day continued, "is divided into thirty-nine classes, including sewing, reaping, baking, plowing, spinning, threshing, and the like. Again it would be simple if these activities did not need interpretation. For example, it is not permitted, while passing through a field on the Sabbath, to pluck and rub a head of grain in one's hand in order to chew the kernels, since the Oral Law says such an action constitutes both threshing and grinding, which are prohibited.

"To tie a knot on the Sabbath is also a sin, unless it can can be untied with one hand. And as for eating, Rabbi Shammai said one cannot eat an egg laid upon the Sabbath without sin. Rabbi Hillel"—here Rabbi Samuel's voice became severe, showing where his own beliefs lay—"held that, since the hen cannot possibly know the Law, there is no sin in eating an egg laid upon the Sabbath day. But I say to you that, if ignorance of the Law does not free a man from sin, it cannot free an animal or fowl. Rabbi Hillel is wrong and sinned himself by making such an interpretation of the Law."

The thought of a sinful egg made Saul smile. He put his hand over his mouth quickly, lest his father or the rabbi notice, then his face sobered, for the sermon had failed to answer the larger question of whether most of what the noted teacher from Jerusalem was saying was not foolishness when viewed in the clear light of the sort of logic he was learning at the university of Tarsus.

## VII

The first year of Saul's studies at the university was nearly over when Lucius called to him as he was leaving one day about noon. Though his written Greek was still far from perfect, Saul had come a long way during the year, the stimulus of his companionship and friendship with Lucius accounting for much of his progress. The Greek youth possessed much the same eager intelligence, the same impatient inquiring mind, as did Saul. And since their backgrounds and outlook were so different, each stimulated as well as complemented the other.

"A drama of the Eleusinian mystery is being staged in the theater," said Lucius. "Would you like to see it?"

"It's pagan, isn't it?"

"*I'm* a pagan, Saul. If you haven't been rendered unclean by contact with me, you will hardly be defiled by watching a play about mythical people."

"Are you sure they're mythical?"

"All mystery religions are mythical. Surely you've heard enough of the teachings here to know that. It should still be interesting—and perhaps exciting."

Saul debated briefly. On one side stood his Jewish conscience but set against it was the lure of learning a new thing, a lure no true scholar could resist.

"The cult of Eleusis is a mystery, revealed only to those who join it," Lucius explained as they made their way toward the open air theater.

"How can we learn anything from it then?"

"What we will see is a play, based on the mystery. It was written by a scholar who was once initiated into the cult."

"Is it anything like the worship of Mithras?"

"Mithras is a degrading religion, fit only for Roman soldiers who make up most of its followers. In one of their rites—they call it the *taurobolium*—the initiate even descends into a pit naked and sits there, while a young bull is sacrificed on a grate above his head and its blood pours down to cover him."

Saul shivered, for to a Jew hardly anything was more defiling than contamination with blood. But there was a certain fascination nevertheless about a man deliberately subjecting himself to a torrent of fresh warm blood upon his naked body.

"The red tide is supposed to wash away all sin and bring him pure into the presence of Mithras," Lucius added.

"I never heard of a Greek god named Eleusis," said Saul.

"The name comes from a shrine at the town of Eleusis on the southern coast of Greece between Corinth and Athens. The goddess—"

"Goddess!" Shocked, Saul stopped so suddenly in the middle of the path that those walking behind them were forced to step off to keep from running into him. "Are you taking me to some pagan ceremony?"

"I told you we're going to see a play! If you don't want to come, go home."

Saul's curiosity quickly overcame his scruples and he started walking again. "What is this about a goddess?" he asked.

"The old Greeks believed Demeter governed the planting of crops and the sprouting of seeds. You've been telling me about these feast days of yours. Don't you have one celebrating the harvest?"

"The Feast of Tabernacles is in autumn, when the grapes are gathered. We live outdoors in booths for several days and drink new wine."

"And no doubt become drunk?"

"Some do." Saul grinned. "But no harm is done since it's an act of thanksgiving to God for the harvest."

"So are the rites of Demeter—and Dionysius, too, for that matter. With the coming of winter, Pluto, god of the dead, was once thought to come up from Hades and bring death to all living things not protected by the Earth Mother, Demeter, and her daughter, Persephone, the Goddess of Vegetation. You have a Hades in your religion, don't you?"

Saul nodded. "It's called Sheol and is presided over by Lucifer, a fallen angel."

"Pluto was supposed to be the brother of Zeus, the chief of the gods in the old legend, so they were probably the same originally. The ancients believed all things would die at the end of the summer, if Demeter didn't raise them again in the form of the seed. It's the same in the cult of Osiris in Egypt, where the young god dies each year and is reborn."

"Are only Eleusinians allowed to participate in this mystery?"

"They were at first. But when Attica yielded to Athens long ago, the Athenians were admitted to the mystery also. Now anyone whose character is moral can become an initiate." Lucius grinned. "But I don't think the cult is as popular as its priests would like it to be, or they wouldn't be writing a play encouraging people to be initiated into the mystery and bring more money into their purses."

"Don't you believe in anything, Lucius?" Saul asked.

"I'm a Stoic. I believe in the supreme power of the Logos."

"Yet you cannot explain what it is?"

"If I could explain it, I might not believe in it," Lucius retorted. "Here's the theater. We'll sit at the back and, if you feel yourself being defiled, you can run away."

Once the actors walked upon the stage and the simple drama began, Saul was so caught up by its symbolic theme that he did not stir. The actors wore masks, as in all Greek drama except the bawdy plays acted in the wineshops. The characters were few: Demeter, the goddess; Persephone, her daughter; Pluto, guardian of the Underworld; and Man, in the form of a young god, implying that through the Eleusinian mystery any man could reach such an elevated state. The latter was portrayed by a handsome youth who carried the products of the harvest, naming him a tiller of the soil and establishing his affinity with it.

A narrator stood at one side during the performance. Using words alone, and the inflections of his voice, he set the stage as effectively as if carpenters and decorators had built it before the drama began. When he had finished the opening oration, the handsome young god spoke:

> "Lead me, O Zeus, and thou O Fate,
> To the goal ordained for me.
> I will follow without shrinking.
> Were I a miscreant, and would not follow.
> I should have to nonetheless."

The opening words of the *Shema* came to Saul's mind: "*Hear, O Israel! The Lord our God, the Lord is one.*"

Now the ominous figure of Pluto came upon the stage and the struggle for the life of the young man-god began. The actors were skilled, the drama tense; silence fell over the amphitheater as the fight continued and the struggles of the intended victim grew weaker and weaker. Finally, he fell before the God of the Underworld and Pluto raised his dagger aloft with a triumphant cry. As it plunged downward, a moan of fear rose from the audience for the dagger seemed to pierce the young man's body and a red fluid which Saul was quite ready to believe was really blood, gushed out over him. Withdrawing the bloody dagger Pluto held it aloft before thrusting it into its scabbard. Then seizing the young god's short robe by the collar, he began to drag his body from the stage.

Now Persephone threw herself upon the body and, foiled by her weight, Pluto turned to attack her. Just then, however, the Goddess Demeter stepped from the wings. Clothed in white, with a tall headdress, the goddess gestured toward Pluto with the jeweled wand she bore and a roar of approval went up from the audience, when the God of the Underworld was rooted to the spot by a power greater than his own malignant spell of death. While he struggled futilely to free himself, Demeter moved to where the young man lay and, reaching down, lifted her weeping daughter to her feet.

"Go!" she ordered the Lord of the Underworld and, suddenly released, Pluto scurried toward the wings amidst catcalls from the delighted onlookers. For a long moment Demeter resisted Persephone's anguished pleas that she bring the young god back to life. Finally she touched him with the sparkling wand and he sat up immediately looking about him as if he had no consciousness of what had happened. When Persephone took his hand, he started to rise but, seeing the majestic figure of the goddess for the first time, prostrated himself upon the stage, and, lifting the hem of her robe to his lips, cried:

> "O Holy and blessed dame, the perpetual comfort of humankind.
> Who by thy bounty and grace nourisheth all the world.
> Thou dost make all the earth to turn.
> Thou givest light to the sun, thou governest the world.
> Thou treadest down the power of hell.
>
> By thy means the stars give answer,
> The seasons return, the gods rejoice.
> At thy commandment the winds do blow.
> The clouds nourish the earth.
> The seeds prosper and the fruits do grow.
> The birds of the air, the beasts of the hill,
> The serpents of the den and the fishes of the sea!
> All tremble at thy majesty!"

"Take care, ye initiates!" The narrator closed the dramatic tale, as Demeter lifted the resurrected man-god to his feet and the actors left the stage. "As the young god was saved, so comes salvation for us from suffering and death."

"What did you think of it," Lucius asked Saul, as the audience, deeply moved by the drama of death and rebirth, filed from the theater.

"I was caught up by the drama," Saul admitted. "Though I didn't understand all of it."

"That's what the play is for, to seize your interest and make you want to know more of the mystery."

"Why must it be mystery? We Jews know who our God is though we may not speak his name. We have only to obey his sacred Law to gain his favor and the gift of eternal life."

"You still have a ritual of worship, with your temple and your Holy of Holies where only the High Priest may go," Lucius reminded him. "You have sacrifices to ransom the firstborn from death and invoke the favor of your god. How can you say your worship is so much different from what you saw and heard just now?"

"It's different—but not different. I suppose that's what troubles me about it."

"This Messiah you were telling me will come one day to establish what you call the Kingdom of God—didn't you say one of your prophets foretold that he will die for your people?"

"It was Isaiah. But scholars aren't sure just what he meant."

"It could be another version of what you just saw, the death and rising again of mankind."

"Say no more of such things!" Saul cried. "Are you trying to turn me from God?"

Lucius shrugged. "There speaks the Jew who tries to shut away the world around him. I thought you had learned more at the university, Paulos. Are you still afraid to doubt?"

Saul didn't answer but turned blindly along another path. Nor did he stop until he reached his house and his own room, where he prostrated himself upon the floor and began to recite the *Shema*, until he remembered that he was in the same position the young god had been in during his invocation to Demeter.

Rising, he went to the shop and began to work the treadles furiously, driving the spindle for spinning cilicium thread—though there was an ample supply of the thread already spun for tomorrow's weaving.

## VIII

Joachim was not surprised when Saul took his place at the spinning wheel the following morning, instead of going to the university as had been his custom for almost a year. He had not missed the many signs during the past few months indicating that his brilliant son was disturbed in his mind. Nor did he doubt the cause for, living and working in an essentially pagan city, Joachim could hardly be unconscious of the many influences at work upon what the Jerusalemites somewhat contemptuously called the "Grecian Jews" of the Diaspora.

The name implied what was no doubt true, that under Greek influences many Jews living away from the homeland had largely lost contact with the wellspring of their faith, just as many of them no longer were able to read Hebrew. Though his own faith, buttressed by his duties as a ruler of his congregation, never wavered, Joachim could understand how Saul's brilliant and scholarly mind might be buffeted by the many currents of thought in the university. He waited until after the brief noonday meal had been eaten and they were sitting in the shade of the ailanthus tree in the courtyard before speaking to his son.

"Have your studies at the university ended for the year?" he asked.

"I ended them—for all time."

"Why?"

"The teachers seek to undermine my faith in God. They would make me a pagan."

"Surely not Nestor. Much of what the Stoics teach resembles our Law."

Saul looked surprised. "Do you know of the Stoic teachings, Father?"

"I read Greek," Joachim reminded him. "I studied their doctrines in order to answer some of the questions our young people ask, when they are no longer sure of their faith."

"And knowing that might happen, you still let me go to the university?"

"Most young men are content to be what their fathers were and believe what their fathers believed, questioning nothing, but I recognized long ago that you have the mind of a scholar. The first thing such a one does is doubt."

"But they teach of mysteries and strange things not mentioned in either the Law or the Prophets."

"The Books of the Torah and the Prophets were written many centuries ago," Joachim reminded him. "We Pharisees have made our own interpretations to cover today's problems very much as the Stoics and others developed their teachings from those of the old gods of the Greeks."

"But where is the truth?"

"I think the truth lies in the simplest relationship between man and God—that of father and son."

"And the Law?"

"The Law came from the Most High as a guide for those who love God."

Saul looked through the open gate at the back of the court where the distant dark masses of the Taurus Mountains were framed as in a painting, with their white crowns of snow set off vividly by the blue sky. It was a familiar scene, just as this was a familiar room and as, until a year ago, everything in his life had been familiar, settled and sure. Now, everything was turned upside down because—he told himself—of his own willfulness in desiring something beyond what had contented him before.

"I have sinned, Father," he said. "I have lost sight of the simple duty of obedience to God and to the Law and have gone astray in foreign places of the mind. How shall I get back the faith I had as a little boy?"

"When you are a child you think as a child and accept all that is told you for the truth," Joachim said. "But when you become a man, you must put away childish ways of thought, as you put away your toys. The thoughts of a child and the thoughts of a man can never be the same, Saul."

"But I must know the truth. My mind will not be satisfied with less."

"The truth about the philosophy of the Greeks? Or about our own faith?"

"About the Law—and God."

Joachim sighed. "I was afraid it might come to this, when I let you study at the university. In only one place can you learn the final truth about our faith—Jerusalem."

The word burst on Saul's ears and in his brain like one of the shooting stars he sometimes saw at night from his sleeping pallet upon the rooftop. Jerusalem, the beautiful and holy! Site of the rabbinical schools and the Porch of Solomon in the temple where the greatest teachers of his people held forth daily. Why hadn't he thought of it when his thoughts had first been troubled by the things he had studied at the university?

"Can I go there, Father?" he asked eagerly. "Can I go to Jerusalem and study?"

"For how long?"

"Until I learn the truth."

"I suppose I realized long ago that you were intended for a higher purpose than being a tentmaker," Joachim said with a sigh. "But I hoped you would find it in Tarsus."

"I shall return—when I find out what I seek to learn."

"I suspect the truth is like what the Romans sometimes call an *ignis fatuus*—a light that constantly eludes one who seeks it in the night. You may never really find it but once you have begun to search in earnest, you can never give up. Where would you like to study in Jerusalem? The School of Shammai?"

Remembering Rabbi Samuel and his dreary discourse on work, enlivened only by the question of whether a hen could sin by laying an egg on the Sabbath, Saul shook his head. "I must have the best, Father. If Rabbi Samuel is an example of that school—"

"I remember his discourse and don't blame you. Then it must be Gamaliel, but I hear that the teachers and priests at Jerusalem have named him Rabban, the greatest of them all, so you may have trouble getting accepted as one of his students."

"I shall convince him. When can I go, Father?"

"Jepthah and I have been thinking of opening a shop in

Jerusalem to sell our tents to pilgrims there and to the Nabateans of the desert country beyond the Jordan. He and Miriam will be leaving in a few months and you can go with them. That way you will have some of your family with you and perhaps Rabban Gamaliel will accept you."

"If he doesn't this year he will the next," Saul said confidently. "Meanwhile I shall see the temple. And once I do, I know I shall never doubt again."

## IX

As a monument to his own energy and to increase trade in his kingdom, Herod the Great had built a great port upon the site of an old location called Strato's Tower. About twenty miles south of where the towering headland of Mount Carmel jutted into the sea, a gleaming new city called Caesarea had arisen. Herod had solved the problem of a harbor by building great quays with stone quarried from the mountain range lying inland from the new city. Breaking the force of the sea, the stone walls formed a protected harbor deep enough for even the round ships of the Egyptian grain fleet to moor at the quays.

Saul's eyes were wide with interest and excitement as he helped Jepthah transfer the bales of tents and cilicium to the backs of a string of pack animals for the trip to Jerusalem. As a Jew, he felt an instinctive revulsion toward Caesarea which, being new and Roman, was thoroughly pagan. But even that couldn't dampen entirely his curiosity about this bustling and obviously important city, with its great amphitheater for the gladiatorial games the Romans loved, its magnificent palaces and column-lined streets. A huge statue of Jupiter Olympus, carved to resemble—and flatter—Emperor Augustus, towered over the harbor. It served, Saul was told, as a beacon for sailors, guiding ships in from the sea like the fabulous Pharos in Alexandria.

They did not tarry in Caesarea. Jepthah rented pack animals in a caravan that regularly traveled the circuit between Caesarea, some of the upland cities, and Jerusalem itself, and before nightfall they had taken the road that led southeastward toward the hill country. Miriam rode upon a mule but Jepthah and Saul walked. And since Jepthah was a stolid and unimaginative fellow, the youth soon left him and moved forward to where the leader of the train, a roly-poly man named Eli with a sun-beaten countenance and deep-set merry eyes, walked with the tether of the lead mule held loosely in his hand.

"I saw you watching everything closely there on the quay when we were loading the mules," Eli said. "Is this your first trip to Jerusalem?"

"My first trip anywhere," Saul admitted. "I've been studying at the university of Tarsus."

"So?" Eli's eyebrows lifted. "Are you not a Jew?"

"I tired of the school conducted by Rabbi Eloichim, so my father allowed me to attend the university."

"And now you're on your way to Jerusalem to become a lawyer?"

"How did you know?"

The plump man laughed. "I guide many like you. They go to one of the schools for scribes and study for a while, but the lessons are hard and Jerusalem is not very exciting, except during the religious holidays. After a few months I guide them back to Caesarea and they take ship for home again."

"I shall be different."

"Don't speak too soon. It's hard for a Jew from the Diaspora to succeed as a lawyer in Jerusalem."

"Why?"

"Judea is a poor land, since Archelaus brought us under the hand of the Roman procurators. The latest is a man called Pontius Pilate, and, like all Romans, he wants to line his own pockets and demands more taxes than we can afford to pay."

"How does that concern those of us from the Diaspora?"

"Many who make the pilgrimage to Jerusalem are rich. They expect to be looked up to, but Jerusalem Jews are very proud and rarely let an outsider into the inner circle of priests and lawyers who really rule the country for the Romans."

"Are they too proud to take our money?"

Eli exploded into laughter. "So you've heard that we prey on pilgrims?"

"My father warned me of it before I left Tarsus."

"Watch out for the moneychangers in the temple particularly. A more rascally lot you'll never see."

"Why are they allowed to bilk people who make gifts to the Most High?"

"Because they're in league with the priests. If anyone dares to speak aloud against the temple authorities, the priests accuse him of rebellion and hand him over to the procurator for execution. In return, the priests help convince the common people that they should bow their necks to Roman rule."

"And no one rebels?"

"Some do. But they are either crucified by the Romans, or driven into the hills to become brigands." Eli nodded toward the mountain range to the east whose foothills they were just beginning to ascend.

"Are these brigands really good men who only seek to remove the bonds of Rome from our people?"

Eli shrugged. "Maybe their motives were pure once, but I notice that they prey on Jew and Roman alike. None of them ever gave me even so much as a gerah. Instead I have to pay tribute to Barabbas, who claims to be their leader."

"Is it possible that this Barabbas could be another Judas of Galilee?"

"Don't speak that name!" the caravan driver said sharply. "I was a young man when he led the rebellion against the Romans, but I remember seeing Jews hanging from crosses before Sepphoris like fruit hanging from a tree. Judas called himself the Messiah and many fools ran after him, but in the end he hung on the cross like any criminal or escaped slave. You'd better get back to the mules bearing your bales, young man. We're starting to climb into the hills and, if a packstrap is loosened because you and your brother-in-law didn't tighten it properly, don't expect me to pay when your merchandise falls off and is damaged on the rocks."

Saul stood by the trail until the mules carrying their bales caught up with him. The packropes were tight, and, having nothing else to do, he turned his attention to the landscape ahead. They had been crossing a fertile and pleasant region known as the Plain of Sharon lying between the sea and the hills. But as the road wound upward now, the view became steadily bleaker and more discouraging, except when they happened upon an upland valley where the spring grass was already green and flowers were beginning to bloom.

Most of the hillsides were covered with the tough burnet thorns that made an effective barrier to both men and beasts. Where terraced vineyards clung to the mountainsides, hedges of the thorn had been planted inside the retaining walls of stone as a barrier to keep stray goats from destroying the green foliage and men from picking the lush fruit in the fall, when it hung heavy on the vines. The burnet leaves were turning green now, a sure harbinger of spring, though the air had grown noticeably cooler as they climbed.

Far to the northeast, a tall mountain peak, its top white with snow, hung against the sky and Saul was thrilled to recognize Mount Hermon from the descriptions he'd read of it. In its foothills, he knew, rose the River Jordan, whose waters had made the great rift through which it flowed seem like a land of milk and honey to the Children of Israel, when they had first looked upon it at the end of their long journey from Egypt.

Soon they entered the district of Samaria. Although geographically a part of the same Roman province to which Judea and Jerusalem belonged, Samaria was another world as far as religion and customs were concerned. Centuries ago, it had been the home of the ten northern tribes of Israel. They had broken away from the tribes of Judah and Benjamin in the south at the death of King Solomon, however, eventually being swallowed up by Assyrian hordes from the east and carried off into captivity.

Those few Jews who had remained in Samaria intermarried with people of other regions brought in by the Assyrians to repopulate the land, thus defiling the purity of the Jewish blood line. And although the Samaritans stoutly claimed to worship only the Most High and had even built their own temple on Mount Gerizim—where, they claimed, certain sacred relics of

Moses were deposited—pious Jews considered themselves defiled by contact with them and avoided the district wherever possible.

The leader of Saul's caravan had no such inhibitions, since avoiding Samaria would have meant a journey of several extra days, and chose a camping place for the night not far from the city of Samaria—lately named Sebaste. As Saul looked upon the hilltop where the ancient city had stood he could almost imagine he was watching King Ahab form there the confederation of twelve kings which had stopped the southward progress of an Assyrian army far to the north at Karkar, in the Valley of the Orontes River. And he pictured in his mind for an instant, before hastily blotting it out, the pagan rites instituted by Princess Jezebel of Tyre, after she became Ahab's queen, rites which had led to her denunciation by Elijah and his prophecy—fulfilled later to the last chilling detail—that the dogs would one day eat the flesh of Jezebel. It was a spot to thrill any lover of Jewish history, even though it now stood in the district of a people hated by all devout Jews.

On the second day of the journey, they watered their mules at the Well of Jacob in the valley beneath the towering height of Mount Gerizim. As the caravan plodded southward, Saul occasionally saw horsemen watching them from higher peaks. Knowing they were almost certainly brigands, he felt a shiver of excitement and fear, but Eli continued on, relying upon the tribute he paid to the man he called Barabbas for protection. Nor were they molested by brigands, although they were forced to pull off the road occasionally to make way for a column of Roman troops. Saul was always careful to avert his gaze from the idolatrous images of Rome borne upon every standard, but he still managed to study the colorful uniforms, weapons, and trappings.

Now and then, as they moved southward along the central ridge that bisected the land between the Jordan and the sea, the caravan stopped for the animals to rest in the shade of a grove of carob, or locust, trees. The foliage, thick and green the year round, cast a welcome shade and though it was somewhat past the main blooming season, the trees were still half-covered with purplish-red flowers which, during the spring, would ripen into large flat pods, horn-shaped in outline. When dried, the pods were gathered and the beans threshed out to serve as food for the poor and for swine and other animals. So universal in this region was the locust tree that the bean had given a name to the smallest Hebrew unit of weight, the gerah, twenty of which amounted to a shekel.

One night, camp was made near Bethel in a protected cup where a spring burst forth from the rocks and the grass was green and rich for the pack animals. Lying by the campfire wrapped in his heavy cloak against the chill at this high level, Saul fancied himself in the camp of Abraham, for the patriarch had stopped at Bethel, when he'd first come into Canaan nearly two thousand years before. And here the father of Israel had sacrificed to God, making this a holy spot for Jews everywhere.

The same bright starlit sky must have looked down upon Abraham, Saul thought, and the lowing of herds from the pastures around them must have made the night come alive. When finally he fell asleep, it was to dream of other exciting events in this area: the great military campaigns of Joshua by which Canaan had been conquered; the battles David had waged here among the hills against the Philistines, forging a mighty nation out of what had been only a loose aggregation of tribes; the Assyrian army of Sennacherib, pushing southward even to the very gates of Jerusalem, only to be driven away when the Lord sent a plague to fell the invaders even while their war machines and scaling ladders were against the walls of the Holy City; the heroic battles of the Maccabees when, though vastly outnumbered, they had defeated the forces of the Seleucid Emperor Antiochus hardly two hundred years before. In his dream, Saul could hear the tramp of marching feet as men went into battle, the clash of weapon against weapon, the cries of the wounded, the shouts of the triumphant. And when dawn brought the camp around him into wakefulness, he rose, eager to push on, for Jerusalem itself lay at the end of that day's journey.

## X

It was midafternoon when the road they were following joined the main route from Joppa on the coast. The traffic increased markedly now, as a steady stream of pilgrims moved eastward. Most were on foot, a few rode mules but rarely was a horse seen, since most of these were commandeered by Roman officers. Only the most affluent and the sick hoping for a miracle of healing rode in carts and wagons. In the opposite direction, a steady stream of vendors passed, headed for the outlying villages to accumulate another load of produce which they would take into the city at dawn to be sold in the markets. It was all new and very exciting for Saul and he pushed on to the head of the column once again, eager for his first glimpse of the Holy City.

The Joppa Gate lay near the northwest corner of Jerusalem. And since the land on that side was the highest in the area, Saul rounded a rocky eminence to find the entire Holy City stretched before him. He caught his breath in a gasp of ecstasy as the sun, reflected from the pillars of Corinthian bronze and from the gilded roof of the temple itself, almost blinded him. The beauty of the temple was even greater than he had dreamed of, in spite of the plume of smoke that hung over it in the late afternoon, product of the daily procession of sacrifices and the acrid smell of burning flesh in the air. In his vast contemplation of this shining pillar of his faith, the awe-struck youth did not even notice the proximity of the grim palace-fortress of Antonia, adjoining the temple so closely that Roman sentries walking their posts upon its battlements could look down into the courts of the temple and march immediately to quench any flame of rebellion that might flare there.

Across the Kidron Valley to the east, the elevation called the Mount of Olives rose in a procession of green terraces to a commanding height, blotting out the vista of the mountains of Moab which Saul had seen occasionally from vantage points in the hills during the day, as they traveled southward. In the depths of the valley, the waters of the brook were red from the sluices that drained away blood and waste from the altars of the temple.

In the richer area of Jerusalem centered around the Mount of Zion and the new suburb north of it, Saul could see the magnificent palaces of the Herod family who, though no longer ruling here, spent much time in the city, the dwelling of the High Priest, and the imposing edifices of affluent city dwellers. Below it, along the slope of what was called the Tyropean Valley, lay the Lower City, where the poor dwelt in their usual squalor.

"Are you disappointed?" Eli asked Saul, as they began the descent toward the Joppa Gate.

"Oh no! The temple is beautiful."

"If you overlook the fact that a Roman fortress is jammed against it. And that the lowest levels are crowded with scoundrels."

"It's still the Temple of the Most High. That's what matters most."

"To pilgrims, yes," the driver agreed. "Many from the Diaspora only get to visit the temple once in their lifetime, so I suppose they couldn't be expected to see the abuses that actually exist."

"If conditions are as bad as you say, why don't men like Gamaliel change them?"

"Gamaliel is a rabbi, a Pharisee who interprets the Law. The temple is run by Sadducees, worldly men who think only of ritual—and collecting the tribute. Why would they change when what they're doing makes them rich?"

"The Law says: '*Thou shalt not steal.*'"

"The Law is for little men to break and powerful ones to mold to their own purposes," the driver said with a shrug. "David stole Uriah's wife, but the Most High forgave him, because he was a king. His son even became king after him."

"But the prophet Nathan denounced David."

"What came of it? Nothing. David took what he wanted and, because he was strong, went unpunished. Get to be the most famous lawyer in some city—perhaps in Tarsus—as quickly as you can, young Saul. Then you can tell others what to do."

"My trade is tentmaking."

"And a good one it is," the older man agreed. "You can always be sure of a living, especially in a seaport where sails must be sewn. But an artisan working alone will never get rich. Judging from the number of bales you and your brother-in-law are bringing into Jerusalem, I imagine your father has many others working for him."

"He owns the largest tentmaking establishment in Tarsus."

"Then go back to Tarsus, when your studies with Gamaliel are finished. It's better than sitting on the Porch of Solomon and depending for your living on what rich pilgrims hand you for giving an opinion about the Law the next teacher down the line will dispute."

Saul was too entranced by his first glimpse of the Holy City to let himself be discouraged. His roving, ever-curious gaze took in everything, as they moved along the street toward the shop Joachim had rented through agents in Jerusalem. It was located on the western side of the Tyropean Valley, where the slope crowned by the temple, giving access to the temple from the Mount of Zion and also from the Lower City to the south, so they could be sure that many people would pass the door each day.

The shop proved to be roomy enough to accommodate several weavers—if business justified later—and in time, Jepthah planned for most of the tentmaking to be done in Jerusalem, though the cilicium that furnished the raw material would still have to be imported from Tarsus, since nowhere did goats with hair of quite such strength and tenacity grow in large numbers. The rest of the afternoon was taken up unloading the bales of tents and placing them behind the wooden shutters that closed the front of the shop at night. Meantime, Miriam had been setting up housekeeping in several small rooms back of the shop where she, Jepthah and Saul would live.

The quarters were considerably less luxurious than their old home in Tarsus, but only two houses away water—brought from the hills through an aqueduct built by the new governor,

Pontius Pilate—poured continuously from a leaden pipe. Many Jews had refused to use the water brought to the city by the Romans, because the procurator had demanded part payment for the construction of the aqueduct from the vast funds of the temple treasury controlled by the priests. But Pilate had proved adamant and, in the end, the luxury of fresh cold water pouring from sources within easy reach of everyone had overcome the scruples of all except the most rigid.

Jepthah and Saul were tired by the time the unloading was finished, but Miriam produced a meal of bread and roasted goat's flesh brought from a nearby shop and washed down with the luxury of a bottle of wine, so they were all soon refreshed.

"I plan to make a sacrifice tomorrow morning," Saul announced as his brother-in-law was wiping his mouth, after eating the last of the savory meat and sopping up the juices with a piece of bread.

"A sacrifice!" Jepthah exclaimed. "This isn't a feast day."

"But it's a special time, our first visit to Jerusalem."

"Sacrifices are for feast days," Jepthah insisted. "If you spend money for an offering now, what will you have when Passover comes next month?"

"I can work to make more."

"Your wages from the shop are supposed to pay your fees at the Scribes' School. Joachim ordered that himself."

"I can sew leather." With an effort Saul controlled his indignation at Jepthah's tone. "Pilgrims must have their shoes mended after walking here from Joppa."

"It's your money," Jepthah shrugged. "But if you have none for the Passover lamb, don't expect to eat ours."

XI

Saul slept little that night and it was not yet dawn when he left the house. He needed no directions to find his way to the temple, even through the darkened city. Crossing the viaduct that spanned the upper end of the Tyropean Valley, he found himself at the southwestern corner of the sanctuary area, called the Royal Court. People were already beginning to move toward the temple from all parts of the city for the morning prayers with which many pious Jews in Jerusalem began the day. A faint light crowning the crest of the Mount of Olives to the east warned of the imminent breaking of dawn, but most of the city was still shrouded in semi-darkness and the depths of both the Kidron and Tyropean valleys were hidden by a blanket of low-lying fog which often developed toward morning during this season of cool nights and warm days.

His heart beating rapidly with excitement and fervor at the prospect of his first gift at the very wellspring of his people's faith, Saul moved with the trickle of the crowd toward the doors of the temple. They had not yet been opened, but just before he reached them, a gong sounded within the structure, followed by a blast from the traditional ram's horn trumpet or *shofar*. At just that moment, the rays of the sun broke across the slopes of the Mount of Olives, signaling the beginning of the day, and a chorus began to chant the *Shema*.

Saul stood with his eyes uplifted, reciting the familiar words of praise and dedication as the chant of the Levites and the music of harps, psalters, trumpets and cymbals filled the air. It was a rare moment of exaltation, a deeper sense of communion than anything he'd ever experienced, even during the ceremony when he'd become a Son of the Commandment. He felt like shouting aloud, regardless of those around him, acclaiming the presence of God, as David had sung it of old in the psalms, until he was jostled by those hurrying into the temple to pray before going on about the duties of the day and rudely thrust back into the everyday world.

Feeling a little ashamed at having let himself be carried away, Saul followed the stream of the crowd moving toward the lower court, known as the Court of the Gentiles because other than Jews were allowed there. Spying a stairway leading to the level beneath the Royal Porch, where were located the stalls of those who sold birds and other living things for the sacrifices, as well as the moneychangers, Saul hurried down the steps.

The denarius he carried clutched tightly in his hand was the equivalent of a laborer's daily wages, and a widely used coin. But even it, along with the doric of Persia, the mina of Egypt, the didrachm of Greece and any other of the myriads of coins in use throughout the Empire, had to be turned into the common medium of exchange in the temple, the Tyrian shekel, by the moneychangers before it could be used as a gift. Each had his own booth with a cabinet before him, upon the top of which stacks of coins were placed, while drawers beneath stored foreign coins received in exchange. Approaching one who beckoned to him, Saul placed his denarius on the top of the cabinet.

"You are from the Diaspora?" The moneychanger was barely civil because the coin was small.

"Yes. From Tarsus."

"I could tell you were a foreigner."

"Foreigner!" Saul's indignation left him momentarily speechless.

"What else? You Grecian Jews don't even speak Hebrew." The moneychanger's fingers had been moving as he spoke. Shoving four gerah across the top of the cabinet, he dropped the denarius into the topmost drawer.

Saul glanced down at the pile of coins. A rapid mental calculation told him he had been given one fifth less than he was entitled to. This, and the fact that the moneychanger had so casually sought to cheat him, only increased the anger aroused in him by the man's manner, but he held tight reign on his temper, remembering Nestor's advice to repeat the alphabet before uttering an angry retort.

"I believe you made a mistake," he said quietly.

"Mistake?" The voice of the moneychanger rose sharply. "Do you accuse me of cheating?"

"You gave me only four gerah, when I'm entitled to five."

"Didn't your father teach you respect for your elders? Begone or I will call the guards and have you beaten."

Saul had seen temple guards posted at the entrance to the porch, easily distinguishable by their colorful uniform from the Roman sentries, whose metal shod feet trod a rhythmic pattern on the walkways of the Antonia above. Charged with keeping order in the sanctuary area, the temple police were responsible to the High Priest and, if what Eli, the caravan driver, had said about the link between priests and moneychangers was true, they might well accept the other man's story. On the other hand, Saul was determined not to be cheated.

"Perhaps I should call the guard and ask him how many gerah one denarius is worth," he said.

"What do you know of money—a mere boy?"

"In Tarsus my father sells sails to all manner of shipmasters. We are paid in coins from all over the Empire."

"Take your money and go then." The moneychanger pushed another gerah across the top of the table, deliberately giving it such a shove that it fell from the cabinet to the floor and Saul was forced to stoop to pick it up. "I would rather give you the coin than argue with you over something so small."

"It is written," Saul said as he picked up the coins, " 'He that is greedy of gain troubleth his own house, but he that hateth gifts shall live.' "

The moneychanger spat a curse after him but, as he turned away, Saul no longer felt any elation. Slowly, he climbed the stairway to the Court of the Gentiles through which people were now moving in a swirling tide, tempted not to make a sacrifice at all. The precious ecstasy of that moment when the music had floated down from next to the highest level of the temple had been destroyed by the argument with the moneychanger and the proof that thievery was being practiced in the home of the Most High himself. Then remembering that he would need all the favor of God to be accepted in the School of Gamaliel, he followed the hurrying crowd to the Place of Sacrifice.

Adjoining the Court of the Gentiles, a balustrade of stone had been built, allowing the central part of the sanctuary to be defended, when rebel groups like those led by Judas the Gaulonite long ago sought to seize control. The balustrade was broken by nine gates, among them those leading to the Court of the Women, the Court of Israel, and the Court of the Priests. Beyond these was the Altar of Burnt Offering.

As Saul moved toward one of the gates that penetrated the

balustrade, he was jostled and almost bowled over by two men carrying a third, who was evidently a cripple, for his legs hung flaccid from his trunk. The two moved swiftly to a position beside the gate leading to the Court of the Women and there deposited their burden, placing the cripple on a worn looking cushion with his back to the stone balustrade. They left him there and immediately the man began calling for alms in a peculiarly shrill and penetrating voice, easily audible above the din of voices.

Saul stopped for a moment to look at the cripple. Then thinking that the man might notice his scrutiny and be hurt by it, he turned to another gate leading to where a row of chests, or "trumpets" had been placed against the wall, watched over by a priest and two of the colorfully uniformed guards. Moving with the shuffling line passing before the chests, he dropped his five gerah into one of them and, still following the line, found himself once again in the Court of the Heathen.

Depressed by the whole experience, which had been almost totally devoid of any spiritual meaning, Saul started to leave the temple and return to the shop, where he knew Jepthah would already be grumbling about his absence. But remembering that the rabbi would probably be holding court by now on the Porch of Solomon, he moved around the east portico toward it. As he had heard, a half-dozen teachers were sitting upon small platforms against the wall, surrounded by their students and here and there a cluster of questioners. Saul decided to listen for a moment to the pronouncements of the learned men but, since none of them seemed to have attracted many listeners, he crossed the porch to where a guard was standing.

"Can you tell me whether Rabban Gamaliel will be teaching here today?" he asked.

"Gamaliel holds court only during Feast Days."

"Which of these is the most learned, then?"

"Take your choice," the guard said with a shrug but Saul's curiosity made him pause for a moment anyway. When he saw a familiar face among the group of teachers, he moved closer in order to hear. The man was Rabbi Samuel, whom he had heard lecture upon the various kinds of work allowed on the

Sabbath during the service at the synagogue in Tarsus. The learned man was answering a question that had been put to him, stating categorically that the removal of a speck from the eye on the Sabbath must be considered work and therefore forbidden. The questioner seemed satisfied with the answer but not Saul.

"What shall a man in pain do then?" he asked.

"It is no sin to wash on the Sabbath," said the rabbi. "Let him wash his face with water and, if the mote be washed out, no sin is involved."

"Even though he only washes to remove the mote?"

"Are you a teacher, young man?" the rabbi demanded acidly and a spate of laughter came from the onlookers and his disciples at his tone.

"No sir." Saul did not let himself be cowed by the note of derision in Rabbi Samuel's voice. "But I expect to be one day."

"A student who questions his master rarely remains a student long. Who will teach you?"

"I am going to enroll in the school of Rabban Gamaliel." It was not quite the truth, but Saul was miffed by the older man's tone.

"Such a question is what one would expect from a follower of Hillel," Samuel snapped. "Be careful, lest you speak blasphemy and suffer because of it."

"I only asked a question, sir. Are not teachers here on the Porch of Solomon to answer them?"

"For that—and to teach impertinent children to be respectful. Go before I call a guard and have you flogged."

Thoroughly angry now Saul turned to the crowd. "I am from Tarsus. I have obeyed the Law and worshiped the Most High all my life," he said. "Today I came to the temple to make my first sacrifice, yet in less than an hour I have been threatened with punishment by the guards, first when a moneychanger tried to cheat me and now when I ask a simple question about the Law of one who claims to interpret it for those of us less learned. Show me my error, and I will submit to a beating by the guards."

"Your error is in accepting the teachings of Hillel, when every man knows the true interpretation of the Law," Rabbi Samuel shouted. "Guard! Guard!"

Saul looked about him quickly, seeking a means of escape, but two guards were already approaching, one from either side of the platform upon which Rabbi Samuel sat. Before they reached Saul, however, the crowd parted and a tall man in the rich robes of a priest stepped into place before the platform.

"What is happening here, Rabbi Samuel?" the newcomer demanded sharply.

"The boy was impertinent, Noble Caiaphas," Samuel's tone was suddenly much less belligerent.

The priest was tall with graying hair, a lean—some might even have said a rapacious—face and blue eyes that were cold with disdain. Saul had recognized the name: Joseph Caiaphas, the High Priest was considered one of the strongest men to hold that office in a long time, considerably stronger than his father-in-law, Annas, from whom he had inherited it.

"Who are you?" Caiaphas demanded of Saul.

"My name is Saul ben Joachim, sire. I reached Jerusalem only yesterday from Tarsus and came to the temple this morning to make a gift. First a moneychanger sought to cheat me, but my father sells many sails so I am familiar with the value of coins and insisted upon my rights."

"Do you always insist upon your rights?" A glint of amusement shone in Caiaphas' eyes.

"My father taught me to be honest—and to expect honesty in return."

"And to insist upon it when you don't get it?"

"Should I do less?"

"No, I suppose not," the High Priest admitted. "What is the trouble between you and Rabbi Samuel?"

"I asked a question and he accused me of being impertinent."

"What was your question?"

"Rabbi Samuel said that to remove a mote from one's eye on the Sabbath is work and therefore a sin, but if the mote can be washed from the eye there is no sin. I only asked if it made any difference whether the face was washed to remove the mote."

"A nice point of law," Caiaphas admitted. "What answer did you give, Rabbi Samuel?"

"That the reason for washing was not important. I could tell he was only asking to be impertinent. He is a student of Gamaliel—"

"I warned you once before about this, Samuel." Caiaphas' eyes were frosty again. "If you must bicker with those who follow Gamaliel and Hillel, do it in the streets, not on the Porch of Solomon. I will have no riots here." He turned to Saul. "And be careful where you ask your questions in the future, young man. Give my respects to Rabban Gamaliel and tell him I recommend you to him as a debater—if not a student."

"I shall, Noble Caiaphas," Saul said fervently. "I certainly shall."

## XII

Saul had arrived in Jerusalem a few weeks before the most important of the great religious feasts, or holidays, of the Jewish people, the Passover. Each spring the nation celebrated the passing over of their houses by the angel of death during the bondage in Egypt, although all other firstborn throughout the land had been destroyed in a single night. This holiest of seasons, when winter had ended and spring was once again upon the land with its promise of rebirth through the sprouting of the seed and the breaking out of new green foliage upon the vine, brought almost as many pilgrims to Jerusalem from distant regions as did all the other holiday seasons together.

Since the presence of so many outsiders in Jerusalem afforded the best market of the year for such items as the tents produced by the House of Joachim, Jepthah was anxious to have the shop ready for them. At his brother-in-law's insistence, Saul deferred beginning his studies until after the Passover and the two worked hard getting the shop ready and their tents displayed.

By the time the shop closed at sundown, the beginning of the Passover season, two-thirds of the stock had been sold at a good profit. Jepthah was vastly pleased with their success and Miriam had already lost much of her homesickness for Tarsus, having made friends with the women in the neighborhood who met at the fountain—the city's equivalent of the village well—where water flowed constantly from the great aqueduct.

Neither objected when Saul suggested that, as a token of thanks to God for their good fortune, they sacrifice a lamb for the Passover and use the flesh for the traditional meal.

At dawn on the day whose evening marked the beginning of the sacred period, Saul was at the Gate of the Sheepfold in the temple to claim the lamb for which Jepthah had bargained cannily the day before. With Jepthah he carried it in his arms through the Sheepfold Gate and entered the Court of Israel, where the Place of Slaughter was located beside the altar. There they wrestled the animal to the stone floor and held it while Jepthah slashed its throat and a priest gathered the blood in bowls and dashed it against the altar. Skilled attendants then dressed the lamb quickly, removing the fat and entrails which were placed upon the roaring fire.

The entire procedure lasted only a few moments, for thousands of such sacrifices must be made before the day was over. Carrying the flesh of the Passover lamb with them, Saul and Jepthah hurried home, where Miriam had already pressed out unleavened cakes of bread ready for baking and prepared a mixture of dates, raisins and vinegar, as well as bitter herbs, symbolic of the persecutions the Children of Israel had undergone at the hands of Pharaoh before Moses led them out of Egypt.

All day as he worked in the shop, Saul's senses had been tantalized by the aroma of roasting lamb and herbs. At sunset, when the holy season began, he and Jepthah closed the shop and joined Miriam in their quarters. There each drank a cup of wine over which Saul had pronounced the traditional blessing, washed their hands with great meticulousness, as custom demanded, and spoke a prayer together.

There had been little time to eat that day—since many pilgrims left the city the morning after the ceremony of the Paschal lamb was finished—and the shop had thronged with buyers. Saul was ravenously hungry but he dutifully ate the bitter herbs and the mixture of dates and raisins, symbolizing the clay Pharaoh had forced their ancestors to make into bricks in Egypt more than a thousand years before. He then read from the scroll of the Torah in Hebrew the thrilling story of a nation's emancipation from slavery. Only when the scroll was rolled up and put away did the ceremonial feast finally begin.

The three felt a little lonely, so far away from their home in a city of which they knew but little as yet, Miriam even wept when Saul prayed for the safety of the rest of the family. But it was a time to make the soul of a devout Jew swell with pride and thanksgiving, this first eating of the Passover in the holiest spot of their faith. And at midnight, when the great shofar in the temple was blown to sound the end of the feast and the Levites began to sing the traditional hymn, the Hallel, Saul felt his heart swell almost to bursting and his voice was husky as he joined in the words:

> *"Praise ye the Lord,*
> *Praise o ye servants of the Lord,*
> *Praise the name of the Lord,*
> *Blessed be the name of the Lord.*
> *From this time forth and forever more."*

# Book II · Jerusalem

## I

On the first day of the week following the Passover, Saul presented himself before Rabban Gamaliel and requested admission to the Scribes' School preparatory to joining Gamaliel's circle of students or disciples. The school, largest in all Jerusalem, was located in a building not far from the shop. The School for Scribes occupied the lower floor under the direction of several teachers employed by Gamaliel, while the upper floor was used in the classes of his disciples, who were learning the mass of involved interpretations of Mosaic Law, making up what was generally called the Oral—or Ceremonial—Law, along the rather liberal principles enunciated by the great Hillel, who had died about the time of Saul's birth.

"Saul ben Joachim of Tarsus." The Rabban was a broad-shouldered man, partially bald, with deep-set, somewhat sleepy eyes masking the sharp intelligence behind them. "What studies have you been engaged in before coming to Jerusalem?"

"I completed all the studies in the school of Rabbi Eloichim in Tarsus. Since my sister and her husband were moving to Jerusalem to open a shop to sell my father's tents, we hoped you would be able to take me as a student."

"Suppose I cannot?"

"Then I shall work as a weaver of tents until you can, sir."

"Other schools might take you earlier, especially since your father is wealthy and a ruler of the leading synagogue in Tarsus."

"I want only the best, sir. I already know something of those schools."

"So? How is that?"

"The first day I went to the temple, I asked Rabbi Samuel a question. He spoke last year in my synagogue and I recognized him, but here he accused me of being impertinent."

"Were you impertinent?"

"I didn't mean to be, sir, but Rabbi Samuel's answer didn't satisfy me. If the High Priest Caiaphas hadn't happened to come along, I think the guards would have beaten me."

"So you're the one?" Gamaliel smiled and for the first time since the interview had begun, Saul dared to let his hopes rise. "The High Priest spoke to me of it, but he'd forgotten your name. He tells me you hoist Rabbi Samuel on the point of his own spear—so to speak."

"I meant no disrespect, sir. It's just that Nestor taught us—"

"Nestor of Tarsus? The Stoic philosopher?"

"Yes sir." Saul could have bitten his tongue for the slip, but it was out. Now Gamaliel would certainly not accept him, knowing he had committed the almost unpardonable sin of studying under a Gentile and a pagan.

"How long did you study under Nestor?"

"Almost a year, sir."

"Did you find him stimulating?"

"Yes, sir. Very much."

"Why did you stop?"

Saul hesitated. He'd gotten safely past the stumbling block of Nestor, it seemed, but he wondered whether even so tolerant a man as Gamaliel appeared to be would accept his having witnessed the pagan mystery play. Yet he could be no less than honest.

"One day I saw a drama of the Eleusinian mystery at the university," he confessed. "It troubled me and I decided I should not study pagan philosophy and religion any more, but should come to Jerusalem to learn the truth."

Gamaliel showed none of the horror Saul had expected; in fact, the sleepiness had altogether gone now from the teacher's eyes. "Tell me about this play," he said. "I've wondered about such things for a long time but never saw such a drama myself."

Saul described the play, his voice warming with some of the remembered tension and suspense of the story. When he finished, there was silence and he flushed as he looked up to meet Gamaliel's thoughtful gaze.

"I—" He stumbled, not knowing exactly how to put his thoughts into words. "I suppose being young, I was carried away by the drama."

"You say it troubled you?"

"Yes."

"Why?"

"Lucius—the friend who persuaded me to attend—claimed that there are similarities between the Eleusinian mystery and our own religious festivals."

"Did you deny this?"

"No sir." Saul took a deep breath. "I could see them, too."

"Anyone who studies the history of our people and our faith with an open mind—as Rabbi Hillel did and as I try to do— cannot help seeing that your friend spoke truly," Gamaliel agreed. "What we Jews call religious holidays—or Holy Days— came into being while we were only a group of families or tribes, moving the flocks and herds from place to place, as our father Abraham did, and living off the land. We gave thanks to God then in feasts which have now come down to us as religious festivals. Did you find the Stoic philosophy disturbing, too?"

"Not very much, sir. The Stoics believe in God and in obedience to him."

"But not through the Law, as we do?"

"That troubled me somewhat," Saul admitted. "I had been taught that the Law represents the whole relationship of man to God."

"And you were troubled because the Greeks seek to apply reason to that relationship instead of a mere set of rules, as we Jews do?"

Saul's eyes opened wide with surprise, for Gamaliel had touched the very root of the vague sense of uneasiness, even of guilt, he'd felt since he had started studying under Nestor. On the one hand his logical intelligence had been intrigued by the Greek concept of reason and logic representing the essence of man's relationship to the Deity. On the other, the rigid tenets of Mosaic Law, drilled into him since babyhood, had interposed a barrier between reason—the Logos of the Greeks—and simple obedience to what Gamaliel had just characterized as a set of rules.

"I had never thought of it that way before, sir," he admitted.

"Then you decided to study here so you would no longer be tempted to follow what your conscience insists is a pagan concept?"

"Yes."

"Suppose I tell you that, if you come to study with me, I shall want you to continue inquiring? That I shall want you to question anything in the Law which doesn't satisfy you? Would you still be willing to study with me?"

"I would like that very much," Saul said quickly.

"Then we shall see how well we can satisfy this curiosity of yours."

"Am I accepted?"

"Of course," said Gamaliel. "Teachers are always glad to get students like you, Saul ben Joachim. You keep us from growing sluggish."

Saul grinned. "Rabbi Samuel didn't want me."

"Samuel represents a point of view that would throttle our faith and limit it to a small caste," said Gamaliel. "Eventually they will become so entrapped by the coils of the Law they seem to worship more than they do the Most High that they will be doomed to extinction. In the distant cities of the Empire, Jews are meeting pagans in business and social life every day and finding them to be earnest men, who are trying to do what is right and good, as the Greek philosopher Plato advised. Rabbi Hillel was a man of broad vision. He saw that we must increase the appeal of our faith, so it will call young men like you who are troubled in their minds."

"What of the priests sir?"

"The Sadducees are concerned mainly with ritual. They feel

that men can be brought closer to God through sacrifice and form. Perhaps they're right—where most people are concerned. Few except the Pharisees concern themselves very much with the Law any more." Gamaliel rose to his feet. "You understand, of course, that most of your studies will be concerned at first with your training as a scribe. Only when this is finished, can you be accepted as one of my disciples."

"I am ready for that, sir."

"I'm sure you are, Saul ben Joachim. What concerns me is whether you aren't ready for more than we shall be able to give you."

## II

Saul had not expected the studies in the Scribes' School to be easy, but he quickly found that they were even harder than he had thought. The first stumbling block came when he discovered how inadequate was his knowledge of Hebrew compared to the other students. Determined to remedy this deficiency as rapidly as possible, he studied every night by the light of a burning oil wick long after Jepthah and Miriam had gone to bed, ignoring his brother-in-law's petulant remarks about the cost of oil.

Busy with his studies at night, and working in the shop by day, Saul didn't have time to look up Joseph of Cyprus. Then one day, school was let out early, because the teacher had other matters to attend to, and he decided not to report immediately to the shop, knowing Jepthah would only put him to work, but to spend a little time seeing some of Jerusalem which he had not yet been able to see.

The air in the teeming narrow streets as Saul strolled along was filled with the hum of voices, bargaining, debating, teaching, or simply gossiping, and he was happily conscious of being part of a busy and colorful world. On the craggy knob called Golgotha the empty wooden scaffolds upon which the Romans crucified the occasional brigands they were able to catch loomed against the sky, but even this grim reminder of death and authority couldn't depress Saul's spirits today. In the Street of the Shoemakers, he stopped to watch an artisan apply leather thongs to the wooden soles of a sandal, the common footgear of the lower classes—when they didn't go barefooted. At one side of the shop, a haughty Pharisee sat in a chair, his bare feet protruding from beneath the elaborately fringed hem of his robe and an overlarge phylactery bound to his forehead. A leather box containing a verse of scripture written on very thin parchment, the phylactery was considered a normal part of the dress of any pious Jew. But those who wished to impress others with their great piety, had taken to wearing overlarge ones, leading the common people to jeer at them as "wearers of the box." With a craftsman's eye, Saul observed the Pharisee's shoes, which the shoemaker was carefully resewing where the heavily waxed thread had been worn through. The leather was obviously expensive and soft, the toe pointed and shaped so it curled up at the tip.

"You there!" The Pharisee's voice was sharp. "Didn't you ever see a pair of shoes before?"

"None like those for a long time, O Pious One," said Saul. "Such leather is tanned in the shops of Tarsus, my home city."

"You are a Grecian Jew?"

"My family traces its lineage back to David, the King," Saul retorted, irritated by the condescension in the other's tone. "My father is a ruler of the synagogue in Tarsus."

"What are you doing here?"

"Working as a tentmaker—and studying in the school of Gamaliel."

"I sit with Rabban Gamaliel in the Sanhedrin." The Pharisee thawed noticeably at the name of the famous teacher. "So you expect to become a lawyer? It's not easy for one from the Diaspora."

"So I have discovered."

"When next you see Gamaliel, give him greetings from Elam," the Pharisee said. "After you become learned in the Law, perhaps I shall employ you in some of my transactions."

Saul moved along, but the Pharisee had stirred his not always quiescent temper and soon he began to ape Elam's manner, walking with an exaggerated version of the gait he'd seen affected by such as he, lifting his robe so it would not be contaminated by contact with any of the common folk, the *amharetz* who of necessity were unable to carry out the meticulous cleansing, the many prayers, and the public giving of alms in small amounts so much liked by Pharisees in the Holy City.

Turning from the Street of the Shoemakers into that of the Silversmith, Saul minced along, still lifting the hem of his robe as he threw himself deeper into the pantomime. His actions did not escape notice for here and there as he passed, a smile broke over the face of a shopkeeper. A silversmith stopped tapping with his little hammer, as he formed a piece of jewelry on his tiny anvil, in order to watch. Being young, Saul was vain enough to enjoy the attention he was getting and stopped to lift his eyes heavenward in prayer, forcing the traffic in the street to flow around him, as he had seen men like Elam do more than once in a crowded thoroughfare.

"Saul! Saul of Tarsus!" a familiar voice shouted and he looked around quickly to see Joseph of Cyprus, his face beaming with pleasure and his red hair shining in the sunlight, beckoning to him from the doorway of a silversmith's shop across the way. Forgetting the pantomime, Saul ran to embrace his friend warmly.

"What were you doing?" Joseph demanded. "Putting on a show?"

"I was imitating a Pharisee called Elam. I saw him just now in a shoemaker's shop."

"Everybody knows Elam," said Joseph. "He comes here every few days and buys a trinket at one shop, then he sells it in another, so he'll have an excuse to parade through the street. How long have you been in Jerusalem, Saul?"

"Since a few weeks before the Passover. I'm studying at the Scribes' School and preparing to become a disciple of Gamaliel."

"Where are you living?"

"My sister's husband, Jepthah, manages a tentmaker's establishment for my father near the viaduct leading to the temple. I live with them."

"I heard that a tentmaker had opened a shop in that area, but had no idea it might be you."

"What about you? How goes the trade of a silversmith?"

Joseph laughed and stretched out his large hands. "I soon discovered that these are better suited for handling a steering oar or raising a sail than making fine jewelry. We sell our products in the larger cities of Galilee, Peraea, and Samaria so I spend much of my time traveling about."

"I spend mine humped over scrolls and writing tablets," Saul confessed. "This is the first time I've been in the Street of the Silversmiths since I came here."

"Jerusalem has much to offer besides work—and religion," said Joseph. "I was about to go to the Actian Games."

"What are they?"

"A festival like the Olympic Games of the Greeks; it was begun by Herod the Great. There are chariot races and athletic contests with running, jumping, throwing and the like. They're held in the hippodrome near the south wall."

Saul could hardly have missed seeing the great hippodrome Herod had built. It was long and narrow in shape, with a track around the inside for chariot races. He had also built an amphitheater, where gladiatorial games had been held during his lifetime, as well as wrestling contests with naked competitors. But since exposure of the body was regarded as a sin by most Jews, those activities had never attracted large crowds, except during the religious holidays, when Jews from the Diaspora attended.

"Aren't such things forbidden?" Saul asked.

"Only by narrow-minded rabbis like the followers of Shammai. They're really very exciting. Why not go with me? I'm sure you'll enjoy them."

"Jepthah doesn't expect me to be at the shop this afternoon," Saul admitted. "I suppose I could go—as long as it isn't forbidden."

"I owe you the price of an admission for taking me to Nestor that day in Tarsus. Come on."

"I'm in your debt for that," Saul assured Joseph as they started down a street leading toward the great hippodrome. "Nestor opened a new world for me."

"Jesus of Nazareth did the same for me."

"Nazareth? Where is that?"

"In Galilee, not far from Sepphoris, where the rebellion of Judas, the Gaulonite, ended. A young rabbi named Jesus teaches there in a way you've never heard in a synagogue."

"Doesn't he preach obedience to the Law like other rabbis?"

"Yes. But he says love of your fellow man comes before everything else."

Remembering Elam, the Pharisee, Saul wondered how he could ever love one so vain and arrogant. "Your new teacher would find no favor with Rabbi Samuel and the followers of Shammai," he said. "But Hillel once said, *'What is unpleasant to thyself that do not to thy neighbor. This is the whole Law. All else is but its exposition.'*"

"Two Sabbaths ago I heard the Nazarene say the same thing in a synagogue in Galilee," said Joseph. "I wish you could hear him."

"Jepthah objects if I waste even a half hour getting back to the shop at the end of the day's lessons," said Saul. "I don't have a chance to see anything except the street between the school and the shop."

"You'll see something this afternoon," Joseph promised as they joined a stream of people moving toward the hippodrome.

"Do you ever run into brigands on your trips?" Saul asked. "When we were coming from Caesarea, the leader of the caravan told me he paid a man named Barabbas for protection."

"A bandit called Barabbas does frequent the hills of Galilee. Many people there believe he will lead them one day in an uprising against Rome."

"Let's hope not," said Saul. "One thing we Jews don't need is another false Messiah like Judas the Gaulonite."

III

Located in a natural depression, the hippodrome was easily reached from the city. It was not quite so large as the amphitheater Saul had seen in Caesarea. A considerable crowd had already gathered and more than half the seats were filled when they arrived. Joseph paid the modest admission charge and they made their way along one of the passages penetrating the walls of the structure, taking their seats in the warm sunlight.

In the open center area, a discus thrower, wearing only a loincloth, was swinging the heavy metal disc, loosening his muscles for the throw. When he was ready, he spun around several times and loosed the discus at the height of his turn. It flew in a long arc, with the sun shining on its polished surface, striking the turf a considerable distance from the thrower. To Saul, it looked like an excellent throw but not to Joseph.

"Watch closely," he said. "The next thrower has powerful shoulders. He should do much better than that."

A muscular young man stepped into the throwing circle, handling the heavy discus as if it had no more weight than a feather. He seemed hardly to exert himself at all, yet when he released the disc, it went far beyond the effort of the other thrower and Saul found himself on his feet, shouting with excitement.

So the afternoon went, with one contest succeeding the other: discus and spear throwing, running at various distances, jumping, leaping over hurdles—it was a parade of thrills and Saul was pleasantly tired merely from watching. Finally came the chariot race that ended the afternoon's events, a feature the Romans had added to the traditional Greek games, along with gladiatorial battles and fights against wild beasts. Mosaic Law forbade wagering but Saul picked his own favorite, a team of four beautiful black horses, driven by a tall young man. Against him was pitted a white team, driven by a broad-shouldered man who, Joseph told him, was a Roman centurion named Cornelius, commander of the troops making up the military garrison quartered in the Antonia.

Very early in the race it became evident that the teams were evenly matched, but the greater experience and skill of the older driver soon began to make the difference. He crowded the other expertly on the turns, seizing every advantage to bring his team across the finish line ahead. And even though the team Saul had chosen was the loser, he could not fail to enjoy watching the work of a master driver. When it was over, Saul sank back exhausted in his seat, his pulse still pumping and his face flushed with excitement from the race.

"I said you would like it," Joseph reminded him.

"Toward the end, I think I was shouting for your friend, the Roman, even though I hadn't chosen him in the beginning," Saul admitted. "He is a superb driver."

"I could hardly call Cornelius a friend although he's a convert to our faith," said Joseph. "But I like him very much."

"Can anyone take part in these contests?"

"Anyone who wishes, but only a few of the Jerusalemites do. The Jewish contestants come mainly from the Diaspora like us."

"What harm can there be in such things as this? After all, the Most High admonishes us to keep ourselves strong."

"I see no harm, but some of the rabbis claim that the Law is broken whenever a Jew and a Gentile contest against each other."

"I shall ask Gamaliel how Rabbi Hillel felt about such things," said Saul. "If it isn't forbidden, I should like to compete, though I don't know how I would get away from the city."

"Why don't you go to the xystus?"

"Xystus—what is that?"

"It's a small arena that Herod built not far from the temple," Joseph explained. "You could reach it easily from Gamaliel's school."

"Do Jews go there?"

"Many from the Diaspora do. With your broad shoulders, you should be able to throw the spear or discus and perhaps wrestle, though you may be somewhat short for running and jumping. I'm leaving for Galilee next week or I would join you."

IV

When he discovered that several of Gamaliel's students regularly visited the xystus, with the Rabban's full approval, Saul no longer felt any hesitation about going there himself. Being of a competitive nature, he enjoyed the brisk exercise in the open air gymnasium located almost in the shadow of the temple. Many of the young Jews he met there were from the wealthy priestly class of the Sadducees or the richer Pharisees. And though, as Joseph had said, his somewhat shorter stature made it hard for him to compete in the races—though compete he did—his broad shoulders and rather strong frame allowed him to excel in throwing and wrestling.

He also became friendly with the centurion who had driven the winning chariot in the race on the afternoon when he had first attended the Actian Games. Cornelius was a convert to the Hebrew faith and a worshiper of the Most High, as he was, so Saul felt no contamination or defilement from being with him. The two became good friends and, in return for what Saul was able to tell him about the things he was learning at the feet of Gamaliel, Cornelius gave Saul instruction in the organization and activities of the Roman army, the armor they used and the methods of battle, as well as in the government of provinces like Judea and Samaria.

Cornelius was in his thirties, had a family, and was independently wealthy, as were many Roman officers. He was also a member of the elite Italian Band, one of the most famous units of the Roman army, and served as deputy in Jerusalem for the Procurator of Judea and Samaria. Through Cornelius, Saul came to meet many members of Jerusalem's Gentile community. He found most of them to be educated men and in their company discovered an intellectual stimulation that was lacking at home, particularly now that Miriam was occupied with the care of a new baby.

At times, particularly after a strenuous afternoon at the xystus or the hippodrome, where he often competed now against Gentiles and the soldiers of the Jerusalem garrison, Saul felt a twinge of guilt at having departed so far from the teachings of his childhood. But in every other way, he was careful to keep the Law as closely as he had ever kept it. Then, near the middle of his third year at the School of Gamaliel, when the frost had just begun to appear on the hillsides in the mornings, something happened that changed the entire course of his life. He came home one evening, after a busy afternoon at the xystus, to find Miriam sobbing and his brother-in-law's countenance black with wrath.

"I warned you more than once that your flaunting of the Law would bring grief and disaster to us all!" Jepthah shouted before Saul had even crossed the doorstep of the shop.

"What is it now?" Saul asked wearily, long since accustomed to Jepthah's tirades.

"The curse of the Lord is upon us because of you." Jepthah's face was suffused with anger as he thrust a small scroll at Saul. "This letter arrived just after the noonday meal, but you were occupied with your Gentile friends and I couldn't find you."

The letter was from his mother, the message brief:

*"Your father is dying of a sudden palsy. The only word he has spoken since it struck him was your name, my son. I implore you to come home at once, though the physicians can give me no hope that he will live until you arrive."*

Saul put down the letter, his eyes blurred by tears. He found it hard to visualize his sturdy, generous father stricken by the hand of the Lord. If any man was free from sin, it was Joachim, so why should he have been taken—unless, as Jepthah had said, it was because of Saul's own sin.

"Don't you even care enough to beg God's forgiveness and pray for your father's recovery—unless he's dead already?" Jepthah demanded. "Your sister and I have been praying for him ever since the letter came."

"I shall pray." The words sounded stiff and strange to Saul's ears. "But first I must arrange to go to Tarsus. Will you go with me, Miriam?"

"She has to care for our child," said Jepthah. "No sin of ours brought this curse upon us. Only you're to blame, you and your fine Roman friends."

"Cornelius!" Saul exclaimed. "He will know the quickest way."

"Would you turn to a Gentile at a time like this instead of people of your own faith?" Jepthah demanded, but Saul didn't listen. Plunging from the shop, he climbed the sloping street toward the Antonia.

At the gate of the fortress, he was stopped by a sentry who refused him admission, until he thought to claim his right as a Roman citizen. Then he was promptly taken to the office where Cornelius was working. When the centurion looked up and saw Saul swaying with vertigo from the intensity of the emotion under which he was laboring, he rose at once and guided the youth to a bench.

"What's wrong, Saul?" he asked.

"My father has been stricken with a palsy and is at the point of death. I must go to Tarsus at once."

"As a Roman citizen, you're free to move about as you wish."

"I was hoping you could help me get there by the shortest route. But if it's too—"

"Wait," Cornelius said. "I was just finishing up some dispatches that will go to Caesarea tomorrow morning by a courier. The brigand, Barabbas, is causing trouble again and I need more troops. Can you ride?"

"Yes."

"Be here at sunrise and you can ride with the courier to Caesarea. A military galley will be calling there shortly and with a letter of authority from me, the captain will take you to Tarsus. But he will have to stop at Seleucia to pick up dispatches from Antioch."

"A military galley would still reach Tarsus far sooner than I could get there any other way," Saul said gratefully. "Be sure the Lord will bless you for—" He stopped suddenly.

"What is it?" Cornelius asked.

"My brother-in-law Jepthah said my father's illness is a curse sent from God, because I have been consorting with Gentiles."

"That is nonsense," said Cornelius. "If I thought the God I worship would strike down a blameless old man because of his son's sin, I would change my religion. You're distraught now and not qualified to judge, Saul. Try not to think too much about this; the important thing now is to get you to Tarsus as quickly as possible."

## V

Hardly a week had passed when a sleek military galley with the emblems of Roman military authority upon its prow nudged to a berth at the quay of the Rhegma in Tarsus. Saul had offered to pay for his passage but the military order from Cornelius, handed him by the courier at the gates of the Antonia in the misty dawn just before they had ridden out of Jerusalem northward on the way to Caesarea, had been all that was needed to insure his passage to Tarsus.

Under other circumstances, Saul would have enjoyed the voyage in the swift galley, but his mind was still numb from the shock of his father's illness and Jepthah's accusations. He had tried to review in his mind his actions since going to Jerusalem but had found no comfort there. He could not deny that during the past several years he had departed considerably from the teachings of the Law given him by his father at home and by Rabbi Eloichim in the school at Tarsus, and torn by sorrow as he was, the conviction had grown steadily upon him that the fault must be his own. Yet he could not help feeling a deep and growing sense of resentment, even of hate, against a God who would punish a father for the sins of a son.

At the moment, Saul's major concern was the need to reach his father's side—if Joachim was still alive—or to sob out his grief and guilt at the tomb if he were not, and comfort his mother as best he could. Leaving the waterfront, he hurried through the busy streets toward his home, but, when he reached it, did not dare to enter by way of the shop with its familiar memories of his father's presence. Stepping through the door of the living quarters, he saw the familiar scene and tears started from his eyes. Then his mother ran from the other room and clasped him in her arms.

"Father?" he managed to ask.

"He lives—God be praised! But it is as if he were dead—with half of his body not moving at all."

"I must see him."

"Don't expect him to recognize you," she warned. "He sees but cannot speak and doesn't know us at all."

Joachim lay upon a couch, his body covered by a sheet. So slight was the rise and fall of the sick man's breathing that at first Saul thought he was dead. Then he saw the sheet move and, falling to his knees beside the couch, cried, "Forgive me, Father! Forgive me!"

The still figure on the couch did not move or give any sign of recognition and when after a few moments his mother touched his shoulder, he rose and followed her into the kitchen, where she had prepared some cheese, goat's milk, and dates for him.

"Tell me how it happened," he said as he started to eat.

"It came like a lightning bolt from heaven," she said and Saul stiffened at the simile. "Your father had just come into the house from the shop for the evening meal. I heard him fall and ran in to find him on the floor."

"He said nothing?"

"He spoke your name once—but nothing else."

Saul took a deep breath and asked the question that was uppermost in his mind. "His tone when he spoke my name— did it sound reproachful?"

"Why should it? Your father was very proud when you were accepted as a student of Gamaliel."

"Jepthah says the palsy is a curse from God."

"Joachim was a good man," his mother said indignantly. "Everyone knows that."

"Not because of him, Mother. Because of me."

His mother stared at him, her eyes slowly filling with horror, as the color drained from her cheeks. "Have you blasphemed against the Most High?" she asked in a whisper.

"Nothing like that. It's just that in Jerusalem there are different schools of the Law. Some interpret it one way and some another."

"But the Law is the Law."

"I thought so, too, when I was a child." He seized her hands and buried his face between them. "Would that I had remained a child. It was all so simple then."

He felt her draw her hands away from his face and, seeing the same look of accusation upon her face that he'd seen on Jepthah's a week ago, felt another surge of anger toward God.

"I must go and buy food for the evening meal," Naomi said. "Stay with your father while I'm gone."

Now that Saul had a chance to look closely at the paralyzed man, he noticed some things he had not seen before: the pulse beating at Joachim's temple; the fullness of the veins in his neck; the slight purplish tint to his skin: the somewhat labored character of his breathing. Though he was no physician, Saul sensed that the picture he was seeing was not normal; certainly it was not like his father as he remembered him, but neither was the visible flattening of the muscles of Joachim's neck from the palsy, or the drawing of his mouth to one side and the droop of one eyelid.

Saul shivered a little as he thought of how active his father had been, how quietly strong both in body and mind. Yet Joachim had been struck down as if by a bolt of lightning from heaven and, remembering his mother's words, he felt a sudden rush once again of the feeling of guilt with which he had lived ever since Jepthah had accused him of bringing down a curse from the Lord. And though he could not help a feeling of resentment, his childhood training reminded him that the anger of the Lord must somehow be appeased. Once he faced that fact, a decision which had been slowly forming in his mind ever since he'd left Jerusalem was finally crystallized. When Naomi returned with food for the evening meal, Saul left the living quarters and went into the shop. The men were at work at the looms, but there was none of the busy hum of activity that had characterized the place when his father had been well and only three weavers were working, where before there had often been six.

The men greeted him courteously, but he sensed a guardedness about their manner which he could not understand at first, for they certainly could not have heard of his guilt for his father's condition. Then he remembered that, if his father died, he would inherit the shop. And since he had gone away from Jerusalem to become a teacher, they no doubt feared he would sell it and were troubled about their future.

"How are your feet, Ezra?" Saul asked the oldest weaver. The old man's ankles had been swollen as long as he could remember from sitting with them hanging in the pit.

"I still suffer from the 'weaver's disease,'" the old man said. "Three months ago, a sore came just above my ankle and wouldn't heal, even with the medicine the physician Elcanah gave me. I was measuring some sails on the quay one day and your friend Lucius sent me to a young Greek physician. He mixed some salve for me and taught me how to bind my legs." The old weaver pulled up the hem of his robe and showed Saul that his feet and legs were wrapped snugly with linen bandages. "The sore healed soon but once I left the bandage off for a week and the skin began to turn red, so I put it on again."

"What about the trade in sails?"

"I cannot walk to the quay on account of my feet and the others don't know how to measure for sails, so we haven't sewed any lately."

"I will go to the quay tomorrow and seek more work for us." Saul put in words for the first time the decision that had formed in his mind. Since his own sin had brought disaster to his father, he must take Joachim's place in the shop. It was the only penance he could think of at the moment.

"We can use the work," said Ezra.

"How about the other weavers? Will they come back if we need them?"

"Until your father became ill, the shop of Joachim was the best tentmaker's establishment in Tarsus and paid the highest wages. Now—" Ezra didn't finish the sentence but Saul knew what he was thinking.

"It will be again," he assured the old weaver. "You have my word for it."

Naomi prepared a delicious meal for Saul's first evening at home, a stew of young bullock meat served with herbs and a rare delicacy even in this prosperous household. There was a dish of lintels on the side, too, with cakes of warm bread from the baker's oven, honey, cheese and a sweet wine.

"I talked to Ezra this afternoon," Saul said when the meal was finished. "Tomorrow I shall take charge of the shop."

"Your father would like that."

"I shall go to the quay, too, and see the shipmasters and shipowners. More money can be made from sails than from tents, but Ezra hasn't been able to measure them because of the sore on his leg."

"Will you take your father's place in the congregation, too?"

"I'm too young to be a ruler."

"But not a leader and a teacher—once your sin is forgiven."

"How could that be, Mother?"

"Rabbi Eloichim is an expert in the Law. Perhaps he can tell you how the curse may be lifted."

"I will see him tomorrow."

"You're a good boy, Saul." Naomi seemed to have forgotten her early withdrawal, when he'd confessed his sin. "Your father would be very proud of you."

Rabbi Eloichim's greeting, when Saul went to the school the next morning, was distinctly cool. The old teacher had never forgiven him for turning to Nestor and the university, both forbidden according to Eloichim's strict interpretation of Mosaic Law.

"Do you doubt that you have broken the Law?" Rabbi Eloichim asked, after Saul had explained the reason for the visit.

"No, I suppose not."

"You've been taught enough to know the answer. Or have they changed it in Jerusalem?"

"No master," Saul gave the old rabbi the title he had used when a student. "It is just that Rabban Gamaliel—"

"A plague on such as he! The followers of Hillel pervert the Law to make its burden easier upon themselves."

Saul didn't argue with the old teacher. In the school of Gamaliel, the study of religion had been a joy and a challenge, while all he could remember from his studies under Rabbi

Eloichim was the daily memorizing of passages from the Torah.

"Your father was stricken because of your sin in consorting with the heathen." Rabbi Eloichim's hard voice shattered the silence. "But if you are properly repentant, the anger of the Lord might still be appeased."

"Tell me how," Saul said eagerly. "I have already arranged to take charge of the shop and I shall try to fill my father's place—"

"Not in the congregation. Surely you couldn't expect that."

"Later perhaps—when I am worthy."

"That may take a long time. Even if your father dies, the burden of guilt will still be on your soul. His death would not free you from it."

"I have no wish to evade anything."

"Then your sins still may be forgiven." The old rabbi had begun to thaw a little. "The physician Elcanah tells me there is little hope for Joachim."

"I pray daily for a miracle." Saul hesitated, then asked a question that had troubled him much of the night. "Would it be a defilement if I asked the advice of another physician for my father?"

"Elcanah has looked after the congregation for years. If he is good enough for—"

"Ezra tells me a Greek physician treated the sore on his leg and healed it—after Elcanah had failed."

"It is true that the one called Luke did cure Ezra," Rabbi Eloichim admitted. "And he is said to have cured many others."

"The Prophet Jeremiah said '*Is there no balm in Gilead? Is there no physician there?*' Surely that means the Most High approved of physicians."

"The prophet was no doubt speaking of the Chosen People, but we who dwell away from the homeland cannot always call physicians who are Jews. I see no harm in consulting a Gentile, if you associate with him as little as possible."

"I shall be diligent," Saul promised. "And afterward I shall perform the ritual of washing and fasting until I am cleansed according to the Law."

## VI

Saul found his old schoolmate, Lucius, at the family's warehouse on the waterfront, going over some ship manifests with the head scribe of the establishment.

"Ezra told me about your father's illness," he said, embracing Saul warmly. "I hope he is better."

"Elcanah gives us little hope. I came to ask where I might find the Greek physician who treated Ezra."

"Luke should be here soon. His class at the university was finished nearly an hour ago."

"Is he as good as Ezra says?"

"I met Luke when I took my father to the Temple of Asklepios at Pergamum last year," said Lucius. "We became good friends while I was there and I invited him here. He had planned to stay only a few weeks but found so much work in Tarsus that he decided to remain for a while and take a course at the university while practicing."

"I was hoping he might be able to help my father."

"He is quite skilled and has helped many people in Tarsus. Why not wait here for him?"

Saul took a seat upon a bench and accepted the glass of wine Lucius offered him. "I'm taking charge of my father's shop," he said. "We would like to make the sails for your ships."

"Of course you shall," Lucius assured him. "We have always found sails from the shop of Joachim better than any others."

"Will you tell that to other shipowners for me?"

"Better still, let me act as your agent—and charge you no commission."

"But how can I repay you?"

"By telling me what you have learned in the years you've been away and describing the places you visited. Since my father died, I've been tied to this room and this desk."

"I thought you were going to be a philosopher?"

Lucius laughed. "As I remember it, you were going to be a lawyer and the leading teacher in Jerusalem, yet look at us now.

Nestor was right when he said the thinking man should serve rather than set himself apart."

"Don't you miss the old days?"

"Of course—as I'm sure you will miss Jerusalem. But the memory of other places will grow dimmer, when you discover how much satisfaction doing a good job here can give you. Besides, I expect one day to become Ethnarch of Tarsus." It was a Greek term the Romans had adopted, signifying the governor of a city or a province.

Saul grinned. "Don't forget what Socrates said about politicians. To him they were all scoundrels."

"I shall pattern my political life after that of Athenodorus." Lucius was quite serious. "He saved Tarsus when it was in danger of being throttled by evil men and his name is more revered than any man who ever lived here. That shall be my goal—that and becoming the most successful shipowner in the city."

"I intend to become the most successful tent- and sailmaker."

"Good!" said Lucius. "We can work together."

Their discussion was interrupted by the arrival of a rather thin young man with a slightly olive complexion and clean-cut features that betrayed his Greek ancestry. He hesitated on the threshold, when he saw that Lucius was not alone.

"Come in, Luke," Lucius cried. "I want you to meet an old friend. Saul is recently from Jerusalem, where he has been studying law, but we grew up here in Tarsus as boys together."

"Your head weaver talked of nothing else but his master's brilliant son who is going to be the greatest rabbi in Jerusalem," said Luke and Saul was immediately attracted by his warm friendliness.

"Saul is going to be the greatest tentmaker in Tarsus instead," said Lucius. "Just as I was once going to be a second Nestor but wound up as a shipowner."

"I was planning to be a pirate, until I saw one crucified on the quay on Troas," Luke confessed. "Somehow the life didn't seem so exciting to me after that, so I became a physician instead."

"You couldn't have chosen a better place than Tarsus," Saul assured him.

"I shall only be here a few weeks longer," Luke told him. "I was on my way to Antioch-in-Pisidia to serve with the Roman army, when Lucius persuaded me to stop here."

"Ezra says you cured him."

Luke shook his head. "Ezra cured himself by wearing bindings I prescribed. If he leaves them off, blood will collect in his legs again and break out in the form of another sore."

"My father is ill with a palsy," said Saul. "I was wondering if you could come to see him."

"Was it a sudden paralysis?"

"My mother says it was like a thunderbolt from heaven." Even repeating the words caused a stab of pain in Saul's heart. "He was stricken several weeks ago and has not moved or spoken since."

"I shall be happy to see him, but I must warn you that I probably cannot help him." Luke's expression was grave. "Most such cases are beyond the competence of even the most skilled physicians and I am hardly more than a neophyte."

## VII

Watching the deft way Luke went about examining his father, Saul felt his hopes rise, even though he had been warned that the case was probably hopeless. The physician took his time with the examination, feeling the pulse beating at Joachim's temple and rolling beneath his fingers the blood vessel that was distinctly visible there under the skin. Moving down along the sick man's neck, he applied his fingers to the veins that swelled there, as if testing the amount of distension in them. When he exposed Joachim's ankles, Saul saw that they were puffed to almost twice their normal size. And, when Luke pressed upon the skin over them, the tips of his fingers sank in and little pits remained after the pressure was removed. Perhaps half an hour passed before Luke rose from the kneeling posture he'd assumed beside the couch during the examination and met Saul's inquiring gaze.

"Your father is suffering from what some people call a

'stroke,'" he said, "because the victim often falls as if he had been struck with a bludgeon."

"What is the cause?"

"We don't know entirely," Luke admitted. "Once I was allowed to dissect the body of a condemned criminal who died in prison with a condition similar to this. I thought I found the answer in a hemorrhage within the brain, but I couldn't be sure."

"You still think there is no hope?"

"The prognosis is grave—I wouldn't want to deceive you about that. But he does seem to have a marked plethora." When Saul frowned at the word, Luke added, "I mean he appears to be suffering from an excess of blood, which might possibly make the paralysis worse."

"This plethora—can you cure it?"

"Perhaps not cure, but it can often be relieved by bloodletting."

"Our Law prohibits defilement by contact with blood," Saul admitted. "But I want everything done that possibly might help my father."

"What about the rest of the family?"

Saul knew his mother wouldn't understand what Luke proposed to do. And if she asked Rabbi Eloichim, as she was certain to do if he told her about it, he had no doubt of the old teacher's verdict, either. The decision must be his and rightly so, since his own transgression of the Law could have brought on his father's illness.

"Please do what you think is best for him," he told Luke. "I will assume full responsibility."

"I shall need a bowl to catch the blood and a towel to put under his arm." Luke opened his instrument case and Saul hurried to the kitchen, returning with a bowl and a towel. Meanwhile, the physician rolled the left sleeve of Joachim's sleeping garment almost up to his shoulder and tied a cord about his arm just above the elbow. To Saul, the veins already seemed distended almost to bursting, but Luke showed no evidence of haste, as he took from the case a slender metal instrument with a narrow blade and a sharp point. Placing the bowl beside Joachim's arm and steadying it with his body, Luke thrust the point of the instrument through the skin of Joachim's forearm and into a vein.

Saul felt himself grow dizzy as a geyser of blood shot upward and splattered into the bowl. He put out a hand to a chair to steady himself but the physician paid no attention to him. Twisting the blade slightly to keep open the small slit he had made through both skin and vein beneath, he held the arm steady and kept the side of the bowl pressed against it. The level in the bowl rose steadily until it seemed to Saul that all of his father's blood was being drained away. Luke continued to keep the wound open, however, gently stroking Joachim's arm upward with the palm of his left hand, as if milking blood from the vein visible there. Finally, when the bowl was more than half-filled, the young physician loosened the cord, removed the lancet from the wound and quickly placed a small pad of cloth against the tiny opening, binding it to Joachim's arm with a strip of cloth from his small kit.

Picking up the bowl of blood, Luke went through the kitchen into the court, where a brick-lined trench connected with the sewer that ran along the street in front of the house. Emptying the bowl into the trench, he poured water into it from a crock on a bench just outside the kitchen door, rinsed it out several times and poured that, too, into the drain. Then he washed his hands and, coming back into the room, dried them on the towel that had been under Joachim's arm. The entire procedure had lasted no more than a quarter of an hour, Saul estimated, and only a few drops of blood were on the towel, the rest having been expertly caught in the bowl.

"I can't promise that this will help him," said Luke, "but you will note that the plethora has already been somewhat reduced. It is my hope that the bleeding may slow the hemorrhage from a blood vessel in his skull that has probably ruptured and caused the paralysis. I know of nothing else to do."

"Will you come again tomorrow?"

"As soon as my lessons at the university are finished." Luke started to close his small instrument case. "Did I hear Lucius say you were in Jerusalem recently?"

"Only a week ago. I was studying there when my father was stricken."

"Did you hear anything about a man called Jesus of Nazareth?"

"Yes." Saul gave the Greek physician a startled look. "Yes. But how did you—"

"I treated a man in the Temple of Asklepios at Pergamum. He came from Capernaum, a town on a lake in a district called Galilee—"

"A friend of mine goes to Galilee regularly to sell jewelry. He once heard the Teacher of Nazareth speak in a synagogue."

"My patient was a Roman soldier who developed symptoms of leprosy after being transferred from a post in Galilee to one in Greece. He says Jesus of Nazareth cures leprosy merely by laying his hands upon the patient."

"I heard nothing about healing," said Saul. "From what my friend said, the teachings of the Nazarene sound very much like what I learned here from the Stoic philosopher Nestor."

"I'm familiar with that philosophy," said Luke.

"Are you a follower of Asklepios?"

Luke shook his head. "Asklepios is supposed to be the patron god of physicians and to visit the sick in the temples devoted to his worship. I spent more than a year at the Asklepia in Pergamum and saw only priests who put on masks to make the sick think the god himself was visiting them."

"Surely they could tell the difference?"

"Not after they had been given a drug to dull their senses and bring on strange dreams. The rite of *incubatio*, as they call it, is practiced in all the temples of Asklepios, but I'm sure the same effect could be obtained from drinking wine with dried poppy stirred into it."

"Then there is actually no such god?"

"I suspect there's only one god, wherever you are," said Luke, placing the instrument case under his arm. "You Jews call him Yahweh. In Egypt he might be called Osiris. In Greece Zeus, or Asklepios, and in Rome Apollo. When you deal daily with life and death as I do, the important thing to know is that some Deity breathes life into each of us when we are conceived in our mother's womb. For that we can always be grateful and pay him the homage due him, whatever his name."

## VIII

Luke had warned Saul not to expect any dramatic change in his father's condition, so he was startled the next morning to see a faint smile momentarily contract the muscles of the sick man's face. The effect was fleeting and Saul could not be sure it had ever happened, but when he looked into his father's eyes, he was fairly certain that a light of recognition burned there momentarily. Filled with a sudden overwhelming tide of gratitude and hope, he stumbled into the courtyard and lifted his face to the sky as he spoke a prayer of thanksgiving.

A croaking sound from the room he had just left made him rush back and he saw that his father's lips were moving, although the sounds he made were unintelligible. Yet the fact that his father had smiled and tried to speak to him so filled Saul's heart with joy and gratitude to the Most High for answering his prayers, that he cried aloud: "Give my father life, O God of Israel, and I will dedicate my own life to thee, to do with as thou will."

The words died away and, feeling a little self-conscious now for yielding himself so completely to emotion, Saul got to his feet. When he saw once again only the same masklike expression on Joachim's face that had greeted him on his arrival from Jerusalem, his feeling of elation began to ebb rapidly and doubt took over instead. As the morning passed, however, there was no longer doubt that Joachim was improving. First the toes of his right foot began to move, then the fingers of the right hand, though as yet there was no real strength in them. Several times during the morning, he made the same croaking sound Saul had heard and shortly after noon, he spoke a word which both Saul and his mother was sure was Saul's own name.

"It's a miracle!" Saul cried, when Luke arrived late that afternoon. "He moved and even spoke my name."

The face of the Greek physician lit up with the warm smile that came so readily to it. "You're right," he said, when he had examined Joachim thoroughly. "The letting of blood has relieved the plethora."

"And he will be well?"

"It's too soon yet to be certain." Luke took a mortar and pestle from his case. Selecting a length of what appeared to be a dried root from a package, he cut it into pieces and began grinding them up in the mortar.

"This is mandragora," he explained. "Some physicians believe it slows the flux of the humours and keeps plethora down."

He ground the dried root carefully, pressing out each lump with the large end of the pestle until the whole had been reduced to a fine powder. At his request, Saul brought a small flagon of wine and, pouring some of it into the mortar, Luke continued to grind, adding more wine until the mortar itself was almost full. Slowly, as he ground, the normal purplish color of the wine changed to brown. Finally, he emptied the contents of the mortar into the flask, shook it up and poured more into the mortar, grinding again until all the powder was dissolved. This done, he poured the contents of the mortar back into the flagon and shook it thoroughly until the brown color was disseminated completely throughout the purple of the wine.

Measuring out half a cup of the mixture, Luke began to feed it to Joachim with a spoon. His hands were as gentle as a woman's, his patience infinite, as he held Joachim's lower lip with his fingers to form a cup from which each spoonful of the mixture could slowly trinkle down the sick man's throat without choking or strangling him. When the dose was finished, the physician got to his feet.

"Give him the same dose of mandragora before he sleeps tonight and again in the morning and at noon tomorrow," he directed. "He is beginning to swallow without strangling, so he may soon be able to drink it directly from the cup. I will come again tomorrow afternoon."

"I don't know how we can ever thank you," said Saul.

"Let us hope you will be as grateful when I ask for my fee," Luke said with a grin. "By the way, Lucius asked me to tell you a ship arrived this afternoon and needs a new set of sails. He said you could measure them tomorrow."

"I will measure them today," Saul said promptly. "Are you going back to the quay?"

"Yes."

"Then I will walk with you."

Saul called a servant to stay with his father and the two of them set out for the waterfront. They made a striking pair, Saul's broad shoulders, sturdy body and almost leonine head contrasting with Luke's slenderness and quick graceful stride.

"You can do me a favor if you will," Luke told him as they moved along the quay around the Rhegma, with its small forest of masts and spars.

"Ask anything and I would still be in your debt."

"I've never seen a case of leprosy cured. If the man called Jesus of Nazareth in Galilee has really produced a cure, I would like to know more about it."

"I will write to my friend Joseph in Jerusalem tonight," Saul promised. "He was starting another journey through that region when I left and should be back by now."

"A cure for leprosy would be a great thing for many thousands of people."

"Perhaps it was magic—or sorcery."

Luke shrugged. "I have no belief in such. A physician—if he is worthy of the name—puts his faith in drugs, the lancet, and the strength and skill of his two hands for setting broken bones."

"Why are you going with the Roman army when you could make a good living here? Do you yearn to be a soldier?"

"At the Asklepia of Pergamum, we saw much illness but few of the injuries a physician is constantly called on to treat," Luke explained. "I feel unsure of myself where they are concerned and a year or two with the army will give me all the experience I need in that field. Besides, there are many places I want to see before I settle down in Troas."

"Troas! Where is that?"

"A city on the coast of Mysia, not far from the mouth of the Hellespont. Some say it's the site of ancient Troy, where Greeks fought against the Trojans after Paris stole Helen—" Seeing the blank look on Saul's face, Luke asked, "Have you never heard of our Greek heroes?"

Saul shook his head. "A Jew is supposed to study only the history of our own people, as set down in the Torah. The beginning of my great sin was when I started listening to Nestor."

"Your great sin?"

"We Jews aren't supposed to consort with Gentiles. My father's palsy is a curse from God, because I strove with Gentiles in a gymnasium in Jerusalem and listened to men like Gamaliel, who are lax in carrying out the provisions of the Law."

"Are you telling me your God would strike an old man down with paralysis, because his son sought to build up his body by running and jumping with others?"

"That's what Rabbi Eloichim says."

"Then Rabbi Eloichim is a fool!" It was the first time Saul had ever seen Luke aroused to anger. "I would have no faith in such a god."

"But we must obey the Law." Saul's protest was only half-hearted, for Luke had put his finger on one thing that had troubled him ever since news of his father's illness had come to Jerusalem. The punishment of Joachim, to whose goodness, generosity and obedience to the Law every Jew and many Gentiles in Tarsus could attest, didn't seem fair by any standard.

"So that's why you've been so disturbed," said Luke. "Surely you know better than that, Saul."

"I've been taught the Law since I was a small child. How can I depart from it now?"

"The commandments your people live by, are a good set of rules for all men," Luke said. "They have been, ever since Hammurabi first had them chiseled on stone pillars for all to read."

Saul stared at the Greek physician half-expecting to see him struck dead on the spot for blasphemy. "Nestor said something like that years ago but I didn't believe he meant it the way it sounded. Are you sure there were rules like ours before Moses?"

"The Laws of Hammurabi were first written down for all men in his kingdom to obey nearly three thousand years ago," said Luke. "When was Moses supposed to have given them to your people?"

"No more than half that long ago," Saul admitted.

"Then the story about your God giving them to Moses is only a legend, Saul. The old tales of the Greek heroes and gods are full of such things. These are rules that men know instinctively."

"But we are punished by God if we transgress the Law."

"Every man is punished if he breaks moral laws—by his own conscience, if not by his fellow men. But nothing in them would strike down an innocent old man for another's misdeeds. It wasn't the anger of any god that almost killed your father, Saul, but a leaking blood vessel, allowing blood to escape just as water will leave an aqueduct if it is broken. When I bled him yesterday, I lowered the pressure in the leaking vessel enough for the blood to stop flowing out. Now do you understand?"

"I—I'm not sure," said Saul. "Whatever the cause, I have offered my life to God in return for Father's."

"How?"

"I shall take his place in the shop, and in the congregation."

"Do that by all means—if it is what you want and what will make you happy," Luke urged. "But not because you feel that you should carry a burden of guilt all your life."

"Tell me more about Troas." Saul changed the subject abruptly, for the prospect of the years ahead, working in the shop measuring and cutting sails and even assuming a seat of a ruler in the synagogue on the Sabbath gave him no pleasure.

"Its beauty must be seen to be believed." Luke's eyes brightened at the thought. "The city is built of granite quarried from the hills back of the shore. Columns from the old palace of King Priam are still standing or lying in the sand and the water and oak trees are everywhere. I plan to build a home in their shadow overlooking the sea, so I can watch ships heading for the mouth of the Hellespont on the way to Byzantium and the

Pontus Euxinus. It's like having a whole world at your doorstep."

"Is Troas much of a city?"

"Not as large as Tarsus, but much of the old grandeur is still there. The Greek theater is now in ruins but the Romans have built baths and gymnasia. The climate is mild and cool at night, with a breeze from the sea."

"I thought Lucius said you came from Antioch."

"I do. The first time I saw Troas was when the ship carrying me to the Asklepia at Pergamum put in there. I knew then I would never be satisfied with any other place for my home. You must visit me there one day and see for yourself."

Saul looked at the ships lining the quay and thought of the shop where tomorrow he would be cutting and sewing new sails for Lucius' ships, and the day after working on tents for the shepherds of the Taurus range to the north.

"I'm afraid my travels are over," he said. Then, as if to reassure himself and give him courage to face the future he quickly added, "But I have seen the Holy Temple at Jerusalem. A Jew can ask no more in this world."

## IX

In the days that followed, Joachim improved steadily. Luke came daily for several more days, then twice a week. Just before his departure for Antioch-in-Pisidia, he bled the tentmaker again to keep down—he explained—any recurring tendency toward plethora. He also showed Saul where to purchase the dried root of mandragora and how to prepare the infusion in wine for Joachim to take.

Saul bade Luke farewell when he joined a detail of Roman troops bound northward for the great military encampment in the Galatian uplands. He knew he was going to be lonely after the departure of the young physician, for, though Luke was a Gentile, the two had achieved from the beginning that rare meeting of the minds in which each stimulated the intellect of the other. Under Luke's guidance, Saul had purchased scrolls in

Greek telling the thrilling stories of the great heroes and their adventures. In turn, Saul gave the physician as a present on his departure, a set of scrolls of the Torah in the Greek translation called the Septuagint.

To allay some of the loneliness he felt in Tarsus after Luke's departure, Saul threw himself wholly into the work of his father's shop. Additional weavers were employed and one man was kept busy now merely spinning the tough goat's-hair into cilicium thread. With the increase in the work force, he no longer spent much time in the shop, but toured Tarsus and the neighboring cities, soliciting tentmaking assignments at the caravanseries where the shepherds camped when they brought their products to market, or at the harbors where ships were tied up. This was the winter season and none of the great round ships from Egypt bound for Rome ventured upon the usually stormy sea. But many small coastal vessels still dared to make the short runs between Tarsus and other cities along the great arc of the Mediterranean shore, so Saul was able to get enough business to keep the shop running steadily.

In Tarsus, Saul was already beginning to take a position of leadership in the congregation to which the family belonged. He read the scriptures often at the Sabbath services and sometimes spoke upon them, when no visiting rabbi was available. But though his natural eloquence made him a favorite for this chore, particularly among the younger members of the congregation, he found little satisfaction in it.

A few weeks after Luke's departure, a letter arrived from Joseph:

*Since last I spoke to you I have become a follower of Jesus of Nazareth, about whom you inquire. I am not one of his disciples. They number only twelve and all are Galileans, except Judas of Kerioth and Simon called Zelotes. The leader is Simon Peter, a gentle man of great strength. I still dwell in Jerusalem, for Simon Peter has assigned me to watch over the activities of the High Priest and others who would destroy Jesus, because he teaches that loving God and one's fellow men is more important*

*for gaining eternal life than obeying every jot and tittle of the
Law. This teaching you no doubt realize is very similar to some
of those of the blessed Hillel.*

*I am sorry I cannot tell your friend, the Greek physician, how
the Master cures leprosy. He performs many cures and miracles,
such as making the palsied to walk, casting out evil spirits and
the like. The secret of his power lies in the fact that he is the
Messiah, the Son of God. We are all confident that he will soon
announce himself to the world.*

*I remember you once said that a caravan driver who brought you
to Jerusalem paid tribute to a brigand named Barabbas. Not long
ago, this Barabbas and his men grew so bold that they created
a disturbance in the Temple. I think they sought to seize Jerusalem then, as Judas the Gaulonite tried to do long ago. But they
failed, too, and Barabbas is now in prison. The Chief Priests
claim that Jesus of Nazareth is also a revolutionary and I believe
they will seek to do him harm.*

*I hope your father will soon be well enough for you to return to
Jerusalem. Please tell him my prayers are for his quick recovery.
May God bless and keep you both,*

*Your friend, Joseph*

The letter sent a wave of nostalgia through Saul, as he recalled the days he'd enjoyed so much in Jerusalem, after Joseph
had introduced him to the centurion Cornelius and the group
who had striven together almost daily at the xystus. But he
did not let himself think about it long, for nothing was to be
gained by yearning for what could not be. Whether or not any
sin of his had brought on Joachim's illness, he had made a
promise to God as a token of thanksgiving for the life of his
father. And however weary he might sometimes be of the life
he had chosen, he would not turn back.

Taking a piece of parchment, Saul mixed ink, sharpened a
quill, and began to write a letter to Luke at Antioch-in-Pisidia.

He told of Joseph's belief that the cures effected by the Teacher of Nazareth were miracles of God's power and not accomplished by any medicine. But he didn't expect the Greek physician to believe this any more than Saul himself believed an obscure rabbi from Nazareth—a town of no consequence in the estimation of the inhabitants of Jerusalem—could be the long awaited Messiah, who would free Israel from bondage and raise it to a position among the foremost of nations, greater even than Rome itself.

## x

The winter passed and the days grew warmer. Joachim improved steadily and was now able to sit in the sun in the court back of the shop and walk a little. By the time of the Passover, he could visit the shop for a few hours each morning and each afternoon, supervising the activities there while Saul was busy gathering orders for new sails and tents.

The most sacred of Jewish religious feasts was the time for particular rejoicing this spring, for Joachim seemed well on the way to recovery. Only a slight dragging of the right foot and a tendency of his mouth to twist a little remained as evidence of his near fatal illness, while the shop, under Saul's leadership, was more prosperous than ever. For Saul, however, there was none of the soaring sense of religious feeling he'd experienced when, with Jepthah and Miriam, he had celebrated the holy season at Jerusalem. Looking back upon it now, he found it hard to believe that only a year had passed.

He put aside his lingering feeling of unhappiness, however, for the sake of his father and mother, not wanting them to dream that he was anything but thoroughly satisfied with the life he had selected for himself in Tarsus. When the Paschal lamb had been eaten, he went alone to the rooftop to listen, while those in the Jewish quarter of Tarsus sang the Hallel, as Jews did at this season wherever they were. And remembering how the choir of Levites in the temple had chanted the sacred hymn from the heights and the music had floated down upon the Holy City, he felt as if the whole world had passed him by.

Two weeks after the Passover, Saul received another letter from Joseph. This time the whole tenor of the message had changed:

*I write this from the depths of a broken heart. Jesus of Nazareth is dead, victim of a plot by the High Priest, who accused him of aspiring to be King of the Jews and turned him over to Pontius Pilate to be crucified. Judas, one of the disciples, betrayed the Master to the authorities. He was paid thirty pieces of silver for the deed, but most of us believe that he did it in the hope of forcing Jesus to announce that he was the Messiah and use the power with which he cured leprosy and other diseases to make himself king.*

*Some say the Master foretold his death in Galilee, and again on the way to Jerusalem. There are those also who claim that he has risen from the dead and has been seen by them, but the guards who were at the tomb say his body was stolen by the disciples. Most of these have gone back to Galilee, lest they also be taken, but I shall stay here in Jerusalem. The temple authorities seem to be satisfied with having caused the Master's death so I don't believe I shall be in danger.*

*These are dark days for those of us who loved and followed Jesus. I am trying to continue his teachings, but few will listen, now that he has turned out not to be the Messiah. Many pilgrims were in Jerusalem for the Passover and, with the Feast of Pente- cost only a month away, the business of a silversmith is good, so I can still earn my living. I was glad to receive your letter telling of your father's continued progress and I hope by this time he has fully recovered.*

*May God bless you all,*

*Your friend, Joseph*

Saul had little time to think about what Joseph had written, however, for a second letter arrived in the same mail. It was from Miriam, telling of Jepthah's having been bedded for some weeks with a fever. And since the Jerusalem establishment was now a thriving one, she asked that, if possible, Saul come to the Holy City for a while to handle the work there.

"What do you say, Saul?" Joachim asked. "Do you want to go?"

"The Feast of Pentecost will soon come. With the seaways open again for the summer, many pilgrims will be going to Jerusalem, so Miriam can hardly run the shop alone. Besides, Jepthah and I had been thinking that we should try to sell our tents to the Nabateans who dwell east of the Jordan."

"Then you would like to go?"

"I will do what you want me to do, Father."

"You must do whatever will make you happiest," Joachim insisted. "You have done well with the shop and your mother and I would like nothing better than for you to stay here, but when I heard you speak in the synagogue last Sabbath, I knew you were meant to be a scholar, not a stitcher of thread and cloth."

"You need me here," Saul protested.

"With the work you have brought into the shop, we will be busy for a long time," said Joachim. "Besides, your friend Lucius offered to buy the shop from me before I became ill. You have made it even more prosperous than it was then, so I'm sure the offer will still hold."

"How can I work out my penance?"

"What is this—penance?"

"For my sin, in consorting with Gentiles at Jerusalem. Rabbi Eloichim says that's why you were stricken."

"Eloichim is an old fool!"

"But the Law—"

"I'm too old to quibble over questions of the Law, Saul. To me it is summed up simplest in the words of the Prophet Micah: *'And what doth the Lord require of thee but to do justly and to love mercy and to walk humbly before thy God?'*"

"Those are the teachings of the Galilean Joseph of Cyprus

wrote me about," Saul exclaimed. "He claimed to be the Messiah, but Pontius Pilate crucified him."

"A crucified Messiah?"

"Joseph says some of his followers claim that he rose from the dead. But the temple authorities say they stole his body from the tomb."

"It's a strange tale," Joachim said. "Perhaps you can learn more about it when you get to Jerusalem."

As I made my journey and was come
nigh unto Damascus about noon,
suddenly there shone from heaven a
great light.

THE ACTS 22:6

# Book III · Damascus

I

Saul's return to Jerusalem was something less than a triumph. Miriam, it developed, had not consulted Jepthah when she sent the letter asking for help and the anticipation of Saul's arrival had been enough to get his brother-in-law out of bed in spite of the fever. Jepthah made no secret of his displeasure at Saul's coming, but Miriam was glad to see him. And the baby, a sturdy little boy who toddled on uncertain feet, crowed with delight when he tossed him in the air.

Miriam prepared the evening meal and afterward they ascended to the roof, as many other inhabitants of the neighborhood had already done. Built so close together that most of them had common walls, the houses in this part of Jerusalem were two stories high and flat roofed. It was a simple matter to step across a low parapet from one roof to the other—a route sometimes called the "Road of the Roofs"—and the early evening hours were a time of visiting and gossip between families. In warm weather, as now, pallets were unrolled on the flat roof and the occupants slept in the open air.

Several neighbors came across the "Road of the Roofs" to greet the returned traveler. One was a merchant named Asa, a strict Pharisee. Another was a potter named Tob, who had once been a slave but had long since been freed. He did a thriving business in fine ware that was much prized by pilgrims, since he used a metal stamp to imprint the outlines of the temple in the soft clay forming the bottom of cups, plates, vases, and other ware, enabling the possessor to indicate, without actually boasting, that he had made a pilgrimage to the Holy City.

"Did you come by way of Caesarea?" Tob asked after Miriam had served them spiced cakes and the sweet thin wine so much preferred in Jewish households.

"No," said Saul. "I had the good fortune to get passage on a vessel directly from Tarsus to Joppa."

"Coming by sea may have saved your life," said Asa. "Ever since Barabbas was freed by the governor, he and his brigands have been exacting tribute from every caravan traveling between Jerusalem and Caesarea—at double their former price."

"Why was he released?"

"It's customary to let the people choose a criminal to be freed from prison at the Passover," Tob explained. "When Pontius Pilate gave the crowd a choice between Barabbas and the Nazarene teacher, they chose to free Barabbas and the Nazarene was crucified."

"A Greek physician who healed my father asked about the Nazarene," said Saul. "He'd heard of him from a Roman soldier with leprosy. Is it true that the Galilean healed many people?"

"He did perform miracles," said Tob. "And I think he was really a good man—"

"How can you say that when he stirred up the people against the temple and against Rome?" Asa demanded indignantly. "Pontius Pilate defiled the sanctuary once with the blood of the Galileans he seized there when Barabbas was captured. If the Nazarene had been allowed to stir up the rabble, it would have been the same thing over again."

"No one has proved that Jesus belonged to Barabbas' band," Tob insisted.

"But he did travel with known traitors," said Jepthah. "The man Judas, who hanged himself, was his disciple and another of those close to him was known as 'the Zealot.' That should be proof enough for anyone that he sought to create an uprising."

"Jesus named himself King of the Jews," Asa added. "I saw it written on the board above his head as he hung on the cross. If he were really the Messiah, as he claimed, how could he let himself be crucified like an escaped slave or a common thief?"

"What happened to his followers?" Saul asked.

"They ran away like frightened sheep," said Asa. "I hear they went back to Galilee."

"But not before they stole his body from the tomb of Joseph of Arimathea and claimed he had risen from the dead," Jepthah added.

"I know Joseph well," said Tob. "He assures me that the Nazarene did rise from the dead."

"Then it was a trick," snapped Asa. "In Samaria I saw a magician named Simon Magus appear to raise the dead, but everyone knew it was a feat of magic. He made no claim to being the Messiah."

"A Messiah from Samaria?" Tob raised his eyebrows. "That would be even harder to believe than one from Nazareth."

"Or anyone else in Galilee," Asa agreed. "When the Messiah does come—and mind you, I'm not unhappy with things as they are—it will be in glory so everyone will recognize him."

"Some of the Nazarene's disciples have returned to Jerusalem," said Tob.

"Who?" Asa demanded.

"The man called Simon Peter for one, I saw him in the marketplace yesterday. They say he is now the leader of those who followed Jesus."

"What a leader he will be!" Asa snorted. "I was in the garden of the High Priest's palace the night they seized the imposter. Simon Peter denied even knowing his master three times."

"Did you say the disciples of Jesus of Nazareth claim that he rose from the dead?" Saul asked.

"Yes. But it's a trick."

"What are they trying to do? Start another mystery religion?"

Asa's head jerked around like a puppet in one of the shows that were often performed during the religious festivals. "What do you mean?" he demanded.

Saul realized too late that he had laid a trap for himself—and sprung it. "Like the worship of Osiris in Egypt," he hastened to explain.

"What do you know of such things?" Jepthah demanded.

"I heard of it in Tarsus."

"When you were studying at the university?"

"Yes."

"Blasphemy," Jepthah muttered. "No wonder your father—"

"Anyone who travels hears of the Greek religions, Jepthah," said Tob. "I witnessed a ceremony to Isis and Osiris when I was in Egypt. They make a celebration of it there, as we do the religious holidays."

"We must do more to counteract such influences in the Diaspora," said Asa. "Only a few days ago, I was telling Caiaphas that we should send more of our Jerusalem teachers to visit congregations in other cities, lest our young people be wooed away from the Law by these new religions of the Greeks."

"I hear the tribute from the Diaspora has been falling off, too," said Tob with a chuckle. "You can be sure that will stir the priests as nothing else would. I'm all for getting some of the teachers away from the Porch of Solomon, though. There'll be less noise in the temple then and perhaps a man can hear himself pray."

"Are you here to stay, Saul?" Asa asked.

"I don't know." Saul saw Jepthah look at him quickly and knew what was in his brother-in-law's mind. "Father gave me permission to go on with my studies, as soon as Jepthah recovers from his fever."

"I am well now," said Jepthah promptly.

"Are you going to study with your old teacher again?" Asa's tone was frosty.

"No."

"So Gamaliel's perversion of the Law finally turned even you against him," Jepthah said triumphantly and Saul let the statement stand, although he was not yet prepared to admit its truth. The years in the School of Gamaliel had been even more intellectually stimulating than the period when he'd sat at the feet of Nestor. But he couldn't erase from his memory the black day when he'd come home from the xystus to be confronted with the letter telling of his father's illness and had heard his brother-in-law's accusation that his own sin had brought it about. And even though Joachim had assured him that such a thing could not possibly be true, he had never quite been able to erase the lingering doubt and feeling of guilt from his mind.

"Say what you will about Gamaliel, his is still an authoritative voice in the Sanhedrin." Tob's voice brought Saul's thoughts back to the present. "Even those who don't favor his interpretations of the Law respect his logic in difficult questions."

"We have organized a Synagogue of the Cilicians since you went away, Saul," said Jepthah. "That's where you should worship. A most respected Pharisee named Elam from the school of Shammai is our leader."

A picture popped into Saul's mind—of a fat man with an overly large phylactery bound to his forehead and long fringes on his purple robe, sitting in the shop of a shoemaker while his shoes were being resewn.

"I don't want to make a choice yet," he said, but he already knew that when he did, it wouldn't be the Cilicians.

"The Synagogue of the Libertines needs a teacher," said Tob. "It's made up of freed slaves and the older rabbis don't want to bother with them because they can't pay much. But it's a wonderful opportunity for a young teacher who wants to make a name for himself. Come visit there with me on the next Sabbath, Saul. They need somene eloquent who can inspire them."

Saul glanced at Jepthah and the disapproval on his brother-in-law's face was enough to crystallize his decision.

"I'll try," he promised. "The worst they can do is walk out."

11

Looking down upon the group of freed slaves gathered in Tob's pottery shed that served them as a place of worship, Saul decided that he had surely taken on the poorest among all of the congregations in Jerusalem—in itself a challenge to a young and ambitious teacher. His major task, he had decided after talking to Tob, was to teach the majesty and beauty of the Law while avoiding the deadening monotony of argument and interpretation with which the Pharisees had encompassed the simple shining truths of the Torah.

When the time came to read, he chose a scroll containing the teachings of the Prophet Micah, remembering the passage his father had quoted to him beginning:

*He hath shewed thee O man what is good. And what doth the Lord require of thee, but to do justly, and to love mercy, and to walk humbly with thy God?*

The congregation was quiet as he read. Having been forced always to be humble among their fellows, these men could understand walking humbly before God. The reading finished, Saul interpreted the message of the Prophet as simply as he could, explaining how the Most High had given the commandments of the Torah to Moses as a guide to men, a path along which they might walk with God. He avoided carefully any involved questions of Pharisaic interpretation, and kept his discourse simple and direct, emphasizing that, through obeying the Law, a man might grow in the estimation of the Most High and earn for himself eternal life.

When he finished, the congregation, including Tob, filed from the building. Only a few stopped to speak to the young teacher and, although Saul was sure he'd done a good job, doubts began to assail him. Had he made the relationship of the worshipers to God too simple, he wondered as he gathered up his scrolls? Had he given his listeners the impression that he was talking down to them? Reluctant to go outside, he delayed until Tob came back in and when he saw that his friend's face was beaming, began to take heart again.

"We've been outside having a meeting," Tob explained. "It seemed better than having it here, where you might be embarrassed by their discussion."

"Discussion?"

"These men were only recently slaves, so they didn't feel

learned enough to talk to such a brilliant teacher. They want you as their regular leader, Saul—if you will accept the position."

"I—" In his relief, Saul could say no more at the moment.

"There will be little pay."

"That doesn't matter."

"Then you accept?"

"Of course. I was afraid they didn't like my sermon."

"They loved it," Tob assured him. "Isak, one of the elders, would like you to share the noonday meal with him and his family, but he hesitated to ask you."

"I shall be happy to go." Saul put the packet of scrolls under his arm. "Will you be with us?"

"I would much rather be, but my wife's brother is coming to take the noonday meal with us. He buys a lot of pottery from me, so I can't afford to antagonize him."

Walking home that afternoon after enjoying the simple hospitality and frugal fare provided by Isak and his family, Saul felt more content than at any time since he'd been called home to Tarsus by his father's illness. At last, he was sure now, he'd found a calling into which he could pour all of himself and in which he would be able to find contentment.

III

The following Sabbath was the Feast of Pentecost. In ancient times it had been called the Feast of the Harvest or the Day of First Fruits, marking the end of the grain harvest which began about the time of the Passover and lasted for some fifty days. Coming at the beginning of summer, when the weather was not yet disagreeably hot in the lowlands, Pentecost was a period of celebration when farmers and city dwellers alike gave offerings of thanksgiving for the harvest of grain.

When Saul rose to read the lesson in the Synagogue of the Libertines on the morning of Pentecost, the hall was packed and some stood outside, unable to enter. But the weather was warm and he had ordered the doors and windows thrown open so everyone could hear. Tob was there and, to Saul's surprise, so was Asa, with a man dressed in the robe of a temple priest. He had no time to wonder why Asa and his companion had come, however, for the service began just then and he started to read.

Opening the scroll containing the first of the five books of the Torah, Saul read the story of how Jacob, having cheated his brother Esau out of his birthright, had fled into the country from which Abraham and his people had come. In the lush pasturelands along the banks of the River Balikh east of Damascus, Jacob had served fourteen long years as servant to his father-in-law, Laban. Being shrewd and willing to work, he had prospered and, when he returned to Bashan and Gilead on the east side of the Jordan north of the crossing near Jericho, he had brought with him flocks and herds of considerable value. Only one stumbling block lay in his path, the fact that his brother Esau might still be angry at him and seize the possessions he had worked so hard to gain.

The congregation listened intently as Saul read how, when Jacob came to the River Jabbok, he divided his herds and flocks, sending half ahead as a peace offering to his brother. And how, alone and afraid on the banks of the stream, uncertain of just what lay ahead, he had been accosted by a stranger with whom he wrestled until dawn broke.

Saul put the scroll back into its case and looked down from the pulpit upon the intent faces of perhaps a hundred people filling the shed. He had dramatized the story as he read, using unconsciously his natural talent as an orator and storyteller. And seeing in their eyes now something of the feeling he'd created in them, he felt himself buoyed up by a sense of power he'd never experienced before, the heady knowledge that he was able to mold minds with his voice and his words. It was a sensation he was to experience many times in the years to come, but never quite so completely as he did now.

"Like Jacob, most of you have known servitude," he told his audience. "Like Jacob, too, you have gained your freedom and some of you have prospered. But while gaining wealth, Jacob sometimes forgot God, by whose favor all of this had come about. Knowing he had broken God's Law in stealing the birthright of his brother, he was afraid. And, fearing Esau's wrath, he dared not enter the land of his forefathers boldly but sent gifts ahead, hoping to appease his brother. God, however, wished Jacob to know it was his Law that had been broken and sent an angel to wrestle with him on the banks of the River Jabbok.

"In our fear lest we be attacked by those against whom we may have sinned, we sometimes forget that our shield and buckler is always the Law," Saul continued. "If we maintain right standing with the Law, then God will favor us in all our endeavors and we will prosper, needing to fear no man. But if we fail to obey the Law, then we are helpless against those who would destroy us because God will desert us.

"As he wrestled there alone that night against the angel, Jacob slowly came to see where his duty lay. First he must give to his brother Esau half the gains he had come to covet so much, not because by doing so he would save himself, but because by righting the wrong he had done Esau when they were youths in their father's household, he would find favor once again in the sight of God.

"The new Jacob had new courage and new strength and was able to wrestle on, when the old would have yielded. In so doing he gained the satisfaction of knowing that, even if he were bested, he had given a good account of himself. And because this was a new Jacob, at the breaking of dawn, the Angel of God said: '*You shall no longer be called Jacob but Israel, for as a prince you have power with God and with men and have prevailed.*'

"The next morning," Saul continued, "Jacob hastened on to meet his brother without fear and without guilt. When Esau refused the gift, the old Jacob would have accepted the refusal and been glad, but not the new Jacob, who had once more gained favor with God and peace within his own soul. Only by obeying the Law in its entirety could he prove his new status; and prove it he did, by insisting that Esau take half of what he possessed. The Torah tells us that because he obeyed the Law in every way, Jacob prospered more than ever before and we are proud to be his descendants and part of the nation that bears the name he was given by the angel.

"You, too, have known servitude and become free." Saul's voice rose as he drove home his final point. "Now you have a chance to live as free men, in the sight of God and of this congregation, if you but follow after the Most High and obey his Law."

After the service, Tob and Asa came up to congratulate Saul but there was no sign of the man in the priestly robe.

"I was telling Isak we must find a larger place to meet," said Tob. "He thinks he knows of such a place, a vacant warehouse once used for storing pottery."

"I would like to see it." Saul was already envisioning a huge synagogue filled with eager listeners, waiting upon his every word.

"Of course this is Pentecost and you may not have as large a crowd next Sabbath," Tob warned. "But the way things are going, Isak and I feel that we will soon need more room."

"I'm sure of it," Saul said confidently. "Jepthah is getting well fast and I can work during the week getting the warehouse ready for our meetings."

IV

It was the custom of the Synagogue of the Libertines to hold their service early in the morning, so it was not yet noon when Saul visited the warehouse Tob had mentioned to him. He found it nearly twice as large as the shed where the congregation had been meeting and, although considerable work would have to be done to get it ready, felt no hesitation in plunging into it, certain that at last he had found the calling for which he had been preparing himself. He paid the rent for two months out of his own pocket, already savoring the pleasure of announcing at the next Sabbath service that the new meeting place would soon be ready.

The day was warm, for the summer solstice was approaching. Walking along the teeming narrow streets of the Lower City, busy making plans for converting the warehouse into a place of meeting, Saul had not noticed a dark cloud hanging above the Kidron Valley to the east until a gust of wind swept through the street along which he was walking, almost bowling him over.

Looking up at the cloud, Saul judged that, if he hurried, he might get home before its full fury was loosed upon the city. But as he moved along the street, the wind became stronger until it was like a giant invisible hand, holding him back and making it almost impossible for him to walk. Struggling on, he rounded a corner and found further progress toward his home blocked by a mass of people filling the street.

The center of attention seemed to be a two-storied house on a corner. People were jammed in the doorway and from inside came shouts and an occasional curse as those outside sought to push their way in.

"What's happening?" he asked a bystander.

"The Nazarenes have returned to Jerusalem."

"Why the excitement?"

"They were meeting in the upper room of that house when suddenly a high wind blew through the street. Some say flames appeared above their heads and they began to speak in unknown tongues."

"They're either drunk or they've come back to make trouble again," said a fat man wearing the fringed robe of a Pharisee. "After they lied about their leader's death, how could anyone believe them?"

"Before he was crucified, the Nazarene promised to return," a bystander volunteered. "Word has gone out that he may appear at any moment."

"I have other things to do besides wait for a crucified rebel to return from the dead." The Pharisee started back through the crowd. "Are you coming, young man?"

Saul was about to follow, when a powerful voice struck his ears. Turning, he saw that a tall, broad-shouldered man had stepped out upon the balcony before the upper story of the house and was calling to the crowd to be quiet, as others filed out behind him. There was an odd sort of majesty about the big man and for a moment, Saul thought the Nazarene himself might have returned.

"It's the Galilean called Simon Peter," the Pharisee said with a snort of disgust. "The one who denied the Nazarene in the courtyard of the High Priest's palace the night he was arrested."

"Men of Judea and all that dwell in Jerusalem." The voice of the tall Galilean carried easily over the heads of the crowd. "Listen to my words and let this be known to you. These men are not drunk as you might suppose, but this is what was spoken by the Prophet Job:

*And it shall come to pass in the last days saith God, I will pour out of my spirit upon all flesh. Your sons and your daughters shall prophesy, your young men shall see visions, and your old men shall dream dreams. On my servants and on my handmaidens, I will pour out my spirit in those days and they shall prophesy. I will shew wonders in heaven above, and signs in the earth beneath; blood and fire and vapor of smoke. The sun shall be turned into darkness and the moon into blood before that great and notable day of the Lord comes. And it shall come to pass that whoever shall call on the name of the Lord shall be saved.*

Being familiar with the passage from his studies, Saul was amazed that the Galilean had been able to quote it correctly.

"Men of Israel hear these words," the man called Simon Peter continued. "Jesus of Nazareth was approved by God among you through miracles and wonders and signs, which God did by him in your midst, nevertheless you crucified him. Now God has raised him up, having loosened the pains of death because it was not possible that he should be held by them. For David said concerning him:

> "'I foresaw the Lord always before
> my face,
> For he is on my right hand, that
> I should not be moved.
> Therefore did my heart rejoice and
> my tongue was glad.
> Moreover also my flesh shall rest
> and hope,

> *Because thou will not leave my*
> *soul in hell.*
> *Neither will thou suffer thine*
> *holy one to see corruption.*
> *Thou hast made known to me the*
> *ways of life.*
> *Thou shalt make me full of joy*
> *with thy countenance.'*"

The crowd was still now for great store was laid upon words of prophesy by priests and ordinary men alike attributed to David.

"Let me speak freely to you of the patriarch David, who is both dead and buried and whose sepulchre is with us until this day," the speaker continued. "Being a prophet and knowing God had sworn an oath to him, that from the fruit of his loins he would raise up the Christ to sit upon his throne, he saw this beforetime and spoke of the resurrection of Christ."

Now the big man's voice rang out like a bell. "This Jesus, God has raised up and we are all witnesses to his resurrection. Being exalted by the right hand of God and having received from the father the promise of the Holy Spirit, he caused what you now see and hear. Therefore, let all the house of Israel know assuredly that God has made that same Jesus, whom you have crucified, both Lord and Christ."

The crowd had been still while the big man was speaking; caught up by the fervor and conviction in his words and by the import of his claim that the crucified Nazarene had not only been the Messiah, the long promised Son of God who would rule in Israel and lead it to the greatest period of glory in its history, but had also risen from the dead and might appear at any moment. Saul found himself strangely moved by the words of Simon Peter, but fought against their influence, sensing that the claims of the speaker were diametrically opposed to everything he had been taught. As he stood there, knowing he should leave but caught up still in the drama of the moment, people around him began to cry: "What shall we do? What shall we do?"

"Repent and be baptized every one of you in the name of Jesus Christ for the remission of sins and you shall receive the gift of the Holy Spirit," Peter admonished them.

Almost bowled over by the rush of men toward the house, Saul was swept to the foot of the steps from the balcony. Seized by a desperate urgency to get away from the scene as quickly as possible, lest he be even more moved by the words of the tall man, Saul began to flail out with his arms, and, bruised and shaken, managed to struggle through the press of the crowd. Finding himself free, at last, he took off in a run, putting the whole disturbing scene behind him.

## v

All week long Jerusalem buzzed with stories of what had happened in the Lower City where the Nazarenes had met. Some accounts described the tongues of fire Saul had heard spoken of, while he was on the scene. Others said Jesus of Nazareth had actually appeared to his disciples in the upper room of the house where they had eaten a farewell supper together before he had been arrested shortly after midnight on the day of the Passover in the beautiful garden called Gethsemane on the slopes of the Mount of Olives. One thing was certain: many people had been swayed by the eloquence of the man called Simon Peter and had joined the following of the Nazarene, the estimates varying from a few hundred to as high as three thousand.

Busy with his plans to convert the warehouse into a synagogue for his congregation and preparing a sermon on false prophets to combat the teachings of the Nazarenes, Saul had little time for rumors. Convinced from what he had heard and seen of the activities of the new sect that trouble with the authorities would inevitably occur again, he planned his sermon as a stern warning to his congregation against being led astray by false doctrines and a reminder that only through the Law, given by God and therefore immutable through the ages, could a man fulfill his whole duty to his creator.

On the Sabbath, the congregation was considerably smaller

than on Pentecost, as he had been warned. Saul brought to his sermon all of his eloquence and fire and had the satisfaction of seeing that, as always, he held the listeners spellbound with his discourse. Tob was in the congregation as usual, but when he met Saul in the yard outside, a scowl had replaced his usual smile.

"I've been inquiring among the people here concerning the smallness of the crowd," he said. "They all agree that many who would ordinarily have come to hear you, have gone over to the Nazarenes."

"But they don't even teach the Law! They claim their leader descended directly from David and that he rose from the dead."

"How do you know that?"

"I heard the one called Simon Peter speaking on the day of Pentecost, when I was on my way home from the new synagogue."

"The way things are going now, we won't need a new synagogue," Tob said dourly. "I am glad we didn't rent it."

"I did."

"With what?"

"Out of my own pocket. After the size of the crowd last Sabbath, it was obvious that we needed a new building."

Tob shrugged. "Maybe you can use it to store tents."

"Surely the authorities won't allow the Nazarenes to go on teaching a false doctrine."

"All kinds of doctrines are taught in Jerusalem. You have only to listen at the Porch of Solomon to know that."

"But they don't even teach obedience to the Law."

"This fellow that calls himself Simon Peter does. He has organized his followers into a synagogue and, as long as they have ten men, they can claim the same rights as any other congregation."

"Why would the Libertines go over to them?"

"The Nazarenes teach that Jesus of Nazareth was the Messiah —and that he will come again to lead those who believe in him. They claim to have made nearly three thousand converts since the beginning of Pentecost. If that's true, they already have the largest congregation in Jerusalem."

## VI

The Court of the Gentiles was filled with worshipers as usual, when Saul crossed it on the way to the stairs leading to the upper level, where the priests carried on their functions. His steps lagged, for the weeks since Pentecost had been bad ones for him. First, he had seen his congregation steadily dwindle in size from Sabbath to Sabbath, although he had spoken out boldly against the new sect, denouncing its members as false prophets and perverters of the Law. And second, a message had come the afternoon before, summoning him into the presence of the High Priest.

The cripple he'd seen being carried into the temple the first time he'd come there long ago was in his usual place beside one of the gates leading through the stone balustrade, his shrill cry for alms still rising above the other noise. At the head of the stairway, Saul inquired where he might find the High Priest and was directed to a door before which stood a guard. When he gave his name and the information that he had been invited by Caiaphas himself to come there, the guard went inside, but returned a few seconds later.

"The High Priest will see you," he said. "Leave any weapons you may have here."

"I am not one of the *sicarii.*" The professional assassins, so named for the long knife, or *sicarius,* each of them carried, were a proscribed group with prices on their heads from both Jewish and Roman authorities.

The man shrugged and opened the door for Saul to enter a richly furnished room, inside which stood still another of the temple guards. The High Priest sat behind a carved ivory table littered with scrolls and tablets. A scribe occupied a stool at one end of the table, while a young priest stood just behind the carved ivory chair of the High Priest. The younger man studied Saul with slightly hostile eyes, but Caiaphas greeted him warmly.

"I've heard good things about you from Asa and the others,

Saul," he said. "The Congregation of the Libertines took on a new life when you became their teacher."

"Until the Nazarenes started drawing my people away."

"Have you lost many?"

"The congregation yesterday was the smallest since I began teaching there. Tob and Isak say many have gone over to the Nazarenes."

Caiaphas gestured toward a cushioned bench in front of the table behind which he sat. "Be seated. And tell me exactly what happened."

Saul described his first sermon to the Libertines and the response, his renting of the warehouse, and his accidental contact with the Nazarenes. When he came to that point, Caiaphas stopped him.

"This wind you mentioned—did it seem unusual?"

"It was very strong. But a thundercloud was hanging over the Kidron Valley at the time and I thought the wind came from it."

Saul noticed that the scribe was writing rapidly with a stylus upon a wax covered tablet and judged that he was taking down the words.

"Did you see any evidence to make you believe there was another explanation?" Caiaphas asked.

"None."

"Was anything about the Nazarenes themselves unusual?"

Saul shook his head, choosing not to mention the strange compelling force Simon Peter's words had exerted upon him.

"No tongues of fire? No one who could have been the man called Jesus of Nazareth?"

"I saw no fire," said Saul. "As for Jesus of Nazareth, I was in Tarsus when he was crucified, so I wouldn't have recognized him."

"Others in the crowd around you would certainly have known him. Did anyone identify the Nazarene?"

"No, sir."

Caiaphas leaned back in his chair, a look of satisfaction on his somewhat vulpine features. "Your account agrees with that of other eye witnesses," he said. "Being from Tarsus, why didn't you join the Synagogue of the Cilicians, instead of the Libertines, when you came back to Jerusalem?"

Saul hesitated momentarily but, unaccustomed to telling anything but the truth, decided to speak frankly. "I didn't like their leader."

"Elam?" Caiaphas' hooded eyes crinkled into a smile and the priest standing behind him giggled. "Why?"

"I dislike ostentation. In my experience it is usually a cloak to cover up ignorance or greed."

"So?" Caiaphas' eyebrows lifted. "You are a philosopher."

Saul flushed. "No sir. But as a tentmaker I deal with many people. Wherever I find much outward show, I usually find little inward worth."

"You are very acute in your observations. Why did you choose to associate yourself with the Synagogue of the Libertines?"

"I intend to become a teacher, so I took the first opportunity that was offered me."

Caiaphas stroked his beard thoughtfully. "It may interest you to know that I have had my eyes on you ever since you bearded Rabbi Samuel that morning in the temple. I suspected then that you might go far and when Gamaliel told me you were the most promising student he'd had in a long time, I watched you even more closely. Then you suddenly left Jerusalem—"

"My father was dying, until a Greek physician named Luke brought him back from death itself."

"So you came back to resume your studies?"

"I returned because my brother-in-law was ill. Now that he is well, I plan to continue my studies and my teaching—"

"Good." Caiaphas' tone was suddenly brisk. "I have work for you that I think you will find interesting. It involves your enemies the Nazarenes."

Saul gave Caiaphas his whole attention now, sensing that the High Priest was coming to the real purpose of the summons.

"The congregation of the Diaspora have been drifting away from their allegiance to the temple," said Caiaphas. "I think it is largely because we have not been sending them teachers who can inspire them with fervor for the temple and its worship. Do you agree?"

"Absolutely," said Saul. "The ones that came to Tarsus always prated about details of the Law and made it seem a burden. I have been teaching my congregation that the Law is a highway along which a man can draw closer to God."

"Exactly my own opinion," Caiaphas agreed. "We must show the people this highroad of which you speak and make them look to it. I think in a few more years, you will be the man to do just that."

"I am still little more than a youth," Saul protested.

"But an uncommonly clear-seeing and persuasive one, judging by reports that have come to me. That's why I want you to join the Scribes of the Sanhedrin."

Saul was too stunned to speak. Not even in his wildest dreams had he thought of becoming one of the select group of young scribes and lawyers who prepared cases for presentation to the highest court of Israel, winnowing the wheat of evidence from the chaff sent up for final decision by the lower courts throughout the nation.

"Do you accept?" Caiaphas asked.

"If you and the court think me worthy."

"That you must prove to us. Your task will not be light either, for I want you to continue leading the Synagogue of the Libertines along with your other duties. Asa tells me the freed slaves trust you and respect you."

"Those who haven't left me."

"You must concentrate particularly on those," Caiaphas told him. "As yet we know of no move the Nazarenes have made outside the Law, but you may be able to learn some of their secrets from former members of your synagogue who have gone over to them. When we can charge the leaders with a capital offense the Sanhedrin can act and the sect will be destroyed."

"Then you want me to spy upon them?"

"I want you to help punish those who are teaching people to subvert the Law," the High Priest said sharply. "I judged you to be ambitious, so I chose you for the task. But if you have any qualms—"

"I have none." Saul saw his chances of remaining a teacher in Jerusalem fading and spoke quickly.

"Then you can start your duties today. Haman here"—he nodded to the priest behind him—"will find a place for you to work. You shall be paid from the funds provided for the Sanhedrin, so you need be a tentmaker no longer."

## VII

Saul's new work proved interesting and challenging but, mindful of Caiaphas' charge that he was to continue his work among the Libertines, he devoted much time to the congregation. As he recovered from his early depression at the loss of so many members to the Nazarenes following Pentecost, he began to regain his old powers of oratory and soon some who had broken away started to drift back. To these he gave particular attention but learned little concerning the activities of the newest among Jerusalem's synagogues.

Simon Peter and his cohorts—numbering twelve once again, since one named Matthias had been elected to fill the place of the traitor, Judas—appeared only to teach that their leader had been the Messiah and, after being crucified, had risen from the dead so that all who believed in him might have eternal life. They were careful not to advise breaking the Law of Moses, according to Saul's informants, although they were not as rigid in their interpretations as some of the Pharisees. This charge, Saul knew, however, could probably have been levied against the majority of Jews everywhere, particularly those who adhered to the more liberal interpretations of Hillel. In one respect, the Nazarenes did differ widely from other Jews, however. This Saul learned one Sabbath when he was leaving the Synagogue of the Libertines and found himself facing his old friend, Joseph of Cyprus.

"Jerusalem agrees with you, Saul," said Joseph. "Although you look a little drawn about the eyes."

"I've been working very hard."

"As an agent for Caiaphas?"

"I am one of the Scribes of the Sanhedrin, an honorable position in Israel."

"You have risen fast," the other agreed. "Teacher of your own synagogue and now an agent of the High Priest."

"I serve the court. Do you deny the authority of the Sanhedrin?"

"Not the court—but the way it is used by Caiaphas to destroy anyone who dares to tell the truth about the priests and the temple. Even Pontius Pilate could find no wrong in Jesus but, because Caiaphas and the others insisted, he was crucified."

"I wasn't here when it happened."

"I'm glad. Else Caiaphas might have involved you in it and your conscience would be troubled forever."

"What about you?" Saul changed the subject abruptly. "When I saw you last you were prosperous—"

"But now my robe is woven of the cheapest stuff, while my sandals have soles of wood and are held on by strings?" Joseph laughed. "The change goes deeper than that, Saul. I'm a new man, a happy man made over in an instant from my very soul outward by the grace of the Son of God. I have even been given a new name—Barnabas, Son of Encouragement."

"But your goods? Your land?"

"None of them matter now."

"Did you lose them?"

"I gave it all to my brethren. With us, all property is held together for the benefit of everyone. No man covets what another has, because no man has more than another."

"Do all Nazarenes do this?"

"Not all. A man named Ananias and his wife sold their property recently but were covetous and held back part of the purchase money for themselves. When Peter found them out, both were struck dead, in an instant."

"Did he kill them?" Saul didn't look at Joseph—or Barnabas as he was now called—lest the other man see in his face some of the excitement the words had stirred within him. If the man called Simon Peter had actually killed others who disobeyed him, he was guilty of murder and could be brought before the Sanhedrin on that charge. And Caiaphas would certainly look favorably upon one who brought him such evidence against the Nazarene leader.

"Peter didn't even touch them." Joseph seemed not to have noticed the eagerness of Saul's question. "The Lord struck them dead for their sins."

"And nobody questioned what happened?"

"Why should we, when everyone knew it was a punishment from God for their sins. But I must admit that since then some, whose faith was not so strong, have drifted away."

"Some of my congregation have returned," said Saul. "They may have been among them."

"And more will follow, if you're always as eloquent as you were this morning. I wish you were with us, Saul. With your mind and your brilliance of speech, you could be one of the Seven in no time."

"I thought there were twelve."

"The Twelve are the disciples, those who were closest to Jesus—with Matthias, who was elected in Judas' place. Seven others have been appointed from the Grecian members of the congregation and will eventually be sent to cities of the Diaspora. Stephen is the most eloquent of the Seven. He's just such a firebrand in the pulpit as you are."

"Are you one of the Seven?"

"No."

"But you were a follower of the Nazarene before his death. Surely that entitles you to a position of special honor."

"None have special honor with us," Joseph explained. "It was so when the Master was alive—"

"Was alive? Don't you claim he rose from the dead?"

"Jesus appeared to Mary of Magdala at the tomb on the morning of the third day," said Joseph. "He was taken up into heaven after his resurrection, but he has promised to return. When he does, the High Priest and his minions will be turned out, the temple will be cleansed, and Jesus will rule as Messiah and king forever."

"Did he promise all this?"

"All that and more. Come with me sometime and hear Stephen preach. Even you will recognize the truth when you hear it from his lips."

"I don't think that would be wise," Saul said quickly. "My congregation might think I have gone over to the enemy."

"Not the enemy, Saul. Jesus considered no man his enemy, and neither do I. Even though you serve the High Priest, I hope we will still be friends. Goodbye."

"Who was that?" Tob asked as Saul watched Joseph's tall form disappear down the street.

"An old friend, a silversmith named Joseph."

"I've seen that fellow among the Nazarenes," said Isak. "They call him Barnabas."

"He wears a shabby robe," said Tob. "I'm surprised that the guild of silversmiths hasn't turned him out."

"Joseph sold everything he had and gave it to the common fund of the Nazarenes." Saul's tone was thoughtful. "Yet I don't think I ever saw a happier man."

"All Nazarenes are mad," said Tob with a shrug. "Else how could they believe in a crucified Messiah."

## VIII

Saul's working day was spent in the building that housed the high court. Since it was adjacent to the temple, he usually stopped briefly to pray in the sanctuary on the way to work and was crossing the Court of the Gentiles one day, when he saw ahead of him the tall form of the Nazarene called Simon Peter, accompanied by a slender, dark-haired man, whom Saul remembered seeing on the balcony with the tall Galilean on the day of Pentecost. They had just entered the Court of the Gentiles and were crossing toward what was called the Beautiful Gate, leading to the inner portion of the temple. Filled with curiosity, Saul followed close behind and thus was able to witness a startling event.

"Alms! For the love of God, alms!" the lame beggar who always sat there cried in his shrill voice, as the two approached the gate. Most of those hurrying through the court paid no attention to him but Simon Peter stopped and the beggar looked up eagerly, expecting a gift.

"Silver and gold I have none, but such as I have I give you," the tall Galilean said. "In the name of Jesus Christ of Nazareth, rise up and walk."

For a moment the cripple didn't seem to understand and even tried to pull his hand away, when Simon Peter took it. Then a strange and utterly incredulous expression came over his face and before Saul's startled eyes, he stood and tottered a few steps holding to the big man's hand. Releasing it then he began to caper about joyfully, his legs seemingly cured of the flaccid paralysis which had immobilized them before.

An excited babble rose from the spectators at the startling miracle. Simon Peter ignored them, however, and with his companion, moved across the court to the wall opposite the Beautiful Gate, where stood several of the platforms from which the rabbis customarily taught. Mounting one of them, the Nazarene leader turned to address the crowd, and the former paralytic moved up close beside him.

"Men of Israel, why do you marvel at this?" the speaker demanded and once again—as on the Day of Pentecost—Saul was conscious of the compelling force in the tall man's voice. "Why do you look at us, as if our own power or holiness made this man walk? The God of Abraham, Isaac, and Jacob, the God of our fathers, has glorified his son Jesus, but you denied him in the presence of Pilate and asked that a murderer be given to you instead. You killed the Prince of Life, whom God raised from the dead, and we are witnesses to it. Through faith, this man whom you see and know has been made whole and strong in the presence of you all."

Simon Peter paused to let the fact sink in that the miracle they had witnessed had been performed in the name of the Nazarene whom he served, then spoke again: "Brethren, I know you did it through ignorance, as did your rulers. But God has already fulfilled those things that Christ should suffer which were spoken through the mouths of his prophets. Repent therefore and be converted, that your sins may be blotted out when the Lord shall send Jesus Christ again to bless you and turn every one of you away from his iniquities."

Engrossed in the words of Simon Peter, Saul had not noticed

a commotion on the outer edge of the crowd, until it parted to admit the captain of the temple guards—a burly man named Abiathar, whom Saul had never liked—and a half dozen of his soldiers. Surrounding the two Galileans, the guards removed them from the Porch of Solomon before anyone could protest— if indeed any had dared. When Saul looked around for the cripple who had been healed, he, too, had fled.

Saul did not go to the chambers of the High Priest that day, for the miraculous event he had witnessed troubled him considerably. But when he talked to Tob about it on the rooftop in the warm summer twilight after the evening meal, the potter had a considerably different view.

"Beggars are always trying to gain sympathy and alms," said Tob. "The man you saw may not have been paralyzed at all."

"I saw him being borne into the temple one morning by two men," Saul protested. "He has been there every day that I can remember since I came to Jerusalem."

"Then an evil spirit laid hold of him and the Nazarene drove it out by magic. This time Caiaphas has them."

"On what grounds?"

"Trust him to find a way. After all, he managed to get the Romans to crucify the Nazarene."

"Then that was contrived, too—as Simon Peter claims."

"Contrived or not, the man was a rebel! He and his followers tried to embroil us with the Romans so it was better that one man should die than a whole nation."

The hearing of the charges against Simon Peter and the other apostle—whose name, Saul learned, was John ben Zebedee —was held before the Priestly Council the following morning. Only if the council demanded their death, would the case come before the full membership of the Sanhedrin.

Annas, the old High Priest who was Caiaphas' father-in-law, presided over the council. Less than a dozen men were present when Simon Peter and John were brought into the chamber. The two had obviously received rough treatment from the guards, for their clothing was torn and there was a swelling over the slighter man's left eye. Yet both faced the council confidently.

"By what power, or in what name, have you done this thing of which you were charged?" Annas demanded peremptorily at the start of the hearing.

Saul had expected Simon Peter to request that a specific charge of breaking the Law be brought against them, for the case was obviously weak on that score. To his surprise, the big man made no attempt to raise the legal technicality.

"If we are examined this day because of a good deed done to the paralyzed man and in what way he was made whole," Peter said, "then let it be known to all of you and to all the people of Israel that this man stands before you today, made whole through Jesus Christ of Nazareth, whom you crucified and whom God raised from the dead. Jesus is the stone that was set at naught by you builders but which has become the head of the corner. Neither is there salvation in any other, for no other name under heaven may we be saved."

Having heard that most of the Nazarene disciples were Galilean fishermen and unlettered, Saul was startled by the reference to the cornerstone. He recognized the source immediately from the Psalms of David; the entire passage read: *"The stone which the builders rejected has become the headstone of the corner. This is the Lord's doing; it is marvelous in our eyes."* Moreover, he knew that most scholars considered this passage to refer specifically to the Expected One, or Messiah.

The members of the council were obviously taken aback by Simon Peter's claim that the prophesy of David supported his cause. Annas ordered the prisoners taken outside, along with the man who had been healed so miraculously. In the heated discussion that followed, Caiaphas argued that performing an act of healing in the temple in the name of a crucified rebel was blasphemy, but few supported him. Most of the council, Saul could see, had been shaken by the quotation from David, whose writings were generally considered to be even more prophetic than those of the recognized prophets. Finally Annas summed up the situation.

"We cannot deny that a notable miracle has been done by these men for it is already known all over Jerusalem," he said. "In order that it may spread no farther, let us warn them that they must not speak henceforth in the name of the Nazarene."

The prisoners were brought in again and Annas commanded them sternly not to teach again from the Porch of Solomon or to use Jesus of Nazareth as their authority. But neither Simon Peter nor John ben Zebedee showed any sign of being intimidated by the command.

"You can judge whether it is right in the sight of God to listen to you more than to God," said Peter. "We cannot but speak of the things we have seen and heard."

## IX

Stimulated by the failure of the Priestly Council to bring charges against the men responsible for the miracle of healing in the temple, the cause of the Nazarenes flourished more than ever. In spite of Saul's eloquence, the ranks of the Synagogue of the Libertines were thinned by further defections to the new group. Nor was it any comfort to him to know that other congregations were suffering even more than his, particularly those whose membership was made up largely of former dwellers in the Diaspora. To them the eloquence of the man called Stephen seemed to have the greatest appeal.

Fluent in Greek and an inspired speaker, Stephen was able to move large audiences with his fervor. Nor was it difficult to see why, for the teachings of the Nazarenes that a divine leader, whose death had been brought about by evil forces, had risen from the dead to bring salvation to his people was strangely like the central theme running through most of the Greek mystery religions that were so popular in the world outside Jerusalem. Like Saul himself, many Grecian Jews had witnessed the rites of these mystery faiths, and their trappings of liturgy and drama, telling the story of the young god slain by the forces of evil and returned to life through divine power—and had been moved by them.

In another way, too, the Nazarenes had become thorns in the flesh of Caiaphas. Peter and John in particular now appeared boldly upon the Porch of Solomon almost every day, preaching that their leader had risen from the dead as the long promised Messiah and naming the High Priest himself a murderer. As their fame spread, more miracles of healing were accomplished and the press of sick and deformed begging to be cured soon became so great that it interfered with the activities of worship.

Anything that took attention away from the altars of sacrifice and the "trumpets" into which offerings in money were dropped inevitably affected the revenues of the temple. When they began to fall off markedly, Caiaphas once again had Peter and John arrested. This time, he brought them before the full membership of the Sanhedrin, counting upon the displeasure of the more conservative members of that court to give him the majority he needed for a verdict that miracles done in the name of a man convicted and executed under the Law must be the work of Satan and therefore blasphemous.

Although Gamaliel was a member of the Sanhedrin, Saul had avoided him since becoming one of the scribes, moved by a feeling of guilt at having swung so far away from the teachings of his former mentor. As he watched Gamaliel weigh the charges carefully, he found himself wondering how the most famous teacher in Jerusalem could possibly accept the flimsy legal basis upon which Caiaphas was bringing his accusations, arguments Saul himself could have demolished in a few words.

When the time came for the accused to defend themselves before the court, Simon Peter, as usual, was the spokesman. To the charge that they had disobeyed the former edict of the court, he said simply, "We ought to obey God rather than men." Continuing, he added, "The God of our fathers raised up Jesus, whom you crucified. Him God has exalted with his right hand to be a prince and a Savior, to give repentance to Israel and forgiveness of sin. We are his witnesses of these things and so also is the Holy Spirit, whom God has given to them that obey him."

Saul could not help admiring the simplicity and forcefulness of the defense, citing the undeniable fact that any man had the right to speak and act as God directed him. To deny that right, therefore, was to deny the right of the prophets who had played such an important part in the history of Israel to speak as God had moved them.

Once again, the court was thrown into confusion by the eloquence and logic of a man who had studied in none of the rabbinical schools, but had been a Galilean fisherman until just a few years before. As might have been expected, many resorted to anger and, since those who opposed the Nazarenes held a considerable majority in the court, Saul expected a verdict of guilty to be rendered at any moment, even though it was quite obvious that grounds for that verdict had not yet been laid. Suddenly, however, a quiet, yet penetrating, voice—one that was quite familiar to Saul—cut through the babble of indignant protests, charges and countercharges. It was Gamaliel who, as Rabban and grandson of Hillel, was the most prestigious teacher and authority upon the Law in Israel.

"Take heed what you intend to do concerning these men," Gamaliel warned. "Once Theudas rose up boasting that he was somebody and about four hundred men joined with him. These were slain, and all who obeyed him were scattered and brought to naught. Afterward, in the days of the census, Judas the Gaulonite drew many people after him but he also perished and all who obeyed him were dispersed. Now I say to you, let these men alone, for if this council or this work they do is of men, it will come to naught. But if it is of God, you cannot overthrow it, lest you find yourselves fighting even against God."

Like Simon Peter, Gamaliel had gone to the very heart of the situation. The force and simplicity of his argument, carrying with it the danger that, in going against God the members of the court themselves might be guilty of blasphemy, carried weight with all except a few who followed Caiaphas blindly. A vote was quickly taken and the charges were dismissed.

## x

Knowing that Caiaphas would be in a foul mood after his second defeat in the campaign against Simon Peter and the Nazarenes, Saul avoided his employer as much as he could during the next several days. Eventually, however, the High

Priest sent Haman, the priest who was almost his shadow, in search of Saul.

"What are you going to do about the Nazarenes this time?" Caiaphas demanded almost before Saul was through the door.

"I, my Lord?" Saul was startled by the question.

"They are taking converts from among your congregation and the Grecian synagogues every day."

"What can I do if the Sanhedrin cannot find them guilty of any crime?"

Caiaphas threw up his hands in a gesture of disgust. "Is it not a crime to lead our people away from the Law?"

Saul could have reminded him that nearly fifty of the Sanhedrin had not seen it that way at the trial, but abstained. Nothing could be gained by turning the High Priest against him at a time when his first venture as a teacher was in danger of a failure. Besides, an idea had just come to him.

"Perhaps we have been trying to convict the wrong people," Saul suggested. "Why not attack the Grecian Jews among the Nazarenes? Since they are already lax in their observance of the Law, they might be more vulnerable than the others."

"That is the first sensible suggestion I've heard in a long time," Caiaphas' gloomy countenance brightened a little. "Grecian Jews have few friends in Jerusalem and probably are not too well liked in the Synagogue of the Nazarenes either."

"I've heard there are divisions among them," Saul confirmed. "The Grecians claim they aren't given as much food from the common store as are the Galileans and the Judeans."

"Good!" said Caiaphas. "If we can start them fighting among themselves, perhaps someone will bear witness to a charge of blasphemy."

"But against whom?" Saul asked.

"Stephen is the leader of the Grecian element among the Nazarenes," Haman, the younger priest, gave the answer.

"Send spies to listen whenever this Stephen is speaking," Caiaphas ordered. "Have them bring me every word he says that might possibly be interpreted as a breach of the Law."

"Are you going to bring him before the Sanhedrin?" Saul asked.

"And have some soft-hearted fool like Gamaliel let him escape?" Caiaphas exploded. "This time we shall make sure he is destroyed."

"How?"

"Leave that to me. You've done well in pointing out where these cursed people are weak, Saul. Be sure that one day you will be rewarded."

Saul's first intimation that Caiaphas had taken his suggestion and made another move against the Nazarenes came one day, as he was finishing up his work on several cases that were to be brought before the Sanhedrin from lower courts. Another of the scribes, a lawyer named Maon with whom he had become friendly, burst into the room where he was working.

"The High Priest has arrested another of the Nazarenes!" he cried.

"Stephen?"

"Then you've already heard it?"

"I knew Caiaphas was considering bringing charges against him. When is the trial to be?"

"Now."

"But the Sanhedrin doesn't meet for two more days."

"Stephen is before the Priestly Council, but the talk is that the temple rabble will seize him from the guards."

Saul knew well the meaning of the term "temple rabble." Beggars, sellers of various objects, even the thieves and pickpockets who did a thriving business in the crowded sanctuary, all paid tribute to the priestly organization that ran the temple itself. And since all were beholden to the Chief Priest and could lose their livelihood if he chose to have them cast out, they constituted a considerable mob which Caiaphas could manipulate as he wished. It was no secret that this same group had been used to create a commotion following the arrest of Jesus of Nazareth and convince Pontius Pilate that a revolt would occur if the Nazarene were not crucified. And Saul had no doubt that the stratagem would work just as successfully with Stephen.

By the time Saul and Maon reached the chamber of the Sanhedrin, the rabble had already gathered outside, clamoring for the death of the Nazarene who had been arrested. As Scribes of the Court, the two were admitted through a side door by a guard. Once inside, Saul saw that considerably less than the twenty-three members necessary for a quorum of the Sanhedrin were present. Nor were the customary trappings attendant upon a formal session of the High Court in evidence, so this was obviously a session of the Priestly Council, called hurriedly by the High Priest for reasons of his own.

Saul had never seen Stephen before, and what he saw now surprised him. The prisoner was slender almost to the point of emaciation, with delicately cut features betraying his Grecian ancestry. He had already been roughed up considerably and blood was beginning to drip from a long scratch on the right side of his cheek, while one eye was swollen almost shut. When he saw the burning light in Stephen's eyes, Saul understood something of why this man was able to exert so much influence over those who listened to him and why the frailness of his body was not important. In the last analysis, as he well knew from his own experience, it was the intensity of a man's spirit that moved men to follow him.

Watching the prisoner before the court, Saul recognized a certain kinship with him, for the same spirit of fire and conviction burned within both. Yet he steeled himself rigorously against feeling any sympathy, reminding himself that the Nazarene, through the eloquence of his preaching, had helped wreck the Synagogue of the Libertines.

One of the two witnesses required to convict an accused of blasphemy had already begun to testify. The man's first words —carefully coached, Saul was sure, by Caiaphas—revealed the gravity of the charge against the accused.

"This man speaks blasphemous words against the temple and against the Holy Law given us by Moses," the witness testified. "I heard him say that Jesus of Nazareth would destroy this place and change the Law."

Nothing the witness could have said was better calculated to stir up the crowd clamoring outside the open doors of the chamber, with only a pair of guards holding them back. To prophesy the destruction of the temple was not only blasphemy, the most heinous crime under Mosaic Law, but also a threat to the livelihood of the temple rabble, who were already shouting for Stephen's death.

The second witness followed the lead of the first, parroting the same charges. Stephen, however, showed no fear of death. Instead, even though he had been beaten severely, his shoulders were proudly erect, his head was high and his burning eyes met those of the council without flinching.

"Are these things true?" Caiaphas asked the accused man in the formal questioning of legal procedure.

Stephen swept the crowded chamber with his gaze. There was almost an air of majesty about him, Saul thought, and sensing it, the crowd was suddenly quiet.

"Men, brethren and fathers listen," he said. "The God of glory appeared to our father Abraham when he was in Mesopotamia, before he dwelt in Harran, and said to him *'Get you out of your country and from your kindred, and come into the land which I will show you.'"*

It was a familiar story, one that both Saul and the crowd had heard many times. Yet such was the spell of the speaker that Saul found himself hanging upon every word, as Stephen told of God's covenant with Abraham, the persecution in Egypt, the escape under the leadership of Moses, the giving of the Law from Mount Sinai, the entrance into the Promised Land, the forging of a new nation in Canaan by Joshua and later by David, and the building of the first temple by Solomon.

The account reached a high point with the predictions of the prophets concerning the coming of a Messiah, and all who listened could not fail to know of whom he spoke, the lowly Nazarene who had been condemned by this same council and escorted to the cross on the hill of Golgotha, by this same rabble.

"You always resist the Holy Spirit," the speaker thundered. "Even as your fathers did of old, so do you now. Which of the prophets did your fathers not persecute? They even slew those who foretold the coming of the Just One and you are his betrayers and murderers. You received the Law by the dispensation of angels, but you have not kept it."

A murmur of anger went through the crowd at this direct accusation of guilt in the death of Jesus of Nazareth. It stopped suddenly when the speaker raised his eyes to the high ceiling of the audience chamber, as if he were looking through the very roof into the heaven above.

"Behold I see the heavens open, and the Son of man standing on the right hand of God!" It was a cry of triumph, of ecstasy. But it was also a sentence of death for, if Stephen spoke the truth, this same council and this same crowd had crucified the Son of God.

Caiaphas made no move to still the angry outcry of the rabble. The guards at the door were easily pushed aside when they surged into the chamber and, seizing the prisoner, began to drag him from the room. Caught up by the rush of the crowd, Saul lost sight of Stephen and found himself thrust for a moment against the table where the council was sitting.

"Saul!" It was Caiaphas. "You and Maon go with the crowd, and make sure the witnesses cast the first stones according to the Law."

## XI

By the time Saul and Maon pushed their way through the door into the street outside, the pack was in full cry about a hundred paces ahead, following a street leading to the gate and the Place of Stoning, an area set aside in all Israelite cities for the execution of criminals guilty of a capital offense under the Law. Through the city gate the crowd surged. Eager hands thrust the doomed man into a niche in the wall where the masonry, pock-marked by the impact of missiles that had missed their human target on other executions, was stained a dull brown by blood spattered upon it.

"Let the witnesses cast the first stones! Make way for them!" Saul shouted, and the two who had testified against Stephen quickly removed their outer cloaks and put them beside Saul, where he could watch them, lest they be stolen by a thief in the excitement. While the crowd was busy selecting stones to cast at the condemned man, the witnesses moved to the forefront. Each carried a jagged stone, since he who drew first blood at an execution could boast of it later.

Although only half conscious, Stephen managed to hold himself upright in the niche by placing his hands against the blood-stained wall for support. For a moment, Saul felt a twinge of pity for the frail man, but the sight of the blood trickling down from the wound in his face began to make its stimulus felt, as it had already done with the crowd. When he reminded himself that Stephen was his enemy, and he had enticed members of the Synagogue of the Libertines away from observance of the Law, which was every man's duty under God, Saul felt a sudden surge of satisfaction, even something resembling joy, that the Nazarene was being punished.

The first stone almost missed its target, striking Stephen on the shoulder and partially spinning him around but drawing no blood. A howl of disappointment went up from the crowd, but the second witness had better luck. His stone caught the condemned man on the left temple, opening up a cut that gushed blood and driving Stephen to his knees. The throw was the signal releasing the others and as a hail of missiles of all sizes and shapes now poured in upon the slender battered figure against the wall, the cries of the crowd rose in pitch, until they resembled the howls of animals tearing a prey to pieces.

Revolted by the savage spectacle, yet feeling his own pulse begin to race with the excitement of it, Saul looked about him for a stone. But the ground in the area had been picked clean by the crowd and he was afraid to leave the cloaks of the witnesses unattended while he searched for one. Maon, his face distorted with the same frenzied joy that had seized the others, cast a stone and ran to look for another. And as the howls of the crowd rose, Saul heard his own voice screaming for blood with the rest.

The crowd had now become a seething mass of men, pushing to the front to cast their missiles and then being shoved back by those coming up behind them. When the supply of stones began to run out, the crowd started to break up into eddies, where men fought against each other for the remaining missiles. Shocked by the naked hate he saw in so many faces, Saul suddenly remembered something which, in the excitement of the execution, everyone else had seemed to forget. The Law forbade violation of the dead and as soon as the victim expired, the stoning must stop, lest the executioners sin by damaging a corpse.

"Cast no more stones lest you make yourself guilty of desecration!" Saul's shouts were unheeded at first, so carried away was the crowd by the blood lust of the execution. When Maon added his voice to Saul's the crowd finally realized what was being said, and the shower of stones trickled to a halt.

"See if he is dead," Saul ordered Maon, but the other scribe shook his head.

"I—I can't stand the sight of blood," he mumbled.

"You witnesses," Saul said sharply. "Get your cloaks while I determine whether this man is dead."

Approaching to within a single step of the battered body, he dropped to one knee, trying to see whether there was any movement of breathing. It was then that he saw the dying man's lips move.

"Lord, lay not this sin to their charge." The words were distinct, though barely audible; then Stephen gave a sigh and the bruised and torn lips were still.

"He is dead," Saul rose to his feet. "Stone him no more."

The crowd began to move away, but an inner sense of decency made Saul stay beside the inert form on the ground until finally, only three persons remained, besides the dead man: Saul, the tall Nazarene called Simon Peter, and Joseph, called Barnabas, by the Nazarenes.

"Why did you stay behind when the others left?" Joseph's voice followed Saul as he started toward the gate.

"It didn't seem fitting to leave him alone."

"We thank you for your compassion, Saul," said Simon Peter.

"Compassion?" Saul heard Barnabas protest as he walked

away. "It was he who watched the cloaks of the witnesses for the High Priest."

Returning to the city, Saul went directly to the temple. "The man is dead," he reported to Caiaphas. "The Nazarenes claimed his body."

"Let them have it. He can do us no more harm now." Caiaphas gave the young man a keen glance. "Was this your first stoning?"

Saul nodded. "The crowd were like animals, fighting over the kill."

"Stephen threatened the destruction of the temple, which is blasphemy. The Most High decreed the method of execution, not any one of us."

"Do you think his death will stop the Nazarenes?"

Caiaphas shook his head. "The crucifixion of their leader didn't stop them. They will have to be destroyed entirely."

"Who will be next?"

"That is for you to decide."

"Why me?" Saul asked.

"You are able and have suffered at the hands of the Nazarenes," Caiaphas told him. "From now on it shall be your commission to harry them however and whenever you can. But limit your persecution to Grecian Jews if you can."

"Why?"

"The Galileans who were disciples of Jesus of Nazareth knew what they faced when they returned here but others will not be so strong in their faith. When you show the rest of Jerusalem how dangerous it is to be a Nazarene, I think they will have trouble making more converts."

"Shall I bring them before the Sanhedrin on charges of blasphemy, as you did Jesus of Nazareth and Stephen?"

"The crowd seized Stephen before the court could give a verdict." Caiaphas' voice was sharp. "You heard the man blaspheme yourself. Still it's probably just as well from now on to imprison and flog them. We must not give Pontius Pilate the idea that priestly authority isn't able to maintain control in the temple and in Jerusalem."

## XII

Saul went about the task Caiaphas had given him with his usual thoroughness. Hardly a day passed during the next several months when he was not able to imprison one or more of the Nazarene congregation and inevitably the number of its members began to shrink, as the Jews of the Diaspora who had been a part of it fled to the cities from which they had come. As Saul's reputation grew, so did his congregation, since he was obviously highly favored by the authorities and able to secure favors for its members.

He had studiously avoided arresting any of the Galileans who made up the inner circle of the Nazarenes, or their leader, Simon Peter. But as the number of the congregation dwindled from the defection of what Caiaphas had called Grecian Jews, it became more and more difficult to find culprits to throw into the already overfilled prison. Such was the situation one Sabbath when Saul left the Synagogue of the Libertines at the end of the service and found Joseph standing in the yard before him. One look at the face of the silversmith told him the situation he had been dreading was facing him now.

"Shalom, Joseph," he said courteously. "What brings you here?"

"The need to be arrested."

"On what charge?"

"I am a follower of Jesus of Nazareth. You have thrown others into prison on that charge, why not me?"

"The Nazarene threatened to destroy Jerusalem and the temple. But I know you have no desire to flout God's Law."

"And the others?"

"It was the task of the courts to decide their guilt or innocence."

"The courts!" Joseph gave a snort of contempt. "Your court is the whip and the bludgeon, the scourge and the grave. Once you were decent and honorable, Saul; I was proud to name you my friend. But now you are like those who destroyed Stephen, a rabid beast snapping at everything in its path."

"I'm only doing my duty under the Law," said Saul stiffly, but Joseph had struck him in a sensitive spot, for he had never quite been able to repress a sense of guilt over his recent actions.

"Whose idea was it to attack only Grecian Jews because they could be drawn away more easily?" Joseph demanded.

"Mine."

"I thought so. It would take a Jew from the Diaspora to predict that others like him might weaken first. You can tell Caiaphas for me that his plan is a failure. In driving the Grecian Jews away from Jerusalem, you and he have done the cause of Jesus the greatest favor you could possibly have done."

"What do you mean?"

"Most of those who left still follow Jesus. We now have churches in Antioch, Damascus, Rome and even in your home city of Tarsus. You and Caiaphas may be the greatest benefactors to our cause since the Master himself walked in Galilee."

## XIII

The dream came first on the night following Saul's encounter with Joseph. The weather was cool, so he was sleeping on a pallet inside the house back of the shop, where he lived with Jepthah, his sister, Miriam, and their baby son, Jared. Relations with his brother-in-law had improved considerably, since Saul had become an acknowledged agent of both the High Priest and the Sanhedrin. Jepthah even boasted now of the connection and made no more demands that Saul work in the shop.

In the dream, he found himself in a spot that seemed vaguely familiar, a section of masonry wall which might have been that of any city. Only when he saw the dark splotches on the mortar and the scars on the wall did he recognize the Place of Stoning outside Jerusalem.

A man was huddled against the wall, with his arms folded about his face, as if to protect his head. Stones of all sizes and shapes lay about and, obeying an uncontrollable impulse, Saul picked up a jagged one, seized by the same savage blood lust that had driven him to search for a stone during the execution of Stephen. The huddled figure in the dream did not move as he lifted the sharp-edged stone and drew back to throw. Only after he had loosed the missile, did the man lower his arms and reveal his face.

It was Joseph! But before the stone found its unprotected target, Saul came awake, sweating and trembling with the sound of his own scream echoing in his ears.

"Saul! Saul!" The voice was Miriam's and he opened his eyes to see her bending over him, her face white with concern. When she reached down to shake him into wakefulness, he seized her hand and clung to it, like a terrified child clinging to its mother. "Joseph!" he gasped. "Did I—"

"Joseph isn't here, Saul. You were dreaming."

He sat up then and wiped the sweat from his face against the folds of Miriam's nightdress. "I had a nightmare—about Joseph."

"Why him?"

"He came to the synagogue today and dared me to arrest him."

"Jepthah was saying yesterday that you will soon get into disfavor with Caiaphas, if you don't seize Joseph. After all, he's one of the leaders of the Nazarene Synagogue."

"But he follows the Law."

"Joseph follows the Nazarene—who threatened to destroy the temple. Jepthah says that is blasphemy and enough to earn him a stoning."

"I'm going up to the roof for a while." Saul pushed himself to his feet.

"But it's cold up there."

"I'll take my cloak."

"You'll bring the fever on you again," Miriam warned. "Remember how you used to suffer from it every year back in Tarsus?"

"I'll take care," he promised. "Go back to bed now. You don't want to wake up the baby."

"He's like his father. A thunderclap couldn't waken him, once he gets to sleep." Miriam looked at her brother closely again. "Are you sure you're all right, Saul? This could be the fever beginning again. There were times in Tarsus when you didn't know us for days."

The nightmare had brought a strange feeling of dread, a sense of some impending disaster which he must try to avoid, but going to the roof did not help identify it. Around him the city lay sleeping but in the darkness, he couldn't see the shining golden roof of the temple from which, as the earthly symbol of the God he served and the immutable truths of the Law, he had hoped to find comfort. Dreading a return of the dream, he hesitated to go downstairs and, instead, remained on the rooftop huddled in the heavy cloak that served in this clime as both an outer garment by day and a cover by night until dawn began to break and the city came awake.

The next night was no better, nor was the third. Each time the place of the dream was the same and at its climax the figure huddled against the wall lowered its arms to reveal the face of Joseph. The eyes were the worst part; filled with reproach and disappointment, they seemed to pierce Saul's heart, reminding him of the happy days long ago when the two had visited the university at Tarsus and later contended as friends in the games of the xystus and the hippodrome.

By the fourth morning, Saul knew he must do something to stop the dream or go mad. When late that afternoon he came home from his work to find Jepthah bargaining with a merchant from Damascus, for the sale of a tent, he suddenly saw a possible answer.

"Tell me, sir," he said courteously to the well-dressed merchant, when the transaction was completed and the tent was being lashed to the back of a pack animal. "Are any of the sect called Nazarenes in your city?"

"Too many!" The merchant spat out a curse. "They preach faith in a Messiah, and the people follow them instead of obeying the Law."

Saul had heard all he wanted to know. The next morning he presented himself before Caiaphas and broached the idea that had come to him, a way of getting away from Jerusalem where Joseph's presence, he was sure now, had something to do with the occurrence of the dream. He did not mention the dream to Caiaphas, but requested that he be commissioned to harry the Nazarenes outside Jerusalem, as he had done in the city.

"Where would you go?" the High Priest asked.

"A merchant of Damascus told me yesterday that the Nazarenes are increasing in number there. With a letter from you to the leaders of the Damascus synagogues, I should be able to arrest some of those who fled Jerusalem and bring them back for trial."

"An excellent idea," Caiaphas approved. "Maon can accompany you and Abiathar will furnish you with a detail of guards to bring back the prisoners. Draw on the temple treasury for whatever money you need for the journey."

## XIV

Saul was able to leave Jerusalem only a few days after he suggested the trip to Caiaphas. What was more, he found himself free of the strange nightmares and was able to undertake the preparations for the journey with his usual energy.

The most direct route to Damascus ran northeastward across the Jordan and through the district called Gilead, beyond which lay the edge of the vast desert. Saul had started the journey with enthusiasm but, as the caravan he and his party had joined trudged across the hot sands of the desert, he found his spirits sinking lower and lower.

Worse than the mental depression, was the return of the nightmare, with the same pattern repeated over and over. Lying shivering in his cloak at night, for the air in the vast desert plateau quickly cooled with the coming of darkness, he fought against going back to sleep after the nightmare awakened him, fearing a recurrence. And when he found himself shaking in a chill, he wondered if he were about to have another attack of the recurrent fever Miriam had warned him about, an illness which often troubled the residents of Tarsus and other swampy areas in the spring.

Noting Saul's discomfort, the caravan leader suggested that

he ride. But the swaying gait of a camel only increased the headache that now troubled him by day, so he climbed down and started walking again. To take his mind off his intense physical discomfort, he began to plan the campaign he would pursue in Damascus against the followers of Jesus of Nazareth. But that brought memories of wives and children wailing as their men were dragged away to jail, the cries of prisoners under the lash, and the bleeding mass that the scourge—a whip of many tails, each tagged with a metal ball—could make of a man's back.

In Jerusalem, Saul had felt little compunction about arresting the Nazarenes who were thwarting his career as a teacher by luring away members of the Synagogue of the Libertines. But the idea of persecuting people whose names he didn't even know was becoming more and more repugnant to him. Nor did his changed attitude escape the eyes of Maon, who sought him out one evening while members of the caravan were gathered around the campfire eating the evening meal.

"Are you ill, Saul?" he asked. "I noticed you stumbling today."

"My head aches from the sun. Or it may be a return of an old fever."

"Are you sure a fever is the whole trouble?"

"Why should anything else bother me?"

"You've been different since we left Jerusalem. If it were anyone else but you, I would say you were having second thoughts about our mission in Damascus."

"That's absurd! After all, it was I who suggested going to Damascus."

"I know," said the other scribe. "And I don't understand why you are so much against the Nazarenes. There are so many sects among the Jews already that another one isn't going to hurt us. If these people are fools enough to believe their leader is the Messiah and rose from the dead, let them."

"If you feel that way, why did you come with me?"

"I've never been to Damascus and I was getting tired of Jerusalem. Besides, I hear they have excellent wine in Arabia."

"Would you condemn your soul to *sheol* by drunkenness?" Saul demanded.

Maon shrugged. "You're too law-abiding for your own good, Saul. Don't you ever feel an urge to forget yourself in wine?"

At the moment Saul would have liked nothing better than to erase his troubled thoughts and his headache, with wine or whatever else was available. But he resolutely put the thought from him.

"Certainly not. I have work to do."

"Do it then," Maon said. "I plan to enjoy myself in Damascus, even if we don't arrest a single Nazarene."

Shortly before noon two days later, the caravan leader called attention to a dull white blur on the horizon and announced that they were approaching Damascus. The hills of the Anti-Libanus range, with the snow-capped peak of Mount Hermon its most dominant feature, had been visible ever since their journey across the desert wasteland south of Damascus had begun. But the sun still beat down from a cloudless sky and with every step, the throbbing in Saul's head seemed to grow worse.

Anxious to reach Damascus before the bazaars closed, forcing him to guard his store of goods through the night, the caravan leader quickened the pace, which only made it worse for Saul. His steps lagged and, when he fell behind, Maon came back to see about him.

"You'd better ride the rest of the way," the other scribe urged.

"I'll make it." Even the effort of speaking sent a wave of nausea through Saul.

"Let me tell the leader you're ill and ask him to slow down."

"No. I'm as anxious to get there as you are."

"Drink some of this then." Maon untied a goatskin bag of water from the pack frame of one of the camels and handed it to Saul. "You look as if you needed it."

Saul upended the spout and drank gratefully. The water was warm from the sun, but it refreshed him somewhat nevertheless.

"Pour some on your head," Maon urged. "The driver says it's not far to the River Barada, so we won't be needing it."

Saul lifted the skin again, letting the water gush over his head and soak the front of his robe. "I'll manage now." He handed the skin back to Maon. "It can't be very much farther."

"Less than two hours, the leader says. I can't wait to taste that Damascus wine."

Refreshed somewhat from the dousing of his face and head, Saul quickened his pace and caught up with the column once again, passing several of the animals at the rear of the column. Damascus was visible now, but to Saul's pain-dazed eyes, it seemed only a blur of white in a field of green, with the brown thread of the River Barada winding through it. Seeing the river, the camels quickened their pace, and one of them passed close to Saul, jostling him and forcing him to seize its pack frame for support.

The jerking movement of the camel's gait jarred him, sending a flash of pain through his head. At the same moment something in distant Damascus, a metal covered roof or other bright object, reflected the rays of the sun so intensely that the flash of it in his eyes blinded Saul. Unable to see, he stumbled over a rock in the path and fell sprawling in the middle of the track, almost under the feet of the rearmost pack camel. Ahead he heard the excited babble of voices as he fell, but none was so loud as the one that rang in his brain, a voice he had never heard before, but of whose identity he was certain at the first sound.

"Saul! Saul!" The tone was gently reproving. "Why do you persecute me?"

"Who are you, Lord?" Saul cried in the agony of the moment, although he already knew the answer.

"I am Jesus, whom you are persecuting. It is hard for you to kick against the goad."

"What will you have me do, Lord?"

"Arise and go into the city and you will be told what to do." As the voice faded away Saul struggled to his feet, surprised to find that his headache was gone, erased in the instant when Jesus of Nazareth had spoken to him within his soul. He shook his head to clear his vision, but only darkness remained before his eyes.

"Saul! Saul!" Maon was shaking his shoulder. "I saw you fall in the road just now and heard you speaking—but no one was here."

"It was the heat." Saul wondered at his own calmness in the face of the blindness. "I must have fainted."

"Can you go on now?"

"If you will lead me. I'm blind."

"Blind! But your eyes look normal."

"It's the sun and the heat. My sight should return soon." Saul couldn't have told how he knew, yet it never occurred to him that he would not regain his sight. That knowledge was part of the sense of peace that had suddenly come over him, the feeling of having shifted his own burdens and his own cares to the shoulders of someone else—forever.

## XV

The Street Called Straight, the major thoroughfare of Damascus, bisected the city. Columned for its entire length and partially roofed over, it was the location for most of the more important shops of the city and the main center for its business affairs. Led by Maon, stumbling in his blindness over the rough stones of the pavement, Saul arrived in Damascus under considerably different circumstances than had been his original intention. Yet none of that troubled him now, for his heart was filled with a great sense of thanksgiving, made over as it were in the instant when he'd seen the brilliant flash of light, had fallen to the ground beside the caravan trail and had heard the gentle voice calling to him alone.

"Who did Caiaphas say we were to seek here?" Maon asked.

"Arza, ruler of the largest synagogue. You can go on there. Someone will be meeting me soon."

"Who?"

"I don't know. He will identify himself."

"First you're struck blind on the road and I hear you talking to someone I can't see," Maon said resentfully. "Now you tell me someone you don't know will meet you. Did you see a vision back there on the road, Saul?"

"No. I was only struck blind."

"Then how do you know these things?"

An inner sense of caution kept Saul from revealing to Maon what had happened to him, knowing the scribe would tell the Jewish leaders in Damascus. Besides, though he had no idea yet just where his path lay from here, he instinctively knew that it would not be one of which the people whom he had originally come here to meet would approve.

More than his mind had been sharpened by his experience on the road to Damascus, Saul realized, as they walked along the busy street. The loss of his sight seemed to have increased the acuity of his other senses. The hum of a spindle and the slap-slap of a loom, as the shuttle was thrown back and forth, told him they were passing the shop of a weaver; the enticing aroma of bread fresh from the oven announced the baker; the taint of burning sulphur in the air indicated the shop of a glass-blower, probably a Phoenician, for the coastal dwellers of that region had raised glass manufacture to a high art; the tinkle of a tiny hammer upon an anvil could only mean the shop of a silversmith or a jeweler; the musty smell of parchment pointed out the establishment of a scribe and seller of scrolls. When the acrid odor of leather told Saul they were approaching the shop of a shoemaker, he felt Maon stop.

"What is it?" he asked.

"A man in that shop is beckoning to us."

"A cobbler?"

"How did you know?"

"I recognized the smell of leather. Lead me into the shop."

Maon turned him to the left but they had walked only a few steps, when another hand took Saul's elbow and guided him over the threshold.

"I am Judas, the cobbler," a deep voice said. "Welcome to Damascus, Brother Saul."

"Thank you, Judas," said Saul. "And thank you for bringing me this far, Maon."

"But—"

"The letter from the High Priest to Arza is in my purse." Saul loosened the strings that held the leather pouch to his girdle and handed it to Maon. "I have no further use for it now, or for the money Caiaphas gave us."

"I still don't understand," Maon protested as he took the purse.

"Whatever mission brought you here, is ended for him," the cobbler explained.

"How do I know someone in the caravan didn't give him a drug to blind him, so you can kill him?" Maon demanded.

"I'm safe, Maon," said Saul. "Go your way and use the gold I brought to buy lodgings for you and the guards."

"Are you sure you want to stay with the cobbler?" Maon insisted.

"I'm sure."

"But how could you know?"

"It was settled a long time ago." Saul spoke with an insight that had come to him in that moment. "When I heard Simon Peter speak from the balcony of a house in Jerusalem."

"All this must be the devil's work," Maon grumbled. "Yes, that's it. A devil took possession of you there on the road."

The scrape of a shoe on the doorsill told of Maon's departure and Judas' low chuckle confirmed it. "Your friend is moving as if the devil he spoke of is at his heels," the cobbler said. "Come Brother Saul, you need rest after your long journey."

"How long will I be blind?"

"I don't know."

"Then who will cure me?"

"Jesus will do that, but through whose hands, I cannot say. You may stay in my home until you are healed—and as long as you wish after that."

"Don't you hate me—for all the trouble I caused the Nazarenes in Jerusalem?"

"Someone asked the Master once what was the greatest commandment," the cobbler said quietly. "Jesus answered, *'Thou shalt love the Lord thy God with all thy heart and with all thy soul and with all thy mind. This is the first and great commandment. And the second is like unto it. Thou shalt love thy neighbor as thyself. On these two commandments hang all the Law and the Prophets.'* No matter what you have done in the past, Saul of Tarsus, you are now my neighbor. I can do no less than the Lord commands."

"Just now—when you just saw me on the street—did you know I was no longer your enemy?"

"No."

"Then how—"

"I saw you once in Jerusalem," Judas explained. "I recognized you out there on the street being led by your friend. But I'm only human and, might have let you pass by, even though I could tell from the way you walked that you were blind. But a voice spoke within my soul and commanded me to take you in."

"Did others hear it?"

"Jesus spoke to us in his own voice, when he was here on earth. Now that he has ascended into heaven, he speaks only in our souls."

"I heard him on the road. He said, 'Saul! Saul! Why do you persecute me?' And when I asked, 'Who are you Lord?' he answered 'I am Jesus whom you persecute. It is hard for you to kick against the goad.'"

"The Master was calling you to follow him, as he called Simon Peter and the other apostles when he walked by the Sea of Galilee."

"But the goad? What did it mean?"

"Jesus must have called you sometime ago, but you kicked against the goad then—as an ox kicks when he doesn't want to be driven. Finally the Master had to strike you blind, so you could no longer resist."

"And I can do nothing but wait?"

"You can rest and recover your strength. You look as if you have suffered from a long illness."

"Perhaps I have," Saul was drawing upon the new wisdom whose extent he was not yet able to perceive. "For longer than I was willing to admit."

## XVI

Past the shop of Judas the cobbler on the Street Called Straight moved the busy world of Damascus. Hammers tapping steadily; the rhythmic creak of wooden handled awls against leather palms, as holes were punched in the leather for sewing; the squeak of resin-coated thread as the sharp-bladed needles pulled it through; the rasp of a knife cutting tough leather—all these were mingled with sounds from the busy thoroughfare outside and the low voices of the workers in the shop.

Saul could hear it all as he sat, praying, beneath the shade of a terebinth tree in the small court around which the living quarters of the family were grouped. Every now and then, the sound of his own name, rising above the voices of the shoppers in the street, told him his presence there—and the reason for it— were being discussed. Occasionally he realized—with his heightened capacity for using his other senses—that people had come into the court to look at him. He could even hear them whispering to each other, though Judas did everything he could to leave him undisturbed.

Saul felt no desire for food, although the cobbler and his wife tried to ply him with tempting fruits, meat and even wine from the vineyards of the Barada Valley. One, two and then three days passed and Saul gradually lapsed into a silence broken only by his mumbled prayers, as he begged God to break the uncertainty concerning the fate that had befallen him. Then a new voice was heard in the court along with that of Judas.

"This is Ananias, Saul." The cobbler touched his shoulder. "He has been sent to heal you."

"Shalom, Ananias," Saul's voice rose on a note of hope and relief. "Are you a physician?"

"I am only a weaver, Brother Saul."

"Then how—?"

"The voice of the Lord instructed me to come here and heal you, just as it told Judas to take you in." Ananias' quiet voice hesitated, then continued. "I will not deny protesting that I had heard of your persecution of our people in Jerusalem and that you had been sent here with authority to arrest us and take us back to trial. But the Lord said, 'Go your way, for he is the chosen vessel for me, to bear my name before the Gentiles and kings and the Children of Israel.'"

Gentle fingers touched Saul's eyelids. "Brother Saul," the quiet voice of Ananias said, "The Lord, even Jesus who appeared to you, has sent me in order that you may regain your sight and be filled with the Holy Spirit."

Light burst suddenly upon Saul's eyes, a light almost as bright as the one that had blinded him on the road, but not nearly so bright as the one that also burst within his soul. He saw Ananias, a plump man with gray hair and kindly eyes, standing close beside him. Beyond the weaver stood Judas, with the workers of the shop looking on.

"I see! I see!" he shouted, filled with a new sense of exhilaration, a desire to tell everyone that he had not only been healed of the blindness which had assailed him on the road, but also the blindness which had for so long kept him from seeing the truth about Jesus of Nazareth.

Seeing a basket of fruit on a table beside him he suddenly realized how hungry he was and seized a pomegranate, biting into it and letting the juice stream down his chin as he chewed the pulpy delicious fruit with vigorous jaws. When Judas' wife handed him a cup of wine, he drank it thirstily.

"You were right, Judas!" he cried in the exuberance of his joy. "The best wine in the world does come from your vineyards—and the best pomegranates."

His hunger quickly satisfied, Saul put down the wine cup and wiped his chin with his sleeve, before turning again to Judas and Ananias. "What shall I do now?" he asked but both looked blank.

"I was told only to heal you," said the weaver.

"And I to take you in and protect you while you were blind," Judas agreed.

"Then I shall testify concerning what has happened to me," Saul cried exuberantly. "I shall tell the world how Jesus spoke to me on the road to Damascus and called me to serve him."

*I went into Arabia, and
returned again to Damascus.*
GALATIANS 1:17

*Book IV · Petra*

I

The warmth of Saul's reception by Judas and Ananias had not prepared him for the resentment he saw on the faces of many, when he rose on the Sabbath in the Synagogue of the Nazarenes to tell the story of how he had been called by Jesus of Nazareth. Nor could he find it in his heart to censure them, for he had personally driven some of them from their homes in Jerusalem and could understand how they might suspect that his being there was a trick to learn names and facts, which he could then use to continue the persecution of which he had been the chief architect in Jerusalem.

Had he still possessed the eloquence that had so moved the Synagogue of the Libertines, he might have convinced even the most suspicious that his story of having been personally called by Jesus was true. But the blinding flash of light that had felled him on the way seemed also to have burned away much of the old Saul—at least for the moment. The brilliant orator, the confidence in his own intelligence, and his own rightness of purpose, which had characterized him even as a student in the school of Gamaliel—all seemed to have been swept away. Instead he was left confused and uncertain, as on the day when, guided by the Roman courier with whom Cornelius had arranged for him to travel, he had left Jerusalem for Tarsus, shaken with guilt for the illness of his father, and hating the God who had been so unfair.

Anxious to rid himself of this new and disturbing uncertainty, Saul sought an answer in what had been the center of his religious life before coming to Damascus. Against the advice of Ananias and Judas, he went to the largest synagogue in the Jewish quarter the following Sabbath. And when the invitation was given for visitors to address the congregation, he rose to tell his story.

Once again he described the voice that had spoken in his soul after his blinding, identifying it as that of Jesus of Nazareth. He went on to tell of his miraculous cure, but before he was finished the murmur of resentment sweeping through the congregation almost drowned out his voice. When the chazan dismissed the congregation, no one came to greet Saul. Instead they drew away the skirts of their robes, as if by touching him they could be tainted with the same madness which they so obviously felt had come upon him.

The rejection by his own people among whom, barely two weeks before, he had been recognized as a promising leader, coupled with the reluctance of the Nazarene congregation to accept his change at face value, convinced Saul that he must leave Damascus, if he were to discover the task to which he had been called so dramatically. Nor did he face the decision with any joy for, even more disturbing than having the whole direction of his life turned around in an instant, was the fact that he had been left floundering, not knowing where his chosen path lay. Judas and Ananias listened gravely when he revealed his decision to leave Damascus, but neither made objection.

"You must go where the Lord sends you," Judas agreed.

"But where? Has the Lord foiled me in my purpose in coming here, only to abandon me?"

"Be sure Jesus hasn't abandoned you," said Ananias. "After all, Judas was moved to take you in when he saw you coming along the street outside, even though he thought you an enemy.

And I was sent to heal your blindness, though I feared you might turn against us, as many in our congregation still do."

"But I have been rejected—first by the Nazarenes and now by the Jews."

"Is it the uncertainty of your purpose that disturbs you most?" Judas asked. "Or the rejection?"

"The rejection. My life has been spent preparing for the role of teacher and lawyer. Now all of it has been swept away and I am left with nothing."

"Not swept away," Ananias corrected him. "Only the direction has been changed. I am sure the Lord has a higher purpose for you, one that will use all your training and all your talents."

"But how?"

"The disciples the Master called to follow him were mainly fishermen. None were highly educated and trained in the Law, and none possessed much eloquence."

"I've heard Simon Peter speak," Saul objected. "No one could say he lacked the power to move people with the story of Jesus of Nazareth."

"Peter tells it well because he lived it from day to day," Ananias agreed. "But I suspect that the story told by Peter and the others who knew Jesus is no longer enough. You are learned, Saul. You can set the coming of the Christ against the background of the Law and the Prophets, as a silversmith builds a setting of precious metal to hold a beautiful jewel."

"But I don't know where to start."

"Start at the beginning," Judas suggested. "By thinking through your own conversion and the way it came about. But leave Damascus first. Maon has been stirring up the synagogues against you; it would be a triumph for him to return you to Jerusalem in bonds."

"Why not go into the desert?" said Ananias. "Caravans leave here every few days from the south and I often send goods to be sold in the markets of Arabia. You can accompany one of them."

"Where?"

"Jesus brought you to my shop when you were blind," Judas reminded him. "You can be sure he will guide you, even in the desert."

Saul left Damascus the next morning with a caravan bound by the southern route for Ezion Geber, there to sell its load of woolen goods to the shipmasters who plied their vessels on the Red Sea between that port and the land of Yemen, from whence had come the Queen of Sheba to visit Solomon. On the return journey, the caravans brought loads of spices, perfumes, fragrant woods, and other valuable stuff to be sold in the markets of the north.

They moved along desert trails, traveling mostly at night when it was cool, rather than during the day when the sun beat down relentlessly from a cloudless sky. Much of the time no road was visible across the sand and the leader seemed to determine his course by instinct rather than any markings. Saul sought him out one evening around midnight, when they paused for a meal, and inquired how the instinct was developed.

"No magic or sorcery is involved in finding one's way across the desert," the hawk-faced, dark-skinned leader said. "The stars guide us."

Saul looked up at the canopy of the heavens where, it seemed, a million stars were shining. He knew vaguely that they were supposed to be arranged in some sort of a pattern, but detailed knowledge of that sort was largely confined to the writings of the Greeks, upon which Rabbi Eloichim had frowned.

"My ancestors were Phoenicians," the caravan driver confided. "Long ago the supply of shellfish for extracting the purple dye that the nobility love so well began to run out near the mouth of the Red Sea. Even then we were sending caravans to cities like Ugarit on the coast of the Great Sea, near where Antioch and Seleucia now stand. And when they reported that the same kind of shellfish was found along that coast, we moved eastward to the shore of the Great Sea, north of where the people your ancestors called the Philistines settled, after they were defeated in the delta country of Egypt. There was plenty of copper on Cyprus but the supply of tin for making bronze soon became limited, so our seafarers began to search for it in the west. They found the tin they needed in Tartessus—which you know as Spain—but the voyage was long and guides were required."

"Which they found in the stars?"

"Eventually, when someone discovered the star the Greeks came to call Phoenikos—after the Phoenicians. It hangs always in the north and never changes, though others move around it."

"But we're moving south."

The leader chuckled. "Phoenikos is not our guide in this portion of the journey, though it will be when we return. Look up there to the south." He pointed to a star more brilliant than the others around it. "That beacon will show us the way to Bosora. Then the twin stars a little to the west of it will guide us to Gerasa."

Saul searched the heavens with his eyes, trying to distinguish the stars the leader was describing, but finally had to rely on the other man's pointing finger to locate them.

"At Gerasa," the caravan leader told him, "we will find a regular road joining the King's Highway leading to Egypt."

"What king is it named after?"

"Who knows?" The caravan master shrugged. "It was called by that name before your people came into Canaan from Ur of Chaldea."

"Then you can travel anywhere in the desert by following the stars?"

"If you know what stars to follow."

"Suppose you don't?"

"Then you must find the right one. Sometimes, a man has to seek for a long time to find his particular star. But once he finds it, he will never be lost again."

"I thought I had found mine," said Saul. "But suddenly it turned out to be false."

"You're young, so don't give up searching. It may lie just ahead of you."

Four days' journey almost due south from Damascus, they came to Bosora, sometimes called Bosra. Located in the midst of a lovely oasis, it was a busy and prosperous city, distinctly Roman in character, with many impressive buildings columned after the Roman style of architecture. Following the twin stars the caravan leader had pointed out to Saul, they turned rather sharply westward and, after a journey of several days, came to Gerasa. Here the Roman influence was even more marked than in Bosora and a considerable garrison was stationed in the city.

The caravan paused only long enough at Gerasa to sell part of its bales of cloth and some swords and knives forged in the famous ironmonger shops of Damascus. Then taking on additional goods, it moved on to the southernmost Decapolis city of Philadelphia, the former capital of the Moabites who had inhabited this area in the time of Moses.

Philadelphia was a thoroughly Greek city, having been the headquarters of Alexander the Great during his march eastward toward Persia and India. Saul could have turned westward from Philadelphia and returned to Jerusalem, crossing the River Jordan near Jericho. But he had not yet found the star of which the caravan driver had spoken. And besides, he somehow knew it did not lie in Jerusalem where by now Caiaphas was certain to have put a price on his head, so he accompanied the caravan southward, following the well defined road the leader identified as the King's Highway.

The first night after leaving Philadelphia, Saul's body was shaken by a severe chill and he realized that he was facing one of those periods of raging fever, alternating with chills, which had troubled him many times before. By the second evening he was delirious, and in the morning the caravan driver was forced to strap him to one of the camels. They were traveling through wooded country now but it was hot and the perspiration evaporating from his sweat-soaked body brought on the chills again.

Saul knew almost nothing of what was going on about him while the caravan covered the distance between Philadelphia and Petra—the longest leg of the journey. Most of the time he seemed to be the center of a world of sky and wasteland, constantly changing with the swaying movement of the camel's gait.

Once he cried out in terror, when the caravan appeared to be passing through a defile whose walls closed in about him, until it seemed that he would be crushed to death. He had the sensation of moving down a long dark tunnel, then suddenly light burst upon his eyes, a rosy colored vista that appeared to be made up of graceful columns and arched doorways, with carved figures jumbled together like a child's castle of sand tumbled hither and thither by a heedless intruder. He shut his eyes against the rosy glare, which had set his head to throbbing all the more, and when he felt his body being lifted from the back of a camel, tried to shout in his delirium that he must go on. Then he felt gentle hands upon his forehead, and a blessed darkness enveloped him.

III

Saul awakened to the sound of voices speaking in Aramaic, the tongue of Jews almost everywhere. His head no longer ached and he was able to move enough to study his surroundings. The walls of the room in which he lay seemed to have been hollowed out of just such pink stone as had formed the jumbled pictures he'd seen before blackness engulfed him. The curving shape of the wall and the absence of windows made him think he must be inside a cave, but it was roomy and cool and very comfortable, more comfortable than he remembered being for a long time.

To one side he saw a brightness that could be a doorway and shortly a shadow momentarily blotted out some of the brightness as a woman entered the cave, bearing a small bowl of some steaming liquid in her hands.

"So you're awake at last?" Her smile was warm and friendly. "Drink this. It will give you strength and help the fever."

He drank the steaming liquid, though even that small effort

brought vertigo. When he was able to look about him again, he saw that the woman was very beautiful, with dark red hair, and brown eyes. She appeared to be in her middle thirties and, though not richly dressed, her garments had been chosen to set off her beauty. Going to a basin of water that stood upon a small stand at one side, she moistened a cloth and put it upon his forehead.

"Your fever has broken and you will feel better soon," she assured him. "Try to sleep now."

"What of the caravan?"

"It went on to Ezion-Geber. You were much too sick to travel any farther."

"Where—where am I?"

"In Petra. My name is Mary of Magdala and my husband is Joseph of Galilee, a physician. The caravan leader knows us and left you in our care. Now rest. You will feel much better when you wake again."

The hot drink had a soporific effect and Saul quickly fell asleep. When he awakened, he saw by the darkness of the cave's opening that night had fallen. A cheerful bed of coals now glowed just inside and upon it was a pot from which came the tantalizing aroma of lintels, onions, and savory herbs, cooked in a stew with goat's flesh. The smell reminded him that he was hungry and he pushed himself up on his elbows to look about him. At the movement a man rose from a cushion on the floor near the wall of the cave. His face was clean cut and intelligent and the dark eyes were friendly. He was slightly taller than Saul, slenderer in build, and perhaps forty years of age.

"I am Joseph, Mary's husband. She went to take some stew to a neighbor who is ill."

"You are the physician who healed me?"

"I am a physician." Joseph filled a bowl with the steaming mixture from the pot and came over to squat beside Saul's pallet. "But as for curing you, I suspect that you have a true intermittent fever, so you'll probably have another chill tomorrow. You've had this before, haven't you?"

"Once or twice a year almost as long as I can remember."

"The infusion I gave you will probably not be able to stop the chill you will have tomorrow, but with luck it should be the last—at least for this attack." Joseph began to feed Saul the stew, handling the bowl and the wooden spoon expertly.

"This infusion," Saul said between swallows. "What is it made from?"

"A collection of the bark from various trees. A friend from India told me about them when I was studying in Alexandria. He assured me that this kind of fever is related to the presence of swampy areas where large numbers of mosquitoes are found."

"Do you have mosquitoes in Petra?"

"None to speak of—and no fever of this kind—which makes me think he was probably right. My guess is that you carry it with you in your body."

"Then it will come again?"

"Probably, unless the infusion of bark is continued for a long time. I haven't seen enough of this kind of fever to be sure."

Mary came in just then, pleased to find her patient awake and taking nourishment. When Saul finished the bowl of stew, she gave him another dose of what Joseph had called the infusion. Washed down with wine, it was not particularly unpleasant and afterward she propped up his head with a pillow so he could see the interior of the cave.

It had been hollowed out of what appeared to be pure sandstone, with layers of lighter color running through the formation. Large enough for several rooms, the cave was quite clean and the few pieces of furniture, a low table, a small chest, and some wicker baskets with hinged tops, were all polished until they gleamed in the firelight.

"Did you say you were from Galilee?" he asked.

"We are Nazarenes—from Magdala," Joseph answered. "Many of our friends in Jerusalem were forced to leave after the death of one of our leaders there called Stephen. There was talk of extending the persecution to other cities and, since Mary knew Jesus of Nazareth well and was the first to witness his resurrection, we thought it would be better to leave Galilee."

"But for Saul of Tarsus, we would still be in our home overlooking the lake," said Mary, somewhat wistfully.

Saul hesitated only momentarily. It was not in his nature to try to hide his identity, even though these people who had taken him in would have every reason now to thrust him out again, if they failed to believe the story of the change that had come over him.

"You need fear Saul no more," he assured them.

"Is he—is he dead?" Mary asked quickly.

"The man who persecuted the followers of Jesus of Nazareth is dead."

"I don't understand."

"I am Saul of Tarsus. I was going from Jerusalem to Damascus, to continue the persecution I carried on in Jerusalem, but I was struck blind when Jesus spoke to me, and called me to serve him. I know you will find it hard to believe—"

"I don't find it hard to believe at all," Mary said quickly. "After all, he accepted me though I had lived a life of evil. It isn't what we were before he called us that counts with Jesus—but what we become afterward."

**IV**

As Joseph had predicted, Saul suffered a severe fever and chill the following day. Mary wrapped him in warm covers and placed heated stones around his body and the fever broke when sweat began to form. By nightfall he was feeling much better and the next day was able to sit up and move around inside the cave. In another day, he felt strong enough to sit in the sun upon the ledge outside and there a scene of startling beauty met his eyes.

Petra, capital of the kings of the Nabatean desert, was a rosy hued and startlingly beautiful city carved from the strange colorfully stratified rocks in vast natural fissure. The entrance to the dry bottomed rocky chasm of Petra, Mary told him, was located in the southern extension of the great rift where, farther to the north, the Jordan flowed to its ending in the Dead Sea.

The so-called Spring of Moses where, it was said, the leader of the Children of Israel had struck the rock with his staff to produce clear and sparkling water upon that epic journey out of Egypt was near the outer end of the passageway that gave entrance to the hidden city. No more than fifteen hundred paces long and in some places barely wide enough for a man and a camel to pass, it was traversed by a road and a brook which, with the spring freshets, sometimes swelled to a torrent, shutting away access to the stronghold entirely through that route.

The narrow rift, whose walls sometimes almost touched above the road and the brook formed the dark tunnel Saul had seen in his delirium. At its inner end, the rift abruptly opened upon the chasm in which the city lay, a vast cup hollowed out by nature during many centuries from the wild and rugged mountain ranges of Edom—as this land had been called in the time of Moses. The center of the chasm contained the major part of the city, but workmen had swarmed up the rocky wall of the gorge in many places, chiseling and excavating a tomb with vast columns, pediments, steps and figures where, Saul was told, the current king would be buried at his death.

Along the face of the jagged cliffs, watercourses had been carved down which the flow of the life-giving spring rains sluiced into cisterns cut into the solid rock. And high up on the side of one of the cliffs, he could see an altar carved from the living rock where the religious ceremonies of the Nabateans were carried out—represented by the God and, Dusares, Joseph explained. They were worshipers of the sun, going back to an ancient faith which arose from man's instinctive understanding that life came from its warmth.

By the end of a week after his arrival in Petra, Saul was able to work and easily obtained employment in the shop of a tentmaker, since the caravans that visited this central point of desert trade were always in need of new tents or repairs to the old. At the insistence of Joseph and Mary he continued to stay with them in their cave home, which was more than large enough for all three. There, during the evenings while they sat with the bed of coals in the entrance to the cave giving warmth to the chill of the night, he listened while Mary spoke of the time when she had been the chief of the women who served Jesus of Nazareth. And as he listened, Saul began to understand at last why he had been sent to this hidden refuge in the rocks far south of the Dead Sea.

From Mary and Joseph, who had witnessed most of the events, or heard them described by those who had been at the scene, he learned the story of the early months of Jesus' ministry, his rejection by his own people in Nazareth—who could not believe the Messiah had come from their own ranks—his coming to Capernaum and the dramatic ministry in the teeming cities around the Sea of Galilee, the miracles he had performed, and the parables he had spoken.

Gradually a picture began to emerge, of a gentle man who had come, not as an earthly Messiah to lead his people to victory and vanquish the Roman overlords, like Judas Maccabeus of old, but the Son of God sent to show men a new way to true kinship with the deity through love one for another.

At last Saul began to perceive a glimmering of the truth Jesus had called him to preach. The full comprehension was not yet his—that would come later. But the seed from which full comprehension would grow had been sown and that alone was enough to lift a great burden from his soul. Nor did the lingering spark of resentment, which had almost led him to the sin of hating God when his father had been stricken ill, simmer within him any longer. For a new Saul had been born in that moment of blinding clarity before Damascus. And at Petra, like a child learning to walk, he began to take the first hesitant steps toward his own particular destiny.

Busy with palm and needle, as he sewed the tough fabrics, free to roam the limitless expanse of universal truth, Saul found the days and nights in the Nabatean stronghold even more pleasant than the period of nearly a year he'd spent at the feet of Nestor, searching blindly—he realized now—for the truth which was only just being revealed to him.

As yet he felt no urge to leave the sanctuary of Petra and the pleasant cave home of Joseph and Mary. His body was growing stronger day by day and his mind clearer; besides, his hosts were intelligent and educated and their minds stimulated him.

As the truth he was to preach thereafter began to take form in Saul's mind, he sharpened its outlines in discussion and debate with the other two, formulating the great conception of redeeming love as the most powerful force on earth or in heaven. Nor did the acceptance of such a radical change in his thinking come easily for him. Trained from boyhood to believe that nothing should come before the Law handed down by a wrathful God on Mount Sinai and graven there in tablets of stone, his mind could not accept the truth that all the old rules had been swept away by the coming of Jesus, his cruel death on the cross and his resurrection.

Saul was preparing early one morning to go to the tentmaker's establishment where he worked during the day, when a messenger came to the cave and called for Joseph. The physician went outside and the two conferred briefly.

"A priest has been injured at the Great High Place," Joseph said when he came back into the cave. "Would you like to go with me there, Saul?"

Saul had learned enough about the customs of the Nabateans during his stay in Petra to know that Dusares was the major deity of this proud desert people and the Great High Place the center of worship. Always curious about other religions, he agreed at once and, with Joseph, followed their guide along a path that wound ever upward across the sheer face of a cliff overlooking Petra. The path was narrow but worn smooth by the many thousands of feet that had climbed to the heights for the ceremonies of worship through the centuries.

This was the first time Saul had climbed high enough into the hills around Petra to obtain a full view of the city. Set apart from the rose red background formed by the towering cliffs of Edom were the buildings of the Nabatean capital, the palaces of its rulers, and the warehouses where merchants stored the vast amount of valuable stuff that came to this central caravan point for transhipment. Across the gorge in which the city lay towered the most massive rock formation of all—a cliff upon which a fortress had been erected by the Nabatean kings for the final defense of the city, in the unlikely eventuality that an invader would be able to fight his way in through the narrow gorge. The only other entrance to the chasm was through a rough jumble of cliffs, valleys, and difficult mountain passes, so it was unlikely that any invader would be able to thread his way in without being detected and destroyed long before the city itself was in danger.

From his vantage point on the path ascending the cliff, Saul could easily see the caves and storehouses hollowed out from the rocks to form the citadel and the soldiers in their colorful headgear and robes walking their posts there. The path he and Joseph were following ended in a level area just below the highest point of the cliff where the altar called the Great High Place stood. Two sentinel pillars, carved from the rosy hued stone, marked the entrance to the sacred place, but Saul and Joseph went no farther, for the priests who served the altar lived in a network of caves and passages well beneath it.

Joseph did not take long to splint the broken arm of the injured priest. As the two descended the cliffside path to the city below, Saul questioned him about the Nabatean faith but the physician could tell him little more than that the God of the Nabateans seemed to be the same as the Sun God, called Aton by the Egyptians and Ahura Mazda by the Persians.

"We're here on the sufferance of King Aretas, because I once treated his ambassador in Galilee," Joseph explained. "I have made it a point not to inquire about their religion. But I did hear that it is their custom to select a young man to be worshiped as a lesser god for the period of a year. Then in the spring, with the planting of the seed and its dying to produce new life, the young god is sacrificed upon the altar up there at the Great High Place, as a ransom for the lives of the people for another year and to insure the fertility of the seed."

"I saw something similar in a drama of the Eleusinian mystery at the university of Tarsus," said Saul.

"Many religions have such ceremonies," Joseph agreed. "In Alexandria, a young man is symbolically—though not actually —sacrificed to Dionysius during an orgy in the spring. And I suspect our Jewish custom of ransoming the firstborn with a gift to the temple is really a substitute for an old, old ritual in which the first male issue was sacrificed to God to appease his wrath."

Mary was unusually silent that night at the evening meal. When she had finished putting away the pot and the utensils for eating, she came to where Joseph and Saul were talking just inside the mouth of the cave.

"Joseph told me you were interested in the sacrifice to Dusares at the Great High Place, Saul," she said.

"Only because everything about religion interests me."

"I once took part in the Great Dionysia at Alexandria, when I was a dancer in the theater there. I played the part of Aphrodite in the ritual marriage between the goddess and young Bacchus."

Saul said nothing, sensing that she felt impelled to tell him more.

"The man playing Bacchus was a Roman who had betrayed me when I was but a girl in Galilee. At the height of the ceremony, I sought to kill him but failed. That failure led me back to Galilee and—Jesus. So you see, we sometimes reach our own particular destiny by a roundabout path."

"*'The Lord shall rise up as in Mount Perazim,'*" Saul said softly. "*'He shall be wroth as in the Valley of Gibeon, that he may do his work, his strange work; and bring to pass his act, his strange act.'* Those words were spoken by the Prophet Isaiah."

"Isaiah also prophesied the suffering of Jesus and his rejection by his own people," said Mary.

"I rejected him, too, when I consented to Stephen's death!" Saul confessed. "Had I not been watching the cloaks of the witnesses that day, I would surely have cast one of the stones that killed Stephen, so I'm equally guilty with the Roman soldiers who drove the nails through the hands of Jesus."

"The Lord was only showing you the way then," she protested. "Whatever guilt you feel, be sure the Master doesn't hold it against you—else he would not have called you to his service, or sent you here to Petra."

"But why Petra? I have done nothing here."

"You have learned of Jesus' days on earth. And I think you have begun to understand now why he came."

## V

Long after the others were asleep, Saul lay awake, searching for an answer to questions that seemed just beyond his grasp, like a tantalizing dream. Finally he rose and, taking care not to disturb Mary and Joseph, put on his cloak against the chill of the night and stepped outside.

The city was asleep, the quiet pervading it now a marked contrast to the bustle characterizing it by day: the babble of voices engaged in trade or gossip; the squawk of camels protesting the order to kneel; the tinkle of jeweler's tools; the clank of pots and pans from the shops of the metal workers, whose ancestors had plied their trade on the shores of the Gulf of Aqaba at Ezion-Geber in the time of Solomon. Tonight, the only sounds were the cough of a camel, the bark of a dog, and the voices of the guards in the citadel near the top of the cliff.

The moon was high over the rim of the gorge in which Petra lay, flooding the whole area with a cool brilliance. Its pale light did not pick up the rosy hues of the sandstone, as did the sun's rays. Instead, the rocky walls, the buildings, and the whole wild beauty of the mountainous cup was painted in shades of gray and black. Saul started to walk, but only when he became conscious of increased effort, realized that his steps had taken the path leading up the cliffside to the Great High Place of the Nabateans.

He hesitated only a moment—before continuing up the steeply climbing path, though fully realizing that the priests there might not look with favor upon the appearance of a stranger in that sacred place. So worn was the path by thousands of pilgrims to the great shrine of Petra that his feet dislodged no stones to go tumbling down the almost vertical cliffs and warn the dwellers in the caves at lower levels of his presence. He did not climb the larger path all the way to the area where he had waited for Joseph that morning. Instead, when he came upon a narrow one somewhat lower down that appeared to give access directly to the great altar, he climbed between crevices in the rocks and finally came out upon the paved space around the sacred spot. Bathed by the cool brilliance of the moonlight, the area was almost as bright as day. He hesitated for a moment at the edge of the paved square. Then, seeing no one and hearing no challenge, moved softly across to the altar itself.

The slab of black obsidian in its center was so highly polished that the white orb of the moon was reflected in its surface as in a mirror. When Saul reached out to touch it, he jerked his hand away for it was warmer than the stone blocks surrounding it, and he recalled Joseph saying the Nabatean priests who served the Great High Place claimed the God Dusares himself lived there and was momentarily tempted to flee. Then he remembered reading in some of the scrolls of Greek knowledge—to which the young physician named Luke had introduced him in Tarsus—that a dark surface always absorbed more of the sun's rays than a lighter one and was therefore warmer in the sunlight than surrounding areas, no doubt explaining the warmth of the black stone hours after the sun had gone down.

As Saul studied the reflection of the moon in the polished black obsidian, the white orb slowly faded and he seemed to see, mirrored in the stone, a strange and colorful scene. A crowd of worshipers filled the level area where the altar stood with a group of richly garbed priests around it. Two of them led a handsome young man to the altar but, even though he sensed what was about to happen, Saul felt no revulsion at watching a forbidden ceremony. For something seemed to tell him this could be a scene from the story of Israel, a re-creation in another time and place of the occasion when Abraham, obeying the order of the Most High, had prepared to sacrifice his son Isaac as a burnt offering to the Lord on a mountain overlooking Jerusalem.

Two burly priests now lifted the human sacrifice and placed him upon the altar. Above him stood the High Priest, his tall headdress making him seem like a giant, as he lifted the ceremonial knife of sacrifice in his right hand. In Saul's trance—as he gazed at the square of polished black stone—he could even hear the great indrawn "ahh" from the crowd when the knife plunged into the heart of the victim.

Blood gushed forth to stain the stones of the altar while the people fell upon the ground before it, giving thanks that they had been redeemed for another year from the wrath of their god through the death of the young man. Redeemed from the hot, burning rays of the sun that could parch the ground and destroy their crops, from storms that could bring the awesome play of lightning across the cliffs and send torrents of rain flooding into the rocky clefts guarding the city, causing floods to sweep across the land, destroying even as they refreshed the earth with new soil for another crop.

As the vivid scene he'd seemed to see in the polished surface of the sacred stone of Dusares began to fade, Saul instinctively lifted his eyes to heaven, half-hoping for some revelation there, but the sky was empty of anything save the moon and stars. Gripped by a sense of disappointment, he was about to turn away when his gaze fastened upon one particular star. It was not as bright as those around it and he could not have told why his eyes had singled it out, until he recognized nearby the giant constellation the Greeks called the Great Bear, though the caravan master had likened it with much more reason to a ladle or a dipper, with its curved handle and almost rectangular body.

As the Phoenician had instructed him, Saul let his eyes travel swiftly across the two stars at the end of the ladle. Passing along the line they formed and estimating six times the distance between them, his gaze came to rest upon the star he'd seen just now and he knew it was the symbol of the north sometimes called Phoenikos.

Perhaps it was not true that the star glowed more and more brightly as he stared at it. Perhaps only the sudden wonder that filled him made it seem that way. But standing there upon the high place above Petra, at a shrine which, whatever the name of the god to whom it was dedicated, could still only be to the glory of One Above All, Saul knew with a sudden rush of joy that the purpose for which he had been selected and for which he had been led to this isolated stronghold in the wilderness, had at last been partially revealed to him. There in the sky, never changing, like the God who had put it there eons ago, hung his own particular star, guiding him to whatever task, whatever fate, the voice that had spoken to him on the road to Damascus had chosen for him. What was more, the vision there at the Great High Place had shown him the truth at last: that God, out of his great love for an erring people created in his image, had sent his own Son as a sacrifice for their sins.

Mary and Joseph were still asleep when Saul returned to the cave. He did not disturb them but, rolling himself up in his cloak, was instantly asleep and awakened only when Mary called him to say that the morning meal of dates, goat's milk, and fruit was ready. Joseph, she said, had left earlier to attend one of the king's wives, in great pain with childbirth.

"I thought I heard you leave the cave last night and return later," Mary said as he was eating.

"I went to the Most High Place."

"That could have been dangerous. We are not of the Nabatean faith."

"Something drew me there—a star. I know now that my path lies northward."

"But where?"

"Where else but Damascus? I had no real chance to tell the whole story of my calling before I left there."

"The Nabateans only tolerate us here because of Joseph's skill as a physician," she warned. "If you stir up the people of Damascus with your preaching, they will put you in prison or perhaps kill you."

"Jesus suffered prison and even death—yet was reborn. How can my enemies triumph over me, when I have already been reborn—on the road to Damascus?"

**VI**

The return of Saul to Damascus created a sensation in both the Nazarene and Jewish communities there. His brief appearance following his dramatic conversion had caused little stir for there he had been uncertain of just what had happened to him and of its ultimate significance, an uncertainty that had been apparent when he spoke from the pulpit. But a new Saul arrived with a caravan from Petra. Self-assured, certain that he had been chosen for a special task by the Son of God, he was possessed once again with the old fire that had moved so many in Jerusalem.

This time his discourse was not on the Law or the Prophets, save where the latter—as in the writings of Isaiah—had foretold the coming of a Savior for Israel and for the world. Instead he took as his theme something Mary of Magdala had told him from the words of Jesus himself: "I am the way, the truth and the life. No man comes to the Father except by me."

To this already startling and revolutionary doctrine, Saul added yet another: that he, who had led the persecution of the Nazarenes in Jerusalem, had been called directly by the risen Lord to serve him. Thus, he placed himself on an equal basis with the disciples whom Christ had previously selected as he walked beside the lake in Galilee and who now directed the church in Jerusalem, an assumption that was certain to stir many in the new faith to anger.

The first part of Saul's doctrine seemed to free Jews from the burden of the Law, with its six hundred and thirteen provisions, although Saul himself continued to keep the Law, as he had always done. As a result, many were moved to announce their trust in the Messiah from Nazareth; others, however, were not so quick to accept the new doctrine. The Pharisees whom Saul accused publicly—as Jesus had done—of making an idol of the Law, particularly considered him the advocate of a dangerous teaching that not only perverted the basis of their religion, but was likely to get those who espoused it into trouble with the Romans for acknowledging allegiance to one crucified as a rebel. As the months passed and Saul continued to preach, not only on the Sabbath but during the week wherever even a few would listen, going from shop to shop in Damascus to tell his story, a deep undercurrent of resentment against him began to build up in many quarters. The leaders of the regular synagogues, who were losing members to the new faith daily—as Saul himself had lost members from the Congregation of the Libertines to the simple eloquence of Simon Peter and the impassioned fervor of Stephen—began to plot to destroy him. Nor were they without support in the Nazarene sector of the community, who resented his claiming equality with Jesus' own disciples.

Busy and happy with his work, Saul did not realize what was happening, until Ananias came to him one evening in the room he occupied at the back of a tentmaker's establishment, where he worked by day. Saul and the weaver, whose hands had brought sight to him in his blindness, had become close friends in the weeks since his return to Damascus. The concern of Ananias told him this was more than just a social visit.

"What's wrong?" he asked.

"Your life is in danger—from those who will not accept the truth."

"Why?"

"Because you have the power to move men's souls and change their lives."

"When has this become a crime?"

"They crucified the Master for it. The leaders of the synagogues—and some from among our own people—are plotting to kill you and make it look as if you were stabbed by robbers."

"I have nothing a robber would want."

"You have your life. These would take it from you for the same reason that Caiaphas arranged to have Stephen killed by the crowd."

"Are you sure?"

"One of my weavers heard them plotting. You must leave Damascus at once."

"Does the Nazarene congregation agree to this?"

"I haven't put it to them," Ananias admitted. "But we're only men, Saul, without your lack of fear. Many resent your naming yourself an apostle and others are afraid you will bring the wrath of the authorities down upon us with your preaching and cause another persecution here."

"'*He came unto his own and his own received him not,*'" Saul said softly. "I am honored, Ananias."

"What do you mean?"

"Never mind. Do you advise me to leave?"

"For your own sake, yes. It's the only safe thing to do."

"I will go tomorrow. To Jerusalem—to see Simon Peter and Barnabas."

"They may resent your naming yourself an apostle, too," Ananias warned.

"Jesus called me with his voice on the road to Damascus and the sight of *his* glory blinded me," said Saul. "If Peter and the group at Jerusalem choose to deny me, I shall start my own church elsewhere."

## VII

Ananias had arranged for Saul to travel with a caravan bound for Galilee along the Way of the Sea but, learning that the guards at the gates of Damascus had been instructed by the governor of the city to arrest him on sight, had arranged at the last moment for the apostle to be let down over the wall of the city during the night by means of ropes. By dint of brisk walking, Saul caught up with the caravan in the foothills of the Anti-Lebanon range. Following the ancient route almost in the shadow of Mount Hermon, they crossed the Jordan north of the Sea of Galilee at the Jisr Benat Ya'kub—the Bridge of Jacob's Daughters. From the lovely harp-shaped Sea of Galilee, where Jesus had walked and taught, Saul followed the favorite route of the pilgrims southward along the Jordan to Jericho, the palm-studded garden spot that served as a winter resort for Herod Antipas and many of the Roman and Jewish nobility.

Leaving Jericho, the road wound steadily upward and westward out of the deep cleft of the *ghor* in which the Jordan flowed. The slaty blue surface of the Dead Sea had been visible every now and then through the hills on his left hand, as Saul trod the road worn smooth long ago by the feet of many thousands of pilgrims, the same road Jesus himself had traveled to meet his tragic destiny in Jerusalem. As always, Saul was rendered speechless by the glory of the golden-roofed temple, seen from the east as he rounded a shoulder on the road across the Mount of Olives. A lone cross occupying the hill called Golgotha, with a limp figure hanging from it, was grim reminder of the fate that could await him in Jerusalem. The Roman sentry on duty at the gate hardly gave him a passing glance, however, for thousands of people came and went through this gate every day. And as he walked the familiar, teeming streets, he thought that nothing had changed—except within himself. But there he was wrong.

Jepthah saw Saul as soon as he paused in the doorway of the tentmaker's shop and snarled a curse as his only welcome. Taken aback by the viciousness of his brother-in-law's attack, Saul stepped back over the doorsill into the street, but Jepthah followed him, hurling curses and accusations at him until a crowd began to gather, attracted by the commotion. From the stream of abuse Saul managed to cull the fact that his father had died during the time he had been in Petra, that the shop in Tarsus had been sold to Lucius, and that his mother was living there, while Jepthah and Miriam had been given the shop in Jerusalem.

Quite obviously Jepthah had no intention of sharing any of the inheritance with Saul and, though he wished to see his sister and her little boy, he finally gave up and turned down the street toward the Lower City. Barnabas, he knew, had been living in the house, from the balcony of which he'd heard Simon Peter address the crowd so eloquently on the Sabbath of Pentecost. Knowing nowhere else to go, he went there and knocked upon the door. It was opened by a slender youth, wearing the linen robe usually worn by young men in the Scribes' School maintained by the temple.

"I seek Joseph of Cyprus—called Barnabas," said Saul. "Does he still live here?"

A woman appeared behind the boy and, seeing the sudden light of fear in her eyes, Saul knew she recognized him. She did not drive him from her threshold, as Jepthah had done, however, but stood aside courteously for him to enter.

"Barnabas should be home soon," she said. "Will you wait?"

"My name is Saul—Saul of Tarsus."

"I know, I saw you once, at the death of Ste— of a friend."

"And you still invite me into your home?"

She smiled then. "You are one of us now. Have you come far?"

"From Jericho today."

"Then you must be tired. I am Miriam and this is my son Mark." She nodded toward a low couch. "Rest there while I finish preparing the evening meal."

The smell of fresh baked bread and boiling beans made Saul realize he was hungry. The boy remained in the room but, though he was polite, Saul saw by an occasional quick glance in his direction that he was consumed with curiosity and finally broke the silence.

"Are you still in the Scribes' School?" he asked.

"Yes. How did you know?"

"Your robe. I was once a student in the school of Gamaliel."

"I wanted to study with Gamaliel, but we couldn't afford it, so I enrolled in the Temple School."

"You must be a very good student. In my day, only the best were accepted there."

"I have the highest marks in my class," Mark said proudly. "But I am no longer enrolled there. Peter and Barnabas thought I should occupy myself by setting down the words spoken by the Master."

"Were you with him?"

"No. Peter has been telling them to me, so I can write them down. That way we will have the teachings of Jesus preserved for others to study."

"Are the disciples still in Jerusalem?"

"James ben Zebedee is here and his brother John, with several others. Philip went to Samaria after the persecution. Peter travels in the surrounding area and I usually go with him, so I may set down the things he remembers about what Jesus taught."

The door to the outside opened just then and Barnabas came in. At the sight of the visitor, his face filled with joy and he dropped the bundles he was carrying to engulf Saul in a bearlike embrace.

"Thank God you're safe," he said. "When a letter came from Ananias saying you were coming here and there was no sign of you, we were afraid something might have happened. I even went to Jepthah to ask about you."

"That explains why he wasn't surprised to see me."

"Or pleased?"

"He drove me from the shop with a whiplash of words."
Saul managed to grin. "I think he would have used a real one,
if he'd had it at hand. I only came back to talk to Simon Peter.
Then I shall be moving on."

"Where will you go?"

"Wherever the Lord sends me."

"Have you any idea where that will be?"

"No. But I'm sure he will tell me when the time comes. How
is it here? Is Caiaphas still troubling you?"

"Not any more. James ben Joseph—a kinsman of the Lord
from Nazareth—now heads the synagogue. He is a strict believer
in the Law and is known to be very pious, so in Jerusalem, we
are just like any other synagogue, such as the Alexandrians, the
Grecians, or even your old group, the Libertines."

"Surely you haven't given up the teachings of Jesus?"

"We will never give those up," said Barnabas. "But James
makes a point of staying strictly within the provisions of the
Law and requires it of others. The synagogue here is very small,
now that many of us are scattered abroad. Even Simon Peter
spends most of his time traveling to other cities and preaching
there."

"Mark was telling me about it. Where is Peter now?"

"In Jerusalem. Tomorrow I will take you to him, but it will
be best if only a few people know where you are. Even though
I'm convinced that the Lord was working through you all the
time to further the growth of his church by making people leave
Jerusalem and spread the Gospel abroad, not everyone in our
congregation agrees with me."

## VIII

Peter had not changed at all, Saul decided when he and Barnabas
went to the house where the big disciple was staying. In fact, he
seemed to be even more confident and assured than during his
dramatic appearances before the Sanhedrin. James—the kinsman
of the Lord from Nazareth who was now leader of the
Synagogue of the Nazarenes—was a spare man, gentle of voice

and manner but very determined. He wore a small phylactery bound to his forehead, in the manner of pious Pharisees everywhere. His greeting was reserved and Saul had the definite impression that the kinsman of the Lord would not be unhappy to see him leave Jerusalem as quickly as possible. Simon Peter, however, was warm and friendly in his greeting and once again Saul was impressed by the magnetic personality of the big man.

"Tell us how the Lord called you on the road to Damascus, Saul," were Peter's first words.

Saul began with the story of his blindness and the voice that had spoken to him, but there James stopped him and made him repeat the exact words of Jesus.

"What do they mean?" he asked.

"I think my conscience had been pricking me for a long time," Saul admitted. "As one pricks an ox with a goad."

"But you never saw Jesus, did you?"

"No. I was in Tarsus at the time of the crucifixion."

"When did your conscience start troubling you?"

"It must have been on the Sabbath of Pentecost, when I first heard Simon Peter speak from the balcony of Miriam's home."

"If I was instrumental in bringing you to Jesus, I am grateful," said Peter. "Go on with your story please, Saul."

Saul told how he had been healed of the blindness in Damascus, of the journey to Petra and his months there, of his return to Damascus and his dramatic escape, when the Jewish leaders there had sought to destroy him. He did not mention the hour he had spent in the Great High Place in Petra—or his conviction that the star he'd seen that night was guiding him.

"Why did you return to Jerusalem?" James asked when he had finished the story.

"I want to help spread the word about Jesus wherever I can serve best," Saul explained. "And since the leaders of the church are here, it seemed a logical place to begin."

"Even at the risk of your life?" Peter asked.

"Jesus called me to serve. Wherever he sends me, I go."

"One thing is certain, you cannot stay here," said Peter. "Your brother-in-law is sure to notify Caiaphas that you are in Jerusalem and your life will no longer be safe."

"We must also think of those who remain here," James pointed out. "It will not help to bring the wrath of the High Priest down upon innocent people."

An answer to the problem posed by his presence in Jerusalem suddenly came to Saul. Nor did he doubt its origin, for it meant traveling northward, in the direction of the star he'd seen that night in Petra.

"I shall go to Tarsus," he said, voicing the thought. "My mother needs me now and, when the Lord has work for me, he will call me there. I wouldn't want to bring down the wrath of the High Priest upon the rest of you and trouble does seem to follow me ever since the Lord called me."

"It follows all who serve him," Peter said simply. "Jesus warned us that whoever would save his life must also be prepared to lay it down for his sake."

"You have chosen a wise course, Saul." James' relief was apparent. "Will you teach in Tarsus?"

"I have the right to speak in the synagogue like anyone else, since I am a Jew."

"And you still adhere to the Law?"

"I am a Pharisee. Since my childhood, I have always lived according to the Law."

"Then be sure you will find favor with God," said James. "Shalom! And may the Lord be with you."

Outside the sun was shining and the well remembered beauty of the Holy City lightened Saul's spirits after his somewhat chilly reception by James. But he could also understand the concern the head of the Nazarene Synagogue naturally felt over the possibility of a recurrence of the persecution.

"You had better travel by way of Joppa," Barnabas suggested. "Peter visited there recently and healed many sick. I will give you the names of some of our people, in case you have to wait for a ship."

"Are you going to stay in Jerusalem?"

Barnabas shook his head. "I shall be visiting Antioch. Soon. The Nazarene congregation there has increased almost as fast as we did here, when Peter and the others first returned from

Galilee after Jesus was crucified. Peter thinks Antioch will soon have to take over much of the leadership from Jerusalem."

"Why?"

"We have made few converts here since James has headed the synagogue. Most of us believe the Master wants the word spread abroad, but James would keep us only a sect within the Jewish faith."

"Like the Essenes?"

"Of the followers of Hillel—though James actually tends more towards Shammai than Hillel."

"He couldn't have chosen a better way to drive away Grecian Jews," said Saul. "Few of them are interested in such an austere faith."

IX

It was spring when Saul returned to Tarsus. Before leaving Jerusalem he had visited a notary and signed over his legitimate title to the shop there to his sister and her son. Though this act of unselfishness meant that he was almost penniless, he knew it would not make Jepthah any less liable to betray him, if he had remained in the city. Not even the prospect of having a price placed on his head by the temple authorities troubled him, however, for the call on the Damascus road had changed both the course and the outlook of his life. And so he was free to enjoy the beauty of the city of his birth seen again in the spring-time.

Flowers bloomed in the gardens, their fragrance enveloping the city, except along the Rhegma, where the acrid smell of cordage and the stench of refuse dominated the air. The same polyglot population filled the streets, talking, arguing, bickering, bargaining in a dozen tongues. For Tarsus was not only a seaport city but also a center for caravans traveling the great Roman thoroughfares leading eastward to Antioch and westward to the Greek cities as well the rough trails northward into the uplands of Cilicia. The sounds of the busy and prosperous city were music to Saul's ears, as he hurried through the streets toward his old home.

Naomi, a little more bent and wrinkled than he remembered, embraced him on the doorstep. Lucius had let her continue to use the house, even though hired spinners and weavers now worked in the shop. And though it seemed empty without his father sitting by an oil lamp in the evening, reading from the scrolls of the Law and the Prophets, Saul was content to be home.

That night he slept on his own pallet and awoke to the sound of birds singing in the garden. He did not dally after the morning meal, but announced that he was going to visit Lucius to see about obtaining employment as a sewer of sails, so he would be able to earn his own keep. He found his boyhood friend in the same warehouse where he'd met Luke years before. And though Lucius was plumper and obviously more prosperous than before, his greeting was as warm as ever.

"So the traveler returns," he said, dismissing the scribe to whom he had been dictating letters. "How long will you be in Tarsus this time?"

"Perhaps years, perhaps only a few months."

"Have you no longing for security? For certainty about the future?"

"My future is already certain. The man I serve tells me where to go and what to do."

"I thought you had become a teacher, a rabbi serving your god by interpreting his edicts to the people."

"I serve the Son of God, Jesus of Nazareth."

"Wasn't he crucified in Jerusalem?"

"Yes. But God raised him from the dead."

"Like the young man we saw killed during the drama of the Eleusinian mystery that day in the theater at the university?"

"What we saw was a play. Jesus is real and eternal."

"One day you must try to explain it all to me," said Lucius. "At the moment it's too complicated for me to understand. Tell me about your travels."

"Besides Jerusalem, I have been to Damascus and Petra."

"Petra!" Lucius' eyes lit up. "Is it true that the Nabateans are carving a whole city from the rock?"

"I saw mainly tombs being carved while I was there. But the cliffsides are honeycombed with caves where many people live, and they are digging new ones all the time."

"Is the only entrance really so narrow that a camel can barely pass through?"

"The main entrance is almost like a tunnel." Saul recalled his first impression of Petra, when he'd been delirious with the fever. "There are several other entrances, but they are located in very rough country and an invader would have trouble reaching the city that way."

"I must go there one day," said Lucius. "I might even journey on southward to Ezion-Geber and perhaps take ship for the Eastern Sea on one of the great vessels that sail to India with the monsoon wind. I envy you, Saul, with nothing to tie you down."

"Most people would envy you—with the proof of your success all around you."

"Wealth doesn't bring the kind of happiness I see in your eyes. I have enough of it now to know."

"You can find happiness the same way I did."

"How?"

"First I gave my life into Jesus' keeping when he called me. Then I signed the shop in Jerusalem over to Jepthah and Miriam."

"You gave away your inheritance?"

"Jesus teaches us not to think of earthly riches. When he was alive, he forbade his disciples to take even a purse with them as they went about preaching and healing the sick."

"I couldn't thrive on such a faith," Lucius admitted. "I am too much attached to my comforts."

"I see that some of them have attached themselves to you."

"A merchant must be well fed. Else people would think he isn't doing well in business."

"We have the same custom among the Pharisees," said Saul. "They boast of their deep piety by wearing tasseled robes and large phylacteries on their foreheads, but Jesus teaches us to judge a man by his inner spirit, not by his body or his outward wealth. On that account, I know you have always been rich."

"I sometimes wonder about that. The more wealth a man gains, the more he thinks he needs and the sharper he becomes in his dealings with others."

"I hope you haven't become too grasping," said Saul. "I came to ask for employment as a cutter and sewer of sails."

"But you have studied at the finest schools in Jerusalem," Lucius protested. "Your mother has boasted to me many times that you are considered one of the most promising young teachers in Jerusalem—with your own synagogue."

"I am no longer their rabbi," Saul confessed. "Even then, the congregation was made up of freed slaves."

"Weren't you a Scribe of the Sanhedrin? With the certainty of a seat on the high court of your people in time?"

"Yes."

"Then how is it that you seek employment from me as a mere cutter and sewer of sails?"

"I gave up everything to follow Jesus of Nazareth."

"Doesn't leaving everything behind trouble you?"

"Not as much as I would be troubled if I hadn't found the secret of happiness on earth and of eternal life."

Lucius studied him for a long moment. When he spoke, there was a note of wonder in his voice—and of envy. "Outwardly you seem to be the same man I knew as a youth," he said. "Yet inwardly, I can see that you are another person entirely."

"That's because I have been reborn in Christ."

"This rebirth you speak of—and this new faith. Is it only for Jews?"

Saul was taken aback by the question, which had never come up before in his experience. Nor did anything he had learned from Mary or from Peter give him an answer.

"When Jesus sent out the disciples to teach he told them to go only to the lost sheep of Israel," he admitted.

"I am a Gentile."

"You could become a proselyte to the Jewish faith. Many Greeks have done that."

"Would it be honest to take up the Jewish faith only so I could become a Nazarene?"

"I don't know," Saul admitted. "I shall have to pray that the answer to your questions will be revealed to me."

"Don't trouble yourself—or your God—over me; I'm afraid I've become too fond of my wealth to give it up anyway." Lucius changed the subject abruptly. "If you really want to work, take over the management of your father's old shop. It's too far from the harbor for me to watch closely, so it brings me little profit. I will pay you a regular tentmaker's wage to operate the shop and, if you make a profit, we will divide it between us."

"Agreed," Saul said promptly. "But you must give me all the sailmaking for your ships and send whatever work you can to me, as we did when my father was ill."

"There speaks the old Saul." Lucius clapped him happily on the shoulder. "It's good to be in partnership with you."

x

The year that followed was a busy and pleasant one for Saul. He threw himself into the task of revitalizing his father's tent-making establishment with his usual energy and shortly it was showing a tidy profit for both him and Lucius. At the synagogue on the Sabbath, he told the thrilling story he'd first heard from Simon Peter and, though the congregation tended to be conservative, having been for so long under the leadership of his old teacher, Rabbi Eloichim, now dead, many listened and followed him home afterward to continue the discussion. As a result, Saul's home soon became a meeting place for the Nazarenes and, profiting by his experience in Damascus, he withdrew from his old congregation and organized another. This grew so rapidly that soon a meeting place larger than Saul's home had to be found but luckily he was able to use a building owned by Lucius.

Busy during the week with his tent- and sailmaking and on the Sabbath with the services at the synagogue, where his eloquence and the thrilling story of a Savior for Israel drew large crowds each week, Saul's life was full and rewarding. Then one afternoon he heard the clank of military harness outside the shop and looked up to see a Roman officer standing in the doorway. He wore the proud insignia of one of Rome's most elite military organizations, the Italian Band, but though his face seemed familiar Saul could not place it for a moment. Then he recognized the centurion of the Antonia garrison at Jerusalem, who had sped him on his way when word of his father's illness had come to him there.

"Cornelius!" Saul rose from the loom, where he had been weaving and came into the sunlight to greet the visitor. "What brings you to Tarsus?"

"I came to see you. Simon Peter sent me."

Saul called to a servant in the house to bring wine and ushered his friend across the courtyard to a bench in the spreading shade of the ailanthus tree.

"How long have you known Peter?" he asked.

"We became friends a few months ago in Caesarea, after I was transferred there from Jerusalem. What about your father? I remember that he was quite ill when I arranged for the galley to bring you here."

"Father was healed then by a Greek physician of Troas named Luke. But he died a little over a year ago, while I was in Petra."

"Peter told me of your conversion and when I mentioned that my galley would stop at Tarsus on the way to Rome, he asked me to pay you a visit. You knew I was a convert to the Jewish faith, didn't you?"

"I remember that from Jerusalem. But I didn't know you were a Nazarene."

"After I was transferred to Caesarea, I heard about Jesus. When I learned that Simon Peter was at Joppa, I sent a messenger asking if he would come there and tell me and my household about the Nazarene. It so happened that the day my messenger arrived in Joppa, Peter had gone up on the rooftop of the house where he was staying and had fallen asleep. As he tells it, he saw in a dream a great sheet containing all kinds of living things lowered from heaven. At the same time a voice inside him said, 'Arise Peter, slay and eat.'"

"Were unclean beasts among then?" Saul asked quickly.

"Yes. Peter said he protested against defiling himself under the Law, but the voice said, 'What God has cleansed, do not call common.' The same thing happened three times before the sheet disappeared and immediately afterward, he was awakened by my messengers. Sensing that there was some connection between the dream and my sending for him, Peter came to Caesarea. After hearing him tell about Jesus of Nazareth, my whole household believed, were baptized and received the Holy Spirit. Peter knew from the dream and from my sending for him just then that it was the will of God for Gentiles to receive the word. From what he said though, he expected to have some trouble convincing the leaders in Jerusalem when he returned."

"You say Peter expressly asked you to tell me all this?"

"Yes. He said you would understand its full significance."

Saul felt as if the bonds which had been shackling him ever since his talk with Lucius had been struck off. Now at last he knew he was free to preach to any who would listen, whether Jew or Gentile.

"I'm also carrying a gift to the believers in Rome." Cornelius took a small scroll from his robe. "Young Mark has been traveling with Peter, writing down the things Peter remembers that Jesus said and did. He made a copy of what he calls 'The Sayings' for me to give to the believers in Rome."

"When does your ship leave?" Saul asked quickly.

"Tomorrow morning, when we finish loading fresh fruit and vegetables for the rest of the journey."

"Would you trust me with the scroll for the night, if I promise to bring it to the quay in the morning?"

"Of course. But surely you already know what it tells."

"While I was in Petra, Mary of Magdala told me something of what Jesus said and did. But there would be many other things that Peter alone would know."

"Keep the scroll overnight by all means, then. You can bring it to my ship in the morning."

It was late that night before Saul finished reading the scroll. While he was reading, he sometimes felt that he was standing beside the Master, listening to his gentle voice telling the simple stories of seeds sown by the wayside and bearing no fruit, while those sown on fertile ground returned more than a hundred-fold; of a house built on the rock of faith standing fast against the seas of doubt, while one built on the sands of uncertainty was washed away; of the single lamb that strayed and was found, causing more rejoicing in the heart of the shepherd than the ninety and nine who had stayed within the fold.

Reading the scroll, Saul felt himself walking the rolling green hills of Galilee, speaking to the people from the mount called Hattin in the hills behind Capernaum, breaking the fish and bread for the multitude on the shores of the lake near Bethsaida, experiencing heartbreak with the news of the death of John the Baptist in Herod's fortress of Machaerus overlooking the Dead Sea, and enjoying the happy days of the religious festivals in the home of Martha, Mary, and Lazarus at Bethany, just out-side Jerusalem. Finally reading how, on the shores of the Sea of Galilee following the return of the disciples there after the crucifixion, Jesus had called to them while they were fishing and had charged Peter to "Feed my sheep," he could not help feel-ing a sense of envy for the man the Lord had singled out above all others to lead the flock. It was true that Jesus had spoken directly to Saul but he recognized that the charge to Peter had been far greater, the specific care of the entire flock, while he had no way as yet of knowing just where his own field of service would lie.

XI

With the shop prospering under Saul's energetic management, and his inspired preaching of the new Gospel bringing converts all the while, the years at Tarsus passed swiftly and pleasantly. Following the visit of Cornelius and the message from Peter opening wider horizons for the teachings of Jesus, Saul began to visit towns and villages in the area surrounding Tarsus. There he spoke in the synagogues to the Jews of each community, telling them the story of the Messiah. As a result, groups of converts to the Nazarene faith sprang up in many towns near the coast, groups who naturally looked to Saul as their mentor.

In Tarsus itself, Lucius became a Christian and through him many influential Greeks of the city joined the new church. But though Saul knew he was doing a great work there and had assured Lucius, when he had first come to Tarsus, that he was content to await the revelation from Jesus of his next task, he was too forceful in his personality, too closely concerned with spreading the faith, not to feel frustrated sometimes about the future.

The death of his mother several years after Cornelius' visit left Saul alone. But though he missed her sorely, he had the satisfaction of knowing that his presence in Tarsus had brought happiness to her latter years. In only one way did she find fault with him, his refusal to marry and produce the grandchildren she desired so much. But Saul was too bound up in the work he was carrying on, too single-minded in the purpose that dominated his life to consider marriage. The devotion he might have given to a wife, he gave to his churches in Tarsus and the surrounding communities. And the desire to succeed, to accomplish, which a wife might have nurtured, was so fully developed in him already that it needed no encouragement.

Though Saul prospered in his partnership with Lucius far beyond his expectations, personal wealth brought him little satisfaction. He gave much of it to the poor, sending part of it also to Jerusalem where, he learned from merchants and returning pilgrims, the shrunken synagogue of the Nazarenes had come upon evil times following the appearance in Judea and Samaria of a new ruler.

The death of Emperor Tiberius shortly after the crucifixion of Jesus of Nazareth had been followed by the crowning of the depraved Caligula. Caligula's madness almost inflamed the Jewish people into bloody rebellion, when he ordered his own statue to be placed in the Holy of Holies in the temple at Jerusalem and worshiped there by the Jews. Before the decree could be carried out, however, Caligula was assassinated by the Praetorian Guards and, in the political jockeying that followed, Tiberius Claudius became Emperor.

Though considered by the Praetorians and most other citizens of Rome to be little more than a moron, Claudius' potentialities as a ruler had been apparent to at least one person there, Herod Agrippa, grandson of Herod the Great. Growing up as a princeling in Rome, Agrippa had been friendly with the lowly and unappreciated Claudius and, when the search for a successor to Caligula began, persuaded enough high-ranking Romans that Claudius would be malleable to have him named Emperor. As a reward for Agrippa's loyalty, Claudius had given Judea and Samaria—the most important provinces in the former kingdom of Herod the Great—to him as his fief. And when the wily and unscrupulous Agrippa shortly managed to have his uncle, Herod Antipas, convicted of treason in Rome and banished, Galilee and Peraea also came under his rule.

The new Tetrarch was a grandson of the tragic Mariamne, a descendant of the Hasmonean line of priest-kings which had begun with the great Judas Maccabeus. As such, he was of the priestly line and at least one quarter Jew, which was more than either Herod the Great, Herod Antipas, or even Herod Philip had been. This naturally made Agrippa much more acceptable to the Jews of Judea than had been either the Roman governors or Herod Antipas. When he started building a new wall around Jerusalem and adding many other improvements to the city, the whole nation joined in singing his praise.

Joseph Caiaphas had lost the position of High Priest in the change of power from the procurators to the new Tetrarch and Agrippa now appointed Simon Kantheros to that post. To further gain the favor of the temple hierarchy, as well as the leaders among the Pharisees in Jerusalem, the new ruler began a fresh persecution of the small remaining colony of the Nazarene sect in Jerusalem, lead by James, the kinsman of the Lord, and by Simon Peter. It was against this background of historical events that Saul opened the door of his home in Tarsus one day to find a tall man with red hair standing outside.

"Barnabas!" he cried and for a moment the two friends were too moved with emotion for further words. Finally Saul took

Barnabas by the arm and led him into the house, calling for the old servant, who cared for him now, to bring refreshment for the visitor.

"You have done well," Barnabas said, looking around the room and out into the court, where the great ailanthus tree still spread its shade over the enclosed area. "How is your mother?"

"She died several years ago, still upbraiding me for not marrying and having children."

"Why don't you?"

"I've been too busy with the Lord's work," said Saul. "Particularly since Cornelius came with news of the revelation to Peter that the gospel can be preached to the Gentiles."

"We've heard good reports of you."

"How does the work go in Jerusalem?"

"James still heads the Synagogue of the Nazarenes and Simon Peter stays there part of the time—I think because he feels that he must support James and the others. But we all know the real future of the church lies elsewhere, particularly in Antioch, where I am living now."

"What about Rome?"

"There is already a large colony of Christians in Rome."

"Christians? I never heard the term before."

"The people started calling us that in Antioch, so we adopted the name."

"It is a good one," said Saul. "You were speaking of Rome."

"The church there is small, but growing," said Barnabas. "Peter sent them a copy of the sayings Mark wrote down from his recollections about Jesus."

"Cornelius showed it to me when he was here," said Saul. "I almost felt as if I were treading the paths of Galilee while I was reading it. I wish there had been time for me to make a copy."

"We have copies in Antioch."

Saul looked quickly at his old friend, beginning to sense now the reason why Barnabas had appeared so suddenly in Tarsus. "But I have no plans to go to Antioch."

"Not even if the Lord should call you there?"

"I will go wherever he calls me, of course. But how do I know it will be Antioch?"

"I think your heart will tell you after you hear what we are doing," Barnabas assured him. "Besides I'm hoping to carry the word soon into Phrygia and Pamphylia. Perhaps even into Galatia and as far north as Bithynia."

"Bithynia!" The word rang a distant bell in Saul's mind, taking him back to the night when he had stood on the Great High Place at Petra and had watched the star in the north. Bithynia—farthest north of the Roman colonies in Asia Minor —had come to his mind when he'd seen the star. It was strange that Barnabas should mention now the beautiful land lying on the shores of what the Romans called the Pontus Euxinus— unless the Lord had put the word in his mouth.

"It's not too far to go," Barnabas' voice brought Saul back to the present. "Some of those who left Jerusalem in the time of the persecution even went as far away as Gaul."

"But I have a thriving business here."

"Think of those waiting to hear the gospel in other lands," Barnabas urged. "Can spinning cilicium and weaving tents possibly compare with the joy of bringing it to them?"

"I shall talk to Lucius in the morning," Saul promised but both he and Barnabas knew he was weakening. "After all I owe him that much."

XII

"But you have everything here," Lucius protested when Saul told him of the call to Antioch. "You're prospering, you lead the Nazarenes in Tarsus, and you have the churches in the surrounding area to oversee. Would you give all that up to become an itinerant preacher and perhaps be stoned by the very people you seek to help?"

"I think that may be why the Lord wants me to go. Life is too easy here and my future is assured. Jesus said those who follow him must always be ready to take up our cross."

"What about the congregation here?"

"It has its own leaders like you, Lucius. Jesus could have escaped danger by remaining in the territory of Herod Philip, after he fed the multitude near Bethsaida and realized that a large element wanted to make him an earthly king, embroiling him with the Romans. Instead, he came back to Jerusalem because it was God's purpose that he go there. I can do no less."

"Are you absolutely certain it's God's purpose for you to go to Antioch?"

"No."

"Then wait until you are certain. If you want to go to Bithynia, I have ships sailing into the Pontus Euxinus regularly to trade at Heraclea, Chersonesus, and even as far east as Trapezus, in the shadow of the Mons Caucasus. You may travel on any of them and stop in Bithynia as long as you desire."

"I shall pray for Christ's will to be revealed to me," said Saul. "But whatever happens, I shall always be grateful to you."

"It is I who should be grateful," Lucius corrected him. "You showed me the way to eternal life."

Long after Barnabas was asleep that night, Saul continued to pray for guidance. But the voice of Jesus did not speak to him again and, exhausted, he finally fell asleep. It was still quite dark when he awoke. The house was quiet and, realizing that he was thirsty, he sat up on his couch, planning to cross the court to the pipe from which water, cold and fresh from the hills, flowed constantly into a small pool. The change of position brought an open window in the northern wall of the house within his range of vision and there, shining as brightly as it had shone that night at the Great High Place of Petra, was the star called Phoenikos.

At last Saul felt all doubt, all indecision melt away for he knew now where his course lay, though of what obstacles might lie before him, he had no inkling. This time Jesus had called him in another way, but the call was as clear as the voice that had spoken to him on the Damascus road.

"I am going to Antioch with you," he told Barnabas, while they were eating the morning meal. "But you must make me a promise."

"What is it?"

"Whatever happens, we must go to Bithynia."

"Bithynia by all means!" Barnabas, too, was caught up by Saul's enthusiasm. "And to the ends of the earth—if the Lord wills."

## XIII

Had the decision been Saul's alone, he and Barnabas would have left Antioch almost at once to carry the gospel of Jesus' resurrection, the doctrine of love, and the promise of eternal life to all who believed. But in coming to Antioch, Saul had placed himself under the authority of the church there and had to follow its directions. Not that there was any clash of wills between him and the leaders of the large Antioch congregation. Rather, the work being carried on was so exciting that Saul found himself caught up in it and was soon working as enthusiastically as the rest.

The seat of government for the Roman province of Syria, which exerted authority over the areas to the south—including Israel under its new Tetrarch, Herod Agrippa—a center of trade, both seaborne through its neighboring port city of Seleucia and overland by means of caravans from east to west, north and south, Antioch was the cultural center for a vast area. It teemed with people of all nationalities and had been governed by a succession of legates who had been intelligent enough to see the value of holding only a loose rein upon the many diverse elements that made up the population.

There had always been a large Jewish community in Antioch and, when many Hellenic Jews had been forced to flee from Jerusalem by Saul's persecution, they had found a warm reception there. The church that was soon proudly calling itself Christian had grown rapidly and was now the largest in the entire Roman Empire. Each Sabbath, Paul preached in the synagogue hall to crowds that overflowed the edifice and stood in the street outside to listen as his voice floated through the open windows. During the week, he went from house to house, telling all who would listen the thrilling account of his call on the road to Damascus and his sudden change from persecutor to eloquent advocate.

Though Saul and Barnabas were anxious to carry the gospel abroad, a succession of events in Jerusalem caused still further delay. One was a severe famine which threatened the Christian community of Jerusalem with starvation. The other was the execution by Herod Agrippa of James ben Zebedee, the gentle apostle who had been one of the first called by Jesus on the shore of the Sea of Galilee, and the simultaneous arrest of Simon Peter.

Saul and Barnabas were on the way to Jerusalem with money collected in the church at Antioch for the relief of the small group whom the other churches still regarded as the mother church, when they learned of the double tragedy. When they reached the Holy City, they discovered that Simon Peter had escaped from prison, where Herod had placed him until a suitable public execution could be arranged.

Some said a miracle had struck off Peter's chains and opened the doors; others that sympathizers among the guards had arranged for his escape into the hill country of Galilee, where capture would be unlikely. In any event, the danger to Peter, as well as to James ben Joseph and the others in the Synagogue of the Nazarenes at Jerusalem was ended for the time being at least by the dramatic death of Herod Agrippa at Caesarea. While haranguing a crowd gathered in the great amphitheater there to celebrate the signing of a new treaty with the cities of the Phoenician coast, the Tetrarch had suffered a sudden seizure and fallen from the imperial box to the floor of the arena, where he had died almost immediately.

Agrippa's death brought Jerusalem once again under the rule of a Roman procurator and sharply limited the powers the High Priest and the temple hierarchy had been enjoying. A bountiful grain crop also removed the threat of famine in Judea and, with the care of the small group in Jerusalem no longer a burden upon the Antioch church, Saul and Barnabas were at last free for the journey they had been looking forward to for almost a year, taking the gospel to cities where it had been taught only occasionally by visitors from Jerusalem and Antioch. Barnabas wished to take young Mark who had come to Antioch from Jerusalem, with them. And, although Saul was not yet sure the boy was seasoned enough to face whatever might lie ahead, he agreed. They set sail one bright sunny day from the busy seaport of Seleucia and headed across the narrow stretch of water lying between Cyprus and the mainland. The decision to begin their missionary work on the island of Cyprus had not been a haphazard one. For Barnabas had come originally from Salamis, its major seaport, and could thus be sure of finding relatives who would welcome them and introduce them to the Jewish community. Though there could be no question now that the gospel and salvation had been made freely available to Gentiles. Barnabas and Saul, however, intended to follow the usual custom of traveling rabbis and speak upon the Sabbath in the synagogues, where they could be sure of having a large audience who would be familiar with much of the background of what they were going to teach and to whom the coming of the Messiah would have a meaning—though perhaps not the one they preached.

The weather was good and, with a brisk breeze to fill the sails, they reached Cyprus on the morning following their departure. Salamis was located in a protected anchorage on the northeast corner of the island. Watching the spread of the city upon the shore as they approached, the plains with their fields of grain and the green of orchards, against the background of the central mountain range that formed the backbone of the island, Saul felt almost as if he were coming home again to Tarsus. And when they alighted upon the quay and he saw piles of fruit, flagons of wine, bales of flax and other produce awaiting shipment to Antioch, along with the products of the coppersmiths for which Cyprus had been famous for at least a thousand years, he felt an instant kinship with the city.

Visitors from Antioch had already told the story of Jesus in Salamis and when word spread through the city that two eloquent preachers of the new faith had arrived, they received an immediate invitation to speak on the Sabbath. Cheered by the reception at their first stop in Cyprus, Saul and Barnabas remained at Salamis for several weeks before taking the Roman highroad along the coast westward to the city of Paphos, seat of government for the entire island. Here they were in a garrison city that was half Roman and half Greek, with only a small Jewish synagogue. But true to their custom, they went to the Jewish meeting place upon the Sabbath and, when the invitation was given for any who might wish to speak, Saul rose and moved to the pulpit.

He had hardly begun to speak when he was challenged by a striking-looking man whose robe was embroidered with strange emblems and whose hands were heavy with rings of gold and silver. In the resultant commotion, the congregation became divided. More than half chose to hear the visitors from Antioch, but those who supported the sorcerer, whose name proved to be Elymas, made so much noise that finally it was decided at Elymas' suggestion to bring the whole affair before the Roman governor the following morning.

Privately, Saul and Barnabas were doubtful about being given the right to teach in Cyprus, once the governor heard that the man they served had been crucified as a rebel by Pontius Pilate in Jerusalem. Nor were their hopes increased when they learned that the wily Elymas enjoyed considerable favor as a soothsayer or foreteller of coming events with Sergius Paulus, the governor. It was with little confidence therefore, that they went to the palace the following morning, and the fact that Elymas was already closeted with the governor did nothing to increase it. Sergius Paulus greeted them courteously, however, and, realizing from his first words that he was a man of intelligence and education, Saul hoped to convince him that they taught no doctrine of revolution but only a religious faith.

"My companion is Barnabas—a native of this island," he said by way of introduction. "My Jewish name is Saul but in Tarsus, where I grew up, I was called Paulus in Latin and Paulos—Paul —in Greek."

"I shall call you Paul," said Sergius. "Did you say you were from Tarsus?"

"Yes. My father was a tentmaker there and I was trained in that trade before I became a teacher."

"Where did you study?"

"I studied our Law in Jerusalem." Saul had a sudden inspiration. "But before that I sat at the feet of Nestor at the university of Tarsus."

"Nestor!" The governor's face showed interest. "Seneca, my old tutor in Rome, used to speak of him."

"They are both Stoics. Nestor taught me something of that philosophy."

"Elymas here claims you are a Jew who stirs up the people," said the governor.

"If showing them the way to eternal life is stirring them up, I am guilty noble Sergius," said Saul. "How else can I make men believe and be saved?"

"What is this doctrine you teach?" Sergius Paulus asked and Saul needed no further invitation to tell the thrilling story of Jesus and of his own call. Several times while he was speaking, Elymas tried to interrupt. Each time Sergius Paulus waved the soothsayer to silence and only when the account was finished, did he turn to Elymas.

"Now you may say what you have to say," he told the sorcerer, who immediately launched into a diatribe, accusing Saul and Barnabas of lying, of claiming a resurrection, when actually the body of Jesus had been stolen away, rehashing the old arguments with which the authorities at Jerusalem had sought to counter the gospel Peter had preached there on Pentecost. He finished his argument by challenging Saul directly.

"If the Nazarene you worship is really the Son of God," he taunted, "why does he not give you the power to perform miracles, such as you claim he performed?"

"Simon Peter has healed many people," said Saul. "I myself saw him cure a paralytic in the temple."

"But you claim to have been called by Jesus himself as an apostle. Why were you not given this power?"

The same question had entered Saul's mind more than once during the years at Tarsus. He had not let it trouble him then, confident that when he was in need of miraculous powers, they would be given him. And when he suddenly felt a new strength flooding through his body he knew Jesus had not deserted him.

"You child of the devil, full of subtlety and mischief," he

told the sorcerer scornfully. "Will you not stop perverting the way of the Lord?"

Elymas quailed momentarily before the tongue-lashing, but recovered his assurance immediately, when nothing miraculous happened. "I see that you are a man of words and not deeds," he sneered. "If you are indeed filled with power from this Jesus, make it known now or name yourself a liar."

"The hand of the Lord is upon you then," said Saul. "You shall be blind, not seeing the light of the sun for a season."

"I cannot see! He has blinded me!" Elymas backed away as if Saul were a viper about to strike, and would have fallen over a chair, if Saul himself had not reached out to steady him.

"Not I but the Lord God has blinded you," Saul said sternly. "You demanded a sign and it has been given you."

As Elymas lunged toward the door, crashing into furniture as he went and blubbering with fear, Sergius Paulus ordered the guard who stood there to lead the stricken sorcerer to his home. When he turned back to face Saul and Barnabas, the governor's face was white and the hand with which he poured himself a glass of wine was shaking.

"What sorcery did you use to blind him?" he asked.

"God blinded him, my lord governor," said Saul. "Elymas demanded the sign and it was given him."

Sergius Paulus wiped the sweat from his forehead with his sleeve and composed himself with an obvious effort. "For a long time I have been seeking a faith in which I could believe without reservation," he said. "None of the mysteries have satisfied me and the worship of emperors is a mockery. Tell me the truth, Saul of Tarsus, and perhaps it will make me free."

"Be sure that it will," said Saul. He and Barnabas remained with the governor all day and before they left the palace, Sergius Paulus had become a believer and was baptized.

XIV

Perga, to which the travelers came after their fruitful mission in Cyprus, was a lovely Greek town with a small colony of Jews and a single Jewish congregation. Located along the sides of two hills, it overlooked an extensive valley with the River Cestrus threading through it and the western extension of the Taurus Mountain range looming behind it. There, though he was eager to move on into the Galatian uplands, Saul was stopped by what he was beginning to believe was his personal nemesis, the intermittent fever to which he was often subject. For days he lay in semi-coma, his body alternately wracked by chills and burning with fever. When finally, the fever appeared to have run its course, as it had done so many times in the past, the first thing he noticed was that John Mark was no longer with them.

"Where is Mark?" he asked Barnabas.

"He went back to Jerusalem."

"Why?"

"The boy is young and this is the first time he has been away from home. His father died when he was quite young and he has always lived with his mother."

"That is no excuse to give up the Lord's work."

"Mark hasn't given it up." Barnabas' voice was a little sharp at Saul's criticism of his cousin. "Just after you developed the fever, word came by a vessel touching here that Peter has returned to Jerusalem. The Romans rule there again and he will be safe, so Mark felt he should be with Peter, in case any more of the sayings of Jesus need to be written down. It was obvious that you couldn't continue our travels for some time, so I let him go."

"The fever has broken now. I can go on."

"You're still half dead. The physician who is treating you gave you up for dead twice."

"I have survived this fever before and I will survive it again. There has been too much delay already. I must be about the Lord's work." Saul tried to push himself up on his elbows but, as on that day when he'd found himself in a similar situation in the cave of Joseph and Mary of Magdala at Petra, discovered that he could barely raise his head from the pillow.

"You see," Barnabas said triumphantly. "You need rest. Move about too soon and you will bring on the fever again and perhaps cause your own death."

In the face of his weakness, Saul could not object and so was forced to remain in Perga for a few weeks while he recovered his strength. It was a pleasant place and, as soon as he was able to sit up, he had Barnabas take him each day to the shaded central square called the *agora*. There, as in all largely Greek cities, men came and went, arguing points of philosophy, geography and any of the myriads of questions that always occupied the Grecian mind.

To the crowds thronging the agora of Perga, Saul told the story of Jesus and debated with those who sought to find a different meaning than that which had been revealed to him. It was almost like the old days at Tarsus when, as a young man he had joined in the give and take of argument at the university. And though he was anxious to be on his way, when finally he was strong enough to leave Perga, he could not say that it had not been a pleasant period. Nevertheless, the star that still hung each night above the heights of the Taurus range beckoned him on and soon he and Barnabas were treading the Roman road that led steadily upward toward the city of Antioch-in-Pisidia, the major population center of the upland plateau of Galatia.

XV

The Passover had just been celebrated and the warmth of spring had been in the air when Saul and Barnabas sailed from Seleucia for Salamis and the island of Cyprus. Now it was summer and the people of the Pamphylian coast were beginning their annual migration to higher ground, partly to escape the enervating heat of summer but also to avoid the unhealthy intermittent fevers that were so common in the coastal lowlands. Bearing a letter from Sergius Paulus, Governor of Cyprus, to his son, Lucius Sergius Paulus, who was the military governor of Antioch-in-Pisidia, Saul and Barnabas joined a group of families on the road.

The party of several hundred people followed the caravan trail only generally at first, since their flocks and herds moved across the grasslands and through the valleys where the verdant green blanket gave them ample food.

Galatia had been given its name because, some three hundred years earlier, three Gallic tribes had entered Asia Minor and settled in this region. After becoming a client state of the Roman Empire, the district had formed a base of operation from which Rome was able to conquer the entire area. Once the real upland climb had begun, the party followed the Roman road hewn from the mountainside during the military campaigns and paved with slabs of native marble and other rocks.

Thickets of oleander and pomegranates, in full bloom now, lined the watercourses in the lowlands. In places plane trees spread a welcome shade over the road, while spring flowers, withered already by the summer heat in the lowlands around Perga, were in full bloom. As they climbed higher, the predominating trees changed gradually to pine and walnut, then to cedar and juniper. A band of horsemen, fierce-looking in their great coats of sheepskin and bearing curved swords of Damascus steel, rode ahead of the group as they entered a region of towering cliffs and mountain passes overlooking verdant valleys and the danger of being robbed by one of the brigand bands infesting most such areas grew steadily greater. This was a large group, however, and so escaped attack, where smaller bands were often cut to pieces and their possessions seized by the brigands. Passing finally through the sparse stands of cedar and juniper marking the higher levels, they came out upon the great central tableland of Asia Minor, a vast plateau above which, still farther north, loomed the snow-capped peaks extending from the Taurus Mountains at its eastern edge to Mount Olympus, legendary dwelling place of the gods of Greece.

Though he and Barnabas walked with the shepherds, the women and the children, and the way was often rough, Saul found himself feeling better every day, as the cool upland air drove the lassitude of illness from his body. Each night, high above the snow-capped peaks to the north, he could see his particular star, but he said nothing of this to anyone, sensing that even Barnabas might think it pretentious of him to assume a personal direction from Jesus. Watching the sun reflected from the snowy peaks of the mountains and listening to the rush of brooks hurrying to the sea, Saul often felt like shouting aloud, as had David of old:

"The heavens declare the glory of God,
And the firmament sheweth his handiwork."

Antioch-in-Pisidia was a *colonia*, having been for many years the military capital of that area. It was more a Roman city than a Greek one, though like all towns in Galatia it had a large Greek-speaking population. The Roman city had been founded by Augustus Caesar on the lower slopes of a majestic peak on the right bank of the river Anthius. It was strongly fortified, with an ample supply of water brought from reservoirs in the foothills of the mountain range through a magnificent aqueduct.

With typical Roman insistence upon order, the city had been built in two large squares, an upper one called the Augusta Platea after the Emperor Augustus and a lower, the Tiberia Platea, after Tiberius. Between the two was a broad flight of steps with three triumphal archways erected in honor of Augustus and adorned with sculptures and statues. Along the face of the archways was a frieze portraying Poseidon, Triton, and other symbols of the triumphs of Augustus at sea.

Also on the square of Augustus was a magnificent temple with a frieze of carved bull's heads connected by garlands of flowers and fruits. It was primarily devoted to the worship of the god Men, a local deity particularly concerned with agriculture, but was also associated in the minds of much of the population with veneration of the deified Augustus.

On their arrival, Saul presented the letter from Sergius Paulus to the young military governor, but found no such interest in his teachings on the son's part, as the father in Cyprus had shown. Leaving the Roman portion of the city, they went to the Jewish quarter which, though not very large, had quite an active synagogue. In Tarsus, Saul had learned that Antioch-in-Pisidia was a very active and influential city for the gaining of proselytes—converts to the Jewish faith who were not born as Jews—containing more of these at that time than any other city in the empire, except perhaps Rome. Naturally he hoped to find many converts among them for the gospel of Jesus had always appealed more strongly to proselytes than to those born into the Jewish faith.

On the Sabbath, the travelers joined the Jews of the highland city in the service at the synagogue. The largest such structure Saul had yet seen in this part of the world, it was built in the traditional manner, with the entrance facing southeastward toward Jerusalem, the "pulpit of wood" in the center where the "reader" could open the Books of the Law and the Prophets in sight of the people, the Ark on the side of the building nearest Jerusalem for the preservation of the scrolls, and seats around it arranged so that all might see—with a special area reserved for the rulers.

As in all Jewish Sabbath services, a portion of the Law was read in Hebrew, then a selection from the writings of the Prophets. The readings were then translated into Greek, rather than Aramaic, since the major portion of those here were as much Grecian as Jewish. This done, the scrolls were rolled up, tied in their protecting cover for return to the Ark, and the invitation given for any who might wish to speak.

As was his usual custom, Saul rose to his feet at once and ascended to the pulpit. His alert gaze had not missed the fact that, just as he had been told, there were many proselytes among the congregation and it was to these that he directed his discourse, spending some time in building the background for the coming of the Messiah, with which the proselytes in particular might not be familiar.

"Men of Israel and you that fear God, listen," he began. "The God of Israel chose our fathers and exalted our people, when they dwelt as strangers in the land of Egypt. He brought them out of it and for about forty years suffered their manners in the wilderness. When he destroyed seven nations in the land of Canaan, he divided the land by lot. After that he gave to our people judges to rule them for a space of four hundred and fifty years, until the time of Samuel, the Prophet. But they desired a king so God gave them Saul the son of Kish, from the tribe of Benjamin. And when Saul was removed, he raised up David to be their king, saying, '*I have found David, the son of Jesse, a man after my own heart who shall fulfill all of my will.'* Of this man's seed has God, according to his promise, raised for Israel a Savior, Jesus."

Saul's voice now took on a new vibrancy. "John had preached the coming of Jesus and the Baptism ceremony of repentance for all the people of Israel. But when John had fulfilled his course, he said, 'I am not he, but behold there comes one after me whose shoes I am not worthy to loose.' Men and brethren, children of the stock of Abraham and whoever among you fears God, to you word of this salvation is now sent. For they who dwell at Jerusalem and their rulers did not know the Messiah, in spite of the writings of the Prophets which are read every Sabbath day. They have fulfilled the prophecies in condemning him and, though they found no cause of death in him, yet desired of Pontius Pilate that he should be slain. When they had fulfilled all that was written of him, they took him down from the tree and laid him in a sepulcher."

He paused to look around at the audiences and, so great was the magnetism of his oratory, that no eye among them was not fixed upon him. "But God raised Jesus from the dead. He was seen many times by those who came up with him from Galilee to Jerusalem and we declare to you now the glad tidings that the promise made to the fathers has been fulfilled by God to us, their children, in that he has raised up Jesus again, even as it is written in the second Psalm, *'Thou art my son, this day have I begotten thee.'*

"Now concerning the fact that God raised Jesus up from the dead, no more to return from corruption, he said, *'I will give you the sure mercies of David.'* And David says also in another Psalm *'Thou shalt not suffer thine Holy One to see corruption.'* For after David had served his own generation, he fell asleep by the will of God and was laid with his fathers and saw corruption. But he whom God raised again saw no corruption."

"Be it known to you then, men and brethren, that through this man Jesus comes forgiveness of sins and by him all that believe are freed from all things from which you could not be free by the Law of Moses. Beware, therefore, lest that come upon you which is spoken of in the Prophets when they said: *'Behold ye despisers and wonder and perish. For I work a work in your days, a work which you shall in no wise believe, though a man declare it to you.'"*

Not a sound came from those gathered in the synagogue, as Saul stepped down from the platform and, rising hurriedly, the chazan gave the benediction. Watching the congregation file from the building and remembering the day when he had delivered his first sermon to the congregation of the Libertines and had met somewhat the same reception, Saul dared to hope the Galatians had been so impressed by what he had to say that they were going out to talk over among themselves this new thing that had been brought to them. He had no opportunity to determine whether such was the case, however, for at the door of the synagogue, he and Barnabas were swept up by a mass of people waiting outside, who demanded to hear again the thrilling story of the Savior of Israel and the Messiah promised by the prophets.

While he answered their questions, Saul examined the makeup of the crowd and saw that most of them were Gentile converts or proselytes. Not one of the leaders of the congregation or the elders who sat upon an elevated platform during the services, had followed them. And even though he was busy answering the questions of those outside, he could not escape the conviction that his message had been rejected by the Jews of Antioch-in-Pisidia, an ominous portent of what was to come.

All that week, Saul and Barnabas were busy telling their story throughout the city, but he could not help noticing that in the homes of the Jews they were treated with much reserve, which in a few places doors were actually shut in their faces. He was not surprised to find the area around the synagogue filled with people, when he and Barnabas went there the following Sabbath. The same thing had happened with the congregation of the Libertines before he had been called by Jesus and he was now accustomed to the effect of his oratory upon crowds of people. What he was not prepared for was the reception given him and Barnabas when finally they managed to push their way into the building.

The Sabbath service had not yet begun, but a heated public

discussion was going on among the elders, with the congregation joining in. At the sight of Saul and Barnabas, an elder named Ezra rose to point his finger at them, denouncing them in a voice shaking with emotion.

"These men are followers of a false prophet crucified by the Romans in Jerusalem as a rebel," he shouted. "I was there when it happened and saw it with my own eyes. The Nazarene's disciples claim he rose from the dead but the guards at the tomb swore they stole his body away during the night."

"The guards lied!" In his anger Saul's own voice grew shrill. "Jesus was seen after his resurrection by more than five hundred people."

A wave of boos and catcalls drowned out his words. Before he could speak again, another of the elders leaped to his feet, accusing them both of blasphemy in claiming that a mortal man, a mere rabble-rouser, was the Son of God. The viciousness of the charge startled Saul, but it was quite to the liking of many in the congregation for they immediately set up a cry of approval.

Some began to move toward where Saul was standing at the foot of the steps leading to the pulpit, obviously intending to attack him physically upon the floor of the synagogue. Stunned by the denunciation of the elders and the barrage of invective hurled at him by the congregation, Saul looked questioningly at Barnabas, who nodded toward the door, indicating that they should escape before the crowd became worked up to the point where they might seize the two travelers and stone them to death for blasphemy. Saul, however, was in no mood to be silenced by threats. Climbing to the platform, he shouted for attention until finally the mob quieted down. When he spoke, the cold fury in his voice was like a lash across their faces.

"It was necessary that the word of God should first be spoken to you, but since you have put it from you and judged yourselves unworthy of everlasting life, we will turn to the Gentiles," he told the Jewish congregation of Antioch-in-Pisidia. "For so the Lord has commanded us saying, '*I have set thee to be a light to the Gentiles, that thou should be for salvation unto the ends of the earth.*'"

The yard outside the synagogue was filled with Gentiles and

proselytes. When they heard the words, easily audible through the open windows of the building, they set up an immediate clamor of approval. Saul said no more but turned, his face set in a mask of pain and anger, and descended the few steps from the pulpit to the floor of the synagogue. Up the aisle he marched, followed by Barnabas. And, in the sudden quiet which had fallen over the congregation at his denunciation, no one raised a hand toward him.

The crowd outside gave him quite a different reception, however. They begged him to address them and, crossing the street, he mounted the porch of a house from which he could see and be heard. There he delivered the sermon he had planned to deliver to the congregation and which they had refused to hear. A few left the synagogue and came out to hear him but most remained behind, cowed by the refusal of the elders to have anything to do with the new doctrine.

That day many came to believe and, when the sermon was finished, followed Saul and Barnabas to the nearby river, where they were baptized. Through it all, Saul was like a man moving in a trance. Watching him, Barnabas realized that in a few hours, he had changed from the young teacher who had eagerly brought the gospel to Antioch-in-Pisidia, to a grim determined man, driven by a cold fury that was even more disturbing than an actual outburst of anger, would have been.

"I shall go no more to the Jews first," Saul announced when the crowd had left and only the two remained standing on the river bank. "They rejected the glad tidings and I shall not bring the word to them again."

"The congregation was stirred up by Ezra and a few others," Barnabas protested. "The old find change difficult; they cling to the Law and see the gospel of Jesus as a threat to it."

"I told them the Master came only to fulfill the Law but they still rejected him," said Saul. "From now on, I have no Jewish name. I shall be called only Paul."

Barnabas started to protest but, seeing the set look on his companion's face, shrugged. "Whatever you wish."

"It is not my wish but theirs. When they reject Jesus, they reject me. I wash my hands of them."

*But when Peter was come to Antioch,*
*I withstood him to his face, for he*
*was to be blamed.*
GALATIANS 2:11

*Book V · Antioch*

I

Though they preached no more to the Jews of Antioch-in-Pisidia, Paul and Barnabas found much favor with the Greek-speaking element of the population and with Jewish proselytes irked by the often absurd provisions of Mosaic Law—as interpreted by the rabbis at Jerusalem. They remained there well into the autumn and gradually, but not so slowly that Barnabas failed to notice it, Paul's teaching took on a different character. Less and less often did he refer now to the Jewish ancestry of Jesus, to Abraham and to Moses, as he had in his initial sermon at Antioch. Instead, the theme of his preaching took on a mystical character in which Jesus, though still the Messiah sent to the Jewish people, began to resemble more and more the young god sacrificed and reincarnated in many of the Greek mystery religions.

Such a doctrine, along with his emphasis upon love—which early Greek philosophers like Socrates and Plato had identified as a powerful changing force in human behavior—found a ready acceptance among Greeks and those under Grecian influence. Barnabas, however, clung instinctively to the old Jewish concept of the Messiah, whose saving power had first been extended to the Gentiles through Peter. More and more troubled, while summer passed and autumn began, by what he considered Paul's drift away from the God of the Jews, Barnabas at last remonstrated with Paul about it as they were unrolling their sleeping pallets one night.

"You no longer preach the gospel we brought from home," he accused his shorter companion. "Have you forgotten Yahweh, the God of the Jews?"

"I am a Jew." Paul stopped in the midst of unrolling his pallet. "I was circumcised on the eighth day and my father ransomed me with a gift to the temple, as Abraham ransomed Isaac by substituting a lamb upon the altar."

"But you no longer tell the story of our people and their relationship to God."

"What would that mean to Greeks?"

"Perhaps not much—but it means something to Jews."

"I preached it to Jews here in Antioch and they refused to listen."

"That was only a small group, the old and the stubborn," Barnabas protested. "Many young Jews would listen, if you spoke of the Messiah."

"Jesus told us to carry his message to all the earth."

"But he also instructed the disciples to go only to the lost sheep of Israel."

"All that has been changed." Saul's eyes took fire with a sudden fervor. "Jesus swept away the old Law and substituted two simple precepts: First, to love God; and, second, to love our neighbor as ourselves."

"Why preach the Messiah at all then?"

"Because Jesus as a man was living proof of God's love. You walked with him, Barnabas. Don't you remember that he said: *'God so loved the world that he gave his only begotten son, that whoever believes in him should not perish but have everlasting life'?*"

"I heard Jesus, the Messiah of the Jews, say that—not Adonai, the Risen Lord of the Greek mystery cults."

"When I preach to Jews I use words with a special meaning to them," said Paul. "And when I preach to Greeks, it is in a way they will understand."

"But this is blasphemy."

"There speaks the Jew in you," Paul retorted angrily. "You're half Greek; where is your understanding of the Greek part of your nature."

"I no longer understand you." Barnabas threw up his hands in a gesture of futility. "One day you're one thing, the next another. Jesus is all things to all men, not one thing to one and another to others."

"I'm what Jesus made me, when he called me to serve him," said Paul. "I can be no other, just as you cannot be other than what you are."

"Don't you ever doubt the rightness of your doctrines?"

"How can I doubt, when the Lord speaks through my mouth and with my tongue." Paul unrolled his pallet and lay down, his head turned to the wall. Obviously, the last word had been spoken as far as he was concerned. He was asleep almost immediately but it was a long time before Barnabas slept, for he was sorely troubled by the small crack he could see developing in the warm accord that had hitherto existed between him and Paul.

The change which had begun that day outside the synagogue at Antioch-in-Pisidia, when the Jewish congregation rejected Paul's doctrine, had gone deeper than Barnabas understood. But somewhere deep inside him was the beginning of a realization, even a dread, that it had already progressed beyond healing. In almost every sense that he could discern, Paul was a new man— as new as the name he had chosen to bear.

## II

By the coming of frost to the Galatian uplands, the leaders of the Jewish synagogue at Antioch-in-Pisidia had managed to stir up considerable opposition to the two missionaries. Gradually, the presence of Paul and Barnabas in the city became a source of conflict, not only among the Jews, but also among those who clung to the old Greek and Roman gods.

Having failed to make any impression upon the young governor and fearful that they might be arrested under Roman law for disturbing the population, thus seeing their work in the entire province and perhaps in the Empire, brought to an end. Paul and Barnabas decided to leave the colonia. Following the Royal Road of Augustus, the Roman military highway through this region, they moved with the steady stream of traffic for two days in the direction of Derbe and Lystra, two major centers located on the Lycaonian Plain. Then at Barnabas' suggestion, they turned off on a less traveled road leading to Iconium, where there was a colony of Jews and a synagogue.

Located in the midst of a considerable plain, surrounded by mountains which at this time of the year were largely covered with snow, Iconium was a pleasant city. The travelers received a warm welcome from many of its Jews and Greek proselytes and made a number of converts. But as had happened in Antioch, a small and intransigent group in the synagogue disapproved of their teaching. Through the winter and spring sentiment against them grew steadily and, when one day their lives were threatened by a mob, Paul and Barnabas decided to leave Iconium.

The principal towns in this region, Lystra and Derbe, lay near the foot of a jutting mass of rock, the Black Mount, that was the most notable feature of the entire central plain. Coming first to Lystra, Paul and Barnabas began to preach in the open space of the agora, the central square found in most cities of Greek origin.

Located at the end of the Roman military highway, Lystra clung to the old gods and its largest single building was the temple of Jupiter. In other cities, Paul and Barnabas had always gone first to the Jewish synagogue and spoken there. But only a few Jews lived in Lystra, not enough for a synagogue. For the first time, therefore, Paul found himself directly opposing a pagan faith, not only in his preaching but in actual fact, since the temple of Jupiter lay across the square from the spot where he had chosen to speak.

Accustomed to a certain amount of immediate approval of their teachings in other cities, Paul was disappointed by his failure to interest any large number of Lystrans during the first weeks of the mission there. His knowledge of the Greek world told him one major reason for this failure lay in the fact that he was speaking to a rustic, backward, and pagan population, largely unacquainted even with the mysticism of the Greek cults toward which Barnabas had accused him of leaning. He soon, too, realized that something other than mere words was needed in order to attract the attention of the Lystrans.

Paul had been startled—and not a little shaken—when the magician of Cyprus had been stricken blind before the governor there. Since then he had instinctively shied away from performing miracles but, when his most impassioned preaching failed to make an impression upon the pagans of Lystra, he decided to employ a more dramatic approach. From their first appearance in Lystra, the most eager listener had been a man whose feet were paralyzed from birth. Like the beggar in the temple at Jerusalem, he was brought by his family to the marketplace each day and left there to beg and Paul now decided to use him as a means of impressing the people of Lystra with the power of the man whose role as savior of the world, he had been preaching to them. When he came to the marketplace one morning, as was his daily custom, Paul approached the cripple.

"Stand on your feet!" he commanded in a voice loud enough to be heard all over the marketplace.

Heads from every direction turned to look at the cripple and the stocky, broad-shouldered Jew, who had been preaching a strange doctrine for several weeks. Sensing the drama of the moment, the crowd moved closer and, when the cripple suddenly leaped to his feet and began to caper about, laughing and weeping with joy at being able to walk for the first time in his life, a murmur of awe swept the area.

"The gods have come down as men!" someone cried and a hundred voices immediately took up the cry, naming Barnabas Jupiter and Paul Mercury, the messenger of the gods.

Some of the crowd raced across to the temple of Jupiter, warning the chief priests of the amazing activities happening at the very gates and shortly a group of them emerged from the building leading a young bull toward the open altar, where it could be sacrificed to the deities who had so suddenly appeared. Only, when he saw the bull and the rich vestments of the priests of Jupiter did Paul realize what was happening and raise his voice in horrified protest.

"We are men like you, with like passions!" he shouted to the crowd. "We preach that you should turn from such vanities to the living God, who made heaven and earth and the sea and all things in them."

The people had begun to quiet down now and Paul was able to climb upon the bed of an empty cart, where he could be heard by all.

"In past times, God allowed all nations to walk their own ways and gave witness of himself to the people by giving us rain from the heavens and fruitful seasons, filling our hearts with food and with gladness," he said. The crowd refused to believe that anyone who could heal a cripple paralyzed from birth was an ordinary man, however, and raised shouts of adoration once again for the divine visitors, while the priests of Jupiter were busy making preparations for the sacrifice upon the altar.

Paul and Barnabas were finally forced to flee from the marketplace to keep from being crowned as gods and escorted to positions of honor in the Temple. By the time they reached their room at an inn where they had taken lodgings on the outskirts of the city, their clothes were torn and Paul was limping from having struck his foot against a rock during their flight. Barnabas had to support him for the last hundred paces, but even though they had been in danger of being injured by the excited crowd, Paul's eyes were shining with excitement.

"We have moved them at last, Barnabas!" he cried. "Now we can really begin to make converts for Christ."

"By letting them name us gods?" Shaken by what had happened, Barnabas' tone was harsh.

"If someone in the crowd hadn't taken us for Jupiter and Mercury, I would have been able to explain to them that we healed the paralytic through the power of Christ. When the furor dies down, they will listen to us as men, not as gods."

"Were you surprised when you saw the man walk?"

"I told him to stand up. Why should I be surprised?"

"Then you never doubted that you could heal him?"

"The Lord spoke through me, as he did in Cyprus with

Elymas. But the next time I shall be better able to take advantage of a miracle and gain the people's attention before it can be turned elsewhere."

"Suppose they still believe we are gods?"

"I will stay in hiding a few days until the excitement subsides," said Paul. "When you assure the priests of Jupiter that we are men like them, they will help us quiet the crowd."

"Perhaps we should go on to Derbe as we had planned."

"And leave virgin ground such as this untilled?"

"What happened today could have been a sign from God—a warning that you are taking the gospel too much to the Greeks."

"Jesus knows all things." Paul's voice was sharp. "Would he have given me the power to heal the cripple, if he didn't intend for me to use what happened afterward to bring these people to him?"

"I only know that what we're doing now is much different from what we started out to do, when we sailed from Antioch and landed on Cyprus."

"We converted the Roman governor there. What more do you ask?"

"We converted him, yes. But we went first to the synagogue and preached to our own people."

"Elymas was among our own people, yet he opposed us at Salamis." Paul's jaw was set in the stubborn line that was becoming quite familiar to Barnabas. "And because he opposed us, I was able to reach Sergius Paulos. We were opposed in Iconium, too, but because of it I was able to come to Lystra and heal the cripple. Don't deny the Lord's work, Barnabas—else he may not again give us the power I used today."

Late that afternoon Barnabas ventured out on the street to determine the nature of public sentiment in the city. He returned just before dark, accompanied by a slender dark-haired boy with bright intelligent eyes.

"This is Timothy," he said. "I have made arrangements for us to stay with his family."

"Why not here?"

"Word has spread through the city that we are at the inn.

The cripple you healed claims to have seen us come down from heaven just before you told him to stand."

"Did you talk to the Chief Priest of Jupiter?"

"Yes. He's afraid to tell the people they're mistaken. I don't think he wants the miracle attributed to any other god besides Jupiter."

"You will be very comfortable at our home, sir," Timothy volunteered. "My grandmother came from Judea a long time ago. We have always worshiped the Most High."

"Had you heard of Christ before we came?"

"No, sir. But I listened to you in the agora and told my mother and grandmother about you."

"You're probably the only one who listened—until today." Paul managed to smile. "Are you sure we will not be crowding your family, Timothy?"

"There's plenty of room," the boy assured him. "I told my mother and grandmother of your teachings, but it will be much better if they can hear them from your own lips."

"We will go as soon as it is dark," Paul agreed. "And be sure the Lord will bless you for taking us in."

Paul and Barnabas were very comfortable at the home of Timothy, his mother, Eunice, and his grandmother, Lois. The father, a Greek minor official, had been dead for several years. He had not been wealthy but had left them a comfortable home and enough income to live on. There was no synagogue school in Lystra, where Timothy could have been taught Hebrew and the Law, but he had been enrolled in the best school there, taught by an old Greek scholar. The boy was an avid reader, just such a one, Paul thought, as he had been when he was of the same age.

Paul and Barnabas spent several pleasant months in Lystra, living with Timothy and his family. After the initial excitement over the miracle died down, they were able to teach again and made many converts among the more intelligent section of the Greek-speaking population, to which Eunice introduced them. Timothy's family, too, were baptized and each day after school, the boy followed Paul around worshipfully.

It was not to be the fate of the two missionaries to continue this peaceful existence long, however. Some Jewish merchants from Iconium came to Lystra at the end of the harvest to buy grain. When they saw Paul preaching, they denounced him and stirred up the civil authorities against the two. The priests of Jupiter were also beginning to see in Paul's eloquence and the power he had shown in healing the crippled man a threat to their own hold over the people.

As Paul was teaching alone in the marketplace one day, Barnabas having gone on to a nearby village, a crowd suddenly converged upon the apostle from the temple of Jupiter, where they had been stirred up by the Chief Priest. Without warning they began beating and stoning him, and with no chance to defend himself Paul was quickly driven to his knees. His last conscious thought was that Stephen must have felt something like this, when the stones had started raining in upon him and the cries of the crowd had echoed in his ears. Then a club struck his temple and he lapsed into unconsciousness.

III

Paul awakened to the sound of someone sobbing nearby. His body ached in every muscle and, when he turned his head, the sensation of swaying brought on by the pain and the movement made him think for a moment that he was back upon a camel during the nightmarish ride to Petra.

"He's alive! God be praised!" It was Timothy's voice, a little thick from crying, and Paul saw the boy's tear-stained face looking down at him, the dark eyes filled with joy.

"Wh— Where am I?" Paul's cut and bruised lips made it almost impossible for him to speak.

"Outside the walls. The crowd thought you were dead, so they dragged you out here and left you."

"Who attacked me?"

"A rabble stirred up by the priests of Jupiter—and some Jews from Iconium."

Paul tried to sit up, but the movement sent waves of pain

and nausea flooding through him again and he was forced to lean against Timothy until they subsided.

"Let me get help," Timothy begged. "Some friends were here just now. They couldn't be far away."

"I can make it by leaning on you. We mustn't let the men who did this know I'm still alive."

Assisted by Timothy, Paul managed to walk, though every step was agony. Fortunately they were not far from the house and, by following little frequented streets, managed to reach there unobserved. Eunice and her mother had been mourning for Paul, but when they saw that he was alive, they busied themselves washing the dirt from cuts on his face and body, where the stones and bludgeons had struck, applying damp cloths to the bruises on his face, and dressing his other wounds with soothing unguents. By the time Barnabas returned shortly after sundown, Paul was feeling considerably better, though every movement still brought pain.

"Who did this?" Barnabas demanded.

"A rabble. They came from all sides, while I was preaching."

"They were sent by priests of Jupiter," said Timothy. "I recognized some of them."

"Then they were Greeks?"

"And some Jews," said Timothy. "I think they were the grain buyers from Iconium who come here every summer."

"If they know you're still alive, they will try again," said Barnabas. "We must leave as soon as you can travel."

"Where will you go?" Eunice asked.

"To Derbe. I was almost there today and the people in the countryside listened eagerly, so we should be safe." Barnabas looked at Paul quickly, expecting a protest. "Remember Jesus himself said, 'When they persecute you in one city, flee to another.'"

By morning Paul was able to walk with Barnabas' help and they set out on the road to Derbe which, like Lystra, lay in the foothills of the Black Mount. Normally it was a journey of less than a day but in Paul's condition the whole day was required. Barnabas spoke little during the journey, his main concern was to get Paul safely to the other city. But when they were in the home of some friends of Eunice and Timothy at Derbe, he voiced his concern.

"How can we serve the Lord, if you get us killed by setting both Greeks and Jews against us?" he demanded.

"What would you have me do instead? Give up the mission?"

"Why not follow the course we followed when we went to Cyprus. Go first to the synagogues where we can speak to people who are familiar with the gospel we preach, or at least with its background, and to proselytes among the Gentiles. That way we will be talking to people who understand us, and we can leave an organized band of Christians behind in each city to carry on the work after we return to Antioch."

"Let us see what success we have in Derbe." Even Paul could see the logic in Barnabas' argument. "Afterward we will return to Syrian Antioch and report on our work before deciding where to go next. But I will not agree for the gospel to be taken only to the Jews. Gentiles, too, must be accepted freely into the church."

It had been the end of summer when Paul and Barnabas were forced to leave Lystra. All during that fall, they remained in the pleasant environs of Derbe, finding no such organized opposition to their teachings as had occurred in other cities along the route. East of Derbe the broad tableland, the Lycaonian Plain, across which they had been traveling since leaving Antioch-in-Pisidia, began to rise toward the base of Mount Taurus. Here, Paul was not far from the Cilician Gates north of Tarsus. Had it been summer, the easiest way back to Antioch would have been to descend from the highlands through the gates and thence down the River Cydnus to his birthplace. From there he could have embarked for Antioch.

It was now mid-winter in the Galatian uplands, however, and the passes were clogged with snow, making travel well nigh impossible. Besides, knowing from the way his own faith had sometimes wavered during the long months in Arabia that the converts they had made in the highland cities would need support and encouragement, Paul decided to revisit the young churches instead of waiting for spring.

Resting in Derbe while he recovered from the near fatal injuries he had sustained at Lystra, Paul had taken time to think about the things that had happened on this journey. With Barnabas, he rehearsed the progress they had made from city to city and particularly the general refusal of the Jews in the synagogues to seize upon the good news of the Messiah, though Greek proselytes and Greeks with no previous knowledge of the Jewish faith accepted freely his teachings about the Risen Lord who had taken upon himself the sins of the world.

Barnabas held fast to the conviction that, before going to the Gentiles, they should go first to the synagogues in each city they visited in the future, giving the congregations an opportunity to accept or reject them. He argued further that the churches they left behind should be, as far as it was possible to make them, synagogues of the Jewish faith with the members subscribing to the essentially Jewish laws of circumcision, diet and ritual. Paul, however, held that all bonds of the Law had been loosed by the death and resurrection of the Lord, making circumcision and the adherence to Jewish Law and ceremonial ritual unnecessary.

Recognizing that the questions involved were fundamental to any success in his mission to the Gentiles, Paul determined to settle the matter once and for all by going directly to the apostles in the Synagogue of the Nazarenes at Jerusalem, the Mother Church of the Christian faith. And Barnabas, always a reasonable man and much troubled by the divisions between him and Paul, agreed.

The road to the coast through the Cilician Gates was impassable because of snow, so they elected to follow the military highroad westward through Antioch-in-Pisidia retracing the route by which they had come. It was mid-winter when they left Derbe and at Lystra, they paused at the home of Eunice, Lois, and Timothy for the weather to lighten, before moving on to Iconium. The first warm days of spring found them at Antioch-in-Pisidia, where they were able to join a caravan of shepherds, bearing a shipment of the fine wool produced by the flocks upon the upland plateaus to the coast for shipment on the first vessels to resume sea travel after the winter storms.

Late spring brought them to Perga, a little distance upriver from the Mediterranean. No ship was available in that city, however, and, remembering his bout of fever there, Paul preferred to move on to Attaleia at the mouth of the river. There they were soon able to take passage for Antioch, arriving in the Syrian capital in the middle of the summer some two years after their departure upon the first great missionary journey to the cities of Asia Minor.

IV

Though Paul and Barnabas had been away from the great church at Antioch for two years, they quickly discovered that it had grown but little during that period. The reason was soon apparent—the presence of a group of Jews from Jerusalem, who claimed the right of the church there to govern all Christians. These Jews had insisted too, that the old laws of circumcision and diet should be followed by all converts, even though both Peter and Paul had preached that Jesus had freed all new Christians from these requirements.

The activities of the Judaizers—as Paul named them, somewhat contemptuously—had caused continual dissension and a split in the Antioch church, with the Gentile element headed by a devout Christian named Titus, following the teachings of Paul.

With characteristic forthrightness, Paul decided to go directly to the heart of the situation by carrying the controversy to Jerusalem where a decision could be made by the apostles there. In this decision, Barnabas supported him, as did Titus, and the three of them, along with others from both factions, soon set out on the journey to the Holy City.

From Petra and Damascus, Paul had come to Jerusalem as a fugitive, convinced of his calling by Jesus but not quite certain of the direction in which his own destiny lay. Though disappointed at being sent to Tarsus at the time, he had made no objection, recognizing that he was something of an embarrassment to many in the Jerusalem synagogue, who vividly remembered his persecutions. This time Paul arrived in Jerusalem as the acknowledged leader of the great church at Antioch and since he and Barnabas risked their lives to carry the gospel to new lands, where it had never been preached before, the two men were, in a great sense, the heroes of the Christian faith. As such, their request for the right to make converts wherever and whenever they could, unchained by any of the old provisions of Mosaic Law, carried considerable weight.

Not all of the apostles were living in the Holy City at the time of the Council of Jerusalem, as this most important policymaking conclave came to be called. James ben Zebedee had been executed by Herod Agrippa and some others had been scattered abroad by the persecutions of Paul and Herod. Peter was there, although he now spent much of his time traveling about the surrounding region, spreading the gospel and looking after new churches. John ben Zebedee, too, was present and of course James, the kinsman of the Lord who now headed the Synagogue of the Nazarenes and was in a sense, spokesman for the Jerusalem Church.

On the morning of the council, Paul rose just before sunrise and went to the temple to pray. Even though Christ had freed those who followed him from the burden of temple ritual and the ceremonial Law, the shining structure there upon the mount still represented to Jews everywhere the dwelling place of their God. Paul had never ceased to regard the temple in that light and he found himself remembering now the first occasion, when he had come here as a youth on the morning following his arrival from Tarsus to begin his studies with Gamaliel.

Had it been the Passover season, Paul would have descended to the lower level of the temple and purchased a sacrifice, since Christian Jews everywhere still celebrated the season when the Angel of the Lord had passed over their homes in Egypt, sparing the firstborn. But this was just another day in the temple and, moving across the court, he sought a quiet place where the small platforms of the rabbis were lined up against a wall of the Porch of Solomon. Standing there not far from where he had engaged in the controversy with Rabbi Samuel and where Jesus himself had taught he raised his eyes to the beams of hewn cedar supporting the roof over the porch and prayed for guidance in the coming meeting of the council.

He did not doubt that considerable opposition would be marshaled against his doctrine that the death and resurrection of Jesus had freed all who would come to him from any restrictions men might place upon them. And, though he felt no hesitation about propounding and defending his own doctrine he wished to do it in a way that would not harm the whole church, as the one in Antioch had already been harmed by the conflict of doctrine. Standing in that holy place praying for a revelation of Christ's purpose he seemed to hear within his soul the same voice that had spoken to him outside Damascus say: "'I am the light of the world. He that follows me shall not walk in darkness but shall have the light of life.'" And needing no other assurance then, Paul left the temple and crossed over the bridge leading to the Lower City.

v

On the previous occasion, Paul had felt that James was anxious to have him out of Jerusalem, so he was not surprised that those claiming that even Gentile converts must be circumcised and obey Mosaic Law were allowed to address the council first. On another occasion, he might have lashed out at them for their stubbornness in clinging to a doctrine Christ himself had nullified through his death and resurrection. But the conviction that had come to him in the synagogue at Antioch-in-Pisidia that day, when he and Barnabas had been accused of blasphemy, had been fortified by the words Jesus had spoken in his soul only a few hours before in the temple. And so he sat silent and let the others have their say, though he knew Barnabas and Titus, among others, were watching him, waiting for him to take the lead in opposing the arguments of those who supported tradition.

Before Paul was required to defend himself, however, another voice was heard, a quiet voice that carried more weight than any other in the councils of the Church.

"You all know that some time ago God made a decision that the Gentiles should hear the word of the gospel from me and believe," said Simon Peter. "God, who knows the hearts of everyone, approved of them by giving them the Holy Spirit, even as he did to us. What is more, he put no difference between us and them but purified their hearts by faith. Why then do you ask God to put a yoke upon the necks of others, when neither our fathers nor we were able to bear it, and when we believe that only through the grace of the Lord Jesus Christ shall we be saved?"

No one among the Judaizers attempted to answer Peter and after a moment, Paul rose to speak. A murmur of disapproval had run through the audience when he stood up but it subsided quickly under the passion and conviction in his voice.

"When we ministered to people in other lands; when we baptized them and they received the Holy Spirit; when we worked miracles among them—did we do it by the Law, or by the faith they discovered through our teachings?" he demanded. "Are any of you so foolish as to believe that, having begun in the spirit, you can now be made perfect in the flesh through the Law? If so, you have suffered many things in vain. To you who say we are accursed, if we do not require the Law of all men, I say that Christ redeemed us from the Law, taking the curse upon himself for us.

"Before faith came we were kept under the Law. As long as we were shut away from that faith, the Law was our schoolmaster to bring us to Christ, in order that we might be justified by faith. But now that faith has come, we are no longer under a schoolmaster; we are all children of God through faith in Christ Jesus. You who have been baptized into Christ have put on Christ and are no longer either Jew or Greek, bond or free, male or female. You are all one in Christ Jesus, so let us stand fast in the liberty with which he has made us free and not be entangled again with the yoke of bondage. In him, neither circumcision avails anything nor uncircumcision but only the faith which works by love.

"The fruit of the spirit is love, joy, peace, long-suffering, gentleness, goodness, faith, meekness, temperance. Against such there is no Law. God forbid that I should glory, save in the cross of our Lord Jesus Christ, by whom the world is crucified for me and for the world. From henceforth let no man trouble me for I bear on my body the marks of the Lord Jesus."

With the words, Paul tore open the front of his robe, so all could see the scars where the stones at Lystra had torn his flesh. Standing there with his breast bared, he was magnificent in his defiance of those who would put restrictions on his doctrine and his eyes bored into those of James who, everyone there knew, was the foremost advocate of the old ways. Not able to meet Paul's challenging gaze, James glanced from one to the other of the apostles gathered around the table, but it was obvious that no vote need be taken.

"Simon Peter has declared how God first visited the Gentiles to select from them a people for his own name." The head of the Jerusalem church spoke almost in a monotone, in odd contrast to Paul's fervent oratory. "To this the words of the prophets agree where it is written, *After this I will return and will build again the tabernacle of David, which has fallen down. And I will build again the ruins of it and I will set it up that the residue of men might seek after the Lord and all the Gentiles who call upon my name.*'

"All of God's works are known to him from the beginning of the world. Therefore it is my decision that we shall not trouble those who turn to God from among the Gentiles, but only write to them, asking that they abstain from pollution of idols, from fornication, from things strangled and from blood. For Moses of old still has those who preach of him in every city and his words are read in the synagogues every Sabbath day."

The decision was a compromise designed to save the face of the Judaizers by allowing some of the less stringent provisions of the Mosaic Law to be required still from converts. But it was also a triumph for Paul, since the requirement of circumcision, a major stumbling block to the acceptance of Gentiles into the Christian faith, no longer existed.

James had given a sop, so to speak, to the Pharisaic element in the church who, while accepting Jesus as the Messiah, had not been able to put aside prejudices ingrained in their minds since childhood. This Paul accepted gracefully and agreed for a letter, signed by James on behalf of the apostles and elders at Jerusalem to be read in Christian churches everywhere. Borne by Silas and Judas Barsabbas from the Jerusalem congregation, who returned with Paul and the others to Antioch for the purpose of reading it there and elsewhere, the letter said:

*The apostles and the presbyters, your brothers, to the Gentile brothers in Antioch and Syria and Cilicia: Greeting.*

*Whereas we have heard that some of our number, to whom we gave no instructions, troubled you with arguments to the unsettlement of your souls, it was our unanimous decision to choose delegates and send them to you with our beloved Barnabas and Paul, men who have surrendered their lives for the name of our Lord Jesus Christ. We have therefore commissioned Judas and Silas who will themselves also deliver the same message verbally. It was the Holy Spirit's decision and ours to impose upon you no further burden beyond these essentials—abstinence from things sacrificed to idols, bloodshed, and fornication. From these you will do well to keep yourselves. Farewell.*

VI

With all the major bonds shackling him to Jewish custom now broken, Paul busied himself in Antioch undoing the damage done by the controversy over the questions of circumcision and the Law. As usual, he preached not only on the Sabbath but wherever he could find people to listen during the week. He was helped no little by the arrival of Simon Peter from Jerusalem with the beginning of spring. And since Peter made a point of associating with the Gentile converts as much as he did with Jewish ones, the schism which had divided the church at Antioch seemed well on the way to being healed. With Peter came Mark. In the years since Cornelius had brought the scroll to Tarsus, the young scribe had set down more of the sayings of Jesus that Peter had recalled and Paul was happy to have these new teachings as a basis for his sermons in Antioch.

The troublesome Pharisaic element among the Christians had been silenced for the time being at the Council of Jerusalem but they had not given up entirely their insistence on accommodation to the old ways. Early in the spring a group arrived in Antioch and began to stir unrest there by encouraging a small faction of the church, who had not yielded even after the letter James had sent by Silas and Judas Barsabbas was read publicly.

Paul was away when the Judaizers arrived, preaching in Seleucia, the nearby port city where a church made up largely of converted Gentiles was thriving. Among the visitors from Jerusalem were friends of both Peter and Barnabas, men who had been active in organizing the Synagogue of the Nazarenes there after the return of the disciples to Jerusalem from Galilee. The real purpose of the visitors did not occur to the warm impulsive Peter, always friendly to any who followed Jesus. And since some of Barnabas' tendencies, too, were in the same direction, he naturally greeted the new arrivals also.

Paul arrived hurriedly from Seleucia one afternoon just before the beginning of the Sabbath at sunset. Very much agitated by something he had learned that very day at Seleucia, he went immediately to the meeting place for the *agape*, or love feast. A prominent feature in Christian ritual, it was a reenactment by the worshipers of the last supper of Christ with his disciples in the upper room at Jerusalem. There Paul found the visitors from Jerusalem, of whose presence in Antioch he'd become aware for the first time that afternoon in Seleucia, sitting apart from the Gentile members of the congregation and Simon Peter with them—apparently, to Paul's disturbed mind, in the capacity of a host.

Grim-faced, Paul strode past the visitors without acknowledging their presence and took a seat in the midst of a group where there were no Jews. All during the meal and the opening part of the service that followed, he sat there, hardly noticing what he ate, while his indignation came to a boil.

Barnabas read the opening part of the service. When the time came for the sermon, he turned as usual to Paul, who rose from his seat and strode, white-faced and stern, to the pulpit. Realizing belatedly, the interpretation Paul must have put upon Peter's presence among the men from Jerusalem, Barnabas sought to speak to him at the foot of the steps leading to the pulpit and assure him that Peter had taken no actual part in promoting the cause of the Judaizers. But Paul brushed him aside and, climbing to the elevated space, faced Peter.

"I speak to you today because the church is in danger." His first words brought the congregation erect in their seats. "Certain people have come among you, seeking to unsettle your faith, the same faith I have taught you and through which you have placed your trust in me. I say to you that if anyone is preaching a doctrine to you contrary to the one you received from God through me, a curse be upon him."

The congregation was silent, knowing these harsh words were directed to one person alone, the man Jesus himself had named the rock upon which the Church would be built.

"You all know that not long ago Barnabas and myself journeyed to Jerusalem because then, as now, false prophets had come among you," Paul continued. "They taught that men could not be saved, as God revealed to me, merely by believing in the Lord Jesus Christ and his resurrection, but must needs be circumcised and keep the Law of Moses. At Jerusalem I laid before James and the elders the way of salvation I have preached to you and to the brethren in Galatia, Cyprus, and Cilicia, and which all of you have believed. The leaders in Jerusalem saw that I have been entrusted with the charge of taking the truths of Christ to the Gentiles and the heathen, just as Peter was entrusted to take it to the Jews—for the same spirit of Christ which had been at work in Peter for his apostleship to the Jews had been at work in me, too, for the apostleship to the heathen. These same leaders therefore gave to Barnabas and me the right hand of fellowship, with the understanding that we should go to the heathen and they to the Jews, asking us only to remember the poor, which we were eager to do.

"Now Peter knew this, and when he first came to Antioch, he ate and associated with everyone, whether Jew or not, whether circumcised or not. Recently other false prophets have also come from Jerusalem, saying that Jews should not eat with the uncircumcised, and now Peter has joined them. So I say to him now, before this congregation: if you are living like a heathen and not like a Jew, although you are a Jew yourself, why do you try to make the heathen live like Jews?"

Simon Peter had sat like a stone, making no move to interrupt during the torrent of words castigating him for what to him had been a mere gesture of welcome and friendship to people with whom he had been associated for many years. When Paul descended from the pulpit and took his seat once again, all eyes turned to Peter expecting him to answer, for nothing so dramatic as the denunication of one apostle by another had ever happened in the history of the church. Peter did not rise in his seat, however, and after a prayer, Barnabas dismissed the congregation.

People gathered around Paul immediately but he shouldered them aside without a word. And seeing the look of pain, as well as anger, on his face as he left the meeting place they let him pass. Only Barnabas followed, catching up with Paul in a room outside the meeting place where, suddenly swaying with the force of the emotion that had brought on the denunication, the fiery apostle sank into a chair.

"How could you be so unfair to Peter?" Barnabas' voice was taut with anger. "The men from Jerusalem are old friends of his—and mine. Some even bear scars from whips in prison where you sent them."

Paul raised his head and, at the agony mirrored in his eyes, some of Barnabas' own anger began to melt away. The two men had been close since their youth and, although they had drifted somewhat apart recently over the doctrinal obstructions that had led to tonight's denunication, they had lived like brothers and shared danger together.

"You don't know the whole story," said Paul.

"What is it?"

"I already knew that the men from James—"

"You cannot say he sent them."

"They're from Jerusalem. And they parrot the same doctrines James has tried to impose upon us."

"He gave the letter to Silas and Judas Barsabbas, freeing us to take Gentiles into the church with only minor restrictions," Barnabas protested. "Are you saying now that James has turned away from the decisions of the council?"

"Perhaps he didn't actually send these men," Paul admitted. "But they are seeking to undermine our work elsewhere. One of them was in Seleucia today, arranging passage for all of them on a ship."

"Perhaps they are returning to Joppa by sea."

"By way of Cyprus, Tarsus, Perga, and Antioch-in-Pisidia?"

"Is this a rumor—or the truth?"

"I heard it from Lycaius. They sought passage on one of his ships."

It was Barnabas' turn to be shaken, for Lycaius was a Christian shipmaster of Seleucia, who would have no reason to lie. "I would still wager that Peter knew nothing of this," he said. "Let us go to him together and ask him about it."

"Peter sat with them tonight," said Paul. "If he would avoid the appearance of evil, why does he associate with those who are evil?"

"You know how impulsive and friendly Peter is. He has known these men for years—and suffered danger with them. He would think of their comfort and welcome them before he would question their motives. Come with me now and we will settle this whole thing."

"Why didn't Peter defend himself tonight?"

"It could be that he is more concerned with the good of the church than with his own place in it," Barnabas said bluntly.

Paul stiffened at his tone. "I bear on my body the scars that proved my concern," he said icily.

"I meant no criticism of you." Realizing that he had gone too far, Barnabas tried to make amends but the rift between them was almost beyond healing. Their differences, which had begun over Paul's break with the Jewish synagogues in the Galatian cities, had finally come to a head.

## VII

The dramatic confrontation between the two strongest apostles in the entire Church sent rumors flying throughout the Antioch congregation. Most of the people sympathized with Paul, for by far the larger part of the membership were of Gentile origin or were Hellenic Jews, who considered him their spokesman. Then a second dramatic event, a true miracle it seemed, took the center of the stage. Word of it was brought by Mark, when he burst excitedly into a group surrounding Paul shortly before noon the day following the denunciation of Peter.

"I saw it!" Mark cried. "I saw it with my own eyes!"

"Saw what?" Barnabas had just joined the group, seeking Paul for a last attempt at reconciliation.

"Peter was walking on the street between here and the river, when his shadow fell upon a crippled man lying in the doorway of a house." Mark paused, moved by the natural ambition of the young to dramatize.

"What happened?" Paul demanded.

"The cripple was healed by Peter's shadow. He got to his feet at once and walked away."

A silence fell over the crowd for everyone understood that the miracle, if it had really happened as Mark described, could be a divine revelation, a vindication of Peter as well as a divine reprimand of Paul. All eyes turned to him, but Barnabas spoke first.

"Are you sure this man was crippled, Mark?" he asked.

"I know it. Only yesterday I saw him begging for alms in the street because he couldn't walk."

"What did Peter do?"

"He paid no attention to the man. But kept walking—toward the road to Seleucia."

Barnabas looked quickly at Paul, whose face seemed suddenly to have turned to stone. Without speaking, Paul turned and left the room but, when Barnabas started to follow, Mark seized his sleeve excitedly.

"Peter is vindicated!" he cried. "The Lord performed the miracle—as a sign that he favors him over Paul."

"Hush!" Barnabas cried, but the words were out and an immediate clamor from the group supported Mark's conclusion.

All that day and the next, Paul remained alone, not even coming to his meals. He spent the time in prayer, as he had done in Damascus before his healing by Ananias, asking for a revelation of God's will and an affirmation or a denunciation of his action. Finally, when no such revelation had occurred to him by the third morning, he sought out Barnabas.

"We will leave for Galatia at once," he announced without preamble. "I'm going to visit the churches there."

"But we agreed to wait until after the Passover."

"If those who oppose us don't wait, we cannot afford to wait either. The churches must be strengthened before their faith can be undermined."

"The seas will still be stormy," Barnabas warned. "Spring has just begun."

"Then we will go by land." Paul brightened at the thought. "That way we can reach the Galatian uplands long before those followers of James get there. And we can visit the churches in Syria and Cilicia on the way."

He did not add that such a route would put them ahead of Peter, if the big apostle sought to undermine Paul's position with the Galatian churches, but Barnabas knew his traveling companion well enough by now to understand what was in the younger man's mind.

"I will tell Mark to get ready." Hoping for a reconciliation with Paul, Barnabas made no further objection.

"I've decided not to take him," Paul said quickly.

"But you agreed earlier—"

"I agreed to consider taking Mark with us. Nothing was decided."

"Why did you choose to leave him behind now?"

"Have you forgotten that he left us in Perga?"

"I told you he was homesick."

"Jesus said: 'No man, having put his hand to the plow and looking back is fit for the Kingdom of God.'"

"But Mark came back from Perga because of Pet—" Barnabas' lips tightened. "That's your real reason, isn't it? Because he's close to Peter and you're afraid Mark will spy on you." Angry at last, he plunged on. "You need to take him, Paul—to remind you of the words Jesus spoke. Do you realize how far you've departed from them, since you were rejected at Antioch-in-Pisidia? It's as if you were preaching a different doctrine altogether."

"My doctrine was revealed to me by the Lord himself. I have no need of sayings that have gone through two minds before they reach me."

Barnabas shook his head slowly—and sadly. "Sometimes I think that to you the God of old, the one who spoke to Moses on the mountain and gave us the Law, is dead. In his place you have raised up some sort of a god of your own making."

"I have raised up Christ upon the cross."

"Your Christ is not the Jesus of Nazareth I knew. Yours is a sacrifice, like the one in the Eleusinian mystery you once told me about or the young god Dionysius sacrificed as a symbol in the pagan ceremony. You have replaced Jesus of Nazareth with a god of your making—with you as his High Priest."

Paul turned on his heel and, appalled finally by his own accusations, Barnabas made a belated attempt to be reconciled with the man who had been his friend for so many years.

"Go to Peter," he pleaded. "Settle this matter with him before the whole Church is split like the congregation here at Antioch, with some saying they follow Peter and others Paul."

Paul turned in the doorway. "If Peter follows James and the others, why doesn't he tell me of it? Instead of joining those who seek to destroy me?"

"Everyone expected Peter to answer you but I'm sure he kept silent rather than split the Church."

"You just said it is split already."

"That can still be healed—if you and Peter are reconciled. After all, it was you who accused him. If you must sit in the highest place, Paul, don't drag the church down with you when you fall. Remember what Jesus said: *'He who would be greatest among you, let him become the servant of all.'*"

"It was not I who separated himself from the rest," Paul said stonily. "How can I be reconciled with Peter and the Judaizers unless I stop preaching what was revealed to me by the Lord himself?"

"We have come to the parting of the ways, then." Barnabas' voice was husky. "I suppose we really came to it almost two years ago at Antioch-in-Pisidia but I refused to see it then. I can go with you no more; from here on our paths lie in different directions."

"You are siding with Peter and the others?"

"I am going the way of the Lord, as I saw it when he was alive, and as I see it now. May God bless you in all you do. Greet our friends in Galatia for me and bid them stand fast in Christ."

## VIII

News of the break between Paul and Barnabas shook the Church at Antioch like an earthquake. Peter had not returned to the city, so there was no further chance of a reconciliation before Paul departed. As his comrade on the second journey, he chose Silas, one of the two men sent from the congregation at Jerusalem to read the letter from James and the other apostles to the churches. By taking Silas and a copy of the letter with him, Paul shrewdly sought to counter any attempt the Judaizers might make to undermine his teachings. Wherever they went, Silas could announce the actual stipulations to which James and the leaders of the Jerusalem Church had agreed in his presence. Moreover, like Paul, he was a Roman citizen and bore the Roman name of Silvanus.

Crossing over Mount Amanus by way of the narrow gorge called the Syrian Gates, Paul and Silas descended to the Cilician Plain. There they visited churches Paul had previously established at Adana, Aegae, and Mopsuetia, located along the main Roman road through that area. The Christians in these towns were close enough to Antioch to be disturbed by the controversy over the question of circumcision and obedience to Mosaic Law. But when Paul appeared with Silas, telling of the compromise worked out at the Council of Jerusalem, they were able to quiet most of this unrest. Pausing only briefly in these cities, Paul and Silas traveled on to Tarsus, where they spent several weeks with the busy and prosperous church of which Lucius was now one of the leaders.

Fearing that the Judaizers from Jerusalem—and perhaps Simon Peter himself—might reach Galatia before them, Paul insisted on pushing northward into the upland region, as soon as the snows melted sufficiently to allow passage. From Tarsus the road followed the valley of the Cydnus for a while before passing through the Cilician Gates, a narrow crevice guarded on each side by precipitous cliffs. North of the gates, the way climbed steadily through deep ravines, and past steep cliffs and copses heavily forested with cedars and pines, emerging finally upon the upland plateau of the great Lycaonian Plain. Far ahead, Paul could see the Black Mount jutting abruptly upward and his heart quickened with the knowledge that in its foothills lay Lystra, the home of Timothy, his mother and his grandmother, where the apostle had spent so many pleasant days on the previous visit.

In the year Paul had been away, Timothy had grown from a gangling boy into a handsome youth. The seed of Paul's teachings had sprouted and flourished in the fertile ground of Timothy's eager mind—like that sown in the parables of Jesus. Long since a Christian, Timothy was eager to join Paul and Silas on the rest of their journey and, when Eunice agreed, he was gladly accepted.

The controversy at Antioch, the seeming turning away of Peter and, finally, the rupture with Barnabas had left Paul depressed. On the trip to Iconium and Antioch-in-Pisidia, Timothy's high spirits were a source of constant pleasure and stimulation to him. He drew new enthusiasm from the boy and came to love Timothy, as he would have loved the son he might have had one day, had his whole life not been dominated by the divine fire kindled within him on the Damascus road. Now at last, he was sure he would be able to go into Bithynia, which he had longed to visit ever since that night in Petra when he'd seen the brilliance of the star called Phoenikos in the northern sky. A strip of territory lying along the south shore of the Propontis—also called the Sea of Marmora—and the Pontus Euxinus, it was said by travelers who had visited the fabled land to be rich in beauty and grandeur, with thriving towns and villages that were sure to form a fertile soil for the seeds of Paul's teachings.

The easiest route into Bithynia, they learned, was to approach its western and more heavily populated section first, rather than thread the mountain passes directly to the north, where they might become prey to the bandits who always haunted such areas. From the western end of Bithynia, they were told, they could later move eastward by boat along the shore of the Pontus Euxinus and perhaps visit the fabled cities of Trapesus and Chersonesus, sowing the seeds of the Christian faith at the farthest northern limits of Rome's Empire in this part of the world.

Summer was at its height when Paul and his companions crossed the River Sangarius near Cotyaeum, following a well traveled Roman road, westward to the heights of the watershed separating the rivers flowing northward to the Sea of Marmora from those flowing to the Aegean. Here they were at the junction of the boundaries of Asia, Bithynia and Mysia, a beautiful region of rolling hills and chalk downs, with the range of the Mysian Olympus—as distinguished from the more famous peak of the same name in Greece—marking the boundary of Bithynia, as the Phrygian Dindymus to the south outlined the borders of Galatia and Asia.

There Paul awoke one night in the grip of a severe bone-shaking chill. And when the next afternoon the sun began to swing in a vast arc across the sky before his pain-dazed eyes, he knew his fever was rising and he must wrestle once again with the affliction that seemed to be his particular Nemesis, much as Jacob had wrestled so long ago with the Angel of Death on the banks of the river Jabbok.

## IX

They were following the course of a stream that tumbled down from the hills on its way to the Sea of Marmora. Paul's companions had gone on a few paces ahead, when he staggered off the path and found a seat upon a rock, but Timothy saw him and hurried back.

"The fever is upon me," Paul gasped. "Bring water from the brook."

Timothy hurried to obey, filling the skin they carried to supply them on the way and bringing it to Paul, who drank deeply. Removing Paul's headcloth, he also soaked it in cold water and placed it on the apostle's forehead as a compress.

"I must get to a physician," Paul told his companions. "Sometimes with one of these attacks I lose my senses for a week."

"There may be one at Prusa," said Silas. "We could go back there."

"No. We must go on." A thought suddenly struck him. "How far is it to Troas?"

"Troas?" Silas frowned. "I don't know."

"Isn't Troas near the site of ancient Troy? The place where the Greeks fought a great battle and captured the Trojans, when they let a wooden horse be taken into the city?" Timothy asked.

"That's the place. How far would it be?"

"I don't remember exactly. Several days journey at least."

"We must go there as quickly as we can."

"But you need rest," Silas protested. "Traveling will only make the fever worse."

"A skilled physician named Luke lives at Troas," Paul exclaimed. "He once saved my father when everyone else had given him up. We must go on."

"We could buy an ass at the next village." Silas' practical nature was one reason why Paul had chosen him as a traveling companion after the quarrel with Barnabas. "You could ride on it to Troas and we could sell it there."

With Paul firmly strapped to the back of the pack animal and supported by Timothy they came at last to Troas and found Luke. By that time the apostle was gravely ill. A week passed before the fever began to subside and Paul awoke one morning to find himself in a strange house. The smell of the sea told him it was not far from the coast and he remembered Luke saying that from a height near Troas he could watch ships passing by on their way to the Hellespont and the Sea of Marmora. Reassured, he dropped off to sleep again and when he awoke, found Luke himself standing beside the couch.

The years had been kind to the physician, kinder, Paul suspected, than they had been to him. Luke was still slender and, though sprinkles of gray showed prematurely at his temples, the same warm light of intelligence and understanding shone in his eyes.

"So we meet again, Saul of Tarsus." Luke pulled up a stool beside the couch. "It was a good thing you remembered that I was going to locate at Troas. Had you delayed much longer in reaching here, it might have been too late."

"The Lord directed me here," Paul assured him.

"The Lord?"

"Jesus of Nazareth—the Son of God. Don't you remember asking me back in Tarsus about his curing lepers?"

"I do remember," said Luke. "Timothy and Silas have told me about what has happened to you since I left Tarsus. They said you were on your way to Bithynia."

"I've wanted to go to Bithynia for a long time."

"Why?"

"Someone told me it's a place of peace and beauty. For several years now my life has been just the opposite."

"I saw the scars on your body, when I examined you. Timothy tells me they came from being stoned at Lystra, so I can understand your wanting to find a place of peace. But surely you know by now that such places exist nowhere except in a man's soul."

"You seem to have found one here."

"Troas has everything a man could want to be happy," Luke

admitted. "I have a comfortable home, the breeze from the sea cools my face in summer and helps to lessen the cold in winter. I am busy tending the sick, but somewhere deep inside me, I still seem to feel a discontent I cannot name."

"I felt it, too, in Jerusalem, when I was an agent for the Sanhedrin, persecuting Christians. But it was swept away, when the voice of Jesus spoke to me on the road to Damascus."

"This voice—are you sure you really heard it?"

"Yes. And I saw the glory of the Lord—so bright that I was blinded."

"Were you in the grip of a fever then?"

"A light attack came upon me as we were crossing the desert between Gilead and Damascus," Paul admitted. "But this experience was real, Luke. The Lord has spoken to me since and the voice has always been the same."

"We won't argue about it. Certainly something has made a change in you." Luke rose from the stool where he had been sitting. "I must visit some patients, but Timothy is here. He will give you a dose of the infusion I have been using to treat you. And some soup. The medicine seems to lessen this type of fever, though I suspect the disease must run its course before disappearing completely."

"I've had several attacks before. Could it have been in my body all the time?"

"Probably. Or you may have gotten it anew while you were in Tarsus. Silas tells me you spent several weeks in the lowlands there when the weather was hot. We do know the fever tends to increase sharply in swampy areas when summer comes."

"A physician friend who treated me at Petra studied at the Museum of Alexandria," said Paul. "He told me of meeting a physician there from India who claimed the fever was caused by mosquitoes."

"I never thought of that, though it's true that the fever is worse in summer in the lowland areas when the mosquitoes are the thickest. We will talk more of this when I return."

The infusion Timothy brought Paul after Luke left was bitter, like the one Joseph of Galilee had given him in Petra.

The boy was bubbling over with joy at Paul's recovery and with excitement over the many new sights and experiences that had been his since coming to Troas.

"Luke is sure that ancient Troy was located not far from here," he confided. "Silas and I went there several days ago. Ruins are everywhere just as they are here at Troas and I was hoping to see the wooden horse the Greeks used to gain entrance to the city. But Luke says it would have rotted a long time ago."

"You like Luke, don't you?"

"Oh yes. I think he's about to become a Christian, Paul. But I mustn't talk to you any more; Luke says you must rest."

Just listening to the boy's eager chatter was a tonic to Paul. He drank a bowl of nutritious broth that Timothy gave him and almost before the boy had pulled the curtains across the window, was asleep.

x

By the third day after his fever began to subside, Paul was able to sit in the sun outside the house. Luke had built it upon an elevation overlooking the sea, in the shade of the great oaks of which he had spoken many years ago at Tarsus. It was a lovely place, with the sea beating against the rocks at the foot of the elevation, making a pleasant harmony with the soft rush of the breeze through the trees. The house itself was not large, but very comfortable. Sitting in the sun, watching Timothy wade in a pool between the rocks or fishing from a low promontory that jutted out into the sea, Paul felt the depression of spirit that had held him since his quarrel with Barnabas begin to ebb farther and farther away.

"Silas told me you have been troubled over the church at Antioch," Luke said one evening as they were sitting outside.

"Today I feel the urge to talk to someone else about it for the first time," Paul admitted.

"Anything you tell me will be kept in confidence."

"No secrecy is needed. I think now that I may have been hasty in my judgment—and am being punished for it."

"Punished? By whom?"

"The Lord—by keeping me from going into Bithynia."

"Once before you spoke of punishment by God for your sins. That time, as I remember it, your father was ill and you felt you were to blame."

"I may have been wrong then," Paul admitted. "A god who loved the world enough to sacrifice his own son as a ransom for it would hardly strike down an old man for another's sin."

"Or turn you aside from a place you long to visit?"

"The situations aren't quite the same. I have put my life into the hands of Jesus, so I must obey only him. I erred in thinking I could settle for a peaceful existence in Bithynia, when the Lord has other tasks for me."

"This quarrel you spoke of with your friend Barnabas. How did it happen?"

Paul told the story, not sparing himself or minimizing his own part in the controversy. "I was hurt," he admitted finally. "Hurt and angry, when Barnabas said I had let God die and had raised up a new god of my own, with myself as High Priest."

"Hadn't you?"

"In my zeal to free those who come to Christ from the hindrances of the Law, I may have shut both the God of our fathers and the Law itself out of my thoughts and placed too great an importance upon my own role."

"How does this new faith you speak of differ from the old?"

"In the element of love and the sacrifice God showed by letting his son die for the sins of the world. The God I worshiped when I first knew you in Tarsus was a god to be feared, because of his wrath and the punishment he meted out to those who broke the Law."

"That does seem to be different from the all embracing love and forgiveness of sin you say Jesus brought to mankind."

"I suppose I went too far in another direction, when I realized that the Law and the old ways had led me to cause the death of men like Stephen," Paul admitted.

"Then you don't deny that the god your people worshiped and feared in past centuries is not the same one you preach to Gentiles today?"

"No. I can't deny it."

"Wherein does the real difference lie?"

"I'm not sure yet," Paul confessed. "It's hard to think of the god who would let Stephen be stoned in the name of blasphemy as the same one who sent his son as a sacrifice for mankind. I can see now that I sinned grievously in judging Peter and Barnabas so harshly. Actually I was taking upon myself the attributes of the god I rebelled against."

"You judge yourself too harshly," Luke said. "Not many men are so strong-willed as you are, Paul. People will always disappoint you by failing to come up to the standards you set for yourself."

"Especially if I fail so often myself when measured against them," Paul agreed.

"I'm not sitting in judgment on you," said Luke. "I'm only reminding you that, if God understands the weaknesses of men and still loved them enough to give his son for them, you can do no less. You cannot preach a religion of love and carry resentment in your heart against those who don't behave as you think they should."

Paul studied the face of the physician for a long moment. When finally he spoke, there was an overtone of gratitude in his voice: "It's strange that you—a Greek and a pagan—should understand God's will and the real mission of Jesus so clearly when even now I'm not entirely sure of it myself."

"You're wrong on one count," said Luke. "I am still a Greek, but I'm no longer a pagan. If I understand the meaning of Jesus of Nazareth, it is that he is in himself the greatest possible gift God could make to men and the ultimate proof of God's undying love and capacity to forgive."

"Then you, too, have come to follow him?"

"I could do no less when, as a physician, I can see that the example he gave us can heal the souls of men in every place and every time."

## XI

Recovering his strength in the warm sunlight of Alexandria Troas, known to the Romans as "New Troy," Paul could look across the hills of Imbros to the higher peak of Samothrace in the distance. Beyond it to the northwest lay Macedonia, hidden by the mists but with its presence always in evidence through the busy shipping in the Aegean Sea. Luke had spent some time in that area and spoke warmly of its busy and prosperous cities, the eager pursuit of learning which had always characterized the Greeks who inhabited the whole area including Achaia to the south and the thousands of islands dotting the sea.

To one who had come so far across mountains and upland plains, often stoned for his pains, the lure of a land to which the gospel had never been brought was great. As yet, however, Paul had made no decision concerning where their journeys would lead them next. It was enough that he was regaining his strength at Troas and once again, as he had so long ago in Tarsus, finding enjoyment and profit in the interchange of ideas with Luke.

While the physician was engaged in visiting the sick by day, the three travelers visited the waterfront of Troas, preaching to the crowds that gathered to buy and sell the cargoes of ships unloading and loading there, or in the agora, at the center of the city. At night, after Luke's servant had served the evening meal, they talked until the stars grew bright and Timothy began to nod. Not for a moment did Paul think that a ministry in Troas, even though it was a busy seaport, was to be his major work in this region. But it was pleasant there and he was content to wait for the Lord's purpose to be revealed.

Remembering the turmoil at Antioch and knowing from experience that a new missionary effort would embroil him with men whose minds were closed to his doctrine, Paul sometimes longed for the peace he'd once hoped to find in Bithynia. He had long since accepted the fact that this was not yet to be, however. In fact, it sometimes seemed to him that the star called Phoenikos, hanging in the northern sky at night above the ruins of ancient Troy and the narrow entrance to the Sea of Marmora, called the Hellespont by the Greeks, had grown dimmer. Then one night he had a dream, a dream so vivid that, when he awakened, he half-expected to see its central figure standing beside him.

The man in the dream was no one he had ever seen before, although the features somewhat resembled what he imagined Nestor, the Stoic philosopher of Tarsus, might have looked like as a young man. The visitor spoke, in Greek, a short message of only seven words: "Come over into Macedonia and help us." But Paul knew instantly that this was the summons for which he had been waiting.

"The Lord spoke to me last night," he announced as they were all eating the light morning meal customary in this region.

Three startled pairs of eyes looked at him. "Where are we going next?" Timothy cried.

"To Macedonia."

"Why there?" Luke asked.

"In my dream a man—a Greek—spoke to me and said, 'Come over into Macedonia and help us.'"

"Are you sure he said Macedonia?" Silas asked. "I don't think there are many synagogues in that region."

"I heard the name plainly," said Paul.

"Will we leave soon?" Timothy asked eagerly.

"As soon as we can arrange passage."

"Philippi is a busy city with the seaport of Neapolis nearby," said Silas. "I've learned that much from talking to sailors on the waterfront."

"Then we will begin our work there," said Paul.

"Mark Anthony defeated Brutus and Cassius on the plains of Philippi after Caesar was killed at Rome," said Timothy. "I studied about it in school at Lystra, but I never thought I would see the very place where the battle was fought."

"We shall hardly come as conquerors." Paul looked at the boy fondly across the low table. "But we will bring an even greater gift—the gospel. We will hate to leave you, Luke," he added. "But the Lord's work must go on, just as yours must."

"I was just thinking, that compared to what you will be doing, my work here seems of little consequence," Luke admitted.

"Why not join us?" Paul suggested. "Nothing would make me happier than having you with us."

The physician looked at the house, the comfortable furniture, the garden visible through the open door, the great oaks shading the whole area and the sparkling blue waters of the sea washing the headland. Paul sensed what was going through his mind for he, too, had given up relative luxury and prosperity in Tarsus to become a wayfarer, dependent for shelter and food upon the generosity of others or on what he earned with the skill of his hands as a tentmaker and a weaver.

"You're under no obligation," he told Luke. "I shall understand if you—"

"I was only thinking of what you said Jesus once told his disciples on Mount Hermon, after Simon Peter had named him the Son of God! *'If any man will come after me, let him deny himself and take up his cross daily and follow me.'* It will take me the rest of the day to notify my patients that they must find another physician. But if you're willing to wait, we should be able to set sail tomorrow for Neapolis, the seaport of Philippi."

## XII

The brief journey from Troas to Samothrace and thence to Neapolis required only two days, but in crossing over into Macedonia, Paul was taking the Christian gospel from Asia, with its leaning toward the Oriental viewpoint in philosophy and religion, to Europe, where Grecian culture predominated. In a way, his move was as much of a departure from the past as had been Peter's visit to the family of Cornelius in Caesarea and the free acceptance of Gentiles into the Christian faith for the first time.

Waterborne traffic was extensive between the seaports of the

Aegean and through the Propontis to the Black Sea, so they had no trouble in arranging for passage on a small sailing vessel bound for Neapolis. Rounding the northern end of the island of Imbros they had a full view of the towering peaks of Samothrace ahead and, bearing somewhat more to the west, where Mount Athos jutted up like a sentinel against the sky, came within the protection of the lee shore of the rocky island and anchored there for the night. Few vessels sailed this area after darkness because of the large number of islands dotting the upper part of the Aegean Sea and the many straits with treacherous currents lying between which made navigation even by day somewhat hazardous.

With the rising of the sun, the sail was hoisted again and they headed with a fair wind a little north of west for Neapolis. A run of about eight hours brought them to the island of Thasos lying just off the Macedonian shore. A fairly deep bay lay somewhat west of the channel, separating the mainland from Thasos. Entering it, they were soon able to dock at the port of Neapolis.

Philippi lay about a four hours' walk inland from Neapolis, across an elevated ridge connecting the mountain range of Pangaeus with the higher ridges in the interior of the district of Thrace. From the high ground of the ridge, they had a final view of the sea, with Samothrace, Thasos and, somewhat farther to the west, the summit of Mount Athos still in sight. But as they began to descend on the farther side, the sea and the mountains soon disappeared from view.

The region around Philippi was a beautiful inland plain, girt with mountains and exuberantly green at this time of the year. Looking down upon the valley between Mount Haemus and Mount Pangaeus, Timothy excitedly described the great battle that had taken place there only a little over a hundred years earlier. To the east was the mountain path by which the armies of Brutus and Cassius had entered Macedonia from the sea. As they descended the ridge, the travelers passed the very spot where the murderers of Julius Caesar had camped beside a stream. To the left was the lowland Mark Anthony had crossed in order to engage them in battle, and opposite it was the hill where Cassius had died and upon which Philippi now stood.

Originally called the "Place of Fountains" by Alexander the Great because of the many streams flowing in this area, Philippi had played an important part in the conflict between the Roman forces of Anthony and Augustus. Given the privileges and appurtenances of a colonia, it was a busy and prosperous city, organized like Rome itself, as were all cities of that status.

Mindful of Barnabas' criticism that in his anger at the Jews of Antioch-in-Pisidia and Iconium, he had departed too much from the concept of Jesus as the Messiah of the Jews, Paul decided to speak first wherever a large enough number of his countrymen could be found to form a nucleus from which the gospel could be spread. The only place resembling a synagogue in Philippi, however, was an open space covered over with an arbor of vines and leaves on the bank of the river, known as a *proseucha*. There devout Jews of the city gathered upon the Sabbath to pray, talk together about the homeland, and, whenever a rabbi happened to be visiting the region, listen to a sermon. Here Paul and his group went on the first Sabbath following their arrival at Philippi; in due time, he was invited to address the small gathering.

Looking at the group there on the banks of the river, Paul saw that they were mainly women, at least half of them Greeks, presumably proselytes to the Jewish faith. There was no formal service except for the customary readings from the Law and the Prophets and a prayer by one of the elder members. When he rose to speak, Paul told the simple story of a Messiah sent to the Jews, the message he had used at the beginning of his ministry in Cilicia and in Galatia.

At the close of the sermon, several of those present begged the apostle to remain in Philippi and teach there each Sabbath for as long as he was willing to stay. And since this was exactly the purpose for which he had come to Macedonia, he and his companions took lodging in the city and began to preach wherever people would stop to listen, in addition to the Sabbath services for those who professed the Jewish faith. The response was heartening and the number of Christians increased rapidly at Philippi during the late summer and fall of that year. But then, as had so often happened before, a controversy swirled about Paul and once again his life was in danger.

One day while the apostle was preaching in the proseucha beside the river, he noticed in the audience a young girl with the brand of a slave upon her forehead. Christianity appealed more strongly to slaves and ex-slaves perhaps than to any other group and he was not surprised to see the girl listening closely to what he had to say.

As the service was ending, two men appeared and, seizing her by the arms, began to lead her from the shelter. Whereupon, she set up such a screeching that Paul's attention was attracted by the commotion. He hurried to the spot where the men were trying to drag the girl away but suddenly, she quieted and said, in a voice that was perfectly clear and quite different from her largely unintelligible mouthings, "These men are the servants of the Most High God. They can show us the way to salvation."

The men holding her were so startled that they released her. Before they could seize her again, she ran from the proseucha and when they started to follow, Paul called them back.

"Who is this girl?" he demanded.

"A slave," said a hulking brute with an evil cast in his eye. "She's possessed with a devil, so she is able to foretell the future."

"Would you set her free?"

"For what price?" the smaller of the two men asked quickly.

"I have no money."

The man spat upon the ground at Paul's feet, throwing dust upon his sandals and the hem of his robe. "You take much upon yourself, Jew," he said. "Why should we give the girl to you, when she can make money for us telling people's fortunes?"

"I might be able to cure her—and give her salvation."

"The girl is worth a fortune to anyone who owns her," the larger man growled. "You only want to profit from the demons that possess her."

Not wanting trouble when the mission at Philippi was going so well, Paul didn't argue with the man. The girl was back on the next Sabbath, however, and followed Paul, when he left the proseucha after the ceremony, crying out again: "These men are the servants of the Most High God. They can show us the way to salvation."

When the two men, who had seized her the previous Sabbath appeared, she ran away again but they did not follow. Instead they started toward Paul with the obvious intention of beating him—until Luke, Timothy and Silas moved up beside the apostle.

"Does the girl belong to you?" Paul demanded of them.

"No one knows who is her master," the smaller man admitted. "Whoever can catch her has the use of her powers."

"Then I, too, have the right to help her."

"We give her food and a place to sleep so we are her keepers," the smaller man said. "Leave her alone—unless you want trouble with the authorities."

"What shall I do?" Paul asked Luke when the two men left. "I can't buy the girl and I can't stop her from following us and crying out the same words whenever she sees us."

"I watched her closely the first time she came to the proseucha," said Luke. "The seizure looked very much like what the old Greeks called the Sacred Disease—epilepsy."

"Would that enable her to prophesy?"

"In seizures like that, the afflicted ones often say strange things and ignorant people consider them to be soothsayers. No doubt the men who claim to be her keepers charge people for her services by claiming she can tell fortunes."

"But if she is ill, she should be treated."

"I'm afraid little can be done for such as she," Luke said. "I've never been able to cure one."

The next day the girl appeared in the agora where Paul and his companions preached daily, crying out again that they were the servants of God. This time, however, she bore the stripes of a recent beating and, seeing them, Paul was moved by pity for her.

"I command you in the name of Jesus Christ to come out of her," he said, using the ritual words for freeing those possessed by demons and forgetting that Luke had said the girl was actually suffering from epilepsy. Whatever the cause of her condition, however, no one could doubt that it was changed by his command. Her face suddenly filled with joy and she fell in the dirt, trying to kiss the hem of his robe.

"You have been healed through the grace of Jesus Christ," Paul told her as he lifted her to her feet. "No man can ever enslave your soul again."

## XIII

Happening as it did in the agora, where crowds of people were constantly moving about, the miracle of the girl's healing created a sensation in Philippi. But the matter did not end there. On their way to the marketplace the next day, Paul and Silas were seized by the two men who had made their living from the slave girl, and dragged before the city magistrates who held court daily in a building at one side of the central square.

Since the two men had admitted that they did not own the girl, but used her seeming ability to foretell the future for their own purposes, Paul was prepared to combat the charge that he had deprived them of her services by healing her. But the two had realized they could not make such a claim under Roman law, so they brought a trumped up charge against Paul and Silas instead, claiming they were stirring the people up with their preaching to a point where a riot might occur.

"These men are Jews and trouble our city exceedingly," the smaller one charged. "They teach doctrines which it is not lawful for us to receive or observe, since we are Romans."

Technically, the charges were legal, for Roman law forbade the worship of gods not sanctioned by Rome itself. But the provision had always been honored in the breach, so to speak, except in the case of Caligula. He had tried to have his own image worshiped in the temple of Jerusalem, only to be foiled by the Legate of Syria, who delayed putting the decree into effect until the assassination of the insane Emperor made it no longer mandatory.

The magistrates were anxious to avoid any commotion that might lead to a riot, however. And since Jews were not well liked in commercial centers of the Empire like Philippi, without listening to any defense they ordered Paul and Silas stripped of their robes and beaten with staves. The beating finished, the two were then thrown into prison, where they were confined in stocks.

It was Paul's first experience with prison. But having escaped a mob in Damascus and survived a stoning at Lystra, he was confident that his work was not to end here on the very threshold of the new world he'd opened for the gospel by crossing over to Macedonia. As if in answer to his prayers, the entire city was shaken so severely that night by an earthquake that the prison was partly demolished. Convinced that the power Paul had used to heal the slave girl had also brought on the earthquake, the magistrates were afraid to do anything more to him and Silas and sent guards to bring them out of prison. But Paul was not going to be thrust out of Philippi like a condemned criminal, when no charge had actually been proved against them.

"They have beaten us, though we were not condemned. And although we are Romans they have cast us into prison," he told the keeper. "If the magistrates would thrust us out now, let them come themselves."

The officials had acted hurriedly the day before, not troubling to discover whether Paul and Silas were Roman citizens. Facing the danger of being condemned for that oversight, they came to the prison, humbly begging the two to leave Philippi. And since a strong church had already come into existence as a result of his labors there, Paul agreed.

Moving westward along the coast of Macedonia, through Amphipolis and Apollonia, the travelers came next to Thessalonica, a somewhat larger city than Philippi standing at the head of the Thermaic Gulf. Here there was a large Jewish synagogue with many Gentile proselytes. One of them whose name was Jason, took them in and on the Sabbath, Paul spoke in the synagogue.

Hoping to create a favorable impression upon the Jewish congregation, the apostle developed at some length the background in the Scriptures for the coming of the Messiah. Using passages from the prophecies of Isaiah and the Psalms of David, he sought to prove that the coming of Jesus of Nazareth, his death upon the cross, and his resurrection had been foretold more than once. To this, he added a prediction of the imminent return of Christ to earth.

Christians everywhere believed in and daily expected the *parousia*, the return of Jesus to sit in final judgment over the world and reign over the Kingdom of God. Because he was speaking mainly to Jews, for whom the Messiah had a real meaning, Paul placed more emphasis upon this doctrine in his sermon to the Jewish congregation at Thessalonica than was his custom, a mistake he was to regret more than once in the years to come. As he had hoped, the initial impression he created was very favorable and many from the congregation, particularly the Greek proselytes, invited him to visit in their homes.

Over a period of several weeks Paul spent much time talking to those who were led to look deeper into the new faith by his impassioned Sabbath sermons at the synagogue. For a while, it seemed that the mission at Thessalonica would be extremely successful—until conservative members of the Jewish congregation, seeing the proselytes being weaned away by the new faith, started an ugly rumor against Paul and his companions, one that was to plague him more and more as his work in Greek territory progressed.

In Philippi, the travelers had been accused of teaching a religion not approved by Rome, a relatively minor offense. But in Thessalonica the charge was brought against him for the first time of teaching the approaching seizure of temporal power by a man who had been crucified for treason against Rome. The politarchs—as the Roman magistrates in this *urbs libera* were called—could not understand a kingdom that existed only in the souls of men. Nor indeed, did the Jews of Thessalonica, who raised the cry against Paul. Eventually, Jason, who had given shelter to the itinerant preachers, was hailed before the magistrates and required to post a bond to insure that they would leave the city and stir up the people no more.

Not wanting to cause trouble for Jason and disturbed by the injection of a political charge against him and his companions, Paul left Thessalonica by night. Following a road across the grain fields outside the city and crossing the shallow bed of the

River Anxius, they passed through a forested area and came out at the base of the western mountain range, from which a short climb brought them to Beroea.

Located on the eastern slope of the Olympian ridge, Beroea was a pleasant town with a fairly large colony of Jews. In spite of his experience in other cities, Paul went to the synagogue on the Sabbath, determined that Barnabas' charge against him of creating a new god and a new religion should not receive further support by his actions there.

Under Paul's direction, the leaders of the Beroea synagogue searched the scriptures thoroughly for predictions concerning the coming of the Messiah. And when they found ample supporting evidence in the writings of the prophets, many were converted to the new faith. Nevertheless, as had happened again and again, those who had driven him from one place followed him to stir up charges of sedition and treason, accusations calculated to make the small Jewish community fearful of getting into trouble with the Roman authorities. Nor were their fears groundless, for about this time, the Emperor Claudius had issued an edict sharply limiting the freedom hitherto enjoyed by the large colony of Jews and Christians in Rome. As a result, many had left Rome and those dwelling in other cities were in constant fear that the oppressive measures might be extended to the entire Empire.

Fearful lest he cause more trouble in Thessalonica, Paul therefore decided to sail directly to Athens, the most important and most liberal city in all of Greece. Silas and Timothy, being less likely to arouse further opposition by those who had opposed the apostle, were left behind to continue the work at Thessalonica, while Paul and Luke took ship at Dium, leaving the snow-crowned summit of Mount Olympus, home of the Greek gods, behind them.

XIV

Not even Rome itself was more beautiful than Athens, with the hill of the Acropolis and its majestic buildings where the greatest minds of the Greek world had walked and taught. Even beauty could not lift Paul's spirits, however, when he and Luke landed there from a coastal vessel one oppressively hot summer day. The impetus of the call to Macedonia had begun to fade now and, uncertain of his future course, Paul wandered the streets of Athens with Luke. He still spoke wherever anyone would listen, but only with an effort for the dullness and headache he often experienced toward the end of the day presaged a return of his old enemy—fever.

Busy with their own concerns and the constant arguments between differing schools of philosophy, particularly the Epicureans and the Stoics, the inhabitants of Athens had little time to concern themselves about an obscure Jewish faith. Particularly when its central theme seemed to be resurrection from the dead, associated in sophisticated Athenian circles with the mystery cults, at which many of them sneered. The number of Jews in Athens was small but, in spite of his experiences at Thessalonica and Beroea, Paul tried to preach to them in their synagogue. Like the Jews in most prosperous trading communities, however, these, too, were conservative and had little welcome for the apostle of a Messiah crucified as a rebel.

Paul's sermons did mark his gospel as different from prevailing lines of Greek thought, and gradually he began to be pointed out—not without derision—as the Jew who preached a new, but obviously unstirring, doctrine. Then one day, as he was wandering through the agora, with the images of Athenian gods all about him, he came upon an altar shrine—and saw cut into the stone below the top, the words: To an Unknown God.

"What is it?" Luke had been walking behind Paul and almost stumbled over him when the apostle stopped suddenly.

"Look there below the altar at the inscription. It reads: 'To an Unknown God.'"

"You will find altars like these in almost every Greek city."

"Don't you see what this means, Luke? Men everywhere look to a god they cannot even name, just as we Jews always have."

"But not necessarily the same one."

"That isn't important. When we tell the Athenians the real

name of the god they have been worshiping and how he sent his son to save mankind, they will surely flock to hear. You told me yourself in Tarsus long ago that men everywhere look to a power higher than themselves."

"No one can deny that," Luke agreed. "But Athens isn't Iconium, or even Thessalonica or Beroea. Philosophers here have more influence than any other group. They aren't likely to give up Stoicism or Epicureanism for a new faith preached by—"

"A Jew."

"Well—yes."

"Everywhere we go in Athens, people are demanding to hear new things. What I preach is new and, when I identify it with their Unknown God, they will surely listen. What is the Greek word for the resurrection?"

"Anastasis."

"Jesus and Anastasis! Today a new doctrine shall be heard in Athens."

Like most Greek cities the agora of Athens was the center of public activities. There, people met in little knots, listening to whoever expounded a new twist of philosophy, pausing awhile to argue with him and with each other, then moving on to another group, who might be discussing something entirely different. It was a lively spot, devoted largely to intellectual pursuits, befitting the peculiar position of Athens as a center for thought in that part of the world.

South of the agora was the Pnyx, a level space where the political gatherings of the Athenians were held. Toward the north loomed the eminence of the Areopagus, while to the east the Acropolis, at once the glory and beauty of Athens, towered over the central part of the city. Statues to Greek gods were everywhere: Zeus, Hercules, Mercury, Apollo, Jupiter, Aesculapius, Venus, Bacchus, Earth, Ceres, and many others. Every god in the Olympain Pantheon had its representative shrine or statue in the area around the central agora of Athens, and at another time, Paul's Jewish upbringing would have made him appalled at the presence of what he considered idols. But he had been so stirred by the discovery of the altar to the Unknown

God that he wasted no time in taking a stand before it and telling the story of Jesus and Anastasis—the resurrection. With the instinctive genius of the divinely inspired, Paul had hit upon the essential weakness of all pagan religions, their failure to stir the souls of men. Only the mystery cults sought to achieve a deeply moving effect upon the human soul, while the worship of the idols ranged about the agora encouraged only the pleasures of the moment. It was true that the teachings of Socrates and Plato concerning the eternal good in man, did more than stir the surface of the human soul. But the gospel Paul preached went deep into the very basic structure of man's longing for immortality, his instinctive desire to do good, always embattled with the animal instinct to destroy.

Once a subject had inspired him, Paul had no equal as an orator. Standing before the stone altar, speaking fervently to the crowd attracted by the sheer moving force of his voice and his personality, he told the story he had crossed a large part of the world to tell, couching it in phrases familiar to Greeks. The vitality of his presentation drew throngs to listen, but years of mere dabbling into philosophy and religion had conditioned the Athenians to a point, where it was difficult indeed to reach far beneath the surface of their souls. Jesus and Anastasis, mistaking the latter word in Paul's rather rough Greek, they took to be only another pair of gods—of which Athens obviously already had plenty.

Paul did attract crowds and inevitably his activities came to the attention of the Council of the Areopagus, an ancient tribunal or court, established centuries before to investigate any teaching calculated to stir or change the placid stream of Athenian thought and custom. When Paul was finally brought before the council, accused of proclaiming strange divinities, the proceedings were not really a trial but rather a hearing to see whether or not he should be accused of crimes against the state in stirring up the people—"corrupting the youth"—in the words of Socrates.

The hearing was held on the Hill of Ares west of the Acropolis and was open to all. Paul was eager to face his accusers, confident that the story he had to tell would sway their minds as it had swayed so many others in the world to the east. But listening to the talk of the people as they were escorted through the crowd to the platform where the Council sat, Luke was not so certain. Being Greek, he knew the intolerance of these self-styled guardians of public thought for anything that did not agree with their own ideas, and their tendency to regard as mere upstarts those whose credentials they did not consider as sound academically as their own.

"What does this babbler say?" one Athenian asked as Paul passed through.

"He preaches strange gods indeed," said another. "Jesus and Anastasis! Whoever heard of them?"

Paul did not underestimate the power of the council either to encourage or to end his ministry in Athens. He was sure, too, that word had come to them of the difficulties he had encountered in other cities; his enemies in Philippi, Thessalonica, and Beroea would have seen to that. But convinced that his doctrine was true, he confidently approached the council.

"Tell us what this new doctrine is that you have been teaching," the presiding officer said courteously. "It seems to bring strange things to our ears and we would know what they mean."

"Men of Athens," Paul faced the crowd. "I see that you are very religious for, as I went about the city, I found an altar with the inscription: 'To an Unkown God.' This god is the Lord of heaven and earth, though he does not dwell in a temple made with hands. He gives life and breath to everything that lives and has made all men of one blood, appointing the places of their habitation in order that they should be able to seek and find him. And lastly, to give assurance of his love for all men, he raised his son, Jesus Christ, from the dead."

To Jews, Paul had preached the Messiah promised by the prophets, a spiritual leader who would institute a true Kingdom of God on earth. To the Greeks of Athens he was now preaching Jesus as a divine force sent to make them new in the sight of God and bring eternal life, very much as was promised by the mystery faiths with which they were already familiar. But centuries of dabbling in religion had made the Greek mind largely incapable of understanding the essential meaning of the Christian faith. And not understanding it, they thrust it aside.

Watching from the edge of the crowd, Luke saw covert smiles begin to appear on the faces of the council members and knew that Paul's arguments, inspired though they were, had not penetrated the rigid walls the philosophers had built around their own minds. Intelligent and educated Greeks had long since given up the concepts of a mighty Jupiter hurling thunderbolts from Olympus and gods who came down to live with men, sharing their passions and their defects. What neither Paul nor Luke realized, too, was that the Greek word Anastasis—resurrection—as used by Paul, had been mistaken by many of his listeners for the name of a goddess closely associated with two of the most depraved types of worship, that of Bacchus and Dionysius, celebrated annually in festivals that were little more than licenses for debauchery. The seeming linkage of such worship to that of a new god called Jesus, or Christ, therefore, could hardly excite much respect among the men charged with deciding what philosophers or what religions could be taught in the agora at Athens.

Encouraged by the smiles of the council, the people began to laugh at the attempt of the sturdy earnest Jew to convince them of truths which, to their mind, had long since been discarded by most Greeks. Finally, when the booing of the crowd drowned out Paul's earnest entreaties, the leader of the council called a halt to the hearing. No vote was taken. To the Greeks of Athens, he had proved himself to be a harmless fellow, not even worthy of being forbidden to have his say.

xv

Paul's failure to stir the Council of the Areopagus marked the end of his mission to Athens; in fact it had never really begun. When a man from Corinth named Stephanas, who had heard the apostle speak and become converted to the Christian faith, invited him to visit that busy commercial city, he decided to accept. But before he and Luke could take ship for Corinth,

Paul was felled once again by the fever that so often returned in summer. Fortunately, this particular bout was mild and, under Luke's skilled care, he quickly passed through the crisis of fever and chills. But his usually strong will had been sapped by his experience in Athens and his strength returned very slowly.

Forced to remain indoors, Paul spent much time resting and talking with Luke, whose understanding of the Greek mind was far greater than his own could ever be. From these talks came the conviction, however distasteful to Paul, that no one else but himself was to blame for his ignominious failure at Athens. Seeking a way to impress the Athenians, he had adapted his gospel to what he considered the type of thought prevalent there. This, he told himself sternly, had been a form of idolatry in itself, a sin for which God had rightly punished him by moving the Athenians to derision. No more, Paul resolved, would he temper his teachings to the thought of the region where he taught. Instead, he would preach only the simple doctrine of the redeeming Christ, who had died for the sins of mankind, and the all embracing love of the Father who had sent him to earth.

Paul's energies somewhat renewed by the rest, he and Luke moved on to Corinth, where the apostle found work as was his custom, in a tentmaking establishment operated by a Jewish couple from Rome named Aquila and Priscilla. But when the Sabbath came and he preached in the synagogue there the crucifixion and resurrection of the son of god at Jerusalem, freeing all men from the burden of the Law, he found the same resistance he had encountered so often before from his own people. And when further access to the synagogue was denied him by the vote of the elders, he shook his robe before the congregation and spoke the words that broke the last bonds tying him to the faith of his ancestors.

"Your blood be on your own heads, for I am clean," he told the Jews of Corinth—though not without sorrow. "From henceforth I shall go to the Gentiles."

*If I be not an apostle unto others, yet doubtless I am to you; for the seal of mine apostleship are ye in the Lord.*
I CORINTHIANS 9:2

# Book VI · Corinth

I

If Athens was the traditional center of Greek philosophy and culture, Corinth was its crossroads of trade and shipping. Located astride a narrow isthmus separating the Aegean and the Ionian Seas, with a great citadel for its defense from attack on either side, Corinth was bursting with life while Athens was slowly dying with its gods.

From the summit of the Corinthian citadel, the view was certain to stir even the most jaded eyes. To the east loomed the mountain crags of Attica and Boeotia, the Acropolis of Athens, and the islands dotting the Aegean. To the west, Mount Parnassus jutted upward in the azure sky above Delphi, where the oracle of old had dispensed wisdom. Corinth itself occupied a small tableland between the two seas, with the harbors of Cenchrae and Lechaum encouraging trade with both East and West.

After being expelled from the synagogue at Corinth, Paul moved his residence to the home of a convert named Justus. The house adjoined the synagogue, however, so he was able to keep a close watch on his enemies. Nor did he allow himself to be overencouraged by the conversion of Crispus, chief ruler of the congregation, and his family, for Crispus' successor, Sosthenes, still bitterly opposed Paul and his work.

Busy in the shop of Aquila and Priscilla earning his living, preaching throughout the city whenever he could find the time, Paul was pleased with the warm reception given his gospel by the Greeks. He was also happy to see Timothy and Silas when they arrived in Corinth, after failing to find him in Athens. But his pleasure was somewhat dimmed by news they brought of trouble in the church at Thessalonica.

Like Christians everywhere, Paul sincerely believed in the parousia—the return of Jesus to inaugurate the Kingdom of God—and looked forward eagerly to it. In Thessalonica, he had emphasized this doctrine particularly. Now, Timothy reported, the Christians there, persecuted by the active Jewish congregation and troubled by attacks upon both Paul and Jesus, had turned to the expected coming of the Son of God as a way of fulfilling their hopes and freeing themselves from persecution.

Though Paul himself believed Jesus might appear at any moment, he recognized that the desire of the Thessalonians to escape from their present difficulties by anticipating the parousia could be disastrous for the growth and strength of the young church. Without delay, therefore, he wrote a letter of advice to the Christians at Thessalonica, dictating it to Timothy, who would read it in the churches and attest to its having come from the mouth of the apostle himself. This was the first time Paul had resorted to a letter, but he proved as eloquent in this form of counseling as he was in the pulpit.

He thanked God for the steadfastness of the brethren at Thessalonica and for the example they had set to others throughout Macedonia and Achaia. He refuted the charges brought against him by the Jews of that city, reminding the Thessalonians that not only had he and his co-workers preached the gospel to them in words, but they had also demonstrated it to them in their own lives, working to pay their own way even while spreading the gospel abroad. And he counseled those so taken up with expecting the coming of Christ that had they neglected everything else to be dependent upon no one but carry on the work he had himself assigned to them.

Finally, to some concerned lest loved ones, who would have

died in the interim between the resurrection and the return of Jesus, might not be able to see the face of the Lord, he gave assurance in these stirring words:

*"Let us who are of the day be sober, putting on the breastplate of faith and love and for a helmet, the hope of salvation. For God has not appointed us to wrath, but to obtain salvation by our Lord Jesus Christ, who died for us that whether we wake or sleep, we shall live together with him."*

## II

Paul had come to Corinth in early autumn. Timothy had arrived from Thessalonica about a month later and, as soon as the letter was completed, returned there immediately. Though happy with the vigorous growth of the church at Corinth, Paul was concerned about Timothy and the situation at Thessalonica. His fears were confirmed; when the younger man returned a few months later, bringing word that many, who should have been working to spread the gospel there, were still so disturbed by fear that Christ would return to find them unworthy that they concerned themselves only with their own troubles. These naturally had infected others and the whole church was now in a turmoil.

Paul was tempted to go to Thessalonica himself and set the minds of the Christians there at rest, but Timothy warned that opposition to the apostle was so great among the Jews of the city that his own life would be in danger. He therefore decided to dictate a second letter to the Thessalonians and, since he could not advise them not to anticipate the coming of Christ, when he devoutly believed it was imminent himself, he searched for some explanation they could easily understand.

Delving deeply into Jewish history, Paul finally came upon a theme prevalent in the writings of the prophets during the period when the Jews had been oppressed by Antiochus Epiphanes. Simply stated, it was that, prior to the arrival of the Messiah, an Anti-Christ, a man of lawlessness and evil often called the Son of Perdition, would appear to be routed by the Messiah when he descended from heaven to set up the new Kingdom of God.

In the second letter to the church at Thessalonica, Paul made perfectly clear the sequence of events he expected to occur in preparation for the second coming of Christ. And when he dispatched Timothy to read this letter to the church there, he confidently expected it to set matters aright. There was no time for rest, however, for a new threat had arisen in Corinth itself.

Almost a year had passed since Paul's arrival in the Greek metropolis. After his decision not to attempt further conversion among his own people, the attempts upon his person and the interference with his teaching, which had characterized the early months of his ministry, had slowly decreased. He had even dared to hope that a reconciliation with the Jews of Corinth might be possible. For, however much he might be convinced that Christ had swept away the old Law, he was still a Jew and could not help being saddened when others refused to accept his teachings, depriving themselves, he was convinced, of eternal life.

All such hopes he might have had were suddenly destroyed, however, when Crispus visited him one evening, as he was resting in his quarters after a day of work in the tentmaker's establishment of Priscilla and Aquila. Paul and the former head of the synagogue at Corinth had become close friends and Crispus was a valuable ally. Today, however, his face was grave.

"Why are you troubled?" Paul asked. "The work here goes well."

"How long would it go well without its leader?"

"I have no thought of leaving."

"It's not your leaving I'm concerned about but your being taken away—forcibly. The talk in the marketplace is that Sosthenes and the rulers of the synagogue are getting ready to move against you."

"They tried it before."

"But not to embroil you with Rome."

"I have broken no Roman law."

"Perhaps not. But in Philippi, you were beaten on a charge

of inciting the populace to riot and the same charge could be brought against you here."

"Why now—after nearly a year?"

"Don't you know that a new governor is on his way to Corinth?"

Paul shrugged. "I'm too busy with the Lord's work to trouble myself about a change in politicians."

"This isn't merely a change. A new proconsul is coming for the whole district. It's not like Sosthenes to have left you alone as long as he has, so I'm sure he has been waiting for just this. All he needs to do now is to stir up a commotion while you're preaching in the marketplace and have you arrested for advocating a doctrine that incites religious controversy."

"Who is the new governor?" Paul asked.

"Julius Annaeus Gallio."

"Isn't he the brother of Seneca—the tutor of young Nero?"

"Yes. But I hear he's not strong-minded like his brother, so he may be easily moved by the arguments Sosthenes will bring against you."

Paul went to the window of the room that served him as a sleeping place; during his waking hours, he was either working at his trade or telling the story of a savior for the world. From the window he could see the star called Phoenikos hanging above the crest of the mountains far to the north. It no longer was a beacon leading him on, however, for he had long ago accepted the fact that the purpose for which Jesus had set him apart did not lie in peaceful areas like Bithynia—at least not for a long time.

"What are you going to do?" Crispus asked.

"What I've been doing—the Lord's work." Paul turned back to face his friend. "Would you have me do anything else?"

"I was thinking that you might leave Corinth for a few months—until Gallio has been in office long enough to become familiar with this part of the world and its problems. I know a few Roman officials; they can inform him that you are no troublemaker."

"But I am." Paul clapped Crispus upon the shoulder affectionately. "I trouble souls and that's the worst kind."

"A few months away from Corinth would be a small price to pay for being able to keep on troubling them," Crispus insisted, but Paul shook his head.

"I shall not say to you, *'Get thee behind me Satan'* as Jesus once said when Peter wished to keep him from going to Jerusalem and the cross," he told Crispus. "I left Philippi because I was not yet sure of my own course, but I intend to stay in Corinth. When Sosthenes accuses me of sedition, I shall make a defense before Gallio."

"If they let you."

"I am a Roman citizen by birth, with the right to be heard by Caesar himself, if I demand it. Gallio is an educated man and a philosopher. Who knows? Perhaps through him I shall be able to end for all time the false charges against Christians of being disloyal to Rome."

III

The new proconsul arrived in Corinth about three weeks before the end of the summer. A few days later, Sosthenes and other leaders of the Jewish synagogue had Paul seized, while he was preaching in the marketplace.

Upon the arrival of a new governor in a city or province, it was customary for court to be held publicly in order that the people might be impressed with his dispensation of justice. For this purpose, the magisterial chair, symbol of Roman justice and imperial power, was carried from place to place in the public squares of the city, where cases were heard and judged publicly.

Paul's first impression of the man sitting upon the rostrum, the elevated platform used in public hearings, was not particularly favorable. Gallio was not a large man and seemed almost dwarfed by the rich purple robe he wore over his toga. Ranged on either side of him were the lictors, bearing their *fasces*, the universal emblem of Roman civil authority. Each was composed of a long-handled battleax with a bundle of staves lashed about it—the staves symbolizing the punishment meted out for lesser offenses, while the ax warned wrongdoers that Rome exercised the power of death over its citizens.

A crowd had filled the agora as soon as word came that the new governor was holding court there. It spilled out into the streets around the square and, watching the people as he was marched under guard through the press of the crowd, Paul saw that by far the major part of them were Greeks. Some, members of the thriving Christian Church established at Corinth, called out words of encouragement to him as he passed. Nor did there seem to be much sympathy with his accusers, for Jews were not particularly well liked in Corinth. Paul knew from bitter experience that he could not expect help from outside sources, however. The decision of the governor was final and, should the verdict go against him, the temper of the crowd could just as quickly turn as it now seemed to favor him.

"Who accuses this man?" Gallio demanded, when Paul's guards came to a stop before the rostrum.

A clerk standing behind the proconsul, lifted a scroll and began to read sonorously:

*"Sosthenes, of the synagogue of Jews in this city, speaks this day against Paul, lately of Tarsus, claiming that he leads people to worship the God of the Jews in a manner which violates their own Law."*

Paul was startled by the narrowness of the charge; he had expected his enemies to accuse him of treason on the grounds that he preached allegience to a ruler other than Rome. Instead, the accusation was limited to a matter of religious law, over which Roman justice ordinarily exercised no more than nominal control.

"Let Sosthenes come forward, and explain the charges against this man," Gallio ordered.

A plump Jew, wearing the fringed robe of a Pharisee, stepped into the open space, and bowed low before the governor.

"He teaches that the Law of the Jewish people concerning diet and circumcision should be put aside."

"Have other sects among the Jews given up this law?"

"Some no longer follow the rules of clean and unclean foods," Sosthenes admitted. "But all Jews must be circumcised."

"Would you force all Gentiles to be circumcised, too?" Gallio demanded sarcastically.

A wave of laughter went through the crowd and seeing that he was losing the case, Sosthenes blurted out: "Paul also claims that Jesus of Nazareth is the promised Messiah of the Jewish people."

"Is this the Messiah promised to the Jews in your ancient writings?" Gallio inquired.

"Yes, my lord governor."

"What rules determine when he shall come? Or who he shall be?"

"Our ancient writings predict it, noble Gallio," said Sosthenes. "But Paul claims that one Jesus of Nazareth was the Messiah."

"And you say that he was not?"

"The Sanhedrin at Jerusalem has so ruled," Sosthenes said promptly and Paul suddenly realized that Gallio was smarter than he'd thought. Deftly, but thoroughly, the proconsul had led Sosthenes into a trap, then closed it upon him.

"Since Jesus of Nazareth has officially been declared by your own court not to be the Messiah, no Roman law has been broken," Gallio announced. "The accused merely states his own beliefs, which you deny. There may be a quarrel between you, but none with the authority of Rome."

"But he preaches that the Nazarene will return as king—"

"Has he returned? Does Paul claim that he lives now on earth?"

"No, my lord."

"Then you have no case." Gallio struck the arm of his chair with the jeweled miniature of the fasces he carried as a token of his office. "If you had charged this man Paul with some misdemeanor or some rascality, I would have listened to you. But since it is a question about words and the meaning of your own law, you must see to that yourselves. I refuse to act as a judge in these matters. The prisoner may go free and henceforth let no man accuse him unjustly of crimes he has not done."

278

Rising from his chair, Gallio left the rostrum, ending the hearing. Nor did he pay any attention when the crowd, filled with glee at the discomforture of Sosthenes and those who had supported him, seized the Jewish leader and began beating him. With a few words, a pagan judge had decreed that the Christian Church was a sect within the Jewish faith. And since the right to worship their God was granted to Jews by Roman law, that same right had now been extended to Christians everywhere.

## IV

With the coming of spring, Paul decided to visit Jerusalem and Antioch in order to be certain that the other apostles fully understood the significance of Gallio's decision. Using the text of the decision as a basis of argument, he also hoped to negotiate an agreement with the temple authorities in Jerusalem whereby Christians would be treated by them as a sect within that faith, very much as were the extremely ascetic Essenes with their monastic communities in the hills overlooking the Dead Sea, or the Therapeutae, who lived just outside Alexandria. For such an attempt at conciliation, no season could be more appropriate than the Passover and, with the resumption of ocean shipping, he took passage for the Holy City.

It was a warm spring day when Paul came again to Jerusalem. Flowers were blooming in protected pockets among the hills and the city was beginning to fill with pilgrims for the most holy of Jewish traditional feasts. He did not go immediately to either the Synagogue of the Nazarenes—as the Christian Church in the Holy City was still called—or to the temple. Instead, he made his way to the tentmaker's shop where he had celebrated his first Passover in Jerusalem with Miriam and Jepthah.

The shop was considerably larger, its size having been almost doubled by knocking out the wall of an adjoining building. The hum of spindles twisting the tough cilicium into thread; the clack-clack of the shuttles, weaving the dark fabric from which tents were cut; the slap of awls against leather palms—none of this had been changed.

Jepthah was not in sight but a slender youth, whom Paul judged to be about twenty, came forward to greet him, just as Paul remembered greeting Barnabas many years ago in his father's shop at Tarsus. The boy was so much like Paul's own father, Joachim, that he knew at once it was Miriam's son—and his nephew.

"Your mother?" he asked. "Is she—?"

"Mother is in the house back of the shop, sir."

"Where is your father?"

"In Petra, selling a caravan load of tents. He should be back tomorrow."

Paul drew a breath of relief. More than anything else, he wished to avoid any unpleasantness with his brother-in-law.

"I am Jared ben Jepthah, his son," said the boy. "May I help you, sir?"

"I am your Uncle Paul."

The boy frowned. "I once had an uncle named Saul—but he became a Christian. My father will not let his name be spoken in our house."

"Saul was my Jewish name. I have been living in Greek lands, so I use the Greek name of Paul instead."

"Mother speaks of you sometimes." The boy's eyes were bright with interest now. "But Father—"

"Jepthah and I never did get along very well, Jared. Please take me to your mother."

Paul spent a pleasant afternoon with his sister and his nephew, who had also chosen to follow the trade of tentmaker. But Miriam was obviously worried lest Jepthah return early, so he did not ask for lodging. Instead he found a place at an inn and the next morning sought out James ben Joseph at the Synagogue of the Nazarenes—a dingy building that gave the impression of profound poverty.

The kinsman of the Lord had just come from the temple, where he went daily to pray. His robe was worn through in many places and he was even thinner than when Paul had seen him last. His greeting to Paul was reserved, as usual, but he showed no real unfriendliness, listening closely to the apostle's account of his experiences since the Council of Jerusalem, the work in Macedonia and Achaia, and the swift rise of the church at Corinth to become an important bastion of the Christian faith.

"The church at Rome has been growing, too," said James. "Peter hopes to go there soon."

"I thought there was persecution in Rome. Two friends of mine, Priscilla and Aquila, were forced to flee to Corinth because of it."

"The Jewish synagogues in Rome tried to poison the mind of the Emperor against us," James explained. "But the trouble lasted only a little while."

"That is good news indeed," said Paul. "Peter should be able to improve the lot of the Christians there even more, when he tells about the decision of Gallio."

"Gallio?"

"I told you about it just now." Paul could hardly believe the man who had headed the congregation at Jerusalem almost since the crucifixion of Jesus didn't realize the significance of his experience at Corinth.

"Oh yes," said James. "I remember now."

"Then you agree that news of the Gallio decision should be brought to the attention of the temple authorities here?"

"I—I'm not sure."

"But it establishes us as part of the Jewish faith—like the Essenes or the Therapeutae. It means that the temple authorities and the synagogues in other cities no longer have any grounds to charge us with treason, as they tried to do with me at Philippi. If they make such charges now they will be condemning themselves."

"No charge of treason has been made against us in Jerusalem."

"James ben Zebedee was beheaded by Herod Agrippa and Simon Peter was arrested on the same grounds," Saul reminded him a little tartly.

"Peter escaped and God struck down Herod for his sins," said James. "Since then the temple authorities have made no move against us."

"Only because the church here is so small and feeble that they don't consider it worth the trouble." Paul was beginning to be exasperated by the older man's passiveness.

"It is true that we are poor," James admitted. "But as long as we obey the Law, the temple authorities do not trouble us."

"They still should be told of Gallio's ruling. With that to support us, Christians need never fear the power of the Sanhedrin again. Will you make it known to the High Priest—or shall I?"

"Leave it to me," said James. "I will counsel with the elders here and decide best how it shall be done."

"But the priestly authorities may not accept the decision without my sworn testimony to it."

"They will accept whatever I tell them as the truth." James changed the subject. "Where are you going from here?"

"To Antioch, to prepare for a mission in Ephesus."

"Peter will be sorry he missed you." Once again—as on a previous occasion—Paul felt that the older man was anxious to have him out of Jerusalem. "May God prosper you and your work, Brother Saul."

Standing outside the building and looking at the dingy structure, Paul found it hard to remember that the Synagogue of the Nazarenes had once been a scene of enthusiastic dedication. Stephen had been the firebrand then and Simon Peter the solid rock of strength from which all had drawn sustenance. Even Saul of Tarsus had not been able to destroy that congregation, he recalled. Instead, his zeal for persecuting them had scattered abroad all zealous men and women who had sowed the seeds of the Christian faith even in Rome itself.

Paul's reverie was broken by a harsh but familiar voice behind him and he turned to see the angry face of his brother-in-law.

"Why did you come to the shop yesterday?" Jepthah demanded.

"I wanted to see Miriam and Jared."

"Liar! You signed the shop away once. Now you want to get it back."

"I want nothing of yours, Jepthah—except your soul for Christ."

"Jesus of Nazareth was a traitor executed by Rome," Jepthah snapped.

"He's the Messiah promised by the prophets." Paul deliberately held his temper in check.

"Do you deny that you teach others to pervert the Law? And that you would corrupt me and my family with your false doctrines?"

"I can show all of you the way to save your souls and give you the gift of eternal life—if you will only listen."

"To your blasphemy against the Law?" Had he been less concerned for Jepthah's soul—Paul would have suspected a purpose in the continual harping upon the Law. But the brief period he'd spent with Jared and Miriam the day before had shown him that the boy had much promise and he was hoping for some sort of a reconciliation.

"The Law was washed away by the blood of Christ shed on the cross," he explained patiently. "That blood can save—"

"Blasphemer!" Jepthah shouted. "You have condemned yourself before witnesses."

Two men emerged from behind a low wall, where they had obviously been hiding. Jepthah's words had been a signal. "You heard him blaspheme, didn't you?" he demanded.

"We heard," the two answered in chorus.

"Only two witnesses are required," said Jepthah. "You have condemned enough men yourself to know that."

"Would you have me stoned because you think I may demand an accounting from you and take some of your paltry wealth?"

"You will never get it! I am a witness, too, and I shall cast the first stone at your execution for blasphemy."

"Neither Herod nor Pontius Pilate rules here any more." Paul's anger at last broke through his control. "The Sanhedrin cannot put me to death without the approval of the Procurator and I am a Roman citizen, so I can still appeal to Rome. Bring charges against me, if you will, Jepthah. But when the Procurator refuses to condemn me on a religious matter, the court will have you and these others seized for bearing false witness.

"Begone!" His voice lashed the other two like a scourge. "Else I shall accuse you myself of bearing false witness and seeking to take my life."

The two men broke and ran. As for Jepthah, the spurious

indignation he had assumed was replaced by the sickly pallor of fear. "You wouldn't destroy your sister's husband and the father of your own nephew," he mumbled.

"Go back to your shop and your precious belongings, Jepthah." Paul felt no anger any more, only pity for the man whose greed so dominated his life. "You never had anything to fear from me before and you have nothing now."

Depressed by James' failure to realize the significance of the Gallio decision and by his encounter with Jepthah, Paul decided not to remain in Jerusalem for the Passover. Taking the road that led to the seacoast, he found passage at Joppa on one of the coastal vessels that went from port to port in this area and arrived in Antioch a few days later, receiving a warm welcome from the congregation he considered his own children.

v

The church at Antioch was now easily the largest and most influential Christian community in the world, although at least one of the churches established by Paul, that at Corinth, was pressing it in the race for size. At Antioch, the Apostle to the Gentiles received two pieces of bad news, the first when Mark arrived from a tour of the Syrian churches.

Mark, who had grown into a tall young man since Paul had last seen him, greeted the apostle with some reserve. But Paul was on a mission of reconciliation and, despite his failure in Jerusalem, was determined that no quarrel should mar his stay in Antioch. Greeting Mark warmly, he asked about Simon Peter.

"The Lord continues to favor him," said Mark. "He is visiting the churches in northern Judea and in Syro-Phoenicia."

"Then he didn't go into Galatia—as he had planned?"

"Peter never intended to visit Galatia. And he knew nothing about the plans of the Judaizers who came here from Jerusalem intending to go there."

"Then I was wrong, when I denounced him for sitting with

those who came from James." Merely confessing his error took a load of guilt off Paul's soul.

"Like Jesus, Peter tries to love and understand everyone," said Mark. "When he sat with those from Jerusalem that night during the supper, he was only trying to make them feel at home."

"When did he tell you this?"

"After you left on your journey. Peter stayed away from Antioch for a while; he thought there would be less discord in the church if he left. When he came back, he preached a sermon telling again how he saw the vision at Joppa and was the first to go to the Gentiles at Caesarea."

"Where can I find him and ask his forgiveness?" Paul asked.

"He should be in Antioch in a few months. There has been trouble in Rome and the churches there have asked him to come and strengthen them with his presence. He will sail from Antioch—if he goes."

"Where is Barnabas?"

"He and I worked in Cyprus for almost a year. Later he went to Alexandria in Egypt. When I last heard from him about a month ago, he said the work there was going well."

"It should," said Paul. "The teachings of Philo have already broadened the Jewish faith in Egypt. And you, Mark?" he added. "What are you going to do?"

"If Peter goes to Rome, I may go with him."

"There is room for you in my work."

"But you—"

"Since I left Antioch, I have felt the staves of lictors on my back and faced a Roman proconsul on a charge against my life," said Paul. "I hope those experiences have taught me to be wiser; they have certainly made me more tolerant of others."

Paul's second piece of bad news was even more disturbing than the first. It came with the arrival of Timothy hurriedly from Lystra.

"The churches of Galatia are in an uproar," Timothy reported. "I lost no time in coming here to tell you."

"But they were strong when I visited them two years ago," said Paul.

"Judaizers from Jerusalem spent last winter in Galatia, undermining our work there."

"Was Peter with them?"

"I heard no mention of him. This group claimed the authority of James and taught that all who acknowledge Jesus must be circumcised and obey Mosaic Law."

"But the Galatians knew of the letter from James. It was read in the churches by Silas."

"The men from Jerusalem arrived after we went on to Mysia," Timothy explained. "They claimed that James and the other apostles at Jerusalem gave them new instructions after the council."

"James mentioned nothing of this to me. I talked to him only a few weeks ago."

"They also attacked your doctrine of justification by faith and claimed you were not called by the Lord, but were commissioned by the other apostles. They said that, since you never saw Jesus, you are of a lower authority than the others."

Two years ago, Paul would have been so angry at the charges that he would have left for Galatia at once. But as he had told Mark, the years had tempered the metal of his zeal with the judgment that came from knowing many people in many countries and coping with the manifold problems that had arisen during his missionary journeys. He did not, however, underestimate the gravity of the news Timothy had brought, knowing from bitter experience that nothing could tear a church apart so quickly as a doctrinal dispute.

"What are you going to do?" Timothy asked.

"Preparations for the mission at Ephesus in the autumn are too far along for me to stop them now," said Paul. "I shall send a letter to the Galatians by your hands, showing them their error and warning them against the blandishments of false prophets."

"The Thessalonians didn't listen," Timothy reminded him.

"That was due to a misunderstanding. When I explained to them in my second letter that the coming of the Son of Perdition must precede the parousia of the Lord, they mended their ways. Besides, I shall visit the Galatian churches myself on the way to Ephesus in the autumn."

The letter Paul began to dictate on the morning after Timothy's arrival in Antioch was an impassioned document. In it the apostle poured out his indignation and his hurt at the failure of his beloved Galatians to cling steadfastly to his teachings, stating in words so simple that no one could fail to understand, not only the essence of his doctrine but the authority given him to preach it:

*I certify to you brethren that the gospel I preach is not from man, for I neither received it from man nor was I taught it, but achieved it by the revelation of Jesus Christ.*

*The life I now live in the flesh I live by the faith of the Son of God who loved me and gave himself for me.*

*No man is justified by the Law in the sight of God; he is justified only by faith.*

## VI

It was late summer before Paul was ready to embark upon his next journey. Timothy and Silas were still in Galatia, so he took with him Titus, the Antiochian who had journeyed to Jerusalem with him years before at the time of the first council there. From Antioch, the travelers followed the familiar route by way of the Syrian and Cilician Gates into the upland districts of Galatia, where the apostle visited the churches and preached again the doctrine Timothy had brought them in his letter. Accompanied by Titus and Timothy, Paul reached Ephesus in early winter. Priscilla and Aquila, his former employers at Corinth, had opened a tentmaking shop there so Paul once again took up his trade. Somewhat later, the group was increased by the arrival of Luke from Troas.

The leading city in the large province of Asia, Ephesus owed much of its commercial success to its favorable location near the mouth of the River Cayster. Its greatest single attraction, however, was the great temple of the Ephesian Diana, or Artemis, lying at the head of the harbor. Considered to be one of the seven wonders of the world, two hundred years had gone into the building of this magnificent structure. The walls and floor were made of marble quarried from the surrounding mountainsides. Its length of more than four hundred and twenty-five feet and its width of two hundred and twenty-five made it one of the largest structures outside of Rome itself. The hundred and twenty-seven columns towering more than sixty feet above the marble floor, the doors of cypress, the roof of cedar, and the staircase that was said to be formed from the wood of a single vine, cut upon the island of Cyprus, easily established it as one of the most magnificent.

No little of the prosperity of Ephesus came from the desire of travelers and worshipers visiting the temple to carry home small images of Diana in silver. As a result, the largest single group of workmen in the city was the guild of silversmiths, their main product being the small images that were sold everywhere. As would have been expected in a sprawling pagan city, Ephesus also abounded with musicians, mountebanks, fortune tellers and would-be sorcerers. The service of the goddess, whose idol occupied the central part of the great temple, required many hundreds of priests, priestesses, and temple prostitutes, plus the movement of all kind of goods through the port in order to supply all the varied needs of the city. Altogether, then, it was a fertile field to which Paul had come, a teeming crossroads where he could appeal to people of many origins and beliefs.

As in most cities of this area, the artisans and tradesmen of Ephesus customarily worked during the morning hours and closed their establishments in the middle of the day, opening them again in the latter part of the afternoon and continuing their activities into the evening. Shrewdly taking advantage of the noonday hours when the streets were thronging with people, Paul rented a hall in the very heart of the city from a teacher named Tyrannus.

The rhetorician used the hall during the mornings and late afternoon hours for the conduct of classes, leaving it free for Paul, who spoke there daily to those resting between the morning and evening work periods or to travelers unable to enter the closed shops. And since the Ephesians, like the Athenians, were always seeking new things and new experiences, the hall of Tyrannus soon became a popular center where Paul and his helpers preached some of their most eloquent sermons.

Paul's impassioned letter to the Galatians setting forth his doctrine of justification by faith in Jesus Christ alone, plus his visit to the churches, had largely settled the unrest in that area, but trouble soon broke out again in the great new church at Corinth. This time, the Judaizers who, as usual, were the culprits, changed their tactics, some claiming to have come from Peter with one doctrine, while others claimed the authority of James for another. Like the Galatians, the Christians of Corinth were soon torn by secularism and the growth of the church there was seriously threatened.

Unwilling to leave Ephesus, where crowds flocked daily to the hall of Tyrannus to hear him speak, Paul wrote a brief letter to the Corinthians exhorting them to stay joined together under the banner of salvation through Christ he had given them. The letter failed to turn the Corinthians away from their divisive ways, however, and word soon came that many Christians were succumbing to the licentiousness which had made the name of the city a by-word in the eastern part of the Roman Empire. During the autumn of his second year at Ephesus, Paul crossed over to Corinth and spent a brief period there.

Conditions turned out to be even worse than he had been told and, although he was forced to return to Ephesus after only a brief visit, he shortly began to compose another letter to the wayward Corinthians. Like all of his writings, it was both eloquent, beautifully couched, and simple:

*When I came to you brethren, I did not come with excellency of speech or wisdom, declaring to you the testimony of God. For I am determined not to know anything except Jesus Christ and him crucified. I was with you in weakness and fear and in much trembling, for my speech and my preaching was not with enticing words of man's wisdom, but in demonstration of the spirit, in order that your faith should not stand in the wisdom of men but in the power of God.*

The now familiar attacks upon his own status as an apostle, Paul demolished with these words:

*Am I not an apostle? Am I not free? Have I not seen Jesus Christ our Lord? Are you not my work in the Lord? If I am not an apostle to others, yet doubtless I am to you, for you are the seal of my apostleship in the Lord.*

Finally the apostle put into perhaps the most eloquent words ever written or spoken the truth that had brought Christ to the cross, the love that made him a sacrifice for the sins of men:

*Though I speak with the tongues of men and of angels and have not love, I am become as sounding brass or a tinkling cymbal. Though I have the gift of prophecy and understand all mysteries and all knowledge, and though I have all faith so that I could move mountains, yet have not love, I am nothing. Though I bestow all my goods to feed the poor and give my body to be burned, and have not love, it profits me nothing.*

*Love suffers long and is kind. Love does not envy. Love does not vaunt itself and is not puffed up. Love does not behave itself unseemingly, it does not seek its own, it is not easily provoked, it thinks no evil. It does not rejoice in iniquity but rejoices in truth. It bears all things, believes all things, hopes all things, endures all things. Love never fails, although, if there are prophecies they shall fail, if there are tongues, they shall cease, and if there is knowledge it shall vanish away. For we know in part and we prophesy in part, but when that which is perfect has come, that which is in part shall be done away.*

*When I was a child, I spake as a child, I understood as a child, I thought as a child. But when I became a man I put away childish things. Now we see through a glass darkly, but then we will see face to face. Now I know in part, but then I shall know, even as I also am known. Now abides faith, hope, and love, these three. But the greatest of these is love.*

Although Paul had vowed after his experience at Athens, not to adapt his gospel to what he thought to be the understanding of the people to whom he was writing, he frequently used examples from the experiences of those living in these areas. One of these had to do with slavery.

According to Greek custom, a slave who considered himself badly treated could seek refuge in certain temples designated as places of refuge, just as certain Israelite cities in the days of the Judges had been labeled Cities of Refuge. There, the slave could be sold to the god represented by the temple and the price gained from the sale paid to his master, after which the slave was free. It was a measure of Paul's instinctive understanding of the people in this area that he was able to use this custom to explain one of the tenets of the Christian doctrine to which he often referred, namely that the slavery one voluntarily entered into with Christ was the highest and most sacred form of freedom.

"One who was a slave when he was called in the Lord is the Lord's freedman," he wrote to the Corinthians later in a third letter. "Similarly, one who was free when he was called is the slave of Christ."

Nor did Paul hesitate to use, in both preaching and in letters his knowledge of the Greek mystery faiths, many of which also promised immortality to the believer and were practiced with ritual ceremonies. Rehearsing the story of the nation of Israel, to whom Christ had come as the Messiah, he reminded his listeners that the Children of Israel had always had their own sacraments, their own sacred meals and litany, even in the wilderness when they were escaping from Egypt. He likened the heavenly bread called manna and the water from the Rock of Moses to the sacramental meals and drinking of wine with which the Greeks of Macedonia and Achaia were already familiar as part of the mystery faiths. Thus, as still another measure of his inspired greatness, Paul was able to take pagan symbols and use them to prove the truth of Christ, an ability that no doubt accounted for much of his appeal to the Grecian mind.

To the troublesome question of the resurrection of the human body, a subject of violent debate in the Corinthian church, as well as in many others, Paul gave a very simple explanation, when he wrote:

*If there is an animal body, there is also a spiritual one. What comes first, however, is not the spiritual but the animal. The first human was a man formed of the dust of the ground; the second is a man from heaven. What the man formed of the dust was, that also are the men formed of the dust. And what the heavenly man is, this also are the heavenly men. As we wore the image of the man formed of the dust, we shall also wear the image of the heavenly man.*

## VII

Two years and part of a third had passed since Paul's arrival in Ephesus, when trouble suddenly erupted there. Busy every morning earning his livelihood as a tentmaker, teaching in the lecture hall of Tyrannus each afternoon to the crowds that gathered there, dictating letters to the Corinthians and others during the evenings and holding his usual services on the Sabbath, the apostle had literally been doing the work of three men and making converts by the thousands.

Paul's presence in Ephesus probably would not have caused discord, however, had it not interfered directly with the business of the most prosperous and important element in the city, the Guild of Silversmiths who did a thriving business manufacturing small images for sale to pilgrims. Like the Jewish faith from which it sprang, Christianity abhorred idols in any form and Paul had denounced the trade in pagan images more than once. When the growth of the church at Ephesus and the influence of Paul's teachings caused a falling off in the lucrative business of the silversmiths, matters suddenly came to a boil.

Paul was measuring a suit of sails at the waterfront, when the controversy erupted, and heard of it first when he returned to the lecture hall. By that time a rabble stirred up by a silversmith named Demetrius, who headed the guild, had ransacked the hall, expecting to find him there. Foiled in that attempt, the mob had seized two Macedonian converts named Gaius and Aristarchus, dragging them to the great theater where a crowd had already gathered to enjoy whatever excitement the situation might bring. Paul was preparing to go to the theater to try and rescue Gaius and Aristarchus, when Timothy arrived, breathless from having run all the way to the shop.

"The silversmiths were about to beat Gaius and Aristarchus to death, when Aristides, the chief magistrate, intervened," Timothy reported. "He told Demetrius that, if they had any charges to make, it should be before the courts, lest the Roman troops be called out to put down the riot."

"Then our brethren have been released?"

"Yes. They're on the way here now."

Gaius and Aristarchus were not too much the worse for their experience, when they reached the hall, although their clothes had been torn by the mob and one had a cut over his eye. But though Demetrius and the silversmiths had been foiled at the moment, no one there had any illusion that the matter was ended.

"Why don't you visit Corinth or Philippi until this dies down?" Timothy suggested to Paul. "The other churches are always asking when you will come again."

"That may be a wise course, Paul." Aquila agreed and the others added their arguments, until the apostle finally agreed to consider the idea and decide the next day. The matter was settled shortly before midnight, when a band of ruffians attacked Aquila's house, almost burning it to the ground before they were driven off by the timely arrival of a detail of Roman soldiers on patrol in the area. The knowledge that he had brought danger to those he loved overweighed Paul's natural reluctance to be driven from Ephesus by force.

"I shall go to Troas," he told Aquila. "Luke will let me stay with him until I decide what to do next."

## VIII

Paul had loved Troas since he had first come there on his second journey, when the fever had forced him to turn away from Bithynia and seek help from Luke. Resting in Luke's comfortable home, preaching in the agora of Troas, after the winter began to wane somewhat and the warm spring sun returned, he was at peace. More important, he had time to think about both the past and the future and crystallize a resolve which, until the sudden trouble at Ephesus, had been little more than a vague longing.

"What do you know about Gaul and Spain?" he asked Luke one evening as the two of them were finishing the evening meal.

"Not very much," Luke admitted. "When I was at Antioch-in-Pisidia long ago serving with the army, some of the officers had been with the Gallic legions and spoke of that region. They said it is a fertile land with a warm climate much of the time, particularly in the south."

"What about the people?"

"The territory around Antioch-in-Pisidia was settled long ago by tribes that came from Gaul," Luke reminded him. "The people should be very much like those in Galatia."

"I've always had a warm spot in my heart for the Galatians."

"And some scars on your body as a reminder of their love for you."

"Those were gained at the hands of Jews. The real Galatians were very kind to me and I found Timothy there."

"He's like a son to you, isn't he?"

"As much as if he were my own flesh."

"Why have you never married?" Luke asked.

"My work doesn't allow it."

"Peter was married—and others of the apostles. Aquila and Priscilla are married, yet no one could serve the Lord more faithfully than they do."

"I resolved never to marry, when I was forced to escape from Damascus and realized that what happened there was a pattern of what I could expect for the remainder of my life," said

Paul. "In Ephesus, I worked far after dark every night. That is certainly no life for a woman."

"You could settle down now. The churches in this area would welcome you as a bishop, or presbyter, over all of them."

"As the slave of Christ, I can only do his will," said Paul. "I don't think that is to be my fate."

"What if the Lord sends you back to Ephesus?"

"I would go willingly, but I'm sure my future course lies elsewhere. If I return to Ephesus, Demetrius, and the silversmith's guild will only make trouble for all who work with me. With me away, they may leave our friends there alone."

"Did you ever think it strange that you seem destined to found churches and then be driven from them by those who oppose you?"

"That is my particular burden," said Paul. "And still another reason why I should never marry."

"Are you thinking of going to Gaul?"

"Yes—after Rome."

"Rome?" Luke looked startled. "When did you decide that?"

"I haven't—yet."

"You couldn't be any more certain that your doctrines would be received in Rome than they were in Athens. The two cities are very much alike, both decadent and dissolute."

"I've tried to analyze what happened to Athens," said Paul. "When I adapted my preaching to what I considered to be the interests of the people and the philosophers, I failed to convince them. In Rome, I would preach only Christ and him crucified, as I have done here in Asia and in Macedonia."

"The Romans have been driving Jews out, not letting them in," Luke warned.

"Aquila and Priscilla heard from friends in Rome before I left Ephesus. Jews are no longer being persecuted there."

"Or Christians?"

"Under Roman law Christians are a part of the Jewish faith and the right of Jews to worship without restriction is guaranteed by it."

"I seem to remember that the first Christian congregations in Rome were established by people you drove out of Jerusalem during the persecution," Luke reminded him. "Do you think they will welcome you?"

"When the Lord called me, Saul of Tarsus died and a new man was born in Christ. Just as when Jesus died on the cross, the old Law died with him and salvation through faith came into the world."

"And you plan to preach that doctrine in Rome?"

"I shall preach it wherever I go, but I plan to stay in Rome only a little while. My work in the West will probably lie in Gaul, Spain—or even in Britain."

"When are you going?" Luke knew Paul well enough by now not to argue further with him.

"In the summer—if all goes well. I must pay a visit first to the churches in Macedonia and Achaia."

At Corinth early in the new year, Paul received news of a severe famine threatening the already destitute members of the church at Jerusalem with starvation. More than a year earlier, he had asked the churches in Galatia, Asia, Macedonia, and Achaia to put aside a fund for the relief of the poverty-stricken Mother Church. With news that this relief was now badly needed, he decided to take the money collected by the churches to Jerusalem himself, before making preparations for his journey westward.

He had spent a leisurely winter, most of it at Corinth, and before leaving the city for Jerusalem, composed a letter to the Roman churches. Dispatched by a woman of Cenchrae named Phebe, who was going to Rome, it was designed to prepare those who might be hostile to him for his coming, and the differences they would find between his gospel and that which they had been taught by those who had fled from Jerusalem at the time of Paul's own persecution.

Leaving Corinth just as spring was beginning—almost four years after he had set out from Antioch on his third journey—Paul spent a week at Troas with Luke before embarking for Miletus, a seaport city about thirty miles from Ephesus. With the apostle on the journey was Trophimus, a Greek convert who acted as a secretary to him during Timothy's increasingly frequent absences as Paul's representative to the churches in Asia.

At Miletus, Paul met with the elders of the Ephesian church

who came there to bring a contribution for the relief of Jerusalem. To them he gave a stirring farewell address, warning of the tribulations that might lie before him on the new venture, with the words: "Now I go bound in the Spirit to Jerusalem, not knowing the things that shall befall me there, except that the Holy Spirit warns me that in every city, bonds and afflictions await me. None of these things move me, neither do I count my life dear to myself, if only I may finish with joy the ministry I have received from the Lord Jesus, to testify to the gospel of the grace of God."

After taking leave of the elders at Miletus, Paul and Trophimus sailed by way of Rhodes, Patara, and Tyre to Ptolemais, known in ancient times as Acca. Disembarking there, they journeyed overland past the promontory of Mount Carmel to Caesarea, lodging there in the home of Philip, an early leader of the church.

They had made good time on the journey and Paul yielded to Philip's entreaty that he speak to the flourishing Christian congregation of Caesarea at the Sabbath service telling them of his success in Asia, Macedonia, and Greece. But before he could ascend the steps leading to the pulpit, a strange figure appeared, striding down the aisle of the building and coming to a stop before the apostle. Tall, almost frail, the newcomer's hair and beard were long and uncombed, characterizing him as a Nazarite, one of a sect of traveling holy men or prophets who went about the countryside preaching.

"That is Agabus." Philip, who was sitting with Paul, spoke in a low voice. "Some regard him as a prophet—or at least a soothsayer. I will lead him to a seat."

"No." Paul was staring at the old prophet with a strange look in his eyes, almost as if he had been expecting to see Agabus. "Let him speak if he wishes."

"Much of the time what he says has no meaning," Philip warned.

"This time I think it will."

Without speaking, Agabus moved close to Paul and reached out to loosen the leather belt with which the apostle's robe was bound at the waist. Taking the belt in his hands, Agabus squatted down and carried it around beneath his ankles and up over his hands, buckling it into place with surprising agility for one so old and frail. Bound there upon the floor of the building, he looked up at Paul, who had been so startled by the old prophet's action that he had not attempted to take hold of the belt.

"Thus says the Holy Spirit." High pitched and reedy with age, Agabus' voice sounded loud in the silence filling the room. "So shall the Jews at Jerusalem bind the man who owns this girdle and deliver him into the hands of the Gentiles."

A murmur of indignation swept the congregation and several people started to remove the old prophet, who still squatted on the floor with his wrists and ankles secured by the leather belt. Paul forestalled them, however, by reaching down to loosen the buckle of the belt, removing it from around the old man's wrists and ankles and securing it about his waist once more. This done, he lifted Agabus to his feet and led him to an empty seat, nodding at the same time to Philip to begin the service.

"The Lord has sent you a warning by Agabus," Philip said when the service was over. "You must not go up to Jerusalem."

"If the Lord wants me to avoid Jerusalem, he will speak to me himself—not through some soothsayer."

"This could be a sign."

"Everywhere I go, people warn me that I shall be cast into prison, beaten—or even crucified. If I obeyed those warnings, Philip, I would get nowhere."

"But some of the old man's prophecies have come true."

"If it's the Lord's will that I not go to Jerusalem, I shall know it soon. Now stop worrying and let's go to your house. I smelled a savory dish cooking, when we left there this morning. It should be ready by the time we get back."

IX

A Christian from Jerusalem named Mnason had been in Caesarea and had attended the service where Agabus made his dramatic and chilling prophecy. He accompanied Paul, Trophimus, and several others to Jerusalem and insisted that they stay at his house. Paul had decided against attempting to see Miriam and her family, knowing his presence would only anger Jepthah, so he accepted Mnason's offer. Besides, he wished for this visit to be a quiet one, a farewell, so to speak, to the Holy City before leaving for Rome on the way to Gaul and Spain.

The morning after his arrival, he turned over the collection he had brought to James. The Jerusalem congregation was indeed near starvation and, perhaps because one could hardly avoid welcoming the bearer of such rich gifts, the kinsman of the Lord seemed more affable than on other occasions. He and the apostles and elders listened attentively while Paul told of the success in Ephesus and other cities, the difficulties of the great church at Corinth, and his attempt to relieve them, both with letters and by going there to reason with the dissenting parties, as he had done in Galatia.

"You have seen how many thousands of Jews have believed, Brother Saul," James said, when he finished the account. "They are all zealous concerning the Law, but we have been told that you teach Jews who live among the Gentiles to forsake Moses, telling them that they need not circumcise their children or follow the customs of our forefathers. They will certainly hear that you are in Jerusalem, so what shall we do?"

"I shall leave immediately, if it is your wish," said Paul.

"No," said James. "We must convince Jews everywhere that you have no wish to destroy the Law."

"Jesus said: *'Do not think that I have come to destroy the Law or the Prophets. I have not come to destroy but to fulfill.'* I have never taught anything else but this—as far as the Jews are concerned."

"Nevertheless, many here in Jerusalem believe you are trying to destroy the Law," James insisted. "Now, I think we may have a way to reassure them."

"You can depend upon me to do whatever I can."

"Four of our men have taken a vow of purity and let their hair grow," James told him. "Go with them, purify yourself, and pay for their gifts to the temple, so their heads may be shorn and the vow fulfilled. In that way everyone will know you really walk in orderly ways and keep the Law."

"I will begin the period of purification tomorrow," Paul promised.

"You have made a wise decision," James assured him. "By doing this and proving you are still a devout Jew, you will do much to reassure our brothers in Rome and insure a welcome from them."

"What are these rites of purification?" Trophimus asked as they were walking back to the home of Mnason. Being a Greek, he was not familiar with Jewish customs.

"It's an old ritual from the days when men could approach God only through the Law," Paul explained. "Jews who wish to give thanks for having been saved from a great peril, such as a severe illness, undertake a special vow. During the period of the vow, the hair and beard are allowed to grow, they drink no wine nor live with their wives, if they are married. At the end of the period of purification, those keeping a vow go to the temple to make a special offering. Their hair and beard are shorn there and burned upon the altar as a sacrifice."

"Why did James want you to take part? You have taken no vow."

"The offering is costly," Paul explained. "By sponsoring the men and paying the cost, I will reassure those who fear that I wish to do away completely with the old customs where Jews are concerned."

"Don't forget the prophecy of Agabus," Trophimus reminded him.

"I haven't forgotten," said Paul. "But James has always hoped to reconcile Jewish Christians with the temple, as I have, and this may be the best way to do it. I cannot fail him now."

X

Paul began the seven days of purification the following morning, with the four men who had taken the vow. It was shortly before Pentecost and, since the weather was warm and the winter storms had long since ended, throngs of pilgrims filled the city. The days passed with no sign of trouble until the temple was closing on the seventh day.

Paul was crossing the second level restricted to Jews, on his way to the stairway leading down to the Court of the Gentiles where he was to meet Trophimus, when he recognized several Jews from Ephesus, members of a small faction in the synagogue there who had always opposed him. He tried to dodge behind a pillar, but one of the Ephesians saw him and ran toward the stairway to cut him off.

Rather than attempt to hide, Paul stepped out from behind the pillar and moved toward his old enemies from Ephesus. He was hoping by the very boldness of his approach to reach the stairway leading down to the lower court, where he could easily disappear into the crowd. But having sighted their quarry when he was almost alone, the Ephesians had no intention of letting him escape. Seizing Paul's robe, one of them held him back while the other raised a cry calculated to inflame the anger of devout Jews, who thronged the court in the last moments before the day's worship was ended.

"Men of Israel help us!" the Ephesian shouted. "This man teaches everyone against the Law and the temple. He has brought Gentiles into the temple and polluted the Holy Place."

The charge was untrue, for Trophimus had not gone above the lower level of the temple where Gentiles were freely admitted. But seeing the Greek convert there and knowing that he was often a companion of Paul, the Ephesians had been on the lookout for the apostle. When they found him on the second level—where only Jews could go—they chose to distort his presence there into something that would inflame the crowd with the false charge that he had brought Trophimus to the upper level.

Having been involved in a similar situation with the death of Stephen, Paul understood fully the danger he faced. Struggling to stay on his feet as hands reached out for him from all sides, knowing that to fall would mean being kicked to death by the crowd, he tried to protect himself from the blows raining down upon him as he was half dragged down the stairway to the lower court and out through the gate. This was promptly shut behind him and his captors by the Levites waiting there, so as to isolate what was rapidly becoming a serious riot and keep the always watchful Romans in the adjoining fortress-palace of the Antonia from violating the temple.

As it happened, what saved Paul was the very watchfulness of the garrison, more alert now than usual because a few months earlier a near insurrection had occurred. Then the Egyptian leader of a brigand band had stirred up a serious riot, hoping to profit from the plunder his men could seize during the disturbance. The disturbance started by the Egyptian had failed, due to prompt and ruthless intervention by the Romans. The man himself had been driven into the wild hill country north of Jerusalem along with his fellows, but the watch had been doubled ever since. And when the sentries walking the parapet overlooking the Court of the Gentiles saw the shouting mob swirl across the court and through the gates into the outer part of the sanctuary area, they reacted promptly.

A shouted order from the decurion in charge sent a detail of soldiers down the stairways leading from the Antonia to the sanctuary. Moving through the cursing, enraged crowd, knocking its members right and left with the shafts of their spears thrust before them—a favorite Roman tactic in controlling a mob—the highly trained soldiers surrounded Paul and quickly secured his hands and ankles with manacles. Ignoring the angry protests of the mob against interference in what they considered a religious matter, the soldiers carried Paul up the steps of the fortress to a space before the gates. There the mob hesitated to go, both for fear of being knocked down by the spearshafts of the Roman soldiers and because to set foot within the courtyard of the fortress was itself a defilement to a devout Jew.

As the soldiers formed a circle around him, Paul finally managed to gain the attention of the chief captain who had come from inside the garrison to see the cause of the commotion.

"May I speak to you, sir?" he asked in Greek.

"Can you speak Greek?" The Roman looked at him in surprise. "Aren't you the Egyptian who has been creating such an uproar here?"

"I am a Jew of Tarsus, a citizen of no mean city," Paul said proudly. "I beg you to let me speak to the people."

"Speak to them if you can," the officer said with a shrug. "But you're wasting your time with a mob like this."

Paul moved out upon the stone pavement at the side of the stairway leading up to the gates of the fortress and, lifting his chained hands, called to the crowd that he wished to speak. For a while the commotion continued but even though chained, the magnetism of his presence was so great that gradually a silence fell upon the crowd.

"Men, brethren, and fathers, hear the defense I now make to you." The fact that he spoke in Hebrew, the tongue in which they were accustomed to hear the scriptures read in the synagogue each Sunday, held the attention of the people.

"I am truly a Jew, born in Tarsus, a city of Cilicia, yet brought up in this city at the feet of Gamaliel," Paul continued. "I was taught according to the perfect manner of the Law of the fathers and was zealous toward God, as you all are this day. I even persecuted those who followed the way of the Nazarenes, binding and delivering both men and women to prison and death. The High Priest will bear me witness and all the elders from whom I received letters to the brethren and went to Damascus, in order to bring those who were there bound to Jerusalem to be punished. As I came near Damascus about noon, a great light suddenly shone around me from heaven. I fell to the ground and heard a voice say to me, 'Saul! Saul! Why do you persecute me?'"

The crowd was quiet now, so compelling was the spell cast by his voice.

"I answered, 'Who art thou Lord?'" Paul continued, "and he said to me, 'I am Jesus of Nazareth whom you persecute.' 'What shall I do Lord?' I asked and he said, 'Arise and go into Damascus where you shall learn what is appointed for you to do.'

"I could not see for the glory of that light and was led by those who were with me into Damascus. There, Ananias, a devout man according to the Law, with a good report from all the Jews who dwelt there, came to me and said, 'Brother Saul, receive your sight. The God of our fathers has chosen you that you should know his will and see the Just One and hear the voice of his mouth, for you shall be his witness to all men of what you have seen or heard.'"

Paul paused for a moment, letting the significance of the term he had used sink into the minds of his listeners. Since the Just One was a name prophets had given centuries ago to the Son of God who would lead Israel to glory, he was testifying that Jesus of Nazareth, who had spoken to him from the heavens, was indeed the Messiah.

"I came again to Jerusalem and prayed in the temple," Paul continued. "In a trance I heard him say, 'Make haste and get quickly out of Jerusalem, for they will not receive your testimony concerning me.' 'Lord,' I said, 'they know I imprisoned and beat those who believed in you in every synagogue and, when the blood of your martyr, Stephen, was shed, I stood by and consented to his death, holding the garments of those that slew him.' But he said to me, 'Depart, for I will send you far hence to the Gentiles.'"

Too late, Paul realized his mistake in mentioning the word Gentile, for the charge made against him by the Ephesians was that he had polluted the temple by bringing Trophimus into the sacred parts of the sanctuary. The word released the crowd from the spell of his voice and, as angry shouts of "blasphemy" came from the back of the crowd, they began to push forward pressing those in the front up the steps leading into the fortress.

The situation could have become serious but the chief captain saw the danger. Shouting to the guards to open the gates of the Antonia, he shoved Paul through into the courtyard. Behind them the soldiers put their shoulders to the gates, closing them and driving the Jews in the forefront of the crowd back down the steps.

Paul was handled only a little less roughly by his Roman guards than he had been by the crowd. Nor did he expect anything better at the hands of the chief captain, a sturdy, graying professional soldier with the broad cheekbones and craggy brows of an Asiatic from beyond the Danube. Speaking with a somewhat guttural accent betraying that Latin had not always been his mother tongue, he directed the soldiers expertly in securing the gates by using the butts of their spears to drive back the Jews who were reaching through the bars.

"Scourge him until he tells the truth about who he is and what caused them to rise up against him," the chief captain ordered the decurion, when finally the commotion had somewhat subsided. "I shall be inside."

The soldiers quickly bound Paul to a post in the courtyard. One burly fellow went to a rack containing the heavy whips, whose multiple thongs were tipped with metal balls, capable of tearing the flesh from a man's back and Paul knew he must act quickly.

"Is it lawful for you to scourge a Roman citizen who has not yet been condemned?" he asked, as the soldier was drawing back the scourge to lay it upon his now naked back.

The decurion in charge of the detail stepped forward and took the whip. "What did you say?" he demanded.

"I asked whether it is lawful for you to scourge a Roman who has not yet been condemned?"

"Are you a Roman citizen?"

"Yes."

"Guard him well and see that no whip is laid upon him," the decurion ordered. "I must talk to Claudius Lysias about this."

The decurion returned a few moments later with the chief captain. Noting Paul's robe of tough, cheap cloth, his wooden soled sandals and the absence of any jewelry or other ornament, the latter looked doubtful.

"Do you claim to be a Roman citizen?" he asked.

"Yes."

"I obtained this freedom by paying a great sum."

"I was freeborn." Paul lifted his head proudly. "My birth is inscribed upon the records at Tarsus in Cilicia."

"See that he is locked up for the night," Claudius Lysias ordered. "I will decide what to do with him in the morning."

The morning was half-gone, when the rhythmic tread of

marching feet sounded in the corridor outside Paul's cell and Claudius Lysias appeared with a detail of soldiers. He unlocked the door and, entering the cell, directed the jailer to loosen the manacles from Paul's feet, though leaving his wrists bound.

"The High Priest Ananias came to see me about you last night," he said. "He wishes you to be brought before the Sanhedrin this afternoon and swears that the matter against you is strictly a religious one, having nothing to do with Roman law."

"That is true," said Paul. "It was so decided years ago by Annaeus Gallio in Corinth."

"The brother of Seneca?" The chief captain looked surprised. "You have friends in high places indeed."

"Gallio is not a friend." Paul could not be less than honest. "I never saw him but once—when I was brought before him in Corinth on a charge made by some Jews there. He decided then that the controversy was purely a religious one and ordered me released."

"Are you willing to go before the Sanhedrin?"

"I welcome the opportunity to defend myself," said Paul. "I have not broken Jewish Law and am free from all guilt."

## XI

The Sanhedrin would not have dared to hear the case of a Roman citizen, with the commander of the Antonia garrison present, in any but its legal form, so a full quorum of the court was present. The presiding officer was an older priest dressed in rich robes. He made no attempt to disguise his hostility, nor did Paul underestimate the gravity of the situation. If the court condemned him on a purely religious matter, Claudius Lysias would be inclined to let the Jewish authorities have their way, rather than try to protect him with Jerusalem already in a ferment. Pontius Pilate had found himself in a somewhat similar situation more than twenty years earlier and had chosen to approve the verdict of what had passed that night for a court.

The presiding officer opened the trial with an impassioned

oration against the prisoner, accusing Paul of creating division in the Jewish church and of blasphemy against the temple by bringing a Gentile into it. He was careful to avoid any charge under Roman law, but the accusation of blasphemy always stirred up violent emotions among the Jews. By the time he had finished speaking, the crowd filling the chamber and spilling through the doorways into the street outside, was shouting for the prisoner's death.

Paul's turn to defend himself finally came and he stepped into the open space before the long curved table behind which the members of the court were sitting.

"Men and brothers," he began with the customary salutation, "I have lived with a good conscience before God until this day."

"Strike him for speaking lies!" the presiding officer shouted and one of the temple guards standing nearby gave Paul a blow full in the face that drove him almost to his knees. Angered at the unjust blow—forbidden by Jewish Law during the trial of a criminal—Paul lost his own self-control for a moment.

"God shall strike you down, you hypocrite!" he shouted at the priest. "Do you dare to sit in judgment over me according to the Law, yet order me struck contrary to the Law?"

"He has reviled God's High Priest!" The guard who had struck Paul shouted and drew back his fist to deliver another blow. He quailed, however, before the withering scorn in the apostle's eyes, and let his hand drop to his side. For a moment, silence filled the room at Paul's denunciation of the court for breaking the very Law under which it sought to condemn him. Then controlling his voice with an effort, he said, "I did not know he was the High Priest. It is written, 'You shall not speak evil of the ruler of the people.'"

Fighting for time, since the temper of the court and its determination to destroy him was all too evident now, Paul's eyes moved slowly along the arc of bearded men behind the long table. Only hostility showed in their faces and he realized that there was no hope of justice from them, no matter how eloquent his defense. Only some kind of a diversionary move could save him now and, when he saw from his quick study of the court that its makeup was almost half Pharisees and half

Sadducees, the priestly class, he had a sudden inspiration as to just how that might be accomplished.

"Men and brothers!" he cried. "I am a Pharisee and the son of a Pharisee. It is concerning the hope of resurrection from the dead that I have been brought before you today."

As he had hoped, his words fanned into flame the ever-smoldering tinder of controversy between the Sadducees, who rejected all idea of a life after death, and the Pharisees, who just as devoutly believed in immortality for those who kept the Law. At once the priests on the court started arguing with the rabbis —who made up most of the Pharisaic faction—and the latter half of the court, who moments before had been ready to vote a sentence of death, were now Paul's defenders.

"We find no evil in this man," a Pharisee said. "If a spirit or an angel has spoken to him, do not let us fight against God."

The argument was the same one Gamaliel had used when Peter and John were brought before this very tribunal years before. Then, the calm tones of the Rabban, the most respected teacher in Israel, had quieted the court and led them to free Peter and John, but now the Pharisaic claim only added fire to the raging argument. Finally, realizing that matters were getting completely out of hand, Claudius Lysias called in the Roman soldiers who had remained outside the tribunal chamber, surrounded Paul with the detail for his protection, and escorted him from the courtroom.

"You seem to cause controversy wherever you go," he said as they were ascending the long flight of stairs leading to the elevated court of the Antonia. "I can understand their wanting to silence you."

"I did it deliberately this time," Paul confessed. "They were determined to destroy me, so it was the only way to save myself from being convicted of blasphemy."

"I've been here for a year, but I still don't understand your Law," Claudius Lysias admitted. "Why is it blasphemy to say this temple will be destroyed, when it has already been torn down and rebuilt several times before?"

"Devout Jews consider it the dwelling place of God," Paul explained.

"Wasn't that idea exploded long ago, too? I seem to remember Antioch Epiphanes entered your Holy of Holies once, but found nothing there."

"Jews believe God dwells in spirit in the temple. We Christians serve the Son of God, whose blood was shed as a sacrifice for others."

"Like the rite of the taurobolium in the worship of Mithras? I went through that once when I was a centurion, but the only change I detected was losing the gold I spent buying the bull and paying the priests."

"We use only water for our baptism," Paul explained. "It symbolizes that the believer is made over into a new person."

"I spent some time once in the region around a fortress built by Herod the Great in the hills overlooking the Dead Sea," said Claudius Lysias. "A strange sect of Jews lived there—"

"The Essenes?"

"Yes, that was the name. They made much of cleanliness and washings. Are you Christians like them?"

"In the beginning many who followed Jesus of Nazareth did come from among the Essenes."

"Jesus of Nazareth?" The officer frowned. "Wasn't he crucified by Pontius Pilate during a rebellion against Rome headed by a brigand named Barabbas?"

"Jesus was accused of that crime," said Paul. "What he really preached was a kingdom of the soul and heart, where every man is equal in the sight of God and loves his brothers as himself."

"The Greek philosophers taught brotherly love," Claudius Lysias said with a shrug. "But if you had served in as many parts of the world as I have, you would know how hard it is to find a man who really practices it."

They had reached the Antonia now and were crossing the courtyard toward a door leading down to the dungeons. But when Paul would have entered with the guard, Claudius Lysias dismissed the soldier and nodded for the apostle to follow him to the parapet overlooking the valley where the brook called Kidron flowed swiftly southward. Across the valley, on the rising slope of the Mount of Olives, Paul could see the garden where

Christ spent the last hour before his betrayal by Judas and his arrest. From where they stood, he could also see the Hippodrome where he had watched the games that day with Barnabas and, winding around the Mount of Olives, the road from Jericho he had followed when he had come to Jerusalem after his escape from Damascus.

"In the year I've been in Jerusalem I have tried to learn something about the Jewish people and your religion," Claudius Lysias said. "The High Priest Ananias accused you just now before the court of saying that the Law your people make so much of was done away with by Jesus of Nazareth. What did he mean by that charge?"

"Before Jesus came, the Pharisees who interpreted the Law had encompassed it about with so many restrictions that men were actually worshiping the Law, when they should have been worshiping God," Paul explained. "We believe Jesus is the Son of God and that he swept away all the conflicting provisions of the Law with two simple commandments; that we should love God with all our soul and with all our might and our neighbors as ourselves."

"Even that rule is impossible for most men to follow."

"There lies the difference between the way of Jesus and the old way," said Paul. "Before Jesus came, whenever a Jew broke the Law, he was considered defiled and had to expiate his crime by making a special sacrifice, or, if the offense were serious enough, by being put to death."

"And this Nazarene you worship changed all that?"

"Through his death on the cross, Jesus pardoned those who have faith in him from all transgressions of the old Law," Paul explained. "All he asks is that we try to follow his commandments, even though we fail—as I did just now, when I lashed out at the High Priest and provoked my brethern to rage in order to save my own life."

"Surely that isn't enough to make the priests hate you the way they do?"

"They hate me because of Jesus," Paul explained. "He taught that all sin can be forgiven through faith and trust in him. Under the old way, the priests who control the temple are paid to invoke the pardon of God for infractions of Mosaic Law. They see in Jesus of Nazareth a threat to the control they have over the people through the temple."

"I'm not sure that is the whole explanation," said Claudius Lysias. "After all, many of the men on the court are not priests, yet they were as opposed to you as was Ananias—until you raised this question of immortality. I wonder if a matter of national pride isn't involved in their antagonism toward you."

"What do you mean?"

"As I see it, the Jews hate the Romans for putting them under subjection—their longing for what you call the Messiah proves that. Now you come preaching a Messiah who will not even lead your people to a new glory as Judas Maccabeus did. Jews have always been proud that they were selected by their god as his chosen people, too, yet you would let him be the god of all who accept a carpenter of Nazareth as his son. You can't expect a proud people to yield up their god to everyone and at the same time accept a Messiah who let himself be crucified by Romans. If I were a Jew, that would be the final indignity. I would try to destroy you, as they have done."

## XII

Early the next morning, the gate of Paul's prison cell was opened by a guard and a young man in the robe of a workman entered. Though he had not seen the youth for several years, Paul recognized his nephew and embraced him warmly.

"Mother sent me," Jared told him. "My father has been plotting with some agents of the temple to destroy you."

"Why? He has nothing to fear from me."

"He claims you are a blasphemer and deserve death under the Law. But mother says he hates you because his success was made possible by your generosity in making over the title to the shop to us."

"Those I have tried to bring the gifts of eternal life to are often the ones who oppose me most," Paul admitted wryly. "This plot you overheard—what will they try to do?"

"Forty men have bound themselves with a curse not to eat food until you have been slain. The Sanhedrin has asked that you be sent before them again for more questioning. Those who have sworn the vow plan to seize you in the chamber of the court and drag you outside the walls to be stoned."

"It has worked before," Paul conceded. "In a mob, no one could tell who were the ringleaders."

"What are you going to do?" Jared asked.

"Will you tell the chief captain of the plot?"

"And betray my father to the Romans?"

"Just tell Claudius Lysias you overheard the plot accidentally, and came to warn me because you are my nephew. He is a capable officer and will know what to do."

Calling the guard, Paul asked that Jared be taken to the Roman commander. About an hour later, Claudius himself entered the cell.

"Your nephew told me of the plot," he said. "Do you think they will really try it?"

"I saw it done once myself," said Paul. "Even if you tried to intervene, I would be dead before your men could reach me."

"The Sanhedrin has already asked to have you brought before them again. If I refuse, they will certainly complain to Felix, the Procurator."

"Then you're going to turn me over to them?"

Lysias shook his head. "It's my duty to protect any Roman citizen from a mob, but I suspect I would do so in your case, even if you weren't a Roman. I shall send you to Caesarea tonight under heavy guard, just in case your enemies are foolish enough to try to take you from us by force on the way. If they want to bring further charges against you, they must lay them before Felix at Caesarea."

Just before midnight, Paul was taken from prison, still manacled, and put on a horse in the courtyard. He was surprised by the size of his escort; it consisted, he estimated, of some two hundred foot soldiers, with about fifty horsemen and a large number of spearmen. Claudius Lysias came out of the fortress while the column was being formed. He carried a small scroll in his hand.

"I have written a letter to Felix," he said. "Listen to it and tell me whether you think he should have any more information about you than I have given him."

Unrolling the scroll, he began to read:

*"Claudius Lysias unto the Most Excellent Governor Felix, Greeting:*

*"This man was taken by the Jews and would have been killed by them, if I had not come with a body of men and rescued him, because I understood that he was a Roman citizen. When I tried to find out what they accused him of, I brought him before their Sanhedrin. But they raised only questions concerning their Law and I found nothing in the charges against him worthy of death or even of being bound. Nevertheless I learned that the Jews intended to seize him, so I am sending him to you and notifying his accusers that whatever they have against him can be brought before you for a decision."*

"You have done all anyone could expect for my protection," said Paul. "I am grateful."

"You understand that I must notify your accusers so they can continue the charges against you in Caesarea if they wish?"

"Of course. That is no more than right."

Claudius Lysias gripped Paul's arm in the Roman gesture of greeting and farewell. "You are a complex individual, Paul of Tarsus," he said. "I wish you could stay here longer, so we could talk more about the things we spoke of yesterday."

"God will bless you, noble Lysias," said Paul. "Be sure that in foiling the plans of my enemies, you are following the will of God."

During the rest of that night the military party guarding Paul traveled northward. When they reached Antipatris, almost halfway to Caesarea, the foot soldiers turned back to Jerusalem, while the horsemen continued on as an escort for the prisoner. Upon their arrival at Caesarea, Paul was taken before the procurator but no extended examination was carried out.

"I will hear your case when your accusers come from Jerusalem," Felix told him. "Meanwhile you will be kept under guard in the *praetorium*."

## XIII

The judgment hall, or praetorium, built by Herod the Great at Caesarea was one of the most magnificent governmental structures in the shining white city overlooking the Mediterranean. Its lower levels contained the cells where prisoners were kept awaiting judgment or execution. But, as a Roman citizen not yet condemned, Paul was given more freedom than would have been the case with a common criminal. The manacles he had worn since his arrest in Jerusalem were taken off, he was fed regularly and well, and even allowed to exercise daily in the courtyard under the watchful eye of his jailers. Compared to some prisons into which he had been thrown, the one at Caesarea was almost luxurious, but he did not allow himself to be lulled into any false sense of security because of it.

From talking to the guards, Paul learned that Felix had been procurator of the province for nearly a decade. During the early part of his term he had been an excellent governor—by Roman standards. He had put down several minor uprisings by the brigand bands infesting the hill country and had moved swiftly to break up the insurrection begun by the self-styled prophet from Egypt, for whom Paul had been mistaken by Claudius Lysias.

Shortly after his appointment as Procurator of Judea and Samaria, Felix had married Drusilla, a member of the Herod family and a sister of Agrippa II, king of nearby Chalcis. Though Agrippa had no power in Judea itself, he was highly regarded by the priestly hierarchy at Jerusalem and, to further ingratiate himself with them, Felix had arranged for Agrippa to be given charge of the sacred vestments worn by the chief priests upon high ceremonial occasions, a responsibility hitherto exercised by the procurator and a source of much ill feeling between the priests and Roman authority.

Because of Felix's close connection with the nearest thing to a royal house in the area, Paul was sure he was familiar with Jewish customs and Mosaic Law and therefore able to recognize the injustice of the charges against him. On the other hand, the governor would have good reason to please the temple authorities if he could. And besides, he was known to have a predilection for taking bribes from those who came before him for judging.

Five days passed before Paul was brought before the provincial court, sitting in Herod's audience chamber. The governor sat upon a dais, a look of weary indifference in his eyes. On either side of the elevated platform stood the lictors, symbols of Roman judicial and civil—as opposed to military—authority. A battery of scribes at tables below the dais were ready to keep the meticulous records that were an important part of Roman justice.

Paul was given a seat before a table at one side of the room, with a guard beside him. Across the room, behind another table, were ranged the High Priest Ananias, several other members of the Sanhedrin, and an impressive looking man—a Roman by his jutting nose and clean shaven cheeks—whom Paul judged to be an advocate employed by the High Priest to help with the accusations. Paul could have employed a lawyer on his own behalf, if he had wished; many such were scattered throughout the provinces, men who had come from Rome after completing their legal training to seek their fortune in the outlying areas. He had chosen, however, to defend himself.

Felix accepted a sheet of parchment from one of the scribes and glanced at it. "Who speaks against the prisoner Paul, a citizen of Cilicia and Rome?" he asked.

The lawyer who had been sitting with the High Priest from Jerusalem rose and bowed ceremoniously. "I, Tertullus, speak for the High Priest Ananias and the Court of the Sanhedrin at Jerusalem," he announced somewhat pompously.

"Of what do you accuse the prisoner?" Felix did not appear impressed by the lawyer.

Tertullus stepped into the open space before the dais. He spoke in Latin, the language of the Roman courts, pronouncing the words slowly so the clerk, who transcribed them into Greek for those who did not understand Latin, could write them down to be read aloud later if necessary. Since Tarsus was an urbs libera, Paul had been taught a smattering of Latin as a boy, so he was able to follow the lawyer's discourse without much difficulty.

"Most Noble Felix," Tertullus said. "Since we enjoy peace and many worthy deeds have been done for this nation through your providence, we accept your judgment with all thankfulness. In order not to be tedious to you, I pray that you will hear us for a few words out of your clemency. We have found this man Paul to be a pestilent fellow and a mover of sedition among Jews throughout the world. Not only is he a ringleader of the sect of the Nazarenes, but he has profaned the temple at Jerusalem. Because of this, he was seized and would have been judged according to Jewish Law. But the chief captain Lysias took him out of our hands with great violence and commanded his accusers to come before you, so that by examining him yourself you may understand all of these things of which we accuse him."

Tertullus then called a succession of witnesses, all testifying to Paul's having been seen in the temple and to various inflammatory statements which they claimed to have heard him make. Felix allowed the vague charges to be made part of the record, though none constituted a breach of Roman law—except perhaps that of causing civil commotion.

When Tertullus finished presenting his witnesses and sat down at the table with his clients, Felix beckoned to Paul to begin his defense. Stepping into the open space before the dais just vacated by Tertullus, the apostle spoke directly to the procurator. He did not attempt to use Latin, where he might have stumbled and been something less than eloquent, but spoke Greek instead.

"Since I know that you have been for many years a judge of this people, I cheerfully answer for myself," he said. "Only twelve days have passed since I went up to Jerusalem to worship. The authorities there did not find me in the temple disputing with any man or stirring up the people in the synagogues and in the city. Nor can they prove the things of which they now accuse me. This I will confess to you, however; namely that I worship the God of my fathers after the way my accusers have called a sect, believing all things that are written in the Law and the Prophets, and hoping as they do that there shall be a resurrection of the dead, both of the just and the unjust. In that way I try to have always a conscience void of offense toward God and toward men.

"After having been away many years, I came to bring alms and offerings to my people but certain Jews from Asia found me purified in the temple, alone with no multitude or any tumult. These should be here before you, if they have anything against me. Or those who are here should say whether they found any evil-doing in me except that, as I stood before the council of the Sanhedrin, I stated that I was on trial concerning the resurrection of the dead. The chief captain Claudius Lysias will also bear witness that what I say is true, for he was in the chamber at the time I was accused before the Sanhedrin and heard everything that was said."

After ten years of the procuratorship, Felix understood his wife's people quite well. He recognized that the accusations brought against Paul were merely dissensions among the many groups in Jerusalem and, like Gallio, could not conclude otherwise than that they had nothing to do with Roman law. Real justice demanded that Paul be released, but Felix was avaricious enough to see how he might possibly profit by not rendering a decision at this time and playing each side against the other.

"Lysias, the chief captain at Jerusalem, will shortly come to Caesarea," he said, when Paul took his seat. "I will ascertain the whole matter from him and give my decision later."

Tertullus and his clients were obviously unhappy with the decision and Paul was not pleased, since it meant that he was still a prisoner at a time when he needed to be preparing for the journey to Rome and to Spain. Following the hearing, he was no longer kept in a dungeon cell, however, but was placed in the care of a centurion of the guard at Caesarea, the form of captivity known as *custodia militaris*. The usual provision that the prisoner be chained to the soldier who guarded him was not enforced in his case and he was allowed to move about the prison and be visited by his friends.

Paul was busy writing letters to Luke and Timothy about two weeks later, when Claudius Lysias entered the room on the ground level of the praetorium where he was held in loose custody.

"Have you been treated well?" the Roman asked.

"As well as a man in prison can consider himself treated."

"Tertullus and Ananias were very much disappointed that Felix didn't send you back for trial. The gossip in Jerusalem is that somewhere in the hills between here and there, you would have been seized."

"By brigands?"

"Assassins—known to those who were with you."

"It could still happen."

"Yes—if you go back."

"What should I do?" With his genius for understanding the human heart, Paul did not hesitate to trust this Roman officer who had already saved his life once in Jerusalem.

"Felix showed me the record of your hearing. Is it true that you brought money from Greece to Jerusalem?"

"Yes, but it was for the Christians there. I collected the offering in the churches and gave it to James, the head of the church."

"All of it?"

"Of course. I've always supported myself." Paul held out his hands to show the calluses on his palms from the shuttle of the weaver's loom. "I'm a tentmaker—as were my father and grandfather before me."

"Did you tell Felix you left all the money in Jerusalem?"

"No."

Claudius Lysias lowered his voice. "Roman provincial governors usually accept their posts to improve their own fortunes. Often, when a case is in doubt, as yours is, the final decision goes to the one with the heaviest purse."

"Bribery?"

"I suppose that's as good a name as another."

"But I have nothing."

"Try to keep that from becoming known," Claudius Lysias advised. "Meanwhile I have been instructed by Felix to take back to Jerusalem the information that the governor is seriously considering setting you free. Tertullus knows the way of Roman justice, if the High Priest doesn't, so the information should result in a substantial offer from the temple authorities."

"Which I cannot meet—even if I chose to do so."

"I think I've taken care of that, too—by telling Felix of the plan to have you murdered. He would hardly send you back now, knowing I would swear to having warned him of the plot against a Roman citizen." Claudius Lysias rose to his feet. "You possess a treasure greater than any bribe Tertullus and his clients can offer Paul—your status as a citizen of Rome by birth. If Felix should be foolish enough to accept the bribe Tertullus is certain to offer and attempt to send you back to Jerusalem for trial before the Sanhedrin, announce in the presence of witnesses that you appeal to Caesar. Felix cannot refuse the right of appeal to a Roman. It's the one final protection we have against injustice, even in the farthest corner of the Empire."

## XIV

After his talk with Claudius Lysias, Paul was surprised when he was taken from his cell a few days later and brought before Felix once again. This time the hearing was held in a small audience chamber in the governor's palace. With Felix was one of the most beautiful women Paul had ever seen.

"I have brought you here so my wife, who is of the Jewish faith, may hear what new things you teach and be satisfied concerning the charges against you," Felix informed him.

Had he been able to choose, Paul would have selected a more sympathetic audience than a granddaughter of Herod the Great. He could only hope that Drusilla had inherited some of the traits of her Jewish ancestors, particularly the lovely Hasmonean princess, Mariamne, whom Herod had married and finally murdered in a fit of rage.

"Most Noble Felix and Lady Drusilla," he began respectfully,

"I would have you know I am a Jew of Tarsus in Cilicia and that I came to Jerusalem while yet a youth to study our Law at the feet of Gamaliel, the most respected teacher of that day."

Drusilla leaned forward, her eyes alive with interest. "Is this the same Gamaliel who was the grandson of the blessed Rabbi Hillel?"

"The same, noble lady. I studied under Gamaliel with the intention of one day becoming a rabbi and teaching from the Porch of Solomon in the temple, but the sudden illness of my father called me back to Tarsus for several years. During that time, Jesus of Nazareth came to Jerusalem and was crucified there."

"For treason on the orders of Pontius Pilate," Felix said heavily.

"The Son of God was sent to earth as a sacrifice for the sins of men. He said himself that he came to fulfill the Law; and his coming was foretold by the prophets of old as the will of God."

"Did you know this Nazarene yourself?" Felix asked.

"Not in the flesh," said Paul. "Actually, after I returned from Tarsus I persecuted those who followed him. But as I was on the way to Damascus, he appeared to me in the heavens—"

"In a vision?" Drusilla asked.

"In all his glory. I saw him and he called me to serve him."

"The man was dead!" Felix snapped. "You have convicted yourself of lying with your own tongue."

"Jesus suffered death like any other man, even though he is the Son of God," Paul explained. "His body was placed in a sepulcher belonging to the merchant Joseph of Arimathea, but on the third day he rose from the dead."

"I'm familiar with the story," said Drusilla. "The Nazarene's disciples stole his body from the tomb to make it appear that he had risen."

"The High Priest Caiaphas bribed the guards at the tomb to swear falsely so the people would not know he and the others had caused Pontius Pilate to crucify the Son of God," Paul corrected her. "Jesus himself appeared to his disciples several times after his resurrection. He was seen by almost five hundred people when he ascended—and later by me."

"Would you have me believe God let his son be crucified like a common criminal?" Drusilla asked. "Such a thing is unbelievable."

"Have you ever seen a lamb offered up as a sacrifice for sin, as is commonly done at the Passover?" Paul asked.

"Of course."

"Jesus took our iniquities upon him on the cross, just as we once thought the sins of men could be expiated through the sacrifice of a lamb or by making a gift. All who have faith in him are granted eternal life."

"What of those already dead?"

"When he returns to establish his kingdom in the hearts of all, those dead in Christ shall rise first. Then we who are alive shall be brought up together with them in the clouds to meet the Lord Christ and live with him forever."

Felix had been eating grapes languidly when Paul began to describe the coming of Christ and the end of the world. Suddenly the bunch dropped from his fingers and some burst, splattering his tunic with juice.

"How do you know these things?" he demanded.

"The Lord has revealed them to me."

"When will this event take place?"

"We know not the day or the hour. But when he does come, I shall go joyfully to meet him with all who have accepted and believe in him."

Felix shivered, although the room was warm. He picked up the bunch of grapes he had dropped, then tossed them aside, as if he had suddenly lost his appetite.

"You are very convincing, Paul," said Drusilla. "But if this Jesus was really the Messiah, why didn't the Chief Priest and the rabbis acclaim him when he first came to the temple?"

"They were blinded because they expected the Messiah to be an earthly ruler, with them as his ministers," said Paul. "They had forgotten the words of Isaiah naming the Expected One a man of sorrows who would take the burden of our sins upon himself."

"Jesus of Nazareth was involved in a revolt against Roman

authority and his own disciples were part of that rebellion." Felix's voice was harsh.

"I have been told that Judas Iscariot—and perhaps Simon the Zealot—did belong to such a group," Paul admitted. "But I have talked to most of the other disciples and I am sure they had no thought of overthrowing Roman authority."

"Jesus tried to destroy the Law of Moses," said Drusilla. "And so have you."

"No, my lady," Paul said patiently. "Before Jesus came, the Law was our schoolmaster, showing us the way to live with each other. But in him a new and better way was revealed to the world—one all men can easily understand. The Son of God gave his life to show men how really great love can be."

"To me it all sounds like words echoing in an empty space." Felix signaled to the soldier to whom Paul had been chained. "Take him away."

"May I ask what you are going to do with me, Noble Felix," Paul said, as the soldier was taking him from the chamber.

"I haven't decided yet. When it's convenient, I shall call for you again."

## XV

Never one to waste time, for he considered every moment not spent in telling others of the gospel as lost, Paul did not worry about what Felix would do with him. Instead he busied himself with other matters. As soon as he had received news of Paul's imprisonment, Luke had taken ship from Troas and soon arrived in Caesarea. Paul was pleased to see him and also Timothy, who reached there about the same time.

Since Luke was a Greek and not known to the priests, he was dispatched to Jerusalem with instructions to talk with people there and seek to discover what new mischief Tertullus and the chief priests might be plotting. Timothy remained in Caesarea, spending part of each day writing letters of encouragement and hope from Paul to some of the churches he had established in various parts of the world.

Paul had been taken prisoner at the beginning of summer and it was early autumn before Luke and Timothy arrived in Caesarea. Luke did not return from Jerusalem for nearly a month, so the nights were already becoming cool with the promise of winter when he reached Caesarea again. He was sun-bronzed from his journey and obviously in good health, but he was far from happy with the news he brought from the Holy City.

"During the past months the whole province has become more and more restless over Felix's greed and misgovernment," he reported. "If the temple authorities didn't hold the people of Jerusalem in check, there would be an open revolt."

"Felix could hardly bribe the Chief Priest to control the people," Paul objected. "The riches of the temple treasury are far greater than Felix's fortune."

"Nevertheless he has bribed them—with something they want more than money."

"What?"

"You. While Felix keeps you shut up here in prison, the agents of the temple and the Sanhedrin have been visiting the churches in Asia, Macedonia, and Greece, trying to destroy what you have built up."

"They will not succeed."

"Probably not. But they may divide the people by preaching false doctrines and saying that, since the Lord has allowed you to remain in prison, he no longer favors you."

"I can do nothing until Felix decides my case."

"Only money means anything to him," said Luke. "Perhaps if I went to the churches in Greece and told the elders—"

"I will not buy my freedom by bribing Felix," said Paul. "In the end, he will have no choice except to make the same decision that Gallio made in Corinth and my release will mean freedom for Christians everywhere."

"Felix may not last that long," Luke warned. "He only became procurator because his brother, Pallus, was a trusted adviser of the Emperor Claudius. Now that Nero rules in Rome, Felix could be replaced any day."

"That might be for the best. A new governor would be certain to recognize my innocence and I should be free to go on."

"To Rome?"

"And Spain."

"You're fit for the journey at least," said Luke. "Even if I weren't a physician, I could see that."

Though almost fifty, Paul was as sturdy as he had been on his return from the desert sojourn at Petra. His stocky frame was well muscled from daily exercise in the courtyard of the prison. And though his hair, which had always been thin, was even sparser now, his eyes—which had troubled him from time to time with a chronic inflammation—were clear and certain. The scars of the beatings at Philippi and elsewhere still showed upon his body but, as he had often said, he wore them proudly like a soldier wearing medals proving his prowess in battle.

## XVI

Months passed and the mild climate Caesarea enjoyed gave way to spring then to the beginning of summer. With the resumption of shipping after the winter storms, Timothy was dispatched as Paul's personal emissary to the churches he had established, assuring them of his continued good health and his intention to go on to Rome and to Spain. Paul kept Luke with him and it was well that he did for, with the coming of hot weather, he was again stricken by the fever that so often accompanied it. All of Luke's skill was required to control the illness and, discouraged by the long term of imprisonment and the failure to see any sign of an early ending, a long period of convalescence was required before Paul regained his strength.

In the province, unrest against the governorship of Felix mounted steadily, as the period of Paul's imprisonment stretched from one year into two. Then one day, the retribution Felix had so long deserved descended upon him with the arrival from Rome of a new governor for the province, Porcius Festus.

Paul had hoped the new governor would hear his plea for justice at once and set him free. Much of the outcry against

Felix had come from Jerusalem, however, and since Agrippa II had built a palace there and spent much time in the Holy City, Festus was concerned lest the young king choose this opportunity to seize power. He therefore remained in Caesarea only three days before going on to Jerusalem.

Luke had been staying in Caesarea at the house of Philip, one of the original Seven. When the two came to the prison almost a week after the departure of Porcius Festus, Paul could see from the concern on their faces that something was wrong.

"I've just had word from Judea," said Philip. "The chief priests have demanded that Porcius Festus send you back to Jerusalem for trial before the Sanhedrin."

"If he could guarantee my safe arrival there and a fair trial, I would almost be willing to go," said Paul.

"The Sanhedrin could always find two men to swear to a charge of blasphemy and turn you over to the mob," Philip warned.

"I can always appeal to the Emperor, as Claudius Lysias advised," said Paul.

"That advice may not be as good now as it was when he gave it to you two years ago," said Luke.

"Why do you say that?" Paul demanded. "Justice is justice."

"It's also as blind as those who administer it want it to be," said Philip. "I talked to an officer who came from Rome with Festus. He says that when Nero first came to the throne, everyone expected him to be an even wiser ruler than Claudius had been."

"It's no secret that Lucius Seneca is the Emperor's tutor," said Paul. "He is the leading Stoic philosopher in the world today, so Nero should have been taught principles much like those of Christ."

"Everyone thought so, especially when Nero began his reign with a proclamation of justice and fairness for all," Philip agreed. "But Empress Agrippina is jealous of the influence Seneca exerts over her son. She wants to rule the Empire herself through Nero and Seneca has tried to counteract her influence by finding a mistress for the Emperor who might be able to control him."

"How could such a sordid business concern me?" Paul demanded.

"Hear on and you will find out," Philip told him. "According to the centurion from Rome, who gave me this information, Seneca found a concubine for Nero, a slave girl named Acte from Asia who may also have been of noble birth. She was an excellent influence upon him until another woman appeared, a dissolute and unprincipled slut named Poppaea Sabina, who was married to Otho, one of Nero's companions in profligacy. The gossip in Rome is that Poppaea deliberately set out to attract Nero and now he is wild with infatuation for her."

"I still don't see what that has to do with justice for me."

"Poppaea Sabina is very close to the leaders of the Jewish community in Rome; some say she even professes to worship God. And Nero doesn't even listen to his ministers any longer, whenever their advice conflicts with whatever Poppaea wants him to do."

"Then you think the Jewish leaders of Rome will oppose me?"

Philip shrugged—answer enough. "Some of the priests who went to Rome to give testimony against Felix stayed on and became favorites of Poppaea Sabina. It is said that every rich woman there keeps a Jew now to entertain her—like a monkey on a chain. Poppaea has the emissaries from Jerusalem."

"Am I to be denied justice wherever I turn?" Paul sank to a bench at one side of his cell.

"The terms of your imprisonment here aren't harsh," Luke reminded him. "It would be a simple matter to escape."

"Where?"

"To the desert—perhaps Petra."

"King Aretas wouldn't give me refuge. He rules in Damascus and the leaders of the synagogue there poisoned his mind against me long ago."

"What about Egypt?"

"I would still be a prisoner fleeing from Roman authority." Paul's moment of weakness and depression at the news Luke and Philip had brought was past now. His shoulders were straight once again and his eyes were clear. "The Lord has revealed to me that I shall visit Rome before going on to Spain. Whatever awaits me there must be his will, so I shall face it without flinching."

"Let me employ an advocate to represent you before Porcius Festus," Luke begged. "He may know some quirks of Roman law that would help you."

"I shall make my own defense—the truth," Paul said firmly. "If Porcius Festus is worthy to be governor of a province, he must see that the charges against me are false."

"And if he does not?" Philip asked.

"Then the Lord will guide me—as he has in the past."

## XVII

Some two weeks after his arrival at Caesarea, the new governor returned to the provincial capital and one of his first acts was to have Paul brought before him. The hearing, held in the audience hall of Herod's praetorium as before, was surrounded by the trappings of Roman authority.

Paul had not seen Festus previously, so he studied him closely during the opening portions of the hearing, while the scribes were noting the date and place, the notable officials present, and the list of witnesses appearing against the accused. What he saw lifted his spirits a little for Festus was obviously a much superior individual to the loutish ex-slave, Felix. Breeding and intelligence showed in the aquiline planes of his face and the direct gaze of his dark eyes. A Roman aristocrat, Festus wore the toga of authority but, unlike Felix, it was spotless and pleated by one of the slaves called *plicatae* especially trained for that purpose.

A number of richly dressed Sadducees from the temple at Jerusalem had accompanied Festus to Caesarea, along with other prominent men, obviously in the hope of impressing the Roman governor. Paul, on the other hand, wore his usual garb—a homespun robe of rough material and wooden soled sandals. The accusers parroted the old charges against him. But a change of High Priests had occurred since the hearing from which Claudius Lysias had rescued the apostle and with it a rearrangement of the temple hierarchy. The testimony of the witnesses was often contradictory and, when finally Paul's turn came to defend himself, he faced the new governor confidently. Certain that a man of Festus' intelligence would already have recognized the triviality of the charges against him, he had determined to make his defense very brief and to the point.

"Most Noble Festus," he said. "You have heard the charges made against me, so it must be evident to you that neither against the Law of the Jews nor against Caesar, have I offended in anything. I therefore appeal to you for judgment."

A startled murmur swept through the crowd. Paul saw Luke frowning in his seat near the front of the praetorium and knew that the physician realized how much he was staking on the assumption that the new governor was both intelligent and honest. From the dais where he sat, Festus studied Paul thoughtfully for a moment, then turned to consult with his advisers. Finally, he faced Paul again.

"Will you go to Jerusalem and be judged there by the Jewish court concerning these charges?" he asked.

It was the one question Paul had hoped would not arise during the hearing. Now that it had been spoken, he could have only one answer.

"I stand at Caesar's judgment seat where I ought to be judged," he said with a sense of relief, now that the die was cast. "As you very well know, I have done no wrong to the Jews. If I am an offender or have committed anything worthy of death, I do not refuse to die. But if none of the things of which I am accused are true, no man can deliver me into the hands of my accusers. I appeal to Caesar."

Festus looked startled and signaled his advisers to confer with him again, but the conference was brief.

"Have you appealed to Caesar?" he asked formally for the official record of the trial.

"I have appealed," said Paul.

"Then to Caesar you shall go. This hearing is ended."

# Book VII · Rome

**1**

The harbor of Puteoli was already in sight when Julius, the centurion charged with transporting Paul from Caesarea to Rome for his appeal to the Emperor, came to the foredeck of the ship, where the apostle was standing with other prisoners watching the approach to the mainland of Italy. The galley slaves of the Alexandrian vessel, *Castor and Pollux*, were pulling steadily in the rhythm beaten out upon a small drum by one of the overseers. Another overseer trod the narrow walkway along the center of the vessel, ready to lay his long whip across the shoulders of any oarsmen who might falter in the rhythm, threatening to entangle the long sweeps and throw the ship off course.

It was still winter, though already warm here in the southern part of Italy. Not much shipping was entering and leaving the harbor as yet, and from his vantage point on the foredeck, Paul could see that the waterfront appeared to be jammed with ships of all sizes and types. The *Castor and Pollux* had sailed early, after being caught by winter storms at Melita and forced to spend several months there before the master judged it safe to continue. Even then, they had journeyed north along the course of Sicily and southern Italy with extreme caution, first to Syracuse, then to Rhegium and finally almost directly northward to Puteoli, the major harbor serving the bustling city of Neapolis.

Across the bay the buildings of Puteoli were visible now, rising in a gradual ascent from the waterfront. A point of land to the north hid Baie, the famous watering place of Roman nobility and playground of the emperors, but the prospect was pleasant enough, with the buildings on shore and the trees bright in the sunlight. The centurion carried a light chain that was already attached to his wrist. At the sight of it, Paul held out his hand for the link to be locked into the ring attached to a manacle upon his own wrist, but Julius shook his head.

"You can remain unchained a little while yet." He was a stocky man with the map of many campaigns engraved on his scarred face and a deformity of the right shoulder, where a horse had rolled over him. "It's the very least I can do, after you saved our lives, when the crew of our first ship would have deserted us at Melita and left us to the mercy of the storm."

"I only gave the warning." Paul had developed a warm feeling of friendship for the centurion. "As I remember it, you were the one who held a sword at the shipmaster's throat."

"I'm a soldier, accustomed to obeying orders, but you are a leader by nature," said Julius. "The Jews of Jerusalem should be listening to you, instead of the priests who seek to destroy you."

"Perhaps this is the Lord's way of sending me where I should go," said Paul.

"Since this shoulder made me unfit to be anything but a jailer, I have taken many to Rome in chains, but never such a one as you," said Julius. "If it were left to me, you would never wear manacles again."

"Bonds placed upon me in the service of Christ are my badges of honor. I wear them proudly. What can I expect in Rome, Julius?"

"Roman prisoners are no better off than most others. Many die before their cases can be heard, especially if their accusers don't come forward immediately."

"Then by not appearing against me my enemies could make sure that I am not free to continue my work?"

"That happens frequently," said Julius. "Fortunately, I have some influence with the Praetorian Prefect, General Burrus, and I know several of the magistrates. I shall report that you saved our lives, when we were shipwrecked on Melita, and perhaps things will move a little faster than usual."

"But I will still have to be in prison?"

"General Burrus might allow you to dwell nearby, with a guard attached to you at all times, but don't get your hopes too high. When I left Rome six months ago, there was talk that the young Emperor is becoming restive and no longer follows the advice of Seneca and Burrus. This new mistress of his, Poppaea Sabina, is said to be closely allied with Tigellinus and some others. People like that are the worst possible influence on Nero."

"I shall not be in Rome long, once my case is decided," said Paul. "The sooner I am off to Spain, the better I shall like it."

The ship was coming into the quay at Puteoli now; the slaves on the side of the vessel nearest to the dock had already drawn in their sweeps and placed them upon the deck against the rail. Those on the opposite side were now manipulating their oars under the direction of the overseers, moving the blades back and forth in the water to propel the boat sideways. When it bumped gently against the quay, ropes were tossed from the deck and secured to bollards.

Directed by one of the overseers, the group of slaves not occupied with the oars took up the gangplank which, while under way, was secured against the rail, acting both as a breakwater for the seas that swept over the deck in a storm and as a means of egress from the vessel. They slid the gangplank over the rail and, when the end tipped downward, those on shore lowered it to the stones where it was secured. All the prisoners except Paul had been chained together. These were now marched off the vessel and across the gangplank to the quay, guarded by the small detail of soldiers commanded by Julius. Paul and the centurion, now bound together by a single light chain, followed.

A small group of men and women who had been waiting discreetly for the docking of the vessel approached Paul. One of them identified himself as Aristos, leader of a group of Christians living in Puteoli. The rest of the prisoners were being marched off to the prison to be quartered there. But when Julius learned that it would be several days before a party could be made up to proceed by land the some three or four days' journey to Rome, he released Paul in the care of Aristos, upon the apostle's assurance that he would not try to escape.

Altogether, a week elapsed before the final journey to Rome began. The apostle had utilized that period to the full, telling all who would listen the story of his conversion and his preaching in Asia and in Greece, ending with his almost miraculous escape from death, when the ship bearing him and his party from Caesarea had been wrecked during a storm on the island of Melita. He found an eager reception to his teachings at Puteoli and was much encouraged when the time came to leave for Rome.

From Puteoli, the route led first to Capua, where they joined the Appian Way. Here the traffic increased markedly, since this was one of the great roadways of the Empire. More than once, the column of prisoners and their guards was forced to leave the stone-paved road and walk beside it, while an elaborately curtained palanquin passed, borne by burly slaves. Sometimes the conveyance was a swift *cisium*, a light and rapidly moving vehicle much like a cabriolet. And occasionally, the rumbling wheels of a heavy carriage or *rheda*, loaded with the family and possessions of some nobleman could be felt upon the stone pavement well before its appearance.

North of Anxur, the road descended from the hills back of the seashore to follow the bank of the canal by which Augustus had drained the Pontine marshes. Luke had been walking behind Paul and Julius, but now he pushed up beside them.

"It would be interesting to know whether draining these swamps had any effect upon the fever in this district," the physician said.

Paul could not repress a shiver, although the day was warm, for Luke's words reminded him of how often the combination of hot weather and low ground had seemed to bring on the attacks from which he had suffered so many times.

"The fever has always been bad here," said Julius. "I don't know what effect the draining had—if any."

The road now ran beside the canal and from time to time they were forced to leave it in order to allow the passage of mules pulling boats catering to travelers who were able to pay for a ride, thus avoiding the rough going by foot or carriage over the worn stones of the Appian Way. But there was no respite for the weary prisoners, although they looked longingly at the passengers on the boat, reclining on cushions and shaded from the sun's rays by gay canopies strung from stem to stern.

The canal ended at Appii Forum. Paul was overjoyed when they were joined there by Priscilla and Aquila—whom he had last seen at Ephesus—with about a dozen other Christians. Julius was anxious to push on with the group of prisoners, so Priscilla, Aquila and the others fell in behind the column. After a few hours' walk they came to Three Taverns, where still another group of Christians waited to welcome the apostle to Rome, word of his coming having been sent ahead by their fellows in Puteoli. At Aricia they paused for the night and, early the next morning, took up the final stage of the journey, an easy walk to the Roman capital.

Not far beyond Aricia, Paul had his first glimpse of Rome, when Julius ordered a rest at the summit of a hill. Most of the party left the road to sit in the shade of an olive grove, but Paul climbed upon a rock, the better to see the city he had been trying to reach for almost three years.

Viewed from this distance, Rome was considerably less impressive than Antioch or Ephesus, although much larger than either. It appeared to be an indiscriminately arranged mass of houses, with here and there the gilded roof of what he judged to be a temple flashing in the sun.

Beyond Aricia, the road descended steadily for a walk of about two hours, then began to cross the considerable plain surrounding Rome. The way soon became almost solidly lined with cemeteries and Julius proudly pointed out to Paul that of the *gens* with which he was connected, since he was the son of a slave of the Julian family who had been given his freedom. To Paul, approaching Rome to fight for his life, the gloomy prospect of the cenotaphs along the way was infinitely depressing. Nor were his spirits lightened when they reached the Porta Capena in the ancient wall and passed beneath an arch where water dripped constantly from the aqueduct passing over it.

Moving onward, they came to what was known as the Sacra Via, the street leading to the center of imperial government in Rome. Here at the Milliarum Aureum was located the golden milestone from which all roads of the Empire originated. In front of it was the famous Capitoline Hill upon which stood the house of Caesar and, beside that, the praetorium of the elite guards. Presided over by General Afranius Burrus, one of the bravest and most respected generals of Rome, the praetorium also housed the central prison for the Empire, where those awaiting verdict by the imperial courts were held.

Paul was consigned to prison with the others of his party, but the next day he was brought before the Stratopedarch Gallinus, one of the magistrates of the Imperial Court. Julius was already there and smiled encouragingly at Paul. Besides the magistrate, only a scribe with his pen, tablets and parchment sheets sat at the table before which Paul came to a halt.

"You are Paul of Tarsus, remanded to Rome in the custody of Centurion Julius by Festus, Procurator of Judea and Samaria, for trial before Caesar?" the magistrate asked.

"Yes, sir."

"Procurator Festus notes that you could have been set free, if you had not appealed to the Imperial Court. Why did you make such an appeal?"

"I was asked to return to Jerusalem and be tried before the Sanhedrin. There was reason to suppose I would have been murdered before my trial."

"Good reason, no doubt." Gallinus' smile was wintry. "I served in Judea for five years. You Jews are a strange people, much given to killing each other over small differences of opinion."

"Proconsul Annaeus Gallio ruled in Corinth long ago that the differences between me and the chief priests at Jerusalem are concerned strictly with doctrine and involve no Roman law," Paul volunteered.

"Gallio—the brother of Seneca?"

"Yes."

"You would get nothing but justice from him." The Stratopedarch picked up a scroll that lay on the table before the scribe and glanced at it briefly, then put it down. "And you shall get nothing but justice from me. Until your accusers appear, you may live outside the prison, provided you are able to pay the rent of a house and the wages and food of the two soldiers who will guard you."

"But—"

"I have been assured that friends of the prisoner will be glad to make such an arrangement," Julius broke in. "They are dependable people, known to me, and will make bond for him."

"Let it be so ordered," said Gallinus. "The prisoner, Paul of Tarsus, will remain in custodia militaris until such a time as his accusers appear."

Outside the prison, Paul drew a long breath of relief. The prospect of being shut up for months, while the priestly hierarchy in Jerusalem, content to have him silenced, delayed making their accusations, had been depressing.

"I have you to thank for this," he told Julius. "How can I ever repay you?"

"All I did was ask Gallinus to give you a hearing and determine whether your case justified custodia militaris, instead of *custodia publica*. Your physician friend tells me you're subject to fevers and I'm afraid the common jail wouldn't be a very healthy place for you."

"But the hire of the soldiers? And the rent of a house?"

"Thank Luke and your friends, Aquila and Priscilla, for that. A centurion barely earns enough to live on."

"Luke left everything behind at Troas, when he chose to go with me. He certainly couldn't afford to pay for all that."

"You forget that he once served as a surgeon to the legions at Antioch-in-Pisidia," said Julius. "In Rome most doctors cater to the rich and the soldiers of the Praetorian Guards have to make out as best they can. They were fortunate and happy to employ a physician of Luke's skill."

"If I'm to dwell nearby, I had better find a home for myself and my guards," said Paul.

"Aquila took care of that," Julius assured him. "I sent a

soldier ahead. When we get there, your chain can be transferred to him."

The house, Paul discovered, was ample for the needs of him and his friends and his two guards, one by day and one by night. Aquila and Priscilla were already waiting for him and a happy reunion followed, tempered only by Paul's feeling of guilt at being forced to accept charity even from old friends.

"If I could remove these chains, I would gladly earn my keep," he told them. "There must be weavers in Rome, if not tentmakers."

"Your work here is far more important than weaving tents or making cloth," Aquila assured him. "As soon as we heard from Luke in Caesarea that you had appealed to Rome, we began to collect a fund for your defense in the churches of Asia and Greece. The only reward your friends ask is that the most eloquent voice ever lifted in the praise of the Lord shall not be stilled."

"It will be stilled only by death; you can depend on that," said Paul. "Even though I am in chains, I shall teach all who will listen."

"Don't be discouraged too quickly, if you find it harder to gain listeners here than at Corinth," Aquila warned. "Rome is a very cesspool of evil."

"Then we must clean it up—as the Greek fables say Hercules cleaned the Augean stables."

"The task would be almost as great," said Priscilla.

"What about the letter I sent to the churches at Rome?"

"It was read," said Aquila. "But not many seem to have listened."

"Why?"

"The churches at Rome were established by refugees from Jerusalem."

"They still follow Christ, don't they?"

"Yes, but in a somewhat different way."

"Are you saying that, until my letter to the Romans arrived, all they knew was what Peter preached at the Feast of Pentecost?"

"That was the only doctrine I had heard, until I met you in

Corinth," said Aquila. "The Christians of Rome look to Jerusalem—to James and to Peter."

Paul sat down on a bench in the small courtyard of the house his friends had rented for him. The guard, who was attached to him by a chain was, perforce, required to sit too. Leaning against a tree, he promptly began to doze. It was humiliating enough for Paul to discover that almost nothing of the fame he had gained as the most eloquent voice preaching the gospel of Christ had any significance here. More than that, the news his friends had just given him meant that he must start over again from the beginning, so to speak, here in Rome.

"We hated to bring bad news so soon after your arrival," said Aquila.

"The fault is not yours but mine. I have been guilty of the sin of false pride."

"But—"

"This is my cross at the moment." Paul lifted his wrist with the chain attached. "I must bear it in penance for my sin."

"You came here to gain your freedom. Surely the Lord wouldn't—"

"I sinned by thinking I am somebody when I am nobody," said Paul. "In the east I had a great church—Antioch—behind me. Now I must build support here for my work in Gaul and Spain, chained to my guard like a sinner bound to the dead body of his sin."

"Do you have any idea where to start?"

"Where I started in the beginning—with the Jews who know nothing of Christ."

"You can hardly take a Roman soldier into a synagogue," Aquila protested. "They would stone you for blasphemy."

"Then we will invite the leaders of the Roman synagogues to come here and listen. You know them, don't you?"

"Of course," said Aquila. "Before I became a Christian, I was one of them. They number some of the most respected people in Rome engaged in trade and the handling of money and loans. If they should go against you, your case before the Emperor might be prejudiced."

"How?"

"Poppaea has many friends among the Jews here. Some say she is really a proselyte, but keeps it a secret because of her affair with the Emperor. Whoever falls into disfavor with her soon leaves—usually for the tomb or the funeral pyre."

"Think what an achievement it would be if I were to induce her to believe." Paul's eyes took fire at the thought. "Not only would her soul be saved but she could influence the Emperor to look with favor upon us in our work."

"You're taking a risk," warned Priscilla. "Poppaea is a venomous woman—and utterly depraved."

"The Lord called me—even though I was persecuting him," Paul reminded her. "No change could be greater than that."

11

The next evening, more than a dozen leaders in the Jewish synagogues of Rome came to the house beside the praetorium at the invitation of Aquila and Paul. They filled the largest room in the house. Seeing the doubt on many of their faces when he came in, chained to a soldier, Paul wasted no time in going directly to the point.

"Men and brethren," he began, "I have committed no crime against our people or the customs of our fathers, yet I have been delivered a prisoner from Jerusalem into the hands of the Romans. Porcius Festus examined me in Caesarea and would have let me go, because he found no reason for a sentence of death in my case. But when the authorities from Jerusalem spoke against the decision, I was forced to appeal to Caesar. For this reason, I have called for you in order to see you and speak with you, though I am bound with this chain for preaching the hope of Israel."

"We received no letters from Judea concerning you," a bearded elder in the front row said. "Nor has anyone from there spoken of you. Nevertheless we would hear what you think concerning this sect of the Christians, for we know that it is spoken against by Jews everywhere."

"Bring as many people as you can whenever it suits your

convenience," Paul told them. "I will preach the whole truth concerning the gospel of Christ so you may understand."

The group that gathered a week later was not as large as Paul would have liked. Looking at their faces, he could see in some the signs of rejection he had so often seen in the synagogues throughout Asia and Greece. He did not let that deter him, however, from giving his usual eloquent account of how the coming of Jesus as the Messiah had been foretold, not only in the Books of the Law but also in those of the Prophets. He ended his sermon with the story of his own conversion, but even before he finished, it was obvious that, though some had been moved by his story, the majority was still unyielding—like the Jews in most of the cities he had visited.

## III

The period of almost two years Paul spent in Rome was both productive and frustrating—with the latter predominating. The mills of Roman justice—at least where it concerned appeals to Caesar—ground very slowly indeed. Until his accusers came from Jerusalem to give testimony against him, the magistrates of the Imperial Court would make no move to free him from the written accusations Festus had forwarded to the court, along with the body of the prisoner. Even so, he realized that he was better off than most prisoners awaiting a hearing, since they were incarcerated in cells. Characteristically, too, Paul chose to regard the chain he wore as a badge of honor, rather than an emblem of either guilt or shame, and did not let it deter him from going about his usual activities.

At the house he had rented, in the public squares of Rome, wherever people would listen, he preached eloquently as usual. But he quickly discovered that Aquila and Priscilla had been correct in warning him against expecting the instant success he had achieved elsewhere. Rome was indeed in the grip of an evil being steadily compounded in the Imperial Palace near which Paul's house stood. And since what was happening there was common talk in Rome, he could hardly fail to be conscious of its progress, particularly since it affected him so much.

As a sect within the Jewish faith, Christianity was protected by the Law of Associations promulgated by the Emperor Augustus. This law gave free rights to all societies and religions so long as they registered, conducted their activities openly, and did not practice subversion. The enemies of the Christians in Rome, largely concentrated in several Jewish synagogues, had tried to prejudice the authorities against them by charging that they carried on secret practices and avoided Roman pagan festivals. No judicial ruling on the status of the Christians had as yet been made in Rome itself, however. And though Paul hoped to achieve such a ruling, as he had done in Corinth, he could make no progress until his accusers appeared or the court decided to quash the charges.

Meanwhile, Paul was heartened by the coming of Timothy from Galatia to be with him and the arrival of Mark from Asia. With them was Aristarchus, a fellow prisoner from Judea, Silas, who had accompanied Paul on the second missionary journey and Demas, a Greek convert. Luke, of course, had come with Paul from Caesarea. Altogether, it was a busy household there in the shadow of the praetorium, with delegations of Christians who had come to Rome to visit the apostle being received daily and letters written to churches throughout the Empire. Nor did Paul give up entirely the attempt to bring the Jews of Rome to a realization that the expected Messiah had come and that salvation for them, as for everyone, lay through him.

The Jewish colony in Rome was a large one, having been established centuries before, when Pompey had brought many of them to Rome as slaves after his successful campaigns in the East. Prized for their intelligence and their willingness to work ceaselessly for their own freedom and advancement, Jewish slaves had always been in great demand, so a considerable body of them, as well as freedmen, had grown up in Rome.

Preserving the old customs and still loyal to the temple at Jerusalem, they exerted a considerable influence on the business affairs of Rome and a section of the city had been adopted by them as their residence. Called the Trastevere, it lay across the river from the Imperial Palace. And since this area was easily reached by way of bridges crossing the river from the central part of the city, Paul was able to spend considerable time there, attempting to show the Jews, too, the way of salvation. For the most part, however, his efforts in this direction were in vain.

To the church at Ephesus, where he had been pastor during those exciting years when he had taught daily in the audience hall of Tyrannus, Paul wrote some of the most eloquent words he had ever set down in writing. Perhaps because of his proximity to the great camp of the Praetorian Guards, and the presence of the soldier chained to him, he gave to the Ephesians—near the close of this letter of pastoral advice the stirring exhortation to:

*Take upon you the whole armor of God that you may be able to withstand in the evil day, having your loins gird about with truth and having on the breastplate of righteousness and your feet shod with the preparation of the gospel of peace. Above all take the shield of faith, wherewith you shall be able to quench all the fiery darts of the wicked, and take the helmet of salvation and the sword of the Lord, which is the word of God.*

IV

The rise of Poppaea Sabina to the position of mistress and virtual ruler of Emperor Nero's emotions had been accompanied by the development of an entirely new structure of political power within the imperial household. General Afranius Burrus, the most admired and loyal military figure in the Empire, had consistently opposed Nero's plan to divorce his wife, Octavia, and marry Poppaea. But with Poppaea pregnant and demanding that her child have the legal status of succession in Empire, Nero finally dared to defy Burrus.

Certain now that she had the upper hand over her imperial lover, Poppaea first arranged with her co-conspirators for Burrus to be poisoned. Next, Octavia was banished to the island of Pandatiri on a trumped-up charge of adultery and shortly killed

—rumor even saying that her head was cut off and deposited in bloody cloth at the feet of Poppaea.

Knowing that the new Empress was in league with many influential Jews in Rome and that, through her, their opposition to him might lead to his own assassination or condemnation upon some trumped-up evidence, Paul decided to take a step he had so far avoided and appeal to the one man who still seemed to have some influence over the Emperor, the philosopher Seneca. To this end, he sent a letter to Seneca asking for an appointment to discuss philosophy and religion with him, citing as a reason for the request, the fact that the philosopher's younger brother, Gallio, had once judged him innocent of any crime in Corinth. Not long after the letter was sent, Paul received a courteous invitation from Seneca, asking him to wait upon the latter at his home.

Though Seneca had been the tutor of Nero and, with Burrus, one of the two most powerful men in the Empire through his influence over the young Emperor, he still lived in the same rambling structure he had inhabited before his rise to power. It was a typically Roman house, with an open court, or atrium, in the center of which water from a pipe poured into a shallow pool. Paul and his guard were ushered into the atrium and directed to seats upon a bench beside the pool by the *nomenclator*—in Roman households with many slaves, one charged with announcing guests of his master was given that title. Through the open door of another room, the apostle could see racks of scrolls and judged that it must be the philosopher's study or library.

While they were waiting, a door opened on the other side of the atrium and a young woman entered. Her hair was dark and she wore a simple white robe, with a strand of pearls about her neck. Against the background of the shrubbery planted around the pool, she made a picture of quiet beauty that was refreshing, after the overdressed and overpainted women who thronged the streets of Rome.

Paul got to his feet and the rattle of the chain attached to his wrist warned the young woman that she was not alone. Startled by the presence of intruders, she first turned toward the door from which she had come but, seeing that only Paul and his guard were there, came around the pool toward them.

"Forgive my rudeness, please." Her voice completed the picture of quiet loveliness. "I didn't know anyone was here."

"The nomenclator told us to wait," said Paul.

"Then Seneca already knows you are here?"

"Yes." Seeing her eyes go to the chain binding him to the guard, the apostle said: "My name is Paul of Tarsus. I am awaiting trial before the Emperor."

"Are you the Paul who preached in Asia?" The young woman's eyes had brightened with interest when he spoke his name.

"Yes."

"I have relatives there; they mentioned you in letters. I am Claudia Acte."

"The Emperor's mis— Forgive me. I have no right to judge."

"I was honored to be Caesar's *concubina*. He gave me my freedom." Actually, the word signified a form of Roman marriage—the most informal and therefore most easily broken.

The story of how Seneca and Burrus had deliberately stirred Nero's interest in the lovely young slave-woman, hoping her quiet goodness and devotion would have a controlling effect upon his often tumultuous passions, was well known throughout the Empire. But Acte had been put aside when she was unable to compete for Nero's rather fickle attention with the wanton charms of Poppaea Sabina. And though she had not been destroyed like Octavia or General Burrus, she had been banished to a villa at Velitrae, where she lived in quiet seclusion. Knowing all this, Paul was surprised that she had risked invoking the wrath of the Empress Poppaea by returning to Rome.

"A freedom you will not enjoy much longer, if you are foolish enough to come to Rome again." The speaker, a gray-haired man with the lined face and deep-set eyes of a scholar, stood in the door to the library. Acte ran to kiss the old man on the cheek and his face softened as he put an arm about her waist and moved across the atrium toward where Paul was standing.

"Forgive me for keeping you waiting," he said to Paul. "In your letter you mentioned that you were a native of Tarsus and I was reading again how Athenodorus freed your city from corrupt politicians during the reign of Augustus."

"I remember hearing Nestor speak of it when I was a student at the university there," said Paul.

Seneca frowned, "The Stratopedarch Gallinus tells me you are a Jew remanded for trial from Caesarea by Procurator Porcius Festus because of offenses committed in Jerusalem. How did you come to study under Nestor?"

"I was born in Tarsus," Paul explained. "A large Jewish colony has been there for many years."

"Since the time of Antiochus Epiphanes, I believe," said Seneca. "That would account for your being a citizen."

"My father and grandfather were citizens before me."

"In what way can I help you?" The old philosopher took a seat upon a bench and Claudia Acte sat beside him. Paul and his guard resumed their seats upon a bench near the pool.

"I have been in Rome for a year awaiting trial before Caesar," Paul explained. "My accusers have not yet come forward—"

"A common trick where the case is weak. An unscrupulous man can bury another in prison merely by not making charges against him."

"I was hoping you might use your influence with the Emperor to have my case brought up for trial, so I may be free to go on with my work," said Paul.

"You have chosen a frail reed to lean on, my friend," said Seneca. "The same evil companions who turned the favor of Nero away from this lovely child are slowly weakening any influence I ever had over him. One day I shall be found dead in my bed—of poison, as was my friend Burrus, or with my veins open."

"They wouldn't dare harm the greatest mind in Rome!" Acte cried indignantly. "Caesar would have their heads."

"Not if it is by his order that the ax falls," Seneca said briskly. "I only hope that when the time comes, you will not share my fate—as you certainly shall if you come here again. Your place is at Velitrae."

"My place is with Nero—if he needs me," Acte said quietly. "I can't believe he ordered General Burrus poisoned."

"What does it matter whose hand administered the poison, if none is raised to punish the culprit," said Seneca. "You and I have lost, my dear. We cannot help Nero—even though we love him for what he could have been. Our task now is to save ourselves—if we can."

During the exchange, Seneca and the girl seemed to have forgotten the presence of Paul and the guard. Unwilling to add his trouble to theirs, which were certainly large enough, Paul got to his feet.

"I hope you will forgive me for coming here, noble sir," he said. "It was an impertinence."

"Nothing is an impertinence—if it gives one man the chance to save his soul by helping another," said Seneca. "If you studied under Nestor, you should know that much about Stoic philosophy."

"But I—"

"And being a Jew, you should also know something about the sacred writings of your own people. Doesn't your Torah counsel you to help others?"

"In the book called Leviticus it is written: *'You shall not hate your kinsman in your heart. Reprove your neighbor, but incur no guilt because of him. You shall not take vengeance or bear a grudge against your kinsfolk. Love your neighbor as yourself: I am the Lord.'*"

"A Stoic might have said it differently, but the thought is the same," Seneca conceded. "I can see that you are a scholar in your own faith. Sit down and tell me why were you accused by the Sanhedrin?"

"Actually, my case was never heard before them. The chief captain of the garrison at Jerusalem sent me to Caesarea because of a plot to assassinate me."

"By whom?"

"The chief priests—and others."

"Why would they want to kill you?"

"Because I preach a doctrine they will not accept. And because the death of the man I serve is upon their consciences."

"The man you serve?"

"Jesus of Nazareth, the Messiah promised to the Jews."

"You are a follower of Chrestus?"

"A Christian, yes." Paul was familiar with the Roman version of the word Christ. "But I have broken no law of Rome."

"Can you prove your innocence?"

"I proved it long ago—before your brother in Corinth."

"Tell me more about that," said Seneca and Paul described briefly his appearance before Gallio and the Proconsul's refusal to listen to the charges against him.

"The Jews of the Empire have been permitted to worship their own god for many years—except for a short period under Claudius and the time when Caligula tried to put his own statue in your Holy of Holies at Jerusalem," said Seneca. "If what you say is true, the Christians are only a sect within the Jewish faith, as my brother ruled, and the Imperial Court will no doubt set you free."

"I'm sure my accusers know that," Paul agreed. "Which is probably why they haven't come forward to present their case."

"Tell me more about the worship of Chrestus," said Seneca. "I have never had the opportunity to study it."

v

Seneca and Acte had listened closely through the long story of Jesus' ministry, his crucifixion and his resurrection, the calling of Paul himself on the road to Damascus, and the apostle's subsequent ministry until the time of his arrest outside the temple at Jerusalem over three years before. Now, the philosopher broke into the narrative.

"Where have you found the greatest response to your preaching?" he asked. "Among your own people or those you Jews call Gentiles?"

"Gentiles. Almost everywhere I have gone, I have eventually been turned away from the regular Jewish synagogues."

"And in Rome?"

"I have failed here—with both." A spasm of pain crossed Paul's face. "Not only do the Jews refuse to listen to me, but I have made few converts among the Gentiles."

"What about the Christians already in Rome?"

"They accept me—as an apostle. But I have found little welcome among them either."

"I could have told you all this would happen—if you had come to me with your story when you first reached Rome."

"But why?"

Seneca glanced at Acte, who had been listening intently, "I think Claudia Acte here knows the answer."

"Our friend is playing the philosopher—and schoolmaster—again." Acte put her hand affectionately on the old man's arm. "He's trying to lead you to see something for yourself that you might not accept, if he told it to you as fact."

"But I don't—"

"I come from Asia and my family is part Greek," she continued. "Your faith has a great appeal to me, especially now that I have so little to cling to. But to a Roman it's too mysterious and set upon too high a plane. That's why you succeeded so well in the East but found so little response elsewhere."

"Exactly what doctrine were you preaching in Galatia and Asia and in the Greek provinces?" Seneca asked.

"I set it all down simply in a letter to the Christians of Rome written in Corinth just before I set sail for Jerusalem the last time," said Paul. "If I may come again I will bring you a copy of the letter."

"I would rather hear it from your own lips," said Seneca. "Tell me the essence of it, just as you would explain it to a citizen of Corinth, a Greek who knew almost nothing about your Jewish faith and the Laws of Moses that seem to be such a stumbling block among the Jews."

"I preach Jesus of Nazareth as the Messiah promised by the scriptures and sent to bring salvation—"

"To Jews only?"

"To all who will believe and accept him."

"A Greek or Roman with no previous knowledge of a Messiah—or what the word means—would have trouble understanding at the very beginning," Seneca objected.

"Many have failed to understand," Paul admitted. "Some will accept the spiritual Messiah I preach, the son sent by God to show men the way to salvation through faith. Others insist on looking for an earthly ruler, to whom men everywhere will be subject."

"And who would bring you into immediate conflict with Rome," Seneca observed. "Wasn't that the charge on which Pontius Pilate condemned Jesus of Nazareth to be crucified?"

"Yes. A placard was even nailed above his head on the cross, naming him King of the Jews."

"There, I think, lies the first stumbling block, particularly for the Jews," Seneca observed. "When you tell them the Messiah is the son and the equal of your god and that nothing but faith in him is required of them for eternal life, it must almost seem that you are saying Yahweh—the God of the Law—has been done away with and a new one has risen up in his place. The Jews have worshiped Yahweh—and his Law—for more than a thousand years. They will not give them up so easily."

"But Jesus has existed since the beginning of time—as the equal of the Father. In fact he once said, 'He that has seen me has seen the Father.'"

"If Yahweh once required his people to obey the Law of Moses but now the son requires only faith in him, how can you say they are the same God, when they require different things of men? Unless Chrestus has usurped the position of Yahweh."

"Not usurped but joined," Paul explained. "When men were no longer able to obey the Law, God sent his son into the world as a new manifestation of his love—and a sacrifice for our sins."

"I am familiar with the ancient Jewish custom of sacrificing the first born male," said Seneca. "Most of the old religions had it. Is this idea of your Christ being a sacrifice the same thing?"

"In a way," Paul admitted. "Long ago, God ordered Abraham to sacrifice his only son, Isaac. But when Abraham was about to slay the boy upon the altar, God let him sacrifice a lamb instead."

"And now you say Yahweh has let his Son be sacrificed, so the sins of all who have faith in him are literally washed away?"

"Then you know about baptism?" Paul asked in surprise.

Seneca chuckled. "Ritual ablutions are a part of almost every religion, my friend. In your faith you use water. In the worship of Mithras, it's the blood of a bull. In the worship of Dionysius, it certainly should be wine."

"But none of those religions have a God who included the life of even the least of men in his plan and pours out his love upon slaves as well as kings," said Paul. "Jesus opened the road to God's love and forgiveness for everyone through faith in him. That is the kingdom he preached, but people insist upon claiming he intended to establish an earthly kingdom as well."

"Things of the spirit are always hard for most people to understand," Seneca agreed. "If that weren't true, there would be no need of philosophers."

"I spent some time once in a Christian family before I entered the Emperor's household," said Acte. "They were Jews, who had left Jerusalem because of a persecution—"

"Probably one I carried out myself, before the Lord called me," Paul admitted.

"They believed Jesus of Nazareth was the Messiah sent to the Jews, but I heard nothing about this doctrine you preach of justification through faith in him."

"I was about to ask you just that," Seneca said. "Don't you preach a different doctrine from what was taught by disciples of the Nazarene after he was crucified—and by Chrestus himself?"

"I preach only what was revealed to me," said Paul doggedly.

"Did you ever study the Eleusinian mystery?" Seneca asked.

"Not the mystery—but I once saw a play based upon it."

"That could account for the similarity between some of the things you teach and the Greek mystery cults."

"I preach only what has been revealed to me," Paul insisted.

"That may be," Seneca agreed. "After all, who knows by what paths a man reaches a final conviction? Probably everything that has happened to him before influences what he decides to do at a given moment. In any event, I think I see now why you have been able to appeal so strongly to those whose background is Greek. And why you have failed so utterly with those who are Jews—or Romans."

"Tell us the answer—if you have it," Paul begged.

"We Romans are a practical people. After all we still worship

Apollo and Zeus—yes even emperors—though intelligent Greeks long ago either gave up religion altogether or began searching for the sort of fulfillment through spiritual effort you seem to have gained through serving your Christ."

"You aren't like that," Paul protested. "Yet you are a Roman."

"A Roman, yes—but I've devoted my life to a purely Greek form of philosophy, that of the Stoics. We Romans control most of the world, but we still haven't forced Roman ideas and cultures—if we have any—on those we conquer. I strongly suspect that if the Romans are to be known for anything important in the history of the world, it will be for helping spread Greek thought, Greek knowledge and culture to the farthest ends of the earth." The old philosopher got to his feet and stretched himself stiffly. "This has been a most interesting discussion, Paul of Tarsus. I hope you will come to see me again, so we can talk further about it."

"And my trial?"

"I don't know what I shall be able to do about that. After all, I'm almost completely out of favor in the Emperor's household. But I still have friends who are indebted to me in other areas of the government. Perhaps they can see that the imperial courts decide to hear your case soon."

Paul had to be content with that. As he was leaving, Claudia Acte walked with him to the door leading to the street. "I cannot help you, but I think you can help me," she said. "Could you possibly come to Velitrae and talk to me more about this faith of yours? It isn't safe for me to come here often."

"I cannot leave Rome," said Paul. "But I have an associate who would be glad to come—a physician of Troas named Luke."

"I know Troas well." Claudia Acte's eyes brightened. "We visited there before my former master brought me to Rome."

"I shall send Luke to see you," Paul promised. "And I hope you will become one of us."

"What I have been in the past would hardly earn me the favor of your God of old," she said. "But your Christ is forgiving and I need a faith now to sustain me in what lies ahead. I think I found that today."

## VI

In the months that followed his first visit to Seneca, Paul returned several times to the home of the old philosopher to sit and talk. With Poppaea Sabina daily gaining more complete control over Nero by appealing to the baser instincts that now dictated much of his behavior, it was inevitable that her favorites should achieve greater influence in the government. And as Seneca retired to the life of philosophic contemplation that was his first love, he found more and more to interest him in the dynamic bald-headed Jew with the broad shoulders and sturdy body, who had stirred the hearts of men in many parts of the world, earning from them a loyalty of such strange intensity that it bordered almost upon worship.

Again and again, Seneca argued that Paul's concept of the life and teachings of Jesus of Nazareth was based upon an amalgam, so to speak, of his strict Jewish upbringing, his early contact with Greek philosophical thought, and the often murky concepts of the mystery religions, with their symbolic rituals encompassing sacrifice, resurrection and the promise of eternal life. But Paul refused to let himself be turned away from his deep conviction that what he taught was an actual revelation from Christ, the gospel that man could not save himself by his own efforts but must yield to the human incarnation of God's love in his crucified Son and have faith in that alone.

Once or twice, Paul thought he might be on the point of convincing the old philosopher. But when he tried to win an actual confession of conversion from Seneca, the Stoic merely shook his head.

"I am too old to change gods now," he said. "Indeed, what god would believe me, if I did?"

"Mine would."

"How could he, when I could never be sure myself that, with death not far away, I didn't choose to follow this Christ of yours merely to save myself."

"He demands no analysis of your motives—only faith."

"We Stoics preach love one for another and the happiness it brings. It seems to me that you Christians, outside of promising eternal life, have little else to offer."

"You're wrong!" Paul cried. "We offer you the consciousness of God's presence in your own soul through his Son. Thus, in a sense, we make you a god."

"Every man his own god?" Seneca shook his head. "It's too late now for me to rise to that sort of bait."

VII

Paul was bitterly disappointed that the passage of the months seemed to bring him no nearer an opportunity to plead his cause before the Imperial Court and gain his freedom. Eager to leave Rome—where even without his chains, he'd never felt any real sense of belonging—and plow what he believed would be fertile fields in Gaul and Spain, he fretted continually at the delay, until Luke was afraid he might endanger his health.

One thing did bring Paul a great deal of satisfaction—the conversion of the lovely Claudia Acte to the Christian faith. She required little persuasion, after the morning spent in talk with Paul and Seneca. Luke visited her several times at Velitrae and one day she came to the outskirts of Rome so Paul himself could baptize her as a Christian.

Though Paul often felt a sense of irritation at Seneca for what appeared to be inaction, as far as speeding up his trial was concerned, he could not know that the old philosopher was actually working slowly to accomplish just that. By speaking a word here and talking with an old acquaintance there, Seneca managed finally, toward the end of the second year of Paul's enforced residence in Rome, to bring the case to the attention of the Imperial Court.

The trial itself was something of an anticlimax. Held before one of the two Praetorian Prefects—Nero was much too occupied with the new forms of debauchery to which Empress Poppaea and her cronies had introduced him, plus his singing and lute playing, to be troubled by such unimportant legal chores—the hearing proceeded rapidly to its inevitable conclusion.

The charges forwarded by Festus were in three categories, each was heard separately. First, Paul was accused of disturbing the ritual of the temple at Jerusalem, a charge he easily refuted by the testimony of Luke who, being a Greek and a respected physician in the praetorian camp, was well known to the judge. Second, he was accused of desecrating the temple but, since no representative of the priestly hierarchy appeared to condemn him, that charge, too, was summarily dismissed. The third accusation, that of being the leader of a sect that conducted treasonous activities against the Empire, was potentially a capital offense and therefore far more serious than the others. To it, Paul devoted the major part of his defense.

He cited first the decision of the magistrates of Philippi not to prosecute him on a somewhat similar charge brought by the owners of the slave girl. Then he went on to the account of his hearing before Gallio who, as a proconsul and the brother of Seneca, was well known and respected in Rome. Finally, he cited a statement made by Herod Agrippa II and Festus just before his departure from Caesarea that, had he not appealed to Caesar in order to save himself from the danger of assassination, he might have been set free.

All of this, plus the failure of the Jerusalem authorities to produce any tangible evidence against him, weighed heavily in the final decision. Paul was declared innocent of all charges that very day. The chains he had worn for almost four years were struck off and, free at last, he could turn his face to the west. Before leaving, however, there was still much to be done.

Silas had recently come from Jerusalem with the disturbing news that, following the untimely death of Festus, the priestly hierarchy there had taken advantage of the lack of a strong provincial government to move swiftly against the small group of Christians still in the Holy City. James, the kinsman of the Lord, had been arrested and brought before the Sanhedrin. After only the briefest of hearings, he had been seized by the temple rabble and cast down the outer steps of the sanctuary. There, his body already broken, he had been stoned by the mob until he was dead.

Simon Peter was rarely in Jerusalem any more, so the Christians there had chosen as the new leader of the church—Simeon, the son of Cleophas and, like James, a kinsman of Jesus' family. Paul was tempted to go to Jerusalem and strengthen the small community there. But Silas and Luke persuaded him against such a course, since it might appear to the Roman authorities that he had gone back to cause trouble in an area that was now in a state bordering upon open rebellion.

Moving southeastward by way of the Appian Way to Brundizium, its terminus on the east coast of Italy, Paul crossed over to Apollonia and there took the Egnatian Way, the great highway leading into Macedonia. Almost a year was taken up visiting the churches in Greece and the mainland provinces of Asia and Galatia, before he was ready at last to journey westward to Spain.

Sailing from Ephesus, he touched at Neapolis only long enough to transfer to another ship, bound for the thriving city of Massilia in southern Gaul. Located near the mouth of the river Rhodanus, Massilia was the terminus of an inland route affording access to the heart of the area he was determined to visit first, before moving southward across the mountains into Spain.

## VIII

The mission in Gaul was like the early days in Galatia and Macedonia. With few Jewish congregations to stir up the people against him, Paul preached freely in city after city throughout this lovely and fruitful land, making converts, baptizing them with his own hands, and organizing active churches. Moving through Gaul, he used the excellent network of military roads, relics of Caesar's conquest and the armies that had followed under later rulers. And where roads did not exist, there were always waterways along which a steady stream of commerce moved, both toward Rome and away from it to the busy market places every city afforded.

Leaving Gaul when the snow melted in the passes of the Pyrenees with the coming of spring, he crossed over into Spain and found an equal welcome there. It was hard to believe that this extreme southwestern corner of the Empire, so little known in Rome and even less in the East, had been a thriving commercial center since the time of the Phoenicians, almost a thousand years earlier. Then it had been known as Tartessus—sometimes Tarshish—after the name of the province drained by a mighty river emptying into the Western Sea near the major seaport city of Gades, or Gadir.

At Tarraco, Carthago Nova, Gades, and Corduva, in the central uplands, Paul labored unceasingly. None of his regular companions had accompanied him on this trip. Luke had been left as an observer in Rome where, being a Greek, he would not be as suspect as if he were a Jew. Timothy had been given the overseership of the churches in Galatia and Macedonia. Silas had returned to Jerusalem, after bringing news of the death of James, and Mark had returned to the homeland to assist Peter, whose age had begun to limit his activities considerably.

Paul did not lack for companions in Gaul and Spain, however, since converts moved with him from city to city, helping to preach the word in these new and fertile fields. It was at Corduva, in the second year of his ministry in Spain, that Luke found him, having taken ship there from Rome seeking the apostle.

Fragmentary accounts of the great fire that had swept through Rome the summer before had come to Paul during his journey through Spain. It had not occurred to him, however, that Nero would believe accusations by enemies of the Christians of Rome, whose lies could easily reach the Emperor's ears through Empress Poppaea. In fact, until Luke found the apostle at Corduva, the inland city which had become the major center for his activities in Spain, he had been too busy to think much about Rome. But one look at Luke's face warned him that his physician had brought grave tidings indeed, for Luke seemed to have aged a dozen years in the less than two since Paul had left him at Rome.

IX

"I have given thanks to God more than once that you were not in Rome this past year," Luke told Paul after they had greeted each other with deep affection. "With you alive and safe here, at least all is not lost."

"Were many of our people hurt during the fire?"

"Those who burned to death were fortunate," said Luke. "The persecution that followed was far worse than the flames."

"Why would Christians be persecuted because fire happened to break out in Rome? The whole central part of the city has long been a firetrap."

"The enemies of Nero—their number is legion now—first sought to put the blame on him," Luke explained. "But when they discovered that he was not even in the city at the time the fire started, they accused the Christians of setting the fire. Nero saw a way to escape his own guilt for not rebuilding much of Rome long ago and shifted the blame to the Christians to take the thoughts of people away from the fire."

"It has ever been the way of the tyrant," Paul agreed.

"Christians were hunted down and seized everywhere," said Luke. "Those thrown to the wild beasts in the arena died quickly. Others were nailed to posts along the streets and roads, their bodies doused with oil, and set afire as human torches to light the Emperor's way to parties."

"Are any of us left?"

"Many survived by hiding in the catacombs."

Like many cities, Rome had found the burial of the dead a major problem. Lest it become entirely surrounded by cenotaphs and literally be squeezed to death by the presence of its own dead, the authorities had ordered tombs excavated from the soft volcanic earth or tufa surrounding much of the city. Thus there had come into being a city of the dead beneath the ground, known as the catacombs, with galleries, rooms and niches carved from the soft rock.

"People have turned against the Emperor since he became a wild beast, killing and torturing without mercy," Luke added. "Even Poppaea died—from a hemorrhage, when Nero kicked her."

"How did you manage to escape?"

"The praetorians gave me refuge and I was able to help some of the others. Mark, at least, is safe."

"I thought he was in Judea."

"He came back—with Peter."

"Has Peter been in Rome?" Paul asked in astonishment.

"Yes. Mark and Silas came with him. The first wave of persecution had already begun to subside by then. But when our enemies heard Peter was in Rome, they accused him before the Emperor of being the leader of the Christians and had him arrested."

"Is he still in prison? Perhaps I can go back and plead—"

"Peter is dead, crucified by Nero with his head down at his own request—lest he seem to emulate Jesus."

Seized by a sudden vertigo at the shock of what Luke had told him, Paul swayed and might have fallen, had not the physician taken him by the arm and guided him to a couch. Pouring a cup of the rich Andalusian wine of this region from a flask on a table nearby, Luke held it to the apostle's lips while he drank.

"I was afraid something like this might happen when you heard the news," he said. "That's why I insisted on bringing it myself."

"What about the others?" Paul's color was returning now and, when Luke felt for the pulse at his wrist, it was regular and strong.

"The persecution has subsided somewhat since Nero went to Corinth for the Isthmian Games. He has become quite a chariot driver, besides being a poet and singer. There is much unrest in the Greek provinces, too, and to pacify them, he has revived the project to dig a canal across the Isthmus of Corinth."

"Doesn't Seneca have any influence on Nero?"

"Seneca retired to his home to think and write. But Poppaea and Tigellinus accused him of being part of a plot to dethrone Nero in favor of Calpurinus Piso and the Emperor ordered Seneca to kill himself by opening his veins."

"I shall pray for his soul. He never became a Christian, but he was very close to believing. And he was a good man."

"Many good men have perished on Nero's orders."

"What about Claudia Acte?"

"As far as I know, she is still at Velitrae—and safe. There was talk in Rome that after Poppaea's death, the Emperor wanted Claudia Acte as his mistress once again, but she refused."

"Then she held fast to her faith?"

"I'm sure she did, but it may cause her death when Nero returns. He's like a mad dog or a ravening wolf turned loose upon all who dare oppose him—particularly Christians. Claudius called himself a god but at least he acted like an emperor. Nero is a demon who would have people think him a god."

"What did you say?" Paul sat up suddenly and swung his legs off the couch upon which he had been lying.

"I said Nero is like a mad dog—"

"No—the latter part."

"Claudius called himself a god but at least he acted like an emperor. Nero is a demon who would have people think him a god."

"It must be true!" Paul got off the couch and strode across the room, his vertigo gone now. "It has to be! There is no other explanation!"

"I—I don't understand."

"Do you remember the second letter I wrote from Athens to the church at Thessalonica?" Paul's eyes burned with excitement, all the dynamic force of his body and his mind seized by the idea that had just come to him.

"Vaguely," Luke admitted. "But not enough—"

"The Thessalonians were spending too much time anticipating the parousia," Paul prompted him.

"The second coming of Christ. Yes, I remember that."

"I wrote to them saying: '*Let no man deceive you for that day*'—the day of Christ's return—'*shall not come until there is a falling away first and the Man of Sin is revealed, the Son of Perdition who opposes and exalts himself above all that is called God or that is worshiped, so that he sits as God in the temple of God, showing himself as if he were God.*'"

"I don't understand."

"From what you say, no Emperor of Rome has ever been as cruel as Nero. He may even have burned the city itself and now he is trying to destroy the Church of Christ by seizing all who believe."

"If you'd been in Rome as I was, you would be convinced of it," Luke agreed.

"Then Nero must be the Man of Sin Christ was speaking of when he said: '*Those whom you gave me I have kept and none of them is lost, except the Son of Perdition, in order that the scripture might be fulfilled.*'"

"I still don't understand," Luke admitted.

Paul shook his head impatiently, a gesture Luke had seen many times when the apostle was fired with enthusiasm for an idea and others did not immediately understand.

"Those are the very words of Jesus, Luke. John ben Zebedee repeated them to me once when I was in Jerusalem."

"But what about the reference to the scriptures being fulfilled?"

"You wouldn't know that, not being a Jew, but I often heard it read from the scrolls of the Prophets in the synagogue when I was a boy in Tarsus." Going to the corner of the room Paul took up a bag containing his few possessions. Rummaging inside it, he came up with a scroll of the Prophets which, like the Torah, he always carried with him in his travels, in order to be able to argue directly from the sacred Jewish writings concerning predictions about the coming of the Messiah. Opening the scroll, he ran down it rapidly, muttering the words to himself. When he came upon the passage he was seeking, he gave a cry of satisfaction and began to read:

" 'And there shall come forth a rod out of the stem of Jesse and a branch shall grow out of his roots. The spirit of the Lord shall rest upon him, the spirit of wisdom and understanding, the spirit of counsel and might, the spirit of knowledge and of the fear of the Lord.' "

Looking up from his reading, Paul asked: "What better description of Christ could you want?"

"It fits what Peter and the others told me of him."

"Then listen to this:

'He shall smite the earth with the rod of his mouth and with the breath of his lips shall he slay the wicked.'

"Don't you see, Luke?" Paul's hands shook with excitement as he rolled up the scroll, wrapped it in its coverings, and shoved it into the bag. "Before he was taken up into heaven on the mount outside Jerusalem, Jesus promised to return and said we will know his coming is near when the Son of Perdition appears. It is now more than thirty years since he was crucified in Jerusalem and who else can lay a greater claim to the title than the Emperor Nero? He has persecuted the church even worse than did Herod Agrippa. Or than I did, when I was an agent of the Sanhedrin."

"No one could deny the title to Nero," Luke agreed. "But are you sure that's what the words mean?"

"The scriptures prove it."

"But if you're wrong—"

"The Lord is coming, Luke! The time we have all looked forward to is almost at hand!" Paul had been striding up and down the room as he talked. Suddenly he swayed again and Luke moved quickly to catch his arm and ease him to the couch.

"Has this happened very often?" the physician asked.

"Only when I get very excited. I'm an old man, Luke. The years have taken their toll, along with the staves of the lictors, the stones of my own people, and the burning fires of the fever.

362

I had begun to give up hope of seeing the Lord before I am gathered to him. Now I know he will come any day."

"You may be right." Luke did not argue; he was more concerned by the two attacks of vertigo and the obvious fact that Paul was not as strong physically as when he had left Rome. Attempting to turn the conversation to a less exciting subject Luke asked about the work in Gaul and Spain. And as Paul told of the new churches established there and the willingness of the people to listen to the gospel, he gradually grew calmer.

They ate a frugal evening meal, as was Paul's custom, and when Luke claimed weariness from his journey, went to bed. It was already dawn and the birds were singing in the trees outside the house, when Paul awakened the physician by shaking his shoulder. One look at the apostle's shining eyes and Luke knew that during the night Paul had experienced one of the vivid dreams he always referred to as visions.

"I saw the Lord himself, Luke! He was coming in glory from the heavens! We have no time to lose!"

"Lose?" Luke was still groggy from sleep.

"We must be there to meet him."

"Where?"

"Where else but Rome? The scripture says Jesus will slay the Son of Perdition with the breath of his lips. What could that mean except that he will destroy Nero and claim the world as his own? With Peter gone and the other apostles scattered abroad, no one else is left to lead the Church and meet the Lord when he comes. I must be there to acclaim him."

X

Standing in the bow of the ship upon which he and Paul had traveled from Spain, Luke was reminded of another spring day when they had approached the same harbor of Puteoli. Then Paul had been in chains on the way to trial before the Imperial Court, but Luke could not throw off the conviction that the apostle was in far more danger now than he had ever been before.

The weeks since they had left Corduva had been hectic ones, beginning with the overland journey to Gades. One of the major ports of Spain, it promised the possibility of obtaining passage to Rome much more quickly than would have been likely in a lesser port on the Mediterranean side. And as if good fortune was smiling upon Paul's journey, they had quickly found a vessel ready to sail by way of the southern route along the coast of Africa.

Passing eastward through what the ancient Phoenicians had called the Pillars of Melkarth—and the Greeks the Pillars of Hercules—separating Spain from Africa, they had followed the northern coast of the province of Mauretania, stopping at Caesarea-in-Mauretania briefly before continuing on to the major port of Utica, almost within sight of the ruins of ancient Carthage. There they had transferred to another vessel for the brief voyage across the Mare Tyrrheneum to Puteoli.

Luke had argued in vain during the journey that Paul might be in grave danger by going to Rome. The persecution of the Christians there, he pointed out, had subsided considerably after the departure of Nero for Corinth and the Isthmian Games, but Paul's return could easily cause it to flare up again. For with Peter and James ben Joseph both dead, the enemies of the Christian Church would certainly try to destroy Paul, now the most important leader of the faith. Paul, however, had ridden roughshod over Luke's arguments, convinced that Nero represented the Son of Perdition to whom Christ had referred and that at last, the Kingdom of God was about to become a reality.

Only the fact that the first ship they could obtain for Italy had been bound for Puteoli had kept Paul from going directly to Ostia and Rome. When they disembarked at Puteoli, he insisted upon leaving at once for Capua and the Appian Way leading northward. The journey proved very tiring, however, and when they reached the junction with the Via Latium a short distance south of Rome, Luke was inspired to suggest that they turn aside to Velitrae and inquire about the welfare of Claudia Acte.

On several occasions Luke had visited the modest villa where the former mistress of Nero lived. He guided Paul there and Claudia Acte greeted them warmly, insisting that they spend the night before taking up the final stage of their journey. Weary and footsore, Paul agreed and shortly they sat down to a delicious meal served in the triclinium of Acte's small villa. Only after the meal was finished, the dishes taken away, and the two servants had retired to their quarters, did she bring up the question of Paul's reason for coming to Rome and his future plans.

"I am watched always," she explained as she shut the door to the triclinium, affording them privacy from the eavesdroppers. "We must be careful about anything we say outside this room."

"Do you think Nero has set spies to watch you?" Luke asked.

"I'm sure of it. After Poppaea died, he asked me to become his concubine again and when I refused, his pride was wounded. He could kill me at any time but that wouldn't satisfy him. He must first find evidence that I am faithless. It isn't true, but there are those around him who will one day perjure themselves to testify against me, as they did poor Octavia."

"We will leave early in the morning," said Paul. "My presence here must not be used against you."

"Rome still isn't safe for Christians," Acte warned. "You will be risking your life if you go there."

"I have no choice. When the Lord comes, I must be there to meet him."

Acte looked startled. "Did you say Jesus is coming back to earth?"

"The signs and portents are strong. I had a vision in Spain telling me I must return to Rome."

"A vision—or a dream?"

"What does it matter?"

"Seneca used to say our dreams are only the fulfillment of what we want to happen," said Acte.

"Would I have seen the Lord—if it had been only a dream?"

"You saw him on the road to Damascus," Luke reminded him.

"And he showed me the task I must perform," said Paul. "Just as he has shown me again that I must go to Rome."

"Surely Jesus wouldn't ask you to risk your life," Acte protested. "Especially after what happened to Peter and the others."

"If it is Christ's will that I lay down my life in Rome, so be it," said Paul. "Can I do less than Peter was willing to do?"

Luke started to speak but let the words die upon his lips. He knew Paul well enough by now to be sure that nothing would be accomplished by reminding him of what was undoubtedly true, namely that the urge to equal Peter's sacrifice was the real driving force that had brought Paul from safety in Spain to almost certain death in Rome.

XI

For a while, it seemed that Paul might be able to inspire the Christians of Rome, though harrowed and in constant fear of death, to emerge from their underground hiding places and once more form an active church. In the vast network of galleries and connecting tunnels beneath the surface of the tufa, particularly on the northern side of the city, many of them had been able to live with some hope of safety, particularly since, with Nero absent from the city, the persecution had lost most of its driving force. But as the days passed, some began to voice openly the fear that Paul's presence might increase the danger to them, when their enemies learned that the most dynamic leader of the Christians was in the city. From that point, it was but a step for one of the Roman Christians, his fear greater than his faith, to betray the apostle to the authorities.

Once again Paul wore chains. This time, however, the fetters were heavy and his cell was located deep inside the praetorium. None dared help him except the faithful Luke who, because he served as physician to the Praetorium Guards, was allowed to enter the prison. As for Paul, he seemed almost to welcome imprisonment and to Luke it sometimes appeared that the apostle was actually courting death, for reasons which Luke suspected but which he did not voice.

The charges against the prisoner were at first vague—merely those of being a Christian. But the citizens of Rome had long since been revolted by Nero's actions in persecuting those he had denounced falsely as the burners of Rome, so there was little real interest among the populace in any action against Paul. Besides, Rome was now being rebuilt in far greater beauty and glory than ever before and some said openly that whoever set fire to the city—whether Nero or the followers of Chrestus— had done its inhabitants a favor.

Knowing the sentiment among the people, Luke dared to hope Paul might be released when the Emperor returned from Corinth. It was reported that Nero's plans for digging the much discussed canal across the isthmus were bogged down because of the growing discontent throughout the Empire over his excesses, his high taxes, and his misrule.

Then in a letter from prison summoning Timothy to Rome, Paul wrote:

*I charge you before God and the Lord Jesus Christ, who will soon judge the living and the dead—I charge you by his appearing and his kingdom, to proclaim the tidings, to be urgent in season and out of season, to reprove, rebuke, exhort with all long suffering and doctrine.*

The phrase "his kingdom" was only an expression of Paul's conviction that the parousia was imminent. But to his enemies, who intercepted the letter, the mention of "Christ" and "kingdom" together were the final proof of treason they needed to condemn the apostle. On this charge, proceedings were set in motion to try him for that crime.

A final proof of Luke's assumption concerning Paul's real reason in coming back to Rome came, when the apostle wrote near the end of the letter to Timothy:

*I am now ready to be offered and the time of my departure is at hand. I have fought a good fight. I have finished my course. I have kept the faith. Henceforth there is laid up for me a crown of righteousness which the Lord, the righteous judge, shall give me at that day. And not to me only but to all who love his appearing.*

Reading the words, Luke realized that Paul was writing his own epitaph. Whether Nero was indeed the Son of Perdition—about whom Paul had warned the Thessalonians and whose coming would presage the return of Christ to earth—made little difference any more. During the years since the vision before Damascus, the apostle had labored steadily toward the day when he would face the Lord in glory and whether Paul saw Christ in person at the parousia, or went proudly to meet him through the gates of death, made little difference now. He would be wearing in his own words, "The whole armor of God," including "the shield of faith, and the sword of the spirit."

## XII

With what they considered a valid charge—in Paul's own words —upon which to demand the death penalty for a man considered a troublemaker for over thirty years, the chief magistrates of Rome moved with unusual swiftness. In midsummer a colorful assembly gathered in one of the great basilicas standing in the Forum, the very heart of Rome. The Praefect of the City presided from the *tribune*, a platform at one end of the rectangular building, down whose center was an aisle with seats on either side. Upon the platform stood the ivory chair of the magistrate, and behind him was arrayed the Council of Assessors, experts in Roman law who would advise him concerning it.

In earlier days, still another body of men drawn from the Senators or Knights and known as the Judices, had acted as a jury, although their verdict was not binding upon the president of the court even then. But Nero's justice—if it could be called that—was embodied only in the person of the Emperor or the Praefect of the City to whom he delegated it much of the time.

An open space was provided before the magistrate for the prisoner and those who defended him, as well as for his accusers. The rest of the basilica, including the galleries, was open to the public who filled it and spilled out into the streets around it.

Paul had forbidden his associates to appear at his trial as

witnesses on his behalf, knowing that by doing so they would only be convicting themselves under the edict outlawing the Christians of Rome. He stood alone as his own defender, calling only one witness, Luke, who was reasonably safe from persecution, to prove his innocence of the first charge against him, namely that he was one of the Christians who had participated in the burning of Rome. Luke quickly proved that Paul had been freed by the Imperial Court of the previous charge against him and had actually been away from Rome when the conflagration occurred.

To the second charge of giving allegiance to a man who claimed to be more powerful than the Emperor and Rome itself, Paul made the ringing defense that Jesus, being God, was indeed above any earthly ruler and that allegiance to him was no more treasonous than the allegiance given by Romans to Apollo, Zeus and other gods.

Finally, as he had once written to Timothy, Paul summed up in the fewest possible words, the very nature of Christ with these words: "God was manifested in the flesh, justified in the spirit; beheld by angels, preached among the Gentiles; believed on in the world, received up in glory."

"This Chrestus you worship was a man," the Praefect said. "Do you claim that he was also God?"

"He was—and is—God made man, for the salvation of men," said Paul.

"Do you also say that Chrestus will return to earth—to judge the living and the dead?"

"I have preached that doctrine from the day I began to serve him," Paul said proudly and a murmur ran through the vast basilica for, in their eyes, he had condemned himself of the charge of treason.

"If you say that Chrestus will judge, when none can judge in Rome except by the authority of the Emperor, then your allegiance to him must be above your allegiance to the Emperor," said the Praefect.

Paul lifted his head and his voice did not quaver as he repeated the words that sealed his doom: "Christ is God, manifested in the flesh, justified in the spirit, beheld by the angels, preached among the Gentiles, believed on in the world, and received up in glory."

"Have you any other defense?" the Praefect asked.

"I proclaim my loyalty to Caesar and to Rome in earthly matters," said Paul. "But in things concerning the Spirit and God, my allegiance is to Christ."

"You have condemned yourself out of your own mouth," said the Praefect, ending the hearing. "I sentence you to death by the ax."

## XIII

The Roman senate had long ago imposed an ordinance requiring ten days to elapse between the sentence of the court in a capital crime and its execution, giving the Emperor time to consider the case and, if he chose to be merciful, remit the sentence. In Paul's case, there was no remission and ten days after his trial, a small procession left the city by way of the Ostian Gate.

A centurion commanded the detail of the Praetorian Guard that marched on either side of the prisoner, whose ankle chains had been removed so he could walk. Behind him was the headsman, bearing the ax which, for Roman citizens, was considered a more merciful form of execution than crucifixion, normally reserved for slaves and for despicable criminals.

Only Luke, of all the apostle's companions, accompanied him on this last journey. A rabble of jeering Romans, eager to see a man meet his death, followed the small procession. Just beyond the Ostian Gate, they passed the pyramid of Caius Cestius and almost a mile farther, came to a narrow lane leading down to a hollow surrounded by low hills forming a small natural amphitheater. Known as Aquae Salviae, it was a frequent site of executions.

Watching from the edge of the crowd gathered in the little hollow where the drama of death was taking place, Luke saw—through the tears that filled his eyes—Paul step forward to the wooden block in its center. The apostle's head was proudly erect and his shoulders were straight, as if he were wearing the invisible armor of God, to which he had often referred.

When Paul's lips moved, the words he spoke were no request for mercy or even pity. Rather they had been spoken long ago by another man on the eve of his own death and repeated to Luke by Paul himself, the words of Stephen when he had said, as the apostle did now: "Behold, I see the heavens opened and the Son of Man standing on the right hand of God!"

The centurion in charge of the detail carrying out the execution stepped forward with a blindfold for the doomed man's eyes, but Paul shook his head and moved directly to the block. Standing there, he looked up at the sky and Luke saw a smile on his face, a smile so radiant that even the babble of onlookers was stilled with wonder. The headsman reached out his hand to shove Paul to his knees, but before he could touch the broad shoulders that had for so long borne proudly the armor of God, the apostle knelt before the block.

Watching as the heavy-bladed ax was raised high, Luke could not help crying out in wonder—as did many others among the onlookers. For the shadow of the falling blade was suddenly blotted out by a blinding glory that shone around the kneeling man.

## AUTHOR'S NOTE

Although hundreds of references have been consulted in recreating, in dramatic form, the life of the only apostle to be called by Jesus himself, after the resurrection and ascension, a few sources should be mentioned as having been especially helpful.

Particularly valuable among these are: *The Life & Epistles of St. Paul*, by W. J. Conybeare and J. S. Howson, Wm. B. Eerdmans Publishing Co.; *The Life & Letters of St. Paul*, by David Smith, Harper & Brothers; *It Began on the Cross*, by Guy Schofield, Hawthorne Books Inc.; *The Cities of St. Paul, and St. Paul, the Traveler and the Roman Citizen*, by William M. Ramsey, Baker Book House.

Those familiar with the author's novel, *The Road to Bithynia*, are reminded that it was a story about Luke based considerably upon traditional material. Since the present volume is a biographical novel, every attempt has been made to follow, as closely as Biblical scholarship and research allow, the known facts in the life of St. Paul, with the least possible use of traditional sources.

*Jacksonville, Florida*
*June 1, 1966*

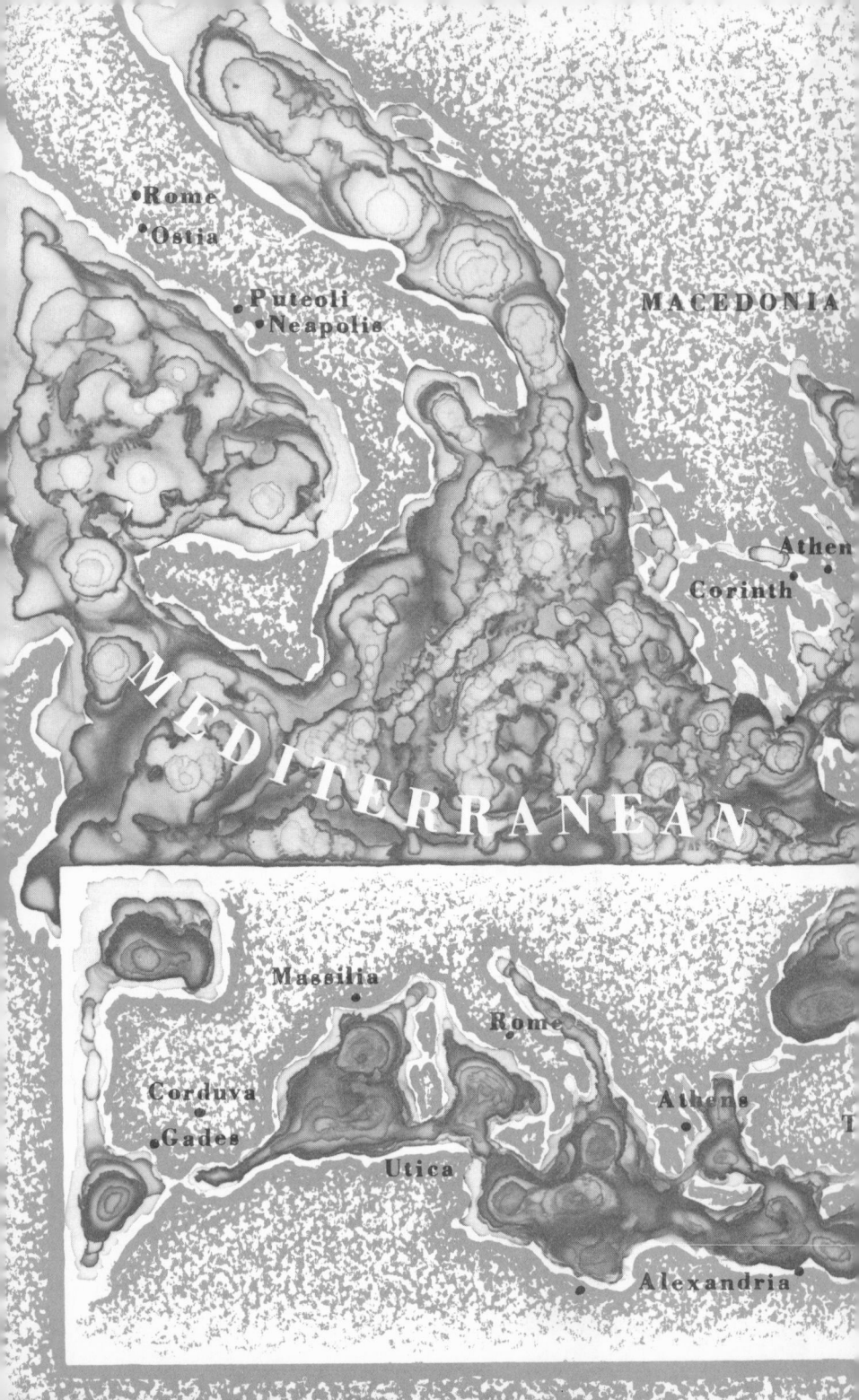